Praise For Loves And Entanglements

"**A**n impressively thoughtful and compelling collection of tales. ...explores the hidden but explosive nuances of romantic longing. ...deftly displays an admirable sensitivity to the human frailty that always accompanies love." —*Kirkus Reviews*

"**A**n entertaining collection of stories... [Lewis Bogaty] has truly outdone himself with his vivid storytelling and impeccable attention to detail." —*Midwest Book Review*

"**A** rare short story collection that manages to be a page-turner from one story to the next.

An intense collection of characters in emotional tumult,...these stories are visceral and subtly brilliant.

Manipulating readers' expectations and emotions with ease, this collection is a masterclass in storytelling structure and execution.

Bogaty's characters, like his plot-crafting, excel in pushing the suspense of a given scene, leaving readers nervously waiting for a blow to land, or the tension to finally snap.

Bogaty has a masterful ear for dialogue and pacing in conversation; he can perfectly tune his writing to the timbre of a fight gone wrong, misguided flirtation, or the satisfying release of temptation finally taken.

Bogaty makes it effortless to escape into each character's life."
—*SPR*

Loves And Entanglements

Thirteen moving stories about relationships — men and women caught in emotions they struggle to understand and control.

**Literary fiction
from award-winning author Lewis Bogaty.**

Obsessed. A woman confronts her terror at the fragility of her marriage as she and her husband engineer a pickup attempt in a restaurant for their woefully-obsessed friend.

Icebound. "'Twin beds' 'Double,' their voices collide." Marooned at a decrepit hotel in a snowstorm, two friends confront their feeling for each other, while her fiancé lurks.

Rabbit's Foot. A woman goes to the Greenwich Village Halloween parade dressed as a hemorrhoid sufferer, meets a snarky Cinderella and a rabbit, and considers the rabbit's odd proposition to spend the night with him.

Namby-Pamby. They met in college just moments after she tried to kill herself. As their paths crossed over the years they grew more and more desperately in love. Now it is her wedding day. She is marrying someone else, and he is there.

The Life That Late He Led. "Sad and touching," the late novelist Evan S. Connell wrote of the story's "angry, baffled, fading actor singing from his apartment balcony to an unlistening world." Connell chose the story for a Kansas Arts Commission/*Kansas Quarterly* Fiction Award.

These and the eight other poignant and gripping stories in this dazzling collection run the gamut from funny to tearful, often in the same story. The tension and suspense from scene to scene, story to story will rivet you. Some stories narrated by women and some by men, they plumb the depths of relationships: sex and passion, exhilaration and pain, love and entanglement. The characters will linger in your mind long after you put down the final tale.

This collection, in an earlier version, was a semi-finalist for the 2021 Elixir Press Fiction Award.

Loves And Entanglements

Stories

Lewis Bogaty

Published by One Marble Desk Publishing.
Published and printed in the United States of America.

ISBN 979-8-9884054-1-2 (paperback)
ISBN 979-8-9884054-2-9 (hard cover)
ISBN 979-8-9884054-0-5 (e-book)

Several of the stories in this collection were previously published in magazines, in slightly different forms:
"Obsessed" originally appeared in *Virginia Quarterly Review*.
"Rabbit's Foot" originally appeared in *Mississippi Review*.
"In The Bears' Den" originally appeared in *Another Chicago Magazine*.
"Blue Heaven" originally appeared in *Calliope*.
"Just As I'm Going" originally appeared in *Confrontation*.
"The Life That Late He Led" originally appeared in *Kansas Quarterly*.
The story won a *Kansas Quarterly*/Kansas Arts Commission fiction award.

For Dorothy
How unimaginably different everything would have been.

Contents

Preface

My first story was published in a magazine of national distribution in 1985. Though I continued to write and publish stories over the years, I never made any effort to put them together into a collection. Then in 2020, during the early days of the pandemic, I took the opportunity to reread all my stories. Some I happily relegated to oblivion, but others, I thought, held up well. These thirteen stories, some written years ago and others quite recently, fit nicely together. So I decided to gather them in one place. A second volume is planned.

The stories here are set during different periods over the past fifty years. Some, as I say, were written a number of years ago; others set decades ago were written recently; and still others are set in the present day. Here you'll find extension telephones in one story, the latest I-phone in the next; ditto machines, restaurants with smoking sections, a phone number you call to hear the weather, and other curiosities that sound as if they are from another century, because, well, they are. I hope the juxtaposition from story to story not only of technologies but of the ways we spoke and behaved over time adds an extra element of interest to the collection. The ethos of the world changes, but emotions, of course, do not.

Obsessed

I'M FURIOUS WITH GARY, even now when he's convinced me it's not his fault. But then, according to Gary, I'm always angry at him. It's pouring rain, and I guess I have to admit I blame him for that too. When we were first deciding, earlier today, to go to this thing, this reading that I really didn't have time for – at Kempton's urging (Gary's friend Kempton) – I *said* to Gary it's going to rain and he said, "Dear, I called the weather three minutes ago..." Well, that's certainly like him. "...and the new 3:00 forecast said some cloudiness, no rain." The restrained, reproachful, why-must-you-be-so-obstinate, I'm-so-rational voice.

"I *know* it's going to rain," I muttered, but I could see we were going to this thing. I had to rush out after a meeting when I knew Arthur wanted me to hang around and discuss the meeting with him. He's going to give me such a hard time tomorrow.

So I start out angry at Gary because I'm going to have to face Arthur in the morning. Then that foul subway jammed with sweating bodies, and I'm running the gauntlet of those awful, pathetic beggars and that stench of urine, and I come out in a thunderstorm. Not just a little drizzle. A torrent of rain. Cats and dogs and crocodiles and hippopotamuses. Inch-deep puddles every step I take. My new pink leather shoes! My toes are probably pink now. I want to kill him.

We are going to a reading of Chekhov stories, read by Swoozie Kurtz, Woody Allen and Cher if you can believe that. I mean I don't even know Chekhov really. Gary's Mr. Literature, but still, Cher? Woody Allen?

Anyway, I *think* we are going to this thing.

When I walk the block from the subway, getting absolutely drenched in the process, I see Gary with Kempton, under the marquee. Gary has a tight-lipped, hunkered-down look about him that I know too well, and Kempton has a big, oh-boy-is-she-going-to-be-pissed grin on his face.

"Dear," Gary says, "you're not going to be too pleased about this, but –" and he laughs. It is a kind of self-conscious chuckle. "Heh, heh, heh."

"They're sold out," I say, my voice registering my complete disgust with him. I see the handwritten sign. I also see the bedraggled people on what passes for a line, waiting for – hoping for – returned tickets. The line winds into the pizza place, then continues under the awning of the drugstore. If he suggests we get in that line, I'll murder him.

Gary follows up fast, before I have time to really boil over. And Kempton is here, which he knows will restrain me somewhat. "We thought some large margaritas might relieve some stress." He chuckles again. "Heh, heh, heh."

I scowl at him.

"We're already here and wet," he says. His anxious look pleads with me to keep the lid on.

I nod, trying to bring to bear the full value of the three and a half years at $75 a session, calm myself, realize that it isn't such a big deal. Things happen.

We start to walk up the block, a dreary succession of drugstores and liquor stores and bodegas, sprinkled with occasional hip restaurants. This is farther uptown than I feel comfortable, but Kempton lives up here.

Kempton is under his umbrella. Gary, as if demonstrating his lack of culpability, doesn't have one, so he is stooping under mine. "You could have called when you got here," I can't keep myself from saying.

"Dear, I did call." And he launches into a long condemnation of my staff and secretarial help for never being at their desks and never delivering messages. As we walk, getting wetter and wetter, he goes deeper and deeper into why it isn't his fault, why he had no way of knowing the reading would be sold out, and repeating the reasons that he couldn't get through to me, now pretty much putting the blame on me.

"Hello Kempton," I say, giving him a big don't-mind-us-while-we-squabble smile. He's been hanging back, out of the line of fire. He pushes his umbrella away from his head to duck under my umbrella and buss the cheek I proffer.

"Hi, Carol."

Kempton's hair is getting long again and he's neglected a two-day growth of beard. He is always at war with his corporate existence, still wanting to think of himself as the graduate student he was a dozen years ago. He never lets his hair get really long, but more often than not it's just beyond what is acceptable for an aging baby boomer with a responsible corporate job. He's come from work, as we have, but he's wearing jeans with his white shirt and sport jacket. His tie is loosened over an open collar.

"So?" I say, giving the signal that I'm OK, under control, ready to be sociable. Kempton's life has been a running soap opera and I know he will have a new installment for us. "Or don't I want to hear?"

We swerve on the sidewalk to avoid the spray from a taxi passing heedlessly close to the curb and sending a geyser our way.

"You don't want to hear," Gary says, dancing away from the water splashing at his ankles. Going "heh, heh, heh." Kempton's obviously been giving him a preview. "You thought it wouldn't get any worse?" Gary says to me by way of teaser, holding the door of the restaurant for us, bowing his head against the rain as we close our umbrellas. His curly brown hair is matted and water trickles down his forehead.

We crowd into the tiny, dry entranceway. "Oh man," Kempton says, shaking his arms like a dog shakes its soaked body.

"Yeah," Gary agrees, trying to brush the water out of his hair.

"I never know," Kempton says, his voice dropping to a confidential, apologetic tone, "if you two are going to groan to yourselves and say, 'Oh God, more of his endless whining.'"

"Don't be silly," I say, knowing full well that this flood is unstoppable. "What are friends for."

"Whine and dine," Gary says.

We can't decide whether we want to eat Mexican or Chinese food, so we decide to sit in the bar and have our margaritas. Gary goes to make a reservation in the restaurant for later, in case we decide to stay for dinner. Kempton and I take a big round table at the window in the bar. It is the table I want. There is something pleasantly melancholy about watching a storm. Cleansing too, as you can almost feel your anxieties being washed away with the soot and grime of the city. But Kempton chose it.

He made some comment about the window, but I know he saw the woman at the next table. I know he took her in, the instant we entered. She is not really anything special, a little thick even around the middle, but the kind of soft features and lots of hair that they can't help themselves from noticing. He is doing his best to make conversation with me, but I see in his watchful eyes a readiness for the opportunity that may present itself. An empty glass sits in front of the chair across from her and we are now both, below the patter of our idle conversation, waiting to see what gender of person is sitting there.

"Gary turned white when he saw that sold-out sign," Kempton is telling me with glee, "knowing he was dead meat and nothing he could do about it." I give him an embarrassed smile. Being Kempton, he sees the vulnerability and pushes it, "'Lorena' Rosner," he says.

"Cool it, Kempton," I warn him. Lorena Bobbitt has dominated the headlines lately for performing a surgical procedure that I, on ever so rare occasions, imagine in vivid detail performing.

I take off my wet shoes, and try to arrange my damp sleeves so they feel less gross against me.

It turns out to be a woman who sits down in front of the glass. I see the pleased look on Kempton's face before I see her. She arrives with two very large margaritas in her hands about the time Gary appears with the word that we are OK for dinner. He's been to the bar himself and sets down three thick mounds of frosted liquor, two with salt, mine without. The woman and Gary seem to have become acquainted at the bar, and I suppress my impulse to be annoyed with him. He and she offer us a fleeting, amused comparison of the size of their drinks, her two tankards and his three smallish glasses, obviously the subject of their introduction. Kempton would like to extend the interaction, of course, but it is self-limiting as they sit down facing away from each other, the woman already talking to her friend.

"Story time," Gary says, turning to Kempton and starting to work on his drink with a spoon. "Tell Mommy and Daddy."

Kempton moans quietly, perfectly serious in his self-absorption. "It's gotten really bad," he says, framed in the rainy day, looking pathetic.

Kempton," I say, "she is trying to give you a message and you aren't taking it."

"That's not true," he responds indignantly, lifting bits of frosted liquor to his mouth on the edge of his straw. "She keeps giving me the message that she likes me, that we aren't just employee and manager. I don't even know how this happened. She is the tattoo and nose ring generation. Look at you smiling. She doesn't actually have a nose ring. She does have a tattoo though."

"Where is it?" Gary asks.

"Why do you want to know where it is?" I ask him.

"I don't know, dear, I just asked a question," he says with a look of exasperation clotting his face.

"I would think," I say, not a little put out, "'What is it?' is the obvious question."

"Dear, please--"

Kempton interjects, "It's a flower, on her shoulder, not exactly original, is it? I hired her specifically because I thought she wouldn't tempt me. She isn't particularly good looking and not at all my type, so it should have been safe.

"I mean, I know," Kempton lowers his voice to say, "this is some kind of obsession. I am not blind. I look at it and say there is no future here, this is not someone I can be with, live a life with." He looks from one of us to the other, his voice starting to quaver, "but I can't stop wanting her."

"Look, why don't you just ask her out," Gary says. "You've been living in this twilight zone for six months already. The worst she can say is no. Then it will be settled. You can get on with your life. You've been frozen in this thing."

"Well, I finally did." He sits there looking sheepish.

"You asked her out? Why didn't you say so instead of holding out on us?"

"It seems like ancient history already. It was weeks ago. She said she didn't think it would be a good idea."

"Because?" Gary asks.

Kempton raises his palms, a helpless look on his face. "She didn't say. If she had just said she didn't find me attractive or she is serious with someone else, maybe that would be it, and I could forget about her. Instead, she sipped her coffee and blinked at me and said she likes me a lot, she really does. She doesn't think of us as boss and employee, she feels like we are very close."

"But?"

"But nothing. That was it. I felt funny for a couple of days like I was back in high school, for Christ sake, and some girl turns you down and you are mortified – embarrassed to face her for the rest of the year. But she treated me as if it had never happened: still just as friendly, almost more flirtatious. And we went along like that for a while, except I was jumping out of my skin."

We sit for a minute, silently, Kempton lost in the details of some painful moment. Then words roar out of him like a car idling too fast suddenly jammed into gear.

"I'll tell you how bad it is; one morning I needed to talk to her about something, and I went down to her office rather than call – so I could look at her."

He laughs. He is right; he does know he is making himself foolish, but at the same time, he is getting high talking about her. "I know every inch of her face, every blemish; every coffee stain on her teeth. I know her body so well I can tell when she has her period. I have this physical need, this craving to see her, to study her. I get anxious if I can't look at her.

"But, as I was starting to say, once I was at her door, I could not face going into her office and hearing her telephone ring. It had gotten so that every time I went in there the phone would ring at least two or three times and I would have to listen to her put on this sweet voice, 'Hi. I'm busy, I'll call you back.' And wonder if one of them was some guy she is screwing. Or all of them. It sickens me just thinking about it. What does she do when she leaves the office? I try to picture every minute of her day. I go home so depressed, picturing her with some whacked out moron with an earring and backwards baseball cap. What I imagine is probably a hundred times worse than what she is actually doing. But she really is always out. I try to remind myself that six months ago she was working for me and she was living her life just the same way, and I was blissfully indifferent. Why can't it be that way now? I can barely remember that there was once a time when her phone ringing didn't hit me in the pit of my stomach."

"So, you were standing in the door of her office – and?"

"So I was standing in the door of her office, unable to go in, talking to her, getting more and more anxious waiting for the phone to ring, and finally I asked her to come up to my office, and she said, with mock hurt in her voice, 'Don't you want to come into *my* office? We're right here.' Her eyes almost laughing at me. 'All right,' I said. What could I say? 'I'm afraid someone is going to call and ask you out.' I keep telling myself it doesn't matter if I am there or not, right? They are still going to call her and ask her out, and she is still going to be out at night doing things whether I am in there when the phone rings or not."

"Think of it this way," Gary says, "every minute you were in there is a minute she couldn't say yes to anyone."

"Thanks, that's very helpful. I went in and sat down."

"And let me guess, the phone rang?"

"No, but I couldn't stand the tension after a second. I yanked the fucking phone off the hook."

"What did she say?"

"Nothing. She looked at me. Not even surprised. Then this knowing, indulgent smile came over her face. We talked about the business question I had come to talk about."

"Oh, she is playing with you. She sees the power she has. And she is liking it."

"It gets worse," Kempton says. He leans back and stretches. As he does, he catches sight of that woman at the next table. After his intimate disclosures, he seems to realize it is silly to hide his awareness of this woman. "She's cute," he says.

"She is," I encourage him. "I think she's interested," I say. "I saw her checking you out."

"Right."

"Why don't you try to meet her? She doesn't have a ring on."

"What am I going to do with you all here and her girlfriend? Forget it. Besides –"

"Yeah?"

"She's not Janey."

"That's good!" Gary and I both shout at once. "That's the point," I say.

"I wish I *could* find someone to pull me away from this thing," he muses. But he is drifting back into his reverie. "It is like she can't commit herself. You know, her father died when she was twelve. Right at the start of adolescence. She could be fixed in adolescence and not willing to risk loving any man again."

"I think you are trying to find reasons for something that doesn't have any deep reasons. Kempton, she doesn't want to go out with you. Stop pouting. I'm just saying what seems obvious."

"It isn't obvious. I know she likes me. There are reasons of some kind."

"She's got a boyfriend?"

"She never talks about one. I don't believe she is serious with anyone. She went on her vacation alone – to Club Med. If she has a serious boyfriend, wouldn't he have gone with her? Wouldn't she mention him? At least sometimes?"

"Maybe he's married."

This hadn't occurred to him and his body stiffens as he sits considering it, realizing that this theory could fit his facts. I think for a moment he is going to start crying.

The woman at the next table has pushed her chair out awkwardly and stumbled up, which catches our attention. I study her, trying to see what the attraction is beyond all that curly hair. She's just a woman, in her mid-twenties, wearing white painter pants and a tee shirt, an ordinary mortal woman, with a cute but unremarkable face, an inflamed zit on her chin, and a chunky shapeless body. There are a thousand like her all around the city.

"Follow her," Gary says.

"Go ahead," I coax.

"What?" I can see him actually debating it momentarily, but he waits too long.

"You two are crazy. I've got no context. This isn't a singles bar. She's not here to be picked up."

She is over at the bar placing an order. "Come on, what do you have to lose? Get up. Come on," Gary says.

I give Kempton a nudge under the table. He just smiles at me awkwardly. By now she is coming back, juggling two drinks and a bowl of chips. "Forget it," he says, "this is silly." But he follows her with his eyes and when she becomes aware of his scrutiny, she gives an instinctive smile, then looks away self-consciously as she sits down.

"Hey," I say, grinning at him, but he shrugs it off.

"She'll have to go to the bathroom," I say. "Follow her down." The look in his eyes tells me he is considering it.

"I hope her bladder capacity isn't too great," he says. "I've got to go already."

"Cross your legs," I say.

"This is silly. I can't do this," he says. "Where was I? One night, we had to work late. It was stuff we couldn't start till four o'clock and it had to get done, and Janey was pissed because she had to cancel plans. Vague plans; she was not specific at all. She never is. She was on the phone for twenty minutes doing it! At least it made *me* happy that she had to cancel them. By about eight we were nearly done and both getting tired. She said she wanted to call her cab by nine. I said very casually it was late enough that we were entitled to dinner if she were interested. She didn't respond. I didn't press. Talked about something else. But when we finally stopped working, she volunteered that she was interested in dinner."

"I'm surprised."

"*You're* surprised? It would have been very easy for her not to," Kempton says vehemently, leaning over the table. "'To want to get home.' Easy easy excuse. She *wanted* to go out with me."

"Or she wanted dinner," Gary says.

"Right," I say.

"She was entitled to dinner without me. There's nothing you can say, is there?"

"She felt uncomfortable eating alone in a restaurant?"

Kempton frowns at me dismissively. "We went to a really nice restaurant. Had drinks, ate, and talked for three hours, till near midnight. She was not the one who made the first move to leave. It was like we were on a date. We talked about personal things, not work. We stayed an hour after we paid the bill. I didn't push anything. Just let it happen. And I felt like she was becoming really attached to me. She touched me with her hand more than once." He reaches over and presses my forearm lightly with his fingers. "I was flying."

"So how long ago was this dinner?"

"It was two weeks ago, and I thought it would all build from that, but then the whole next week she avoided me. She was totally cold. I realized I blew it. I should have taken advantage of the moment and made a real move. Gone home with her. That night I could have had her. But I didn't, and then things were just worse.

"I started to see that she enjoys the power of my wanting her, so I resolved to deprive her of that. From then on, I was businesslike, uninterested. Sure enough, after a few days, she ambled in as casual as could be, but with this sheepish grin on her face. 'I feel as if I haven't seen you in ages,' she said. Gave me this awkward, eager twitch of her mouth. I stared at her for a minute. She looked so forlorn, I started to feel sorry for her. 'Am I getting that report on Wednesday?' I asked her. She nodded, her eager grin turning to an uncertain frown. Then I picked up the phone and spoke to my boss about another matter. After a minute or two, she slunk out."

Kempton pauses, giving me a disgusted look that says "your whole sex is responsible for my misery." He gazes out at the rain, which in the darkened street, in the lights of passing cars, sparkles and shines like the falling, fading embers of fireworks.

"It got so every interaction was fraught with an unbearable intensity. My palms were sweating from the moment I walked into the office in the morning. I was living with this certain knowledge that something would explode, but I didn't know when or how.

"And then it happened. A couple of days ago I called her to give her some work. My heart was thumping the minute I picked up the phone. I got a busy signal. I slammed down the receiver and cursed just as my boss walked in. 'She's on the phone again,' I spat out. I regretted it the moment I said it, but it was a reflex. Unfortunately, I'd been complaining about her telephone chats since the day I hired her, before I had even the slightest interest in her. And now my boss had finally had it."

Kempton shakes his head forlornly. "I spoke to her about her phone usage. She was furious, but I had no choice. My boss insisted.

"That was it. Whammo. She blew up. 'I'm tired of this,' she screamed, standing there in her prim little navy blue suit.

"I think we must have glowered at each other with identical expressions of rage."

Kempton laughs a little self-conscious Gary laugh. "I should have just kept quiet, but I couldn't stop myself. I looked her in the eye and said, 'You never cared about anybody but yourself a day in your life.'"

"You said that?" Gary marvels.

"'Who am I supposed to care about if not myself?' she screamed. 'What do you want from me?'

"We looked at each other then, because we both knew the answer to that, and we seemed to have had this tacit understanding that we would not mention it. But now I had opened it up and I went the whole way. I said, 'Could I just ask – why? It might help me if I knew why.' I tried to help her. I said, 'It could be that you're just not attracted to me. That would be an easy answer I could understand.' She stood there gazing at me like a zombie.

"'It could be that we work together, or the age difference.' I said to her, 'I don't believe you're in love with someone else.'

"She took a breath, was silent for a moment with her eyes on the floor. Then she looked at me and said, 'It is a lot of things. It is not entirely untrue that I am seeing someone else.' My insides just fell when she said that. I can't tell you. 'It is just a lot more complicated than that.' What does that mean? I looked at her, all but begging her for more. 'I'm gonna go now,' she said. It was only getting less clear. I wanted to howl with frustration."

"She just got up!" I say.

Kempton's and Gary's heads jerk up as she turns the corner.

"Shit," Kempton says.

"Go, Go. Go," I urge him. "Hurry up."

He hesitates, with his eyes fixed on us. We are by now sitting rigid in our chairs, frozen, expectant, wondering if he will do it. Then he shoots out of his seat.

Gary and I laugh at first, then sink into the sudden vacuum his leaving has created, as the babble of voices in the bar now flows over us.

"Live drama. Isn't this better than Swoozie Kurtz and Cher and Woody Allen?"

"Don't push it," I warn him.

Gary starts to speak, but realizes silence is safer.

"What do you think?" I say.

"I don't have the slightest clue. What would you do?"

"Walking to the bathroom in a restaurant? Blow him off."

"I can't believe we prodded him into this."

"She did notice him. She smiled at him."

Gary gives me a look.

"Actually, I meant what do you think about the other thing."

Gary shakes his head slowly. "He thinks he can pin her down so she makes sense," he says.

"Maybe she doesn't want to go out with him, but she just enjoys being adored," I say.

Gary reaches out and takes my hand, caresses it, and then starts to squeeze it with a passion that doesn't seem to have anything to do with me. I withdraw my hand and we sit without talking.

I realize I am quite anxious, waiting for Kempton to return. My palms are sweaty. I also feel weird sitting here with Gary, participating in another man's seduction. And then I feel like it is going to be very embarrassing if she blows him off after we pushed him.

"Here they come." Gary whispers.

"Yeah?"

"They aren't together."

"Yeah?" I say impatiently. "Tell me."

"He's about ten steps behind her. He's not smiling. Actually, he's got a bit of a crazed look on his face."

"Oh, God. What about her?"

"I can't tell. She's sort of smiling, I guess."

"Maybe he never did it."

Kempton sits down woodenly and silently.

We look at him with eager eyes.

He raises his glass, holds it tipped up to his mouth, and nibbles at the icy slush.

"Well, should we go eat?" Gary says, looking at his watch, trying to make the best of it by ignoring it.

"What happened?" I say, flustered.

Kempton doesn't answer. He is like a statue. Just staring straight ahead at the window, at the ceaseless rain scrubbing away at the city. "Kempton?" I say.

He gives me a look that says, "Wait." After a minute he turns toward their table.

She is hunched forward in her seat, all smiles and frizzy hair and that zit on her chin. She is nodding at him.

"My friend approves," she says. "You get the OK." The other woman has dug a pen out of her pocketbook and produced a napkin. The object of desire is writing on the napkin.

"Really?" Kempton blurts out before he realizes it.

"Let's go." I nudge Gary and we quit the scene discretely. Standing up, I become aware of just how blitzed I am on the margaritas. As I follow Gary to our table, negotiating on unsteady legs the narrow passages between rows of happy people, a blackness overtakes me. I am glad for Kempton, but it depresses me.

I sag dizzily into my chair, take the oversized menu from the maître de, and try to focus. All around me I see seductive young women engaged in animated conversations. A strikingly attractive woman in a yellow dress several tables from us at the border of the smoking section draws my eye again and again. She is so aware of herself, pushing her flowing hair back, gesturing with arched fingers as she speaks. I know Gary noticed her the minute we sat down, and tried not to let me see him glancing over there.

Kempton comes to the table with a smug, composed look on his face. But when he sits down, he can't keep from breaking into a grin and pounding his fist on the table in exultation.

He feels immortal, Mr. Stud. Sitting back in his chair, he surveys the room, his eyes coming immediately to rest on the woman in the yellow dress. "Ohhh," he sighs. Right now, he thinks he can just walk up to that table and she too will give him her phone number.

"Don't be greedy," I say.

Gary says, "Go for it."

"Gary," I say.

Kempton is shaking his head slowly, smiling in his slightly inebriated euphoria. "I wonder how her bladder is," he says.

He sits down, but then stands up, "And speaking of which...." He wanders off in the direction of the men's room.

I feel really bad; a foggy, cobwebby feeling that clings to me but that I can neither grab onto nor wipe away.

Gary is shaking his head. "That was pretty amazing, wasn't it? I don't know what's wilder, his thing at work or this. What's the matter?" he asks.

I squint at him, trying to get hold of this feeling. Then, peering at his no longer quite so boyishly smooth face and his brown hair now flecked with gray, I do. "You wish it were you, don't you?" I blurt it out before I have even realized I am thinking it. But once I say the words, they take me over.

"What?"

"Come on, admit it."

"Admit WHAT?"

"As sick and miserable as his life is, you're jealous, aren't you? You wish it were you going out with that woman. It's exciting thinking about it, isn't it? Not knowing how the night might end, with this total stranger, whether you'd sleep with her. You miss it, don't you, the uncertainty, the excitement? The newness."

"No."

"No, right."

Gary is saying something but I'm not even listening, and then Kempton is back, radiating his joy. I smile at him. He and Gary start talking about stocks, and I turn myself inward. I try not to look at the people at the other tables: the woman in the yellow dress tossing her hair, and beyond her, two young women smoking cigarettes, careless of their lives, of the wrinkles around the lips the smoking will bring in time, but not now. Young and powerful and confident, they are talking with great animation. Their skin is radiant, their juices plentiful. They are frightening in their come-and-get-me outfits. It was so easy for Gary to engage the woman at the bar when he was picking up the drinks, and with a ring in plain view on his finger.

I feel as if I have come to a place of clarity in my thoughts I have never been before. And I feel a relief of a strange sort flowing over me, a relief I craved in all my sessions with Ellen, all that anger and anxiety floating around the couch just out of reach.

"What have I done, Dear? Jesus," Gary says suddenly.

"Nothing. You haven't *done* anything." So once again, I am the ogre, the hormonal bitch on wheels. Kempton is squinting at me and Gary is hunkering down.

***

Life is so deceptive. You believe it is always building to something. You think it has a form to it. Everything that happened that night seemed climactic, overflowing with portent. But it was all illusory: false hints of shape flattening into time gone by formlessly.

Kempton went out with that woman. It had seemed, at that moment, that night with us, charged with possibilities. But already when he called her to set it up, she was very tentative. He suggested dinner, a movie, a club, but she wouldn't commit herself to more than drinks on a Wednesday night. And when they got together, the encounter was a non-event. It turned out that she had been so drunk that night at the restaurant that she didn't really remember him at all. They had nothing to say to each other. After no more than an hour, they were both happy to end the evening. It only made him long more helplessly and bitterly for Janey.

Nothing ever came to a head with her either. The inscrutable Janey never gave up her secret. Neither did she succumb to the power of his desire. She went on working for him for another year of roller coaster days of pain for them both, all of which he described to us in agonizing detail and tried desperately to parse in subsequent dinners around town. Then, quite out of the blue, she moved to Wyoming. Several months later, Kempton received a postcard from her picturing Old Faithful. In the scrawl he knew so well, she wrote that she was working in Yellowstone as a tour guide, enjoying the pure outdoor air. Signed it "Affectionately, Janey." He never saw her again. I suggested to him that perhaps the reason for her reticence had been a serious sexual disease. He found a certain compelling logic in that explanation, so in the end he adopted it and felt sorry for her, and glad things hadn't worked out.

Gary and I seem to just keep going on in the same old way. Whatever awareness I gained under the influence of those margaritas that night didn't change anything. I see Ellen each week, spend my $75, $85 now. But I still feel incredibly anxious when I see those young women and know he is so quietly, innocently, surreptitiously, yearningly aware of them. It is so powerful. I never feel really safe.

Icebound

"I F IT GETS A little worse," Jonathan said, "we'll have to stop for the night."

Jonathan and Doranne – she hadn't been called Dora Anne since she was a child – were driving in a blizzard that was not supposed to be, that was mere light rain when they left the graduate apartments where they both lived. They had been switching off the driving, and now, still less than halfway to Cleveland, Jonathan was behind the wheel of Doranne's sub-compact, lamenting the fact that she didn't have snow tires.

Doranne, forced to sit still for the first time in months, mesmerized by the falling flakes, was pondering the abruptness with which decisions made in the summer snuck up on one in the dead of winter.

"You can have your last fling," Jonathan added.

"What?" Doranne asked.

"I said you can have your last fling."

"You'd try it too, wouldn't you?" she said, not that the thought hadn't occurred to her in the year they'd known each other.

Jonathan was steering by the feel of the ruts in the two feet of unplowed snow. They had skidded seven times already, by Doranne's count, and were now experiencing an indifference to danger that came with their fatigue. Doranne used a soggy Kleenex to dab at the fogged inside of the windshield, but it no longer made any difference. Snow and ice were caked on the outside, and though the defroster blasted away, only amorphous gray shapes showed through.

"It's like it was watching a television screen without an antenna back in the day," Doranne said abruptly.

"Why might they call that snow, do you think?" Jonathan said, rolling his eyes at her.

"Watch the road, would you."

The car danced across a ridge and settled back in the groove. "God, Jonathan."

"Doranne, did you know that if you put a penny in a jar every time you do it for the first three years you're married and take a penny out every time after that for the rest of your life, you'll never empty the jar?"

"Thank you for sharing that."

"Unless you get divorced, of course (which fifty percent of all couples will). Did you know that ninety percent of all people marry within twenty blocks of home? Still. Even today."

"What is this? 'Ask Mr. Romantic?'" Doranne said. She set the Kleenex on the dash and rearranged herself cross-legged on the seat. Jonathan's angular body looked to her like a coiled spring. His long legs were cramped up even with the seat as far back as it could go. "I guess I'm not marrying within twenty blocks of home, am I?"

"You're a trend setter."

"Jonathan, would you cheat if you were engaged to a woman in another city?"

He ran his fingers through his red hair and beard-in-progress. "No."

Doranne stared at him.

He nodded to punctuate it.

"You're such a liar. I know you'd cheat. Why do I really believe Rusty isn't?"

"Because you have found your perfect match," Jonathan suggested.

This vacation week together she and Rusty were going to set the date and finalize all their plans. Which meant, of course, her leaving school.

"You got your ice, so plunge ahead," Jonathan sang at her in a Marilyn Monroe voice, glancing down at her finger.

Wasn't it supposed to be different for women now? The closer she got to Cleveland, the more her stomach felt as if ice cubes were bouncing around in it. She reached for her cigarettes on the dashboard and lit one.

"Thank you for not smoking."

She ignored him. "You know what it is?" she went on. She let a long trail of smoke eddy out, and when she had finished, she realized she didn't know what she wanted to say.

"You're just up tight because you met him in a singles bar and you can't believe you actually got engaged. He was supposed to be a one-night stand, right?"

"He's intelligent," she said, and then was sorry she said it. She dragged on her cigarette and twirled it between her fingers, pondering. No one had ever adored her so completely. She thought she had shed her closetful of storybook ideas about the prince she would marry. She was going to be thirty years old. She had slept with more men than she could even remember. She was lucky as hell to be disease-free. But the truth was, she still wanted him to be perfect. He wasn't perfect. On the other hand, she was thirty years old and it was time already.

The sound of packed snow scraping the bottom of the car filled their enclosed world. The radio had lost all stations an hour ago, and they were sick of the limited music they had on their phones.

"We should get off," Jonathan said. "It's really becoming impossible. I'm serious."

"And what? It's not going to stop. Look at it."

Jonathan looked at her and frowned. He was just hitching a ride. It was her car. His life, but her car.

"No, we have to keep going," she said firmly. "Rusty'll be hysterical as it is." She looked at her watch and calculated how late they were. They had not had cell coverage for the past hour and a half.

"Telephones do exist in this state. You know, those old fashioned things. At places people stop."

"No. Just drive."

Doranne dragged deeply on her cigarette.

"Your secondary smoke is going to kill me," Jonathan said. "Close and intimate with you is a funeral pyre. And I never even liked The Doors."

"Rusty is very possessive," Doranne said, squinting anxiously at the falling snow.

"Yes, we know that; we do know that."

"He hates even hearing your name. When you and I got off the plane together whatever holiday that was, you can't believe the drive into the city. He couldn't understand how I had never mentioned you if we looked so chummy getting off the plane. 'Rusty,' I said – what could I say to that? – 'There are two hundred people in the graduate apartments. I know most of them. I talk to most of them. I even laugh with some of them. I talk to everyone in the dance department too. It is my department, after all,' I said. 'They don't matter. They're all faggots,' he said; he just passed it off. 'I mean welcome home, I'm glad I came, Rusty.' He hates you."

Jonathan nodded vigorously, gunning the gas. "And for all that, do I get any?"

"Jonathan!" she screamed, too late.

The car jerked suddenly out of the ruts, out of control for real this time. Doranne moaned as they slid sideways at a shadowy signpost that appeared and disappeared as their headlights wobbled toward it. The yellow smudges of a truck's lights that had been behind them blinked furiously ahead. They spun in circles across the highway as the piercing blast from the truck's horn vibrated through their bodies. Doranne screamed. Her hands pressed tight to the dash, "Why doesn't he stop?"

"He probably can't," Jonathan yelled as they spun forward again. Jonathan jammed the gas. The car surged ahead, still fifty miles an hour on the dial, out of the skid. Jonathan grinned and let out a whoop. "I can't do it *that* well in any video game!"

Doranne sat rigid, but she felt limp. "Let's get off," she said quietly when she found a voice, "at the next exit."

"Hark the echo," Jonathan said, still breathing hard.

They turned onto the exit ramp and Jonathan wiggled his eyebrows at her.

"Just get that out of your head."

Doranne opened her window. The snow and cold air swirled in, blowing her hair. How would she explain this to Rusty? It infuriated her that she would have to. She rode with her head out, looking for the "food and lodging" promised by the sign at the exit. There was nothing. No town, no gas station. Just white-covered country road. They drove slowly on until they came to an old wooden hotel that looked more like a small barn.

Jonathan, driving all but blind, turned into what was decidedly not the driveway, and the car slid one last time, in a wide, slow, gentle semicircle, down a bank onto what must have been the front lawn of the hotel. It came to rest, after a groan of metal against snow, in sudden, overwhelming silence.

"Well," Doranne said, "I guess we are not going to Cleveland tonight. Oh Rusty, you'll love this."

Steamy heat was Doranne's first sensation when the hotel door closed out the wet snow. Her attention focused on the sound of plinking that came from half a dozen buckets placed under leaks in the roof. Then, as they stood hesitating, she saw the ten or so faces staring at them in silence from the bar on the left side of the cavernous room. "This isn't real," Doranne whispered. The glow of the fire in the stone hearth straight ahead was the only inviting aspect of the entire scene before them. Where were they, anyway? She had no idea.

Doranne thought about turning around and leaving, but then, with a sinking feeling, she remembered the car marooned on the front lawn.

A corpulent man with tiny eyes buried deep in ridges of flesh, separated from the row of eyes and approached them slowly. He looked to be in his sixties, and wore a tee shirt and work pants.

"Evenin'," he said.

Doranne smiled awkwardly. "Snow's too bad to drive. Do you have rooms here? Or just food?"

The man nodded. "Road's closed, 'cording to the highway patrol. Worst night I've seen in years."

Doranne said, "We couldn't even see the road anymore at all. We thought your front lawn was the driveway."

"It's bad; bad night. We'll get it out for you in the morning." The man turned, and walked slowly toward the counter. "One or two?"

Doranne thought the guy was loony if he imagined they were going to stay two nights.

"One," Jonathan answered too quickly, and Doranne finally grasped what had been asked.

The man, turning back, looked from one of them to the other. "Married?"

Jonathan nodded before Doranne could react, and then she could hardly contradict him.

"Sixty-five the night."

"That's fine," Jonathan said. Doranne glared at him.

He whispered to her, "Cheaper this way," as he filled out the card the man handed him.

"Twins or double?" the man asked. "We got both," he said proudly.

"Double's fine." "Twins." Their voices collided.

Doranne flushed with confusion as the man's little eyes rested on the two of them. "Twins. We want two beds."

"Twin," Jonathan relented. "But, honey, my snoring *has* been a lot better lately."

"Two oh four," the man said, "follow me," and began climbing up the creaking stairs.

Doranne jabbed Jonathan hard in the kidney.

"It's OK, Mrs. Rusty," he whispered.

"What?"

"Mr. and Mrs. Jonathan Rusty. That's us, dear. That's how I registered."

They entered the room. Doranne held her tongue until the man was gone. "This is just what I need," she said, slamming her suitcase onto the bed and throwing her things out in handfuls.

"This is what I call sparse," Jonathan said, looking around the cold room.

"I'm going downstairs." Doranne scowled, and walked out.

Entering the lobby, she hesitated when she heard the buzz of conversation from the bar area, but she plunged ahead and took a seat by the fire. She curled up with her legs under her, melting in the warmth, watching the locals at the bar, old men mostly, who discoursed with Mr. Heliston, as the proprietor seemed to be called, and joshed with his wife as she served them beer. Everything seemed so simple here. Doranne was envious.

She caught Mrs. Heliston looking at her, and before Doranne could look away, the woman was walking toward her with a warily efficient smile on her bright red mouth. "How we doing here?" she asked. Her voice was very loud, rumbling through lips that seemed frozen to a locked jaw.

"Fine," Doranne said. She smiled up at the woman, feeling scrutinized.

"So, you two newlyweds, I bet?"

Taken aback, Doranne allowed as it was "pretty recent." She folded her arms around herself more tightly to hide her fingers under her armpits."

"Well, I wish you a good one. Twenty-seven years, Jim and me been together. Through thick and through thin. And every daggone minute of it heaven." She let out a guffaw at about the same time the old men at the bar responded with laughter of their own.

"You hush up, Harry Smith, you old bachelor." Mrs. Heliston started back toward the bar, with a nod to Doranne, who sat smiling for a moment, and then decided she had better call her beloved while she still had a smile on her face.

The pay phone in the corner was hardly private, but their room had no phone. She couldn't put it off any longer. The sound of the coins tripping the mechanism seemed so loud she was sure everyone there would hear every word. She tried to speak softly, but Rusty kept shouting, "What, I can't hear you." It didn't matter because mostly she was listening to his tirade.

"I can't help it if it's raining there," she finally exploded at him. "There are two feet of snow here. The Interstate is closed. Closed. What do you want me to do? You think I'm making it up? Honey – honey! No. No." She looked around. He was announcing that he was coming to get her.

"Don't come! You can't. If we can't get there, how the hell can you come here? What? We? Jonathan. You know Jonathan. I told you. What should I do, sleep in the car?"

"This is just great," she said to Jonathan, who had come gliding up to her, with a "Hi honey" and a peck on the cheek. "He says he's coming to get me."

"I hope he'll take me too."

What does he think, I'm making up a blizzard? They heard all that, I suppose. God, what'll they think? It's so embarrassing. You're such a jerk, Jonathan. I hate men, all of you. Why couldn't you just get two rooms? Don't talk to me." She pushed him away and walked back to her chair by the fire. Jonathan followed at a safe distance and sat down on the arm of the chair. The telephone was ringing. Jonathan stroked his beard and told her she took things too seriously. "This is an adventure," he said.

"More like a nightmare." She had this vision of Rusty arriving at two a.m. with fists flying.

Mrs. Heliston, who had been in the kitchen all this time, walked out with a tray and came toward them smiling. Meanwhile, Mr. Heliston had answered the telephone and returned to the bar. Thank goodness it wasn't Rusty, Doranne thought.

Mrs. Heliston set the tray on a table nearby. "I *thought* your husband would be down by now," she said, showing extra teeth for Jonathan.

"Wrong," Doranne said to herself.

"I thought you two nice people might like something warm. On the house, of course."

"Cocoa," Doranne said. "Oh how wonderful. Jonathan, isn't this nice, and cookies."

The phone was jangling again. The sound was grating and intrusive. The man finally answered it. Why was Doranne not surprised to see him walking toward her?

"Excuse me, folks, one moment, if I could. Do either of you make something out of Loohman, Loochman, something like that. I told him the first time there's no one here of that name. Asking if we had any snow here. Now he calls, says Rusty. Wants Lukman. I said there's Rusty here. I can't tell if he's Rusty or wants Rusty or what. It make sense to any of you all?"

Doranne stood up, sighing, and strode to the phone, her fists clenched at her sides. He was yelling at her as soon as she said hello. "Don't you dare," she said, trying to speak softly, glancing at the old couple and Jonathan.

Mrs. Heliston frowned toward Doranne, who tried to lower her voice, who did lower her head, who felt trapped in this public spat with her intended while her "husband" watched.

"Rusty, if you do, it's the end. I'm telling you that now. If you can't have that much faith. I'm not getting back on that road. Rusty. NO. Don't you dare. I know – the name – I'll explain it later." She was whispering through gritted teeth. "I said later. I can't talk now. Good – bye."

She saw, as she started back, the stiffness returning to Mrs. Heliston's face. Her red smudge of a mouth twitched a smile, and she walked smartly to the kitchen.

Doranne felt as if she were in a Marx Brothers movie, or maybe a Bela Lugosi movie.

Back in the privacy of their connubial bower, Doranne lay on her lumpy mattress with her hands under her head, watching Jonathan pull down his bedspread. It was all so absurd. "You know," she said, "I keep expecting Rusty to show up any minute."

Jonathan looked at his watch. We have a few hours at least.

"Don't joke."

"Well, if he does come, don't expect me to lie here listening to you two grunting and groaning."

"You're disgusting."

Jonathan started bouncing on the bed. "Don't you feel like we should have a pillow fight or something?" he said.

"You know," Doranne announced, we're into serious second thoughts here."

"Can I help?" Jonathan said. Doranne heard his bed creak and then saw him looming over her.

"Go away, Jonathan. I need to think."

"Let me just lie against you and fantasize while you think."

She laughed, but she found herself letting him lie down. He stretched out peacefully, and without realizing it, she began to stroke his head. Then, as she lay there lost in thought, she found herself pressing tighter against him, forgetting who he was. But when she remembered, she found that he had fallen asleep.

"You jackass," she said, jabbing an elbow into his ribs to wake him. He looked up at her, blinking, probably thinking he was still dreaming, as her hair fell across his face.

⚬

It was a crunchy, still, blue-skied morning that they stepped out into. Cotton candy white everywhere. "Oh, isn't it just gorgeous," Doranne said.

"Doranne, do you remember when you were pure as the driven snow?" Jonathan asked her.

Doranne had a happy, mischievous, snowball-throwing smirk on her face as she grabbed Jonathan's hand and took him running. She kicked up the white powder and it sprinkled prickly cold in their faces.

She spread her arms and spun slowly. Perhaps Rusty was on the road now. Perhaps he was sliding on an ice slick somewhere, marooned. He was far away as she whirled, and drifting further. "Oh, what a glorious day." She let herself tumble into Jonathan's arms and they spun together for a time.

Rabbit's Foot

S HE WAS SUPPOSED TO be Snow White. She had chosen the costume. But she no longer felt like wearing it. If they were still going to the Halloween parade in the Village, Sandy just wanted to be obscure. So she dressed as Rosalyn Snitow, proper suburban housewife, hemorrhoid sufferer; victima de hemorroides, the subway ads proclaimed.

Johnny was sulking. He probably felt stood-up as a Dwarf with a Víctima de Hemorroides. But for now, she ignored him, just tuned him out.

As they stood on Christopher Street in the heart of Greenwich Village, jostled and jolted in the vast swirl of cadavers and weird creatures, Sandy was again and again surprised to find herself not at all obscure. True, she did have a large name tag pinned across her prim blue sweater. But so what? Who was Rosalyn Snitow that anyone would know the name? She was wearing Rosalyn's white turtleneck under the sweater. It had been easy to do her hair like Rosalyn's. But nothing indicated her status as a víctima, nor anything about the remedy she preferred. She had forgotten to buy some Preparation H.

Nevertheless, first a couple of ghouls broke up in hysterics at the sight of her, and then a cluster of boys in drag, dressed to the hilt of old fashioned girlhood, prancing and preening in flowing dresses – gowns actually – and wearing white lacy gloves and spike heels, cheeks painted ruby red, hairdos to kill for, one after another they pinched her rear, and, with a shake of their balloon boobs, yelped, "Ohhh!" or something vaguely smutty. Apparently everyone actually looked up and read on the subway. Rosalyn Snitow, the lady with the pain in the ass, was a personality. Sandy smiled for the first time in days.

She was not pregnant now. Hadn't been for a week, and she was sure that repulsive doctor butchered her. At first she had been ok. She even found herself chattering boisterously as she walked down from the recovery room with the other women, down the stairs to the dutifully waiting, quite worried really, Johnny. It was fetching the way he looked at her, all nerves and concern. She put her arm around him, and as they walked out of the clinic she regaled him with the tale of the twenty of them in that room cursing men. Johnny made a sad face and she hugged him. "Well, I hated you a little. I'm sorry," she said. It wasn't bad at all right after.

But then as the days passed, the memory of that doctor grew hideous. He butchered her. His black pinhead eyes blinking at her as she looked up at him admitted everything.

She had really been pregnant. Her body hormones were acting like she still was. And this dark ugly ooze kept flowing from her. She couldn't have been pregnant. Other people had abortions. Like other people got sexual diseases, venereal disease, venerable disease her grandfather used to call it. She had never been sure if he was joking or not. She tried so hard every day to act the part of a grown up, but she felt like a little, lost girl.

"Sandra Jane," her mother said, "whatever you're doing, you stop it this minute." Her mother was standing scrambling eggs with her back to the children. Sandy had opened her blouse to flash her newly swelling breasts at her little brother, who, with a mouthful of Cheerios sputtering out, wailed, "Mooommy, make her stop." "What did I do, stinkball?" "You know," he said accusingly, stuffing more Cheerios into his mouth.

Should she tell her brother? He was a doctor. Maybe he'd know if the procedure had gone ok. No. She couldn't. She just couldn't. She was supposed to go in for a post-abortion checkup, but she couldn't face it. She wasn't going to keep the appointment.

She and Johnny were such innocents. When she had bought the home test, Johnny devoured the instructions, all curiosity, all scientific. The words he read to her floated by; they had nothing to do with her body. Nor did the science experiment they set up then.

Afterwards, fooling around in the bedroom, waiting the al-lotted time, they lost track until she happened to glance at the clock. They scrambled up and fell all over each other hurrying to the dining room table where it all became suddenly real. Why was it looking like that. It wasn't supposed to. Johnny picked it up and looked at it. From every angle. Then he stood there blinking.

When he instinctively looked at her belly, she started to cry. He was good then, holding her and stroking her head, his fingers passing gently through the tear-wet curls that stuck to her neck. She said, "We're two mature college-educated people. I'm not supposed to get pregnant." He guided her limp form to the bed and she lay with him. He told her softly that it would be all right, and she snuggled into his promises.

"You'll take care of me?" she asked. He nodded and caressed her forehead with slow, even finger-tip strokes. As she half dozed in his protection, feeling all stuffed up and like a little girl staying home from school with the flu, a kind of serenity blocked out the new knowledge. She heard the sound of the cars that whooshed by and she found herself counting them. She heard the clock on her wall ticking and the radiator pipes pinging. She and Johnny were lying on her queen-sized bed, on the crumpled sheet with the pink and purple flowers, her bower. As usual, she hadn't gotten around to making the bed. The whoosh of the cars told her it was raining now. It had been dark and foreboding all day, but she felt warm and cozy in Johnny's arms, in the brightly lighted room.

She drifted and she drifted, as his hands played over her body, until all at once, she could feel – in the warmth and closeness and what they had done – passion growing, rising up in her, in him, pressing her against him, tightening the grip of his hand against her.

Abruptly, thoughtlessly, they fell at each other. She was clammy, hungry, sour-mouthed from crying, unable to get enough; overpowered by the awareness of his baby inside her. And he too – he whispered, "My baby, mine; we made it," and her tongue shot through his mouth frantically. As he entered her, she rose up off the bed to meet him, her arms pulling him deeper into her, the two of them poised in mid-air, as he pulsated his seed rhythmically into her baby.

The abortion was the right thing to do, for sure. But that doctor.

"Miss Snitow, poor dear, well we all have our crosses to bear." She looked up and it was a not-half-bad Jesus stooping under his.

"Hey, turn the other *cheek*, baby," a passing sheik put in. That cracked Johnny up.

The sheik looked at the laughing Johnny and told Sandy, "Beware Dwarfs."

She sighed. "I wish you had told me that earlier."

The mad, costumed throng swarmed by. It was endless, garish, and all at once too much. Sandy just wanted to be away from it. "Let's go," she said to Johnny, and nudged him, and pulled him.

"Wait," he said, tweaking the long, wart-covered nose of a witch, laughing and flirting.

Sandy was gone. She melted into the wall of people. Johnny noticed nothing; she knew he would wander around looking for her eventually, then go home mad.

Sandy smoked a cigarette that she bummed from a stewardess wearing shoes that were anything but sensible – a fag from a fag, she thought irreverently. She hadn't smoked in years. She inhaled deeply. She closed her eyes and let the smoke eddy out. She sat down on a brownstone stoop and watched the backs; the tide of watchers, surging and flowing.

When the cigarette was finished, she walked to an Italian restaurant that had a garden in back. There, off the parade's route, the street was hauntingly silent, but the restaurant's garden was bustling. She found a little table for two. For herself. The weather was unseasonably warm, and the garden had probably not been open in a month. What with the parade, the few waiters were overwhelmed. Sandy didn't care about the service. A bucolic serenity irradiated the night in this courtyard surrounded by smudged old brick buildings. Leaves lay under foot, and the full moon shone bright through a fittingly Halloweenish mass of high cloud. Sitting with her hands under her legs and her shoulders hunched in, she stared at the leaves on the ground, crackling them with her shoes slowly and methodically.

God, the two of them were sick. It turned them on so much to do it without the diaphragm. They'd be kissing and cuddling, and pressing close against each other when she would dutifully mumble that she had to put her diaphragm in. But then his eyes would start to shine and she would feel this quiver and thrill course through her. He would probe and pull back, probe and pull back, watching her, staring into her wide-open eyes. "No," she would mumble, feeling his heart pounding through her as he whispered, "Make baby," and she whispered back, "Your baby," and he probed again and with the head of him just squeezing through she would thrust forward, taking him into her. Then crying "baby" at each other, they would fuck till the sweat poured off them, and after the explosion they would lie there feeling like total idiots, swearing they would never do it again. And all week she would worry, and the next week. And, because she worried, she would be late and then he would worry, and when the blood came, finally, they would thank God and swear they would be good.

At the next table, a big one in the center of the garden, eight revelers were telling the harried waiter that no, they had distinctly specified one of the pizzas was to be half anchovies and half peppers, not one pizza with peppers and the other anchovies. The second as well as the third were supposed to be all mushroom. Cinderella said sharply, "You know, I asked you twice, 'Do you understand?' and you just nodded like I was a stupid child."

"All right, Cindy, let it go."

Sandy, at her corner table, giggled. Could Cinderella really be named Cindy?

The waiter raised his outstretched palms.

"Look," a bunny rabbit said, "leave the anchovy pizza. We'll forget the peppers. Just bring us the second mushroom."

He went off and Cinderella muttered, "These two'll be ice cold by the time he gets back."

"Start, start, go ahead."

Cindy pulled at a slice of the pizza. It tore away sloppily and she used a finger to break it, then curled it up and felt at the edge tentatively with her tongue. "Well, I don't want to burn off the whole roof of my mouth," she said tartly to her audience of seven.

"That *would* be a shame," said a prissy cowboy.

"All right, enough," said a pirate, and after an awkward pause, half the table – clearly aspiring actors all – began talking about auditions past and future while the other half had somehow gotten caught up in an earnest discussion of their sex lives. The rabbit was telling Cinderella and a blonde woman in a tuxedo that sex had lost its allure, not to mention the danger it presented in a world without trust. He received patronizing nods in response. He took his ears off and Sandy thought he was a sweet looking boy. He had short curly brown hair and warm brown eyes.

Cinderella was grunting while attempting to break a strand of cheese that dangled putty-thin between her mouth and her pizza slice. It stretched finer and finer but would not crack.

The rabbit talked on oblivious of her plight. "Sex isn't hard to get, but what I really want, you girls just won't give. You'll let me fuck your brains out, but if I ask you to caress my back or rub my feet you'll resist like I have broken every rule of etiquette. At the least there will be payment due. I once went out with a woman who timed rubbing my back. I got five minutes and then she damned well expected her five.

"Why should you get more than you give?" said Cindy trying to pick the strand of cheese off her face.

"Why is everything measuring? Besides, if it is, then she didn't factor in the effort I had to put into getting her off. For that matter, she didn't even like having her back rubbed. She was ticklish. It was just the principle of it. Well, there's some justice. I think she became a dyke, so now *she* has to work to get someone off.

"You're an asshole," the tuxedo said.

"Do it yourself," Cinderella suggested, chewing finally. "You could masterback, or masterfoot."

"Did you ever wonder why you can't do that? It's funny, isn't it, but it doesn't feel the same. There must be some scientific reason."

"You're strange."

"You know," the bunny reflected, "I think I would pay cash for it."

"Prostifoot."

"How about it, Cindy, what would it cost me?"

"What, are you crazy? That is demeaning as hell."

"Why? No kissing or anything, no sex, just sleep in my bed with me and massage my back and feet till –"

"Till you come."

"Till I fall asleep."

"I've heard that line before."

"It's just a massage."

"Right and the kind of masseuses – masseusi?-

"Massage parlor persons," the tuxedo declared.

"We know the kind of massage persons who sleep in."

The cowboy had now grown interested in this conversation. "How much are you offering?"

"Uh, uh, has to be a woman. Has to be a woman. I mean it won't do anything for me if –"

"Rosalyn Snitow?" Cinderella read the sign across Sandy's prim sweater. "Who's that?"

Sandy was standing over them, gazing at the earless bunny rabbit.

"How much?" she inquired.

The silence at the table was sudden, the attention rapt.

The rabbit smiled self-consciously, apparently not quite sure how to deal with a fanciful idea turned so abruptly concrete.

"I don't know," the rabbit said finally. "I'm not looking for a, a prostitute. I'm sorry."

"He's looking for a footitute," someone called out.

"I thought it was a prostifoot."

"Chickenshit," the pirate goaded him. He looked Sandy over. "She's cute, David." He played his eyes over her. "Quite cute."

"I'm not one," Sandy said. "Your terms; absolutely no sex."

The rabbit sat silently.

"So how much?" Sandy asked again.

"The pirate asked Sandy, "How much do you think?"

"I don't believe this," Cinderella muttered, with disgust in her voice. "Go away, would you."

Sandy was tempted to do just that. Now that the initial impulse, maybe it was anger at Johnny, maybe an attraction to this guy, maybe a need to do something outrageous to blow everything else out of her mind; whatever the impulse was, now that it had brought her here, she realized she didn't want to be doing this. But it had a life of its own, and she couldn't make it stop.

"Well, look," the rabbit said, "Why don't you give me your phone number and I'll call you sometime."

Sandy shook her head. "There is no sometime. There is only now."

"Oooh, profound," Cinderella whispered.

"Right now," she said sharply, "$200." She blurted that out so unexpectedly, she surprised herself. Having said it, she thought, wow, an extra $200 would be great.

"I don't have $200 on me."

"I'm sure you have a cash machine card."

"Can't you see she's a pro?" Cindy said. "God knows what she's after. Tell her to go away."

The cowboy was whispering at his end of the table. A conference was in progress. When it ended, the pirate said, "We'll chip in $25 each."

"Ted!" the bunny shouted.

"Not me," Cindy said.

"Well, without Cindy, then, if you can make $50, you're in."

"Not *in*," Sandy corrected.

"I'll give an extra $25," the cowboy said grinning. "Now all you need is twenty-five bucks, and I know you have that."

Suddenly green bills started floating out over the anchovy pizza.

"Fuck you, Ted, just fuck you," the bunny said, and fingered his fork, passing it over the plate, slowly; jabbing absently at clumps of dried cheese. Sandy saw that the bunny was seriously considering it now. He looked her over. "My place or yours?" he said with a laugh.

Sandy bent down and gathered the bills, folding them, and shoving them in her back pocket. "Yours," she said.

He shrugged, and grinned a sheepish grin. "Why the hell not. Come on, let's go." He took her arm and with a haughty glance at the teasing table of his friends, hurried her out of the chaotic streets of the Village.

They were in his neat, clean apartment, in the bedroom. She was undressed except for her pink panties and he, his name was indeed David, except for his white jockey shorts.

He had told her she didn't have to go through with this if she didn't want to. He was gentle and kind and sweet and she felt safe with him. Now they were in bed and she was rubbing his foot, first one and then the other, and he was lying back, sighing with pleasure.

She never felt safe with Johnny, that was for sure. Her brilliant engineer lover, her self-involved, inconsiderate, headstrong child. He kept her forever on edge. Never had they even considered having the baby. Never would he commit himself to her. But nothing made her feel as alive as the intensity of their bodies struggling to be one.

"Don't you have a girlfriend?" she asked curiously.

"Uh uh."

"Why not?"

"What can I tell you? I'm too choosy. Women are too choosy. Sometimes you just don't meet anyone for a while. What about you?"

"I'm sort of seeing someone, yeah."

"So you're not the one I've been looking for all my life?"

"Guess not," she said.

"Oh well, this feels awfully good anyway. Why are you doing this?"

Sandy didn't answer. "Other foot," she said.

"You must have a strong maternal instinct," he said, switching feet.

"Do you ever think about having children?" she asked abruptly.

"Sure, sometimes, I guess. Maybe. Eventually."

I can't, she thought.

In the end, she was tired and she lay against him on his chest, this unfamiliar person named David, this guy out of all the guys who had been on that street that night. He had offered to rub her feet for a while, but she told him no, he had paid for this service. What had they said, prostifoot. She chuckled.

They lay together for minutes, tranquil peaceful minutes, with the rhythmic sound of his heart beating against her. Then the thump in her ear, the ear that lay on his chest, got louder. His hands, which had been idly stroking her, started to exert more pressure.

And now, she saw, she had done it again, she had brought on a moment, another moment in that risky work in progress she could not let alone called her life, when her luck would be tested. She would not agree to sleep with him; she couldn't. But would he accept that nicely? Or would there be a scene now? Would she have to explain, tell him about the abortion she had just had? Even that would only mean anything if he cared what happened to her. They were strangers to each other, utterly utterly strangers. You could do anything to a stranger. Would he force her? Would he rape her? Or would he just throw her out in a rage? What would Johnny do if it were he? She thought she knew the answer to that.

They lay together, the sound of his heart and the feel of it, enwrapping her. And now she herself felt her heart pounding.

When he lifted her face to his, she found herself kissing him. When he went for her panties she didn't react at first, and then she said "no." And he – he stopped. He smiled at her. And they tried to sleep.

"Are you awake?" he whispered. She was. They began to talk, hesitantly at first. But knowing that she would not see him again, and under the spell of the Halloween witchery that had brought her to him, Sandy felt her inhibitions evaporate, and a desperate need to express things that she never could to anyone. So it seemed did he. They talked until dim pink light appeared through his grimy window. And then they dozed again, emotionally spent.

When she awoke in the now bright morning, Sandy didn't know where she was at first. She gazed around at the theater posters on his wall. And she remembered. David. She smiled. She *was* lucky.

Sandy dressed and, with a last glance at him asleep in the bed, closed the door softly behind her. The air was crisp and cool. When she got home – she lived with Johnny mostly, but she kept her own apartment – she sat in her rocker in the stillness of the morning. Halloween was over. Reality reasserted its ugly primacy. She didn't want to go back to that clinic.

The sun had just entered its daily twenty minute solstice, poised over a lone brownstone between two high rises, whence it streamed through her middle window in a beacon that flamed the length of the room, all the way to the kitchen, where the hanging copper pots grew long purple doubles on the wall. She wished the world still contained signs. Maybe it did. She rocked quietly, watching the dust play in the flowing light, and when the twenty minute beacon was gone, she went into the bedroom to the phone.

She noticed her answering machine for the first time then, blinking madly with calls. She had been sitting trying to work up the courage to call that clinic and cancel her appointment, and she hadn't thought to check the machine. Now she played the messages:

-Where the fucking hell are you? ... You witch... You know I spent a fucking hour looking for you. You are such a shit. I have a mind to BEEP.

-Sandy, are you home? .... Damn you bitch.

-Sandy, damn it, where the fuck are you? ...You know I've been through a lot with you the last weeks. I don't think it's very nice the way you're treating me in return. ... It's not my fault you got BEEP.

-Sandy, honey, are you OK? I'm really getting worried now. Are you there? Are you just not answering? Come on, San, I just want to know if you're OK ... BEEP.

-Honey, I know what it's been like for you. I've tried to act like it wasn't anything so you wouldn't be more upset. But I know, honey, I really really do know. And I hurt so much myself and for you. I know it can't be as much as you hurt – but so much. I feel so guilty for BEEP.

-Hi, it's six in the morning. Do you know where your Dwarf is? He sure wants to know where his hemorrhoidal Snow White is ... Sandy? ... BEEP.

-Sandy, hi. I'm sitting here by the window, watching the sky get light ... I love you, Sandy, more than anything in the world. I'm nothing without BEEP.

-Sandra Jane Fayer, there's a lonely little boy sitting by himself out here – missing someone very, very much .

-Hi. Well, this is my last message. Because I have only one thing left to say. It's just this. And I don't want your machine cutting me off in the middle, so I'll call you back.

-It's just this, will you marry me?... I'm serious.

The machine went silent. What, she wondered, was the operative part of this remarkable piece, the prelude or the finale? Art, in the end, is not divisible, she thought; it is all one Johnny. Sandy flipped through her wallet and came upon the paper that said "David – 663-9477." She smiled and dropped it on the table, now finding the card from the clinic. With the phone crooked under her neck, she punched in the numbers. The two, three, four rings seemed endless.

"Clinic."

"Hello, this is Sandra Fayer. I'd like to cancel my appointment."

"Fayer, Fayer, yes, 11:00, Dr. –"

"I don't want to see him."

"Excuse me?"

Then it occurred to her to ask, "Does the other doctor have any time free?"

"No, I'm sorry."

"Oh."

"Of course you can see him at his office, if you like."

"Oh, really?"

"I'm afraid he does charge though a full fee there."

"That's OK, that's OK." Never to have to see that clinic again. She just happened to have some spare cash.

Sandy sat in the waiting room with the bulging women, many with bawling children in tow. She felt as if she were hollow. A shell sitting on the hard wood chair. She sniffed in. "Blow out," Johnny always told her. "That's what tissues are for." But it was one of her nervous habits. Another was pushing her hair back, she realized, as she gave a quick poke for the dozenth time.

"Miss Fayer?" the man with the chart called tentatively, searching the waiting room with his eyes.

She let out a breath. He was an adorably sweet-looking old man with gray hair and bushy eyebrows over soft kind eyes.

When she was in the stirrups, every muscle tight as a knot, he saw, and caressed her head and told her to calm down, relax. When the tears began pouring out, he talked to her, kindly, lullingly. Told her it was sometimes harder emotionally for adult women than teenagers. He told her it would be OK. She did not tell him she was afraid of what he would find.

As he worked, she watched his face, but she couldn't divine anything. No frowns, no momentary looks of dismay. And afterward, dressed again, when she sat down in his office to hear, she was shaking. The dimly-lit office had the quiet, masculine feel of a study: the dark mahogany desk behind which the doctor sat scratching with a fountain pen; the leather chairs that squeaked when either of them moved. She heard the captain's clock tick-tocking. She read the doctor's diplomas and societies without taking any of it in until he looked up and cleared his throat.

"You're fine," he told her. "Everything is coming along just as it should." She sat, shocked, for a moment.

"Really?" she asked him at last, and choked through the tears that started coming, "You're not just saying that?"

He smiled at her. "Oh, you're afraid – the plumbing? Went haywire or some such thing?"

She looked at him, her eyes burning, her mouth all pinched up, tears streaming down her cheeks, and nodded.

"You're healing beautifully, so don't you give it another thought. You are fine, Miss Fayer, really. Come on now, smile. I won't let you leave until you take this tissue, blow your pretty red nose, and give a big smile."

Sandy laughed through her tears.

"That's good, that's better. Now I want to you to call me in a week and tell me how you feel. Will you do that?"

"Ogay," she promised, and blew her nose. "Thank you, doctor, thank you so much." Lucky, again, she thought.

Returning home exhilarated, she felt as if she could get beyond what had occurred. She would not curl up in a cocoon. She would not let herself. She found two new messages on her answering machine. Without listening to either, she knew they were from two people. And that they mattered to the course of her life. She sat down at her phone. She knew Johnny's number by heart. On the scrap of paper on the table before her was the other number. She sat another moment, gazing off. She felt lucky.

Then she picked up the phone and dialed.

Dinner Out

WE WERE ALL STARVED by the time we got to the restaurant. The line was not long, but we were pressed uncomfortably into the alcove between the inner and outer doors, and it was cold. I squeezed through and got the attention of the tired-looking woman doing the seating.

"Ten minutes," she said.

I said, "Is that really ten or is it really more like twenty?"

"No, ten, maybe less."

I hoped so. Nothing was right in my little world. I hated my job, but felt trapped by the money they forked out in large portions. Tonight I had been looking forward to a relaxing dinner with my best friend, Carla. Although, if truth be told, a certain edginess had come to the surface of our relationship, or more to the point, lack of relationship, since Carla's younger sister announced she was getting married. And then Carla called to say her friends were joining us for our quiet, relaxing dinner.

I went back to the vestibule and shrugged. "Ten. Let's wait, OK?"

Carla looked at Tama and Charl, but it was our choice. They were the friends from out of town, and had no basis for a decision. They both bobbed their heads agreeably.

I was already in a mood not to like them. Their chopped names annoyed me. Tammy? Tamara? And Charl. Saying his name was like having my head snapped back in mid-word. Once at least tonight, I would have to call him Charley. They were holding hands, cramped in a corner by the continually opening door.

In ten minutes we'd worked our way in from the vestibule. I had been exchanging smiles and an occasional word with the cute, curly-haired woman behind us. She was holding the place on line for the cluster of people waiting out in the street by the pile of garbage bags. One of the group, a real princess, came in and asked her friend – Laura, she called her – what the story was. Not happy with Laura's answer, the Princess said, "Go talk to Rico." When Laura hesitated, she said, "Wait here."

I said to Carla, "They aren't going to get seated before us, no matter who they know, or there's going to be a scene."

"Cool your jets, would you." Carla scowled at me. "Don't get your bowels in an uproar over nothing." As an afterthought, Carla said with a smile, "She *thinks* she has an in."

When the Princess came back, harried Rico having held out his hands palms up, she hovered, not with her curly-haired friend behind us, not quite on line, but clearly ahead of both us and the party of two in front of us. Carla saw my look and started saying something over-cheery to Tama. Tama had these hairs growing out of her nose. When she smiled at Carla, they stuck out further and glinted.

Charl and Tama were oblivious of the Princess. They were puppeteers, did kids' birthdays and shows at fairs and colleges. Carla and Tama had been graduate students together at Michigan and had remained close. Charl was a relatively recent accretion of Tama's. He had been her student in a puppeteering class she gave in New Paltz for a while. They were living in an old barn they had been renovating for as long as I had heard about them. I had not met them before this.

"Ah, so I finally meet the Nicky of Carla and Nicky," Charl had said enthusiastically, his eyes fixed on me, his face shining, his arm outstretched. I had shot Carla a withering look. She rolled her eyes in a "Don't accuse me; I never tried to make out we were lovers" expression. His handshake was one of those disgustingly powerful, firm, lasting ones.

Charl was trying to make conversation with me now, but I was preoccupied with that hovering Princess cutting ahead of us. He asked me what I did. I hated that instantly limiting, defining question. Hadn't Carla told Tama, who surely told him? Not only that, I saw the Princess's ears perk up, and I muttered to wait until we sat down.

I went after that weary hostess again. "So what's going on?" We'd been waiting half an hour.

She said, "I have two fours in here and one in there paid their bills and haven't left. We cleared all the dishes. What can I do, yank the table cloth? They're sitting and sitting and sitting. I'm really sorry about it." The line behind us was now out the door and down the street.

Suddenly, Charl tuned in. He pointed toward a table for four in the rear where an elderly man and woman sat. They just sat. Charl stared at the man; the man gazed back. Charl was getting wound up. He started talking in a stage voice about inconsiderate people. The man sat there like he was Rico's prize customer, a Mafia cliché with his stocky, sagging body, round, bald head, bushy white eyebrows, tough-guy features. He was lounging at his cleared table. Charl wouldn't get off him.

A party of eight right near us was going through the motions of imminent departure, counting money, adjusting clothing.

Tama said to Carla, "The wedding's next month you said?"

"They aren't getting that table," I said to Carla, loud enough so the Princess could hear.

She had moved back from the traffic alley, very casually, positioning herself at the front of the line. Meanwhile, her friend Laura, who had left some time before, returned with the whole party, and they all stood idly with the Princess. Their mere number was imposing.

"It's two pushed together," I said to Carla. "They can pull them apart and give us one."

"It could be one long table," Carla said.

Another few minutes passed and I said to the hostess, "Is this the table we're getting?"

"No," she said. "That's the only big table we have. I've got to save it for large parties." She nodded at the Princess and company. "I'm really sorry. There's another one, beside the three I told you about. This one is paying the bill now. It can't be more than just another minute or two." I saw the Princess shift her weight. She had heard the table was hers, and she was comfortably relaxed now.

I joined Charl in glaring at the Mafioso, but it certainly failed to move him.

When the people at the big table rose, the Princess, having ignored my stream of accusation for half an hour, turned to me with her over-mascaraed eyes and said, "They won't seat four at that table. I would never try to cut ahead of you."

I said, "I think you would if you thought you could." I waited for Carla's elbow in my ribs, but instead I heard a grunt of assent from behind me.

"That's a terrible thing to say," the Princess replied. "You don't even know me." Her male retainers were squinting in our direction.

"We know you," Carla said.

I looked at Carla with mild surprise. She looked surly and embarrassed at the same time.

As their group straggled off to sit down, we turned our eyes as one on that bald king of gangland, lounging with his arm over a chair back, his dark eyes taking in the scene spread before him. His wife sat like a little white lump. I hadn't seen him speak to her once.

Charl began declaiming again in a stage voice. Charl was very tall, six foot three I judged, and I'm sure he was projecting nicely. He kept up a patter of jibes such as, "Some people are just incredibly inconsiderate, you know, Tama."

Tama sniffed. She had a long thin nose and she never blew it. She sniffed constantly, which made the little hairs dance.

The tired hostess gave me a tired smile. She had our menus in her hand. At long last, we were shown to our table, which turned out to be two away from the Mafioso's. I thought Charl would quiet down in such close quarters, but the imminence of an audience seemed to spur the puppeteer on. No matter what Carla attempted to discuss, we were confronted with the very loud, equable voice, persistently irrelevant to the discussion. To Carla's question, "Have you guys ever been to Zabar's?" came the non sequitur, "I do agree, Carla, that some individuals, often hairless, can show a disdain for their fellow men and women."

My stomach growling, I was peering around for the bread, the butter, the water. Carla gave me a look I knew. It said, relax, *now*. Don't you dare ruin the rest of my night. I sat back, but I kept watching waiters scurry by without stopping. I wasn't pleased.

"Tell me about Myra and Brad," Tama urged Carla in her little voice. She was stroking Charl's wrist.

"Look at that," Charl whispered, leaning his long torso across the table, as a waiter, with Rico beside him, stopped at the Mafioso's table. "They're asking him to leave and he still won't go." The Mafioso, apparently angry, exchanged words with Rico.

I leaned toward Carla and said, "So do you think Rico is discussing with him the finer points of Racketeer-Influenced and Corrupt Organizations?" Tama and Charl were looking at us, waiting. Carla shook her head. "Ignore him. Not worth explaining. Pathetic lawyer joke, not important. Dumb, extremely witless."

"Humph," I said.

We continued to await our waiter. Another table opened, people were seated, served bread and butter and water. I muttered.

"Tell us about Myra's shower," Tama said.

"Let's stare at him," Charl urged, turning to look at the Mafioso. He continued loudly, "I mean, this is so obnoxious. Some people have no courtesy at all. Totally self-centered."

Tama was trying to shush him, without success.

I said, "He's going to put a contract out on you if you don't shut up."

"He doesn't care," Charl said extra-loudly. "He couldn't care less about anything but his own stomach. He's too busy digesting. He can't even *think* of moving until every morsel of food has been digested. I wonder what he had. It's so long ago they probably washed all his dishes already. We'll probably be eating off his dishes."

Our waiter finally came with bread, butter, water. He took our order. Rico escorted him, telling us how sorry he was for the delay. Charl thanked both of them profusely. The waiter had just snapped up the last menu and turned on his heals when I looked in the direction of the Mafioso, and did a double-take.

Charl must have seen my face because he stopped speaking. He craned his long neck forward, and when he sat back, his face had gone white and he was sliding down in his seat.

"Don't you feel bad," I said softly. "Don't you feel like shit."

Charl took another quick glance. "Oh my God," he said through gritted teeth. He buried his face in his hands, and shook his head back and forth. When he looked out at us between spread fingers, I could see that he truly did wish he might disappear.

"They're just now being served," he whispered. "They've been waiting all this time?" He sat staring at me with his jaw frozen open. Eventually he spoke. "Why weren't napkins and silverware on the table then?" he said, angry at being misled. "I feel awful," he finally said. "The poor guy must be starved half to death the whole time I've been harassing him. I have to go over and apologize." As he started to rise, Tama and Carla simultaneously reached for his shoulder. "No!" they said in unison.

"Don't worry," Carla said with unassailable logic. "He probably has no idea he's the one you were riding. He probably wonders who's the bastard who won't leave."

"Now what?" I said, looking the other way.

One of the women in the Princess's coterie was watching us and whispering. They were all, one after another, sneaking glances in our direction. Of course, the whole restaurant had been eyeing us at one point or another, but why now? Then one of them, a little bony thing in a loose tee-shirt that said "Hungarian Pastry Shop," was standing over us. Her voice was soft; she spoke with, if not quite a lisp, a whistle. "Excuse me, but are you Charles Peters?" she said, looking intently at the one and only. Aha, I thought, the unchopped Charles did exist.

"I'm Doris Schmerling – from Madison."

Charl's face, when her face and her name and the place registered, lit up, and he was bolting around the table, wrapping the frail creature in a bear hug, to the chagrin of the harried waiters trying to squeeze through the narrow aisle. "Doris, God, I can't believe it."

"Do you remember Ginny McBride and Tom Goldstein?" she asked, leading him toward the table of eight. And then there was a chaotic minute of rearranging and we were all being moved to a table that had just opened, that was being pushed together, even as it was being cleared by a waiter, with the table of eight. Plates and glasses and silverware and bread basket were being transferred by Charl and Doris. It was as if the unhappiness oozing from Carla and me, even the loving resignation of Tama, were rendered impotent by Charl's enthusiasm, and against all our wills we were sitting with these people, listening to Charl's resonant voice telling the entire restaurant his tales of the puppet stage. Carla asked me from across the table to pass the butter and I glared at her, unmoving. Tama, next to me, passed it.

Both sides sat awkwardly silent, as Charl and Doris boomed and lisped for all of us. I chewed at my bread, silently stewing, silently cursing Carla for her friends. We were hearing a litany of who had married whom, and who was still with whom, and who was now gay, in the great Midwest.

"Hello again," I heard the Princess say. She had been at the end of their table, so she was sitting next to me.

I looked at her with a wry smile. "I said we'd get this table," I muttered. She pressed her lips tight to keep from smiling. She had nice full lips, very red except in one corner where the lipstick had been wiped. I thought that if I were sleeping with her, I would make her wash all that makeup off first.

"Are you always so obnoxious to strangers?" she asked. Her eyes were dark brown; they had deep circles under them that the makeup almost disguised and I had not noticed before.

"To a certain kind of person," I said in a playful voice. Somehow, those circles under her eyes had made me feel differently about her. She was probably working impossible hours similar to mine, determined to be a success in some hyper-competitive firm. I started to feel a certain kinship with her. Like me, she had just been trying to take control of the chaos around her.

"Ah," she said, and whirled some spaghetti onto her fork and into her mouth. "And to what kind of person are you a gentleman?" she asked. Her eyes darted between Carla and Tama. She didn't, I realized, know who belonged where.

I was looking into those dark brown eyes. I was imagining how she would taste, how she would smell, whether her nipples were large or small, how wet she got, what she liked. Her teeth were very large, very white. She was showing them to me. We sparred playfully a little more. Carla was eating in silence. My hand inadvertently brushed the hairs of the Princess's arm. She didn't move away, and our arms pressed together for a moment. Her heat made me feel a flush of excitement.

"So what *do* you do?" she asked, from under half-closed eyelids. I had been right about her ears perking up earlier. Or should I respond to the double entendre.

Her guy was saying something to her then and she turned the other way. I went back to eating, glancing up at Carla.

"You are such a predictable asshole," she mouthed. Tama looked up at her, squinting.

When we left the restaurant, it was late. The line had dwindled. There were only one or two parties waiting. The pace of the waiters was less frantic. The cool night was refreshing; the now empty street tranquil. The air was misty. The black vinyl garbage bags piled in mounds at the curb in front of every restaurant had a glistening jewel-like quality. We turned the corner into a crowd.

We had to humor Charl. He wanted to stop and watch a street magician. I'd seen them so many times – I'd even seen this particular one's whole rap last year or the year before that.

Tama was saying to Carla, "We haven't even talked about the wedding, which is what I've been dying to hear about. When is it? Is your mother thrilled? Do you like the guy? He'll be a member of your family. Myra must be in heaven."

"He's very sweet," Carla said with a pleased smile, "I like him a lot. Myra picked herself a real winner. They are so cute together, all in love. And Mom absolutely adores him."

Carla, my closest friend in all the world for the last four years, Carla's little sister was getting married, while Carla tick-tocked into serious biological clock time. She'd take me to the wedding naturally, and that would make it just so much worse. Her mother happened to think I was the greatest thing on earth. The one inexplicable blind spot of a quite intelligent woman, Carla often mused in my presence.

We said goodbye to Tama and Charl, who said what a real exciting, fun New York time it had been, much livelier being out with real New Yorkers in real New York places. Even the embarrassing incident with the hungry bald guy, Charl said, was great. They would have fantastic stories to use in their puppet show ad libs.

Carla and I walked on without speaking for several blocks after we dropped them.

"So," Carla said tersely then, as we stopped for a light, "Get her number?"

For a moment I didn't respond. Then I nodded.

In The Bears' Den

I T IS 6:30 IN the morning of a day that will be sultry. Golda sleeps on her futon, on the floor of her living room, where she dreams. In her dream, a hulking man is swinging a mallet wildly, grinning at her, showing her his yellow teeth. He fills a version of her bare apartment. This version contains her queen-sized mattress on the floor of the bedroom. It contains the futon on which she sleeps in the living room. It does not contain her five-year-old son who lies in the center of that vast mattress on the floor of the real bedroom. It does contain, filling one wall, the mahogany cabinet which the real room does not contain. The cabinet covers the entire length of the cramped apartment, as it would if it were there. It is a glassed-in breakfront containing her fine china, mostly bowls, the china that was her grandmother's. It is – and this, in the funny way of dreams, she does know and considers thoughtfully – the one possession of hers that she absolutely wants from her husband, who lives with her possessions several floors down.

In this dream she is having, the undeterrable man, who has a beard and longish hair and towers over her, and who swings a mallet methodically, is smashing her breakfront. She flinches as the cabinet crunches under the weight of the blows, leaving exposed the jagged flesh of unvarnished wood. She considers (in her dream, in the curious way of dreams) who this man would be if this were a dream she were analyzing. She concludes only that he would not be her husband.

The dishes and bowls that had been stacked so neatly shatter under the random strokes of the man's unremitting, violent hammer blows. Shards fly. The bowls explode. When the man has powdered the entirety of the collection of china, he rapes her.

Golda wakes, sun streaking her; she is gulping for breath. She lies there weak. When she collects her thoughts, she realizes that she is lying on her futon in her bare living room on a day that will be sultry; she remembers that her son is in the bedroom this week, a small bit of warm flesh denting the center of oceanic mattress. Her dream is already fading. She is not able to tell whether or not it was a nightmare. She cannot grip her feelings yet. She is just now realizing she has had a dream and struggling to recall the details. She can visualize the man only vaguely. She is filled with an intangible sense of discomfort, anxiety. As her state of wakefulness becomes more and more complete, she is, as she is when she awakens every morning, on the edge of panic.

She hears the stirring in the bedroom, then the sound of feet padding across the floor and the warm arm hugging her as the little body flops down next to her and falls almost immediately asleep. "Time to get up, honey," she says, stroking his damp hair. He whines crankily and presses tighter to her. She dreads the battle today more even than usual. If only she could convince him it were a Saturday for just half an hour. On Saturdays, when she can sleep late, nothing keeps him in bed.

The phone rings. It will be her lover, who has grown impatient with her inability to stop suffering. Her lover will tell her she has floated too long. He presses her relentlessly now to take her dishes – the precious bowls that were her grandmother's; to take an easy chair or two so she has some place to sit; to take a box spring so the mattress is not on the floor where it gets so filthy. He wants her to steal things. He wants her to break and enter. He wants her to clean out her husband's apartment, the apartment that was hers. They are her things, he says. They are joint property, he says. In her possession rather than her husband's, they will precipitate movement. They will make things happen. They will help to extricate her from this drifting cage in which she has been bound. She lets the phone ring until it stops.

She thinks she shouldn't do anything that will weaken her position. "What position?" she hears her lover fuming. She flinches from his anger. She is paralyzed in a moment of fear. She strokes her son's head.

"Mommy, don't cry," her son yells at her, confused, angry.

"I'm not crying, sweetie. I have something in my eye."

"No you don't."

"Come on, sweetie, you have to get up now. We'll be late."

"I don't want to go to school. I hate riding the subway."

"All little boys love the subway, honey."

<hr>

Golda dreads the subway tunnel with its dank, antediluvian air, air that has never touched blue sky, steamy air that smacks her and drips down her breast as it is pushed through the tunnel by a train that is yet a distant rumble.

In the swarm of perspiring, angry people, she clings to her son, whose forehead bears the worried frown of a little old man. She has dragged him to the dark front of the platform, where the crowd is thinner. But here the pools of urine reek at her. She wishes she could give her son disposable sneakers to change when they leave this orifice. The train hurtles in, shoving her hair off her face, exposing her. She clasps her son's hand hard, yanking him through the doors, fearful of being disconnected from him, terrified to imagine his being left on the platform, abandoned, not knowing where to go or how.

This car is, miraculously, only half full. Golda guides her son to two empty seats, where they settle themselves. In the pallid light, stations flicker by, island worlds bulging with humanity. Her son chatters, half to her, half to himself.

"Ladies and gentlemen, can I have your attention," a white-haired woman arrests Golda's wandering thoughts. Her voice is strong and clear, without emotion, without any bashfulness or self-consciousness. In matter-of-fact sentences, she tells her tale of woe. Golda gives a dollar bill from her purse. She can't afford it. She has to get through this week on $11. The weeks she has her son, all her money goes to his food. The weeks she doesn't have him, she eats the leftovers from the week she did. The woman evaporates and more stations flicker by.

A man in a filthy torn coat appears, gripping a soiled paper cup. "Spare change," he calls out in a surly voice. Golda instinctively places her arm across her son as the man pauses in front of her. He has stopped because a tall burly man with a beard and a blue wool hat pulled down over his ears has taken out a wad of bills and peeled off a single. "Let me have fifty cents," the hulking man says to the bum, smiling, showing his teeth.

Golda feels a sense of guilt that she has closed her heart to this dirty, sad man. Up close, he looks forlorn. That he was not as articulate as the woman should not have kept her from helping. The beggar is searching in his pocket for two quarters. He finds them and hands them to the burly man, who abruptly flips his dollars back into his pocket. "Git away or I'll bust out your lights," he tells the open-mouthed beggar, as he places the beggar's fifty cents ostentatiously in his pocket. And with that, he holds the pole, swaying with the raging train, grinning through the beggar now, as if he no longer stands before him, as if he is not real.

Golda holds her breath, her eyes fixed on the burly man's grinning face, his yellow teeth, the blue wool hat pulled down around his ears. The beggar is poised in uncertainty. In this moment of choice he determines ultimate things. His eyes show that he knows this. His unclear mind pulls him back and forth, and Golda, terrified of the outcome, blocked from any retreat, any way to spare her son, watches helplessly the battle in the beggar's adrenalin-soaked mind. And Golda too, in this moment, grapples with the urge to protest this outrage and the necessity of forbearance.

A chinless woman, scowling at the burly man, waves a dollar at the bewildered beggar who takes the money and, the spell broken, goes, with a sidelong glance at the face beneath the blue wool hat.

A man with his wife and baby breaks the silence, doubling over in laughter. "That's not funny," screams his wife. The husband cannot stop. "That's not funny," the wife repeats, and the stations pass by. The wife's voice merges with the rhythm of the tracks. "That's not funny," she repeats and repeats. The man in the blue wool hat stares at a particular bit of stainless steel in front of him, riding the subway. Golda glares up at him from her distance.

⚬

"So, do you know why the cops shot the polar bear?" Golda's boss asks her eagerly even before she has unlocked her desk drawer. He is a heavy, frumpy man, sagging, with bulging eyes and thin red hair. Her son is safely at school. Golda is three minutes late for work. Her stomach turns even thinking about the polar bears. Several days before, a young boy had sneaked into the zoo after closing time with two friends. This one foolish boy, up to no good, climbed into the polar bear enclosure. The three polar bears, a male, a female, and a cub, after dragging the boy to their den, ripped him apart and ate him. The police, arriving after the boy was dead, but while the two adult bears were still tussling over the remains of his body, shot all three bears dead in a hail of more than forty bullets, causing great controversy in the city.

Golda had not been able to get the images out of her mind. She pictured the scene over and over: the largest bear – lumbering, dirty, white – rearing up; muddy paws crushing the little boy to the night-cold rocks; the yellow teeth probing his bare chest as he called out to his friends to get help, urgently telling them that the bear was biting really hard; the crunch of bone as his chest opened; the red spurting onto the pure white fur; the terrified screams that roused some distant person to make the phone call that brought the police; the boy crying for his mommy, half-conscious as he was dragged, almost a piece of meat now, to the darkness of the den, where his last feeble kicks attracted the eyes of one of the bears to his legs; the boy's leg raised in the air as the wet foaming mouth closed on it with a sickening crunch; the curdling howl as the face, the horrified eyes, disappeared into the other bear's saliva-dripping mouth; the stillness then, broken only by the grunts of the bears as the two mouths groped, the two bears jockeying, growling possessively, tugging at the limp flesh of the torso while the baby bear sat nearby, patiently waiting for its turn.

"They thought it was Camilla Dunquist," Golda's boss tells her, grinning. His eyes search her for a flicker of a smile. Abruptly, his face contracts in a spasm of laughter, phlegmy-sounding. Camilla Dunquist, Golda remembers, was a very large woman, who, in the process of refusing to be evicted from her apartment, was shot dead by a heavily armed contingent of policemen who were later acquitted in a court trial of any misbehavior. And ever since, the Camilla Dunquist jokes had ricocheted through the city.

"Come on, Golda. Lighten up. That was funny." Golda doesn't know what to say. She is working temporary jobs at nine dollars an hour. She can't afford to jeopardize her relationship with her boss, which would in turn jeopardize her position with her agency. "I guess I don't have much of a sense of humor anymore," Golda says. "I'm sorry," she adds.

Golda works through her lunch hour. She can't afford to eat, as she tells her lover when he gets angry at her for not eating.

He calls her while she is printing out a letter. He is checking to see if she is eating, angry that she is not.

And once angry, he presses her to steal what is hers.

"It has so little value," she says.

"You are lying on the floor drinking out of cottage cheese containers," he says. "While he lives it up."

"All right, I'll do it, OK. Listen, my boss is coming. I have to get off." Golda hangs up the phone, working at freezing her face.

The images keep coming back; make her queasy. The way they autopsied the bears right there – taking out the head and legs of the boy from the stomachs of the bears. She feels as if she has to watch her son every moment, not let him out of her sight. She is afraid her husband is too lax on his watch.

<hr>

It is eight o'clock at night now, and it is still sultry.

"This is not right," Golda says to herself. She is leaning against the window of her husband's first floor apartment and peering into the bedroom. No one is home, she is sure. Her husband and his lover have a meeting tonight. He told her son about it when he called him. "This is not right," she repeats aloud.

Golda returns to the lobby, nods to the porter at the door. She hesitates halfway between her husband's door and the elevator. The bastard, she says to herself, decisively, and walks briskly to his door, standing on tiptoes to peek in. The living room is completely dark.

"This is not right," Golda mumbles, clutching the key he does not know she still has. It is moist with the sweat of her palm and she turns it over in her hand, finally slipping it into the lock and jerking open the door. She hurries into the dark room, giddy and aflutter. As her eyes adjust to the dim light from the street, she sees her mahogany cabinet looming expansively across the width of the room. In the murky silence of ticking clocks and whirring refrigerator, Golda stands hunch-shouldered, staring at her bowls. Her small figure is a ghostly luminescence in the glass of the cabinet.

What is she doing here? she wonders. She cannot carry these things by herself. She feels as if she is floating through a dream where nothing makes sense. She opens the cabinet and runs her fingers across one of the dainty china bowls. She sets it on a coffee table and falls heavily down on a leather easy chair that she knows with despair is beyond her ability to drag.

She walks with sudden momentum into her son's room. She stands, shivering all at once, looking at his toys and clothing strewn about his room in this apartment that is no longer hers but is still his.

She feels weak, and stretches out on his bed. His bed here is more comfortable than where he sleeps in her apartment. Lying back, head on his pillow, she takes in his room. He has a chest for his toys here, and a desk and lamp and a clock and a closet

– a room of his own. "It isn't fair," she cries out, banging her fist on his sheet with the fairy tale motif, her eyes falling for a moment, and lingering, on the golden-haired fairy godmother, her smiling face, her bright red lips, her silver wand.

Golda lies for many minutes on her son's bed, gazing at his toys, staring finally at the menacing wrathful monster poised on three legs on the dresser, reflected in the mirror back into the recesses of the wall.

She picks up the telephone and dials her lover's number. "Hello?" she says.

He seems preoccupied. And, now that she has called, angry at her. He asks her when she is going to have her lawyer file for divorce, her lawyer who knows how little money she has, who so obviously just wants her to agree to whatever terms her husband and his powerhouse lawyer set. "And what about your possessions?" he presses the relentless question. "Make things happen. Force the lawyers to move." All she wants is consolation.

Golda picks up a stuffed animal and strokes it. "I don't know," she murmurs. "I'm so tired. I just can't take this anymore. This uncertainty. Why are you so little help to me? Why do you yell at me?"

Her lover does not answer. She feels bad for having said this. He has been good to her. It has been too long and he is getting impatient. He has a right to be impatient. This isn't what she led him to believe her life would be like. He is not the kind of person who can understand what holds her so suspended between here and there. But he has stuck with her beyond his understanding.

"I'm upset about the bears," Golda offers.

"Yes," her lover answers. "To kill those bears that lived in that zoo all those years! Twenty years," he says. "They could have used a tranquilizer gun."

"What?" Golda says. "That's not what I meant."

Golda's mind plays over that awful scene, that nightmare that has become a part of her waking state – those yellow groping teeth nudging her. She doesn't hear what her lover is saying. She puts down the telephone, feeling for the cradle but missing it – hearing the receiver sliding to the floor with a clatter that sounds louder than in reality it is.

She thinks she hears voices in the other room, the room where she once entertained company; and a silence as the phone falls. Then she hears distinctly the sound of feet moving slowly toward the room she is in, toward her son's room. She looks at her watch. "My God," she thinks. And picks herself up, moving to the window, heaving it open with one graceless motion, lowering herself clumsily, and disappearing into the forest of garbage bags and cars and buses and traffic lights and street lamps outside.

Looking back, she catches a glimpse of them, the pair of blond heads, bleached white in the play of light, thrust out the window, strands of hair blowing in the gentle breeze. "Was anything taken?" she hears him say to this woman for whom he left her.

"They've been at the bowls in your cabinet, and they seem to have moved a chair, and someone's obviously been lying on the bed in here talking on the phone."

Golda thinks this woman is ugly, and she knows her to be a cold person. Her son should not have such a stepmother. It isn't fair.

Blue Heaven

I HEARD THE ANNOUNCEMENT of my office closing at 6:30. Now, at 7:26, I am still listening to the radio, sitting at the window, wrapped tight in my afghan. Fifty billion schools have closed and been announced. And my office. But so far, nothing of Rick's office. He's been checking on line, carrying his phone around the house, but so far his HR hasn't made up its mind. I like listening to the names being read on the radio as I watch the snow.

Out there, in the white seamless world, the flash of red quickens me. One of our pair of cardinals comes to the feeder, cocks his crested head, first to this side, then to that, takes two quick pecks. He darts away, powdering a mound of snow with his fiery red wings. As he flies off, I first spy the female flying after him.

"The cardinals," I call out.

I hear the sound of running water as Ricky sticks his head out of the bathroom. "What's that? Was that us?"

"No, Rick, nothing yet. It was the cardinal." He grunts and the door closes.

My leg is falling asleep. I get up and hobble, push open the bathroom door, feel the steam sealing my skin, enclosing me. "I want you home today," I say. He is bent over the sink and I press up against his back. I form myself to him, wrap my arms around him, tweak his nipples. I hear the cat's squeak of greeting and feel him rubbing up against my leg. "Hi, Cutie," I say into Ricky's neck.

"Delbert and I want you to cuddle all day and watch the snow with us," I say to Ricky.

Ricky rinses the toothpaste out of his mouth and says into the fogged mirror, "You and Bertha, you mean?"

This week, for some inexplicable reason, we started calling the baby all the names we've never understood how any parents could give to a child they loved.

If it's a boy, we are going to call him Daniel. We are having more trouble on the girl's side. I like Deborah. The D's are for my grandfather Donald who died last year. Ricky likes Rachel. My grandfather's middle name happened to be Raymond, so Rachel's OK too.

Evan spent an hour on the phone with me yesterday pushing for Michelle or Nicole. He said he'd never seen an unsexy Michelle, and the kinkiest best time he ever had was with a quiet little coquette named Nicole. I said I wasn't sure those were exactly the criteria we were planning to use. And then I was mad at myself for wondering if he thought I had been just Jell-O; what did they have that I didn't?

Clinging to Ricky now, thinking about Evan, I feel for a moment a strangeness that makes me shiver. I press myself tighter to him. The white bathroom tiles are moist, starting to drip. The bright light hurts my eyes. In the beaded mirror, Ricky blurs. We have entered, the two of us together, this still, white tunnel nine months long, and when we emerge, everything will be somehow unalterably different. Irrevocably. I feel this. I know this. Forever. In ways I try and try to imagine.

Ricky bundles up. He has on the Bean duck boots I bought him. In his down coat, he is a gray form held together by wire-rimmed glasses.

"Be careful," I say. "Gussy and I will worry."

"Wait a minute, is that a boy or a girl, Gussy?"

"Augusta."

"Ah. Well, you and Roscoe shouldn't worry. I'll be careful."

I smudge his glasses with my nose in trying to kiss him under the hood.

At ten, my mother calls to ask how I'm feeling. I've been having good and bad days. Today is good. I'm half asleep when she calls, reading through one of the two dozen baby care books with which we've managed to encumber ourselves. I take my phone and get up to watch the birds at the feeder. A whole flock of chickadees and a few tufted titmice are taking turns sweeping in and flapping off with sunflower seeds clamped tightly in their beaks. The snow isn't so bad where she is, mom says.

At eleven, I get an unexpected phone call from Evan. Cutie is meowing, so I let him out. He steps gingerly, shakes his foot, then plunges, sinking and hopping, creating a trough as he goes. Evan says he read a novel in which some wrinkled old prune – therefore unquestionably wise, he says – (how about a modicum of political correctness, Evan) gave the advice that if you set a biscuit on the back of your tongue as soon as you wake up – don't chew it now, just let it sit there and melt – you won't get nauseous. I don't tell him morning sickness is only at the beginning. I tell him I'll try it. He has become unnaturally attentive.

The silent snowfall continues till early afternoon. I watch, entranced, out of the window, listening to a playlist of "mellow midday jazz" I asked Alexa to play. I imagine our child at ten, at sixteen. It is a girl I find myself picturing. (We chose not to know; *I* chose. I'm not sure why. I don't really like surprises.) A Michelle, I admit reluctantly, not a Deborah. Zits and too much unevenly applied makeup. I feel my stomach knotting

– her kicking – at hungers and guilts and angers she barely understands at sixteen. Will she, her angers, hurt me terribly?

"Cutie, where are you?" I want to hold my cat. I open the back door, white prickles of snow on my hand leaving moist, glistening spots. As if I had conjured him, he appears before me with a squeak to announce his presence, and scurries in.

"Hi, Cutie," I say. "Had enough of the snow? Did you wipe your feet like a good boy?"

He is stretching lazily, yawning. The fur on his legs is curly wet. As I smile at him, I notice him start to twist his tongue as if something is stuck in his mouth. I see a spot of red under his whiskers. In his mouth. He jumps away from the suddenness of my move.

"Come here, Cutie," I say. "Let me see." He is still working his tongue as I bend down to squint at him. Up close, I see that a tiny red feather is caught in the corner of his mouth.

"Cutie!" I scream at him. He darts under me, gallops across the living room, and slides hard into the brick of the fireplace. Scrambling to his feet, he stands poised, wide-eyed, looking up at me, licking his lips with his pink tongue. He meows softly, terrified that I have turned on him. I feel bad for him, but the shudder is ricocheting through me.

—◆—

On Saturday, the sky has cleared to a deep brilliant blue. Standing on tiptoes, sinking into the snow, wishing, as ever, that I were taller than five foot two, I let the seeds slide from my fist into the feeder. I have never seen Evan turn his eyes on the street to look at a tall woman. Richard, on the other hand, is fond of telling me I am not his type – too short. That's why we'll work out, he says.

I stretch up another fistful, my sunglasses sliding down my nose, which is starting to run. Impatient now, I tip the whole bag of sunflower seeds into the feeder. Seeds tumble and scatter, disappearing into tiny dark dots in the crust of white. I feel more than see the female cardinal waiting nearby, watching.

The door clatters closed behind me as I hop, teeter, trying to get my rubber boot off. It's stuck to my heel and when it comes off I make a sort of unbalanced, springing dive across the kitchen and into the living room, and end up standing in front of Evan, catching my breath. He is sprawled on the couch playing channel roulette, which he knows I hate. When we lived together, I once tossed his remote out our eighth-story window. He came over to drop off that novel – apparently the old woman is a wealth of advice – and now it looks like he's planning to stay for dinner. Ricky is very tolerant about Evan, very trusting. I'm not sure why I let him come.

Evan begins crooning at me teasingly, wickedly, and horribly off key the words to the old song, "My Blue Heaven."

Yes, I want to say to him, what number does baby make? Three, not four. I show him a sneer.

Evan is pleased with himself. I am struck, as so many times before, by his angel hair, his blond eyelashes, his liquid blue eyes I thought once upon a time could float right into me.

"Tell me about marital bliss."

I give him a dramatic sigh of annoyance, but he is in one of his moods. He won't be deterred. He stares, eyebrows raised, waiting, demanding to be told how someone other than he has changed my life.

"I don't feel less crazy. It's more like I have a warm blanket around me I can duck my head under." I smile at him. "You'll find her, your Nicole, Michelle."

"You thought you wanted to marry *me*."

"It's different."

"*How* different?" he demands.

As I watch him petulantly flick the channel changer, I feel for just a moment as if I am back in the time three years ago when I was living with him in a studio apartment, with the loft bed and no place to put things except on top of each other in ever-ascending piles. As hard as I try, I can't recall our ending. The last thing I can recall is the fire, a big apartment-building fire on a bitter cold winter night. We were striding up the street in our usual condition of ambiguity – holding hands, but mouths squawking ferociously at each other. We turned the corner before we were aware we had been smelling smoke.

"This is amazing," Evan said as flames shot ten feet above the roof. We stood for half an hour in the cold, watching. Everyone had been evacuated, so there was no sense of imminent danger, rather an almost serene sense of viewing art, of spectacular beauty. Like a Turner painting of a volcano erupting, city version.

I was the only one who saw the yellow cat perched on a window sill on the eighth floor. His back arched in fear, he looked, from my distance, utterly calm.

I turned to Evan. He was looking furtively at a cute dark-skinned, short woman. It was cold out, but she had no coat. She wore a white tee shirt and her arms were folded very tight below her breasts. It dawned on me that she had probably lived in the building. The cat remained motionless, watchful, unnoticed in the bustle of activity.

For seconds, I could only stare up, my mind fixed on the cat's incongruous stillness.

"Excuse me," I said, finally breaking free of my paralysis, grabbing the arm of the policeman who was leaning on his car, flirting with the woman. "Do they know about that cat?"

Still grinning at the woman, he looked where I pointed, and, seeing, palmed his radio, pressed it into his lip, and mumbled. The woman looked at me and smiled politely. She had a tooth missing in the middle.

"They do now," the cop said, nodding at me.

As I stared eagerly upward, the cherry picker of a fire engine – which had been at roof level – began slowly to descend to the eighth floor. I said to Evan, "How could someone just leave their cat?"

Evan was not interested.

"Why are you pulling me, damn it, I want to see! Let go of me."

I watched as the fireman leaned toward the window, a silhouette against the yellow leaping flames, and stretched out his arm gingerly. Some people clapped as the cherry picker descended, with the radiant fireman waving over his head a limp, very unhappy, very alive ball of fur.

⬤

"The funniest thing happened," my mother is telling me on the phone. "Your father sent me an anniversary card. He didn't write anything, but the postmark was Florida. I guess he's still living in Miami with that strumpet." My mother doesn't know that I talk to my father on the phone almost every week. It's been a secret I've had a hard time keeping. He'll call and then I'll be talking to her and catch myself from saying "Daddy says –" as if it were the old days.

I can hear her moving around in the kitchen. From the sounds, I think she is scrubbing the sink. "Can you believe it?" He must have been drunk and thought it would be a good joke, a kick for old time's sake."

"Mom, can't you think that maybe he was just feeling nostalgic, just for a minute, and in a mellow mood, and thinking of you?" I say.

"He's crazy," she says. "'Dear Ida,' he wrote. And signed it 'Jack.' And it wasn't like a card from a husband to a wife. It was – wait, I'll read it to you."

"No, mom, don't go and get it."

"Oh, all right. It was something like, 'To the two of you on your anniversary. May all the years to come be as blessed with love as this year,' or something like that. You don't see anything the least bit sadistic there? You never did have any idea about your father. You never had any idea about men period. I don't know how you managed to find someone as nice as Rick."

⸎

Ricky is in the bedroom organizing me. He slipped over a pile of my papers in the dark last night and now he is putting up a shelf.

My papers have started to spread across the floor since I've been working at home the last month – since a few weeks after the snowstorm. I've seen the female cardinal once since I've been home: on the terrace, pecking at the seeds under the feeder. I am still trying to forgive Cutie, trying to tell myself it is his nature.

Ricky comes in looking proud of himself. "Done," he says, and wraps me up in his arms, bending so his middle doesn't press too hard on my bulging belly. He leads me into the bedroom, and shows me the shelf. It's very nice.

"What's wrong with it?" he asks

"Nothing," I say. "It's great." It is quite perfect. "It's a shelf."

In the afternoon, rain falls, and then it turns to snow as the day gets colder. The radio says the roads are freezing. I say, "Maybe you shouldn't go to work tomorrow." Ricky says he has to.

In the morning, Ricky says, "How is Algernon doing?" as he walks into the whiteness, away from me.

"OK," I say, stepping out with him, pulling my robe tight, then stepping back in, holding the door open.

The car leaves thin rings of white smoke behind it. The snowfall is deep and I can hear it rubbing against the tires. The car disappears from view behind the curtain of flakes. But I am still with him. I can't explain it. It feels so real. Ricky likes to chew gum when he drives. Half a dozen sticks of Juicy Fruit are scattered across the dashboard. I concentrate on the road, smell the pervasive fragrance of Juicy Fruit. I am having a baby with Ricky.

As we descend the hill, I find myself pressing with my brake foot. The light at the bottom of the hill, when we see it flickering through the snowfall, is red, but we are not slowing down. My foot is jamming my nonexistent brake to the floor. Ricky's brake is to the floor also. We are sliding slightly from side to side, and accelerating. Now we are starting to spin; suddenly out of control. All at once I know we are going to hurtle through the red light.

Ricky is cursing to himself, squinting to try to see out the windshield. Is he panicked? Does he think about me and the baby? I can't tell. I can't know.

I can't speak. I am trying, but only sounds like a deaf person makes come out of my mouth. I squeeze my eyes closed as we fly through the intersection. I hear the wail of a horn, then a second one. I brace myself for the impact, thinking horrifying thoughts about losing my baby. And my husband.

"That was lucky," Ricky says to himself as he rolls slowly to a stop.

Hot And Sour

THE SNOW WAS FALLING in big fluffy romantic flakes. Veronica stuck out her tongue to catch some. She was holding Josh's hand as they walked over the slippery cobblestones of DUMBO. She had never seen cobblestones in the two years she'd lived in New York since graduating from Brown, and she thought this would be a fun jaunt. "There won't be any crowds, that's for sure," she'd said. He had rolled his eyes. "I wonder why."

She wore inappropriate shoes. She was only 5'2" tall, and her priority was to look taller regardless of any inconvenience. Josh knew that, and thought it was silly. He loved her exactly the way she was. Who was she lifting herself for? He just smiled as she lost her balance and he held her up.

She at least was dressed warmly. She must have had five layers of sweatshirts and sweaters under her down coat, and snow pants over the short skirt she had told him she was wearing for him, for later. She looked fat although she was a slip of a thing. All that showed of her face were her mouth and red nose, and occasionally her piercing blue eyes, which kept disappearing into her slightly too-large knit hat's face mask as the eye slits shifted. Her long black hair was dotted with white, melting flakes.

He on the other hand was freezing. He had thought a down coat, gloves, and a warm hat with ear flaps, plus flannel jeans and a flannel shirt would be enough. He simply hadn't accounted for the wind along the river. And getting old, of course.

The plan, her plan anyway, was to walk back across the Brooklyn Bridge. "It will be so romantic with the skyline, the snow falling." She slipped again and he put an arm around her as he held her up. Then he put the other arm around her bulk and kissed her. The wet from her running nose made his face even colder. She wiped his face off with the end of her scarf and then reluctantly took off her glove to dig out a tissue to blow her nose.

"You're shaking," she said.

"It's fucking freezing."

She looked at the looming vague outline of the Brooklyn Bridge against the lowering sky.

"Not happening."

She nodded. "I guess that was a wee bit much, huh?"

"Yah think."

"We'll come back in the Spring," she exclaimed. He wished he had her confidence. Then she looked at him, with less confidence. "Will we?"

"We will," he said vehemently. "Damn it, nothing else matters to me. Just you. Just you." They kissed again as the snow swirled around them, and they clung to each other on the deserted cobblestones.

"Oh God you're shaking like a leaf," she said. "Let's get to the subway."

They ran to the F Train, Josh pulling her along, holding her up. Back in the East Village, they stopped in front of a Chinese restaurant. "Here OK?" he asked.

She hesitated. "You don't come here?"

"No," he said. "This is your neighborhood, not mine."

"Never?"

"No."

She scrutinized him. "Why did you choose this place then?"

He frowned. "No idea. I spotted it. Looks warm."

She considered, then nodded. As an afterthought, she said, "It's a good place." He opened the door and they stepped in.

Both let out an involuntary gasp of relief as the door closed behind them. They stood for a moment, holding hands, letting the heat roll over them.

The place was packed. They found themselves shoehorned into a tiny table in an odd corner toward the back, and lucky to have it. Five minutes later the line stretched out the door into the cold and snow.

Josh laughed as she took off layer after layer, finally revealing her Brown tee shirt and the white skirt.

"Very nice," he said. As she turned from him to sit down, a fleeting smile creasing her lips at the excitement he couldn't quite hide with that flat statement.

He added his coat and hat to the pile of stuff on the third chair. As he bent over the chair, she reached up and ran her fingers through his long brown hair, patting it down where static had made it stand up. Then they both gulped down hot tea.

"Did you check your cell?" she asked.

"I promised you I wouldn't. Anyway, I turned it off." She smiled approvingly. Then he added, "She won't call."

Veronica squinted at him skeptically.

He gave her a reassuring nod.

Veronica played at eating her hot and sour soup with chopsticks. Josh watched as she worked on a mushy piece of tofu that kept breaking into smaller and smaller bits. Since she was Veronica, she persisted until she'd managed to pinch every floating speck. It took a while, but the two of them were in no hurry to venture back into the cold. When only the liquid remained, she experimented with using the chopsticks on that too. She bent over to take a snake-like lick as the chopsticks broke the surface of the soup. Josh chuckled. She winked at him as her tongue again flicked out.

He was already halfway through his helping of shrimp with chili sauce when she ran out of patience with the soup. She picked up her bowl and drank the liquid. She ladled some chicken with broccoli and what he'd left her of the shrimp – pretty much half – onto her plate.

They watched the crowd and the hypnotic snow outside the steamy windows. They made their way through the serving bowls in a comfortable silence. She had one of her inappropriate shoes off, and she'd worked her foot under the hem of his jeans. She rubbed her foot against his leg idly as they ate. Eventually he looked up and sighed. "I'm stuffed."

She grunted softly in response, and continued eating.

He watched her deftly wield her chopsticks for a time, then slid his chair back, reached down for her foot, and hoisted it up, causing her to drop a broccoli floret. Her frown as the broccoli splashed into the sauce became just the suggestion of a smile as he began massaging her foot.

After a while, helping herself to more chicken, she nodded at his fortune cookie." He gently lowered her foot, and reached forward to crack it open. He read it, raised his eyebrows, and gave her a look.

"Well?"

He read, "'Many women find you attractive.'"

"Hah!"

"What?"

She rolled her eyes, but on reflection, as she finished up her broccoli, she said, "I'm sure they do."

With nothing left to eat, they eventually bestirred themselves. Josh watched, intrigued, as her little body again became vast. "I dread this," he said. They stepped out. Four or five inches now covered the sidewalk. She clutched his arm and they made their way to her apartment as darkness fell. Once slimmed down again, they settled onto the sofa in the living room with a blanket over them, though the apartment was quite warm. Just the memory of the cold was enough to demand more warmth. They clung, squeezing out every bit of warmth the other offered.

She had been right about that out-of-season skirt, he thought, as their hands strayed to various parts of each other's bodies. Soon enough, they found themselves in the bedroom wrapped around each other without the skirt or any other clothing, under a mass of blankets. Afterward Josh was dozing off when Veronica got up to go to the bathroom.

She returned to find Josh staring at his phone.

"I guess I was wrong," he said sheepishly, as she tensed up. "She's been calling me."

"Oh God." Veronica sat down in a chair.

"No worry, really. But I should call her back. I'll put it on speaker. No secrets. Ever. OK? But you have to keep quiet no matter what? K?"

"I don't know. Do I want to hear?"

"I want you to...I think."

"Why? You and her should be private. You and she. I wouldn't want someone listening in. It's like a violation."

"Hah." Without considering his words, Josh blurted out, "You think *that's* a violation." He saw her face and said, "I'm sorry. That was an awful thing to say." She nodded, looking down at the floor.

"This isn't about you," he said.

She raised her eyebrows.

"Well, you know what I mean."

She looked at him, silently.

"Well of course it's about you," he said.

Josh hit call, and smiled at her reassuringly. She found herself not only nervous but curious, and it disturbed her.

They heard the phone connect, and then loud breathing. And then abruptly, "Where in the fuck have you been?"

"Where? I...I..."

"I've been calling all day."

"Calm down."

"I'm not calming down. Tell me where you are. What the hell is going on?"

"Priscilla."

"Don't you Priscilla me. Damn you."

"OK, fine." He was silent then.

"Well?"

He hesitated.

"Well?"

"Priscilla."

"I'm still waiting."

"If you really want to know."

"Yes, I really want to know."

"I'm out. I'm with a 22-year-old." He felt an unexpected surge of relief that left him weightless. "Her insights, her sensibilities, beyond her years, astonish me." He looked at Veronica, and smiled. She stared back at him wide-eyed.

And then uncontrollable words spilled out from where the weight had been. "She has jet black hair down to her waist. She was wearing a short white skirt, until I yanked it off her. I've been fucking her brains out. She has a thin little waifish body. She's only five foot two. I adore everything about her." He paused for a moment, looked Veronica in the eye and nodded emphatically. "And dazzling blue eyes."

Veronica turned away, a look of horrified disbelief on her face. It was an effort for her to keep quiet. "What are you doing?" was what he could see she wanted to shout.

"And oh my God. She is insatiable." Veronica put her hands over her face.

The room constricted in the long silence that followed. The heat; the refrigerator; the muffled street sounds grew loud.

"I presume this creature has a name?"

Veronica began shaking her head violently.

"Tell me, damn it. Come on."

"Uhhhh."

"Name, tell me her name."

"Why do you want to know that? Why does it matter?"

"OK, she has no name. So are you done now?"

"I guess." He sagged into the pillow.

"Really, I'm serious. I've been worried out of my mind."

"You don't believe me?"

"Joshua, I was starting to get really nervous. People do have heart attacks at your age. It's not like you to be totally unreachable. And then I heard about the snow. An accident."

"Ohhhh, just what I want to hear. I'm only 44, for Christsake. I'm two years younger than you. Do you feel a heart attack coming on? You're fucking psychotic."

"Neurotic maybe. I wouldn't argue with that. Joshua, I didn't know what to think."

"I'm sorry. I have the landline going directly to voice because the robo-calls have been coming every five minutes. And you know I don't carry the cell around the apartment. I forgot to turn the sound on after we were at the movies yesterday. Relax. I was actually wondering why I hadn't heard from you."

"No you weren't. I told you I wouldn't have time to call."

"Uh, right," he said cautiously. Then, "Well I guess that wasn't exactly true."

"I needed to hear your voice." She laughed a bitter laugh. "That really worked."

"I dozed off. Otherwise I might have thought to leave a message."

He winked at Veronica, who was shaking her head. "Everything is good. No heart symptoms. How is it going out there?"

"That wasn't nice of you."

"What wasn't?"

"Your fantasy girl."

"You're right. It wasn't. I'm sorry."

"You still get me hot, after all these years."

They were silent, and in the awkwardness, Josh blew Veronica a kiss and mouthed, "I love you."

Veronica gave him a look.

"So tell me how it's going there."

"I could dye my hair black instead. I thought you like it blond. They say black makes you look older. Do you think I'm fat?"

"It's fine blond, or gray, or anything. No. You know you're not fat."

"Do you wish I were shorter?"

"You're being ridiculous. You know that, don't you?"

"I know," she started and then paused, considering how to say it, "that I'm finally really starting to look old. Gray hair was only the beginning. My neck..."

He groaned. "Yeah, 92 at least. Could we talk about your trip."

"I'm sorry. It's going well...." Several minutes later Josh hung up and blew out a breath, sinking back on the bed.

"You're horrible."

He smiled sheepishly.

"No I mean it. How can you lie like that. It's like you didn't miss a beat. How can I ever trust you after listening to that?"

"I didn't lie. Everything I said is true. We did doze off, didn't we?"

"Yeah but..."

"Except about turning the phone off *at the movie.* Actually I did turn it off there. During the movie, even if I did turn it back on, so half true. Every other single thing. Absolutely truthful." He looked at her.

"Listening to you talk, I feel demeaned. Like I'm nothing but a sex object."

"I was saying that to her. You know it isn't even about the sex. It's being in your presence that makes me feel alive. It never ceases to amaze me. The affect you have on me."

She sighed with frustration.

"Look, you don't know. You have no idea what it's like living with a borderline personality. You can't begin to imagine."

"Is she really? Or are you just making up a diagnosis?"

"I'm not a shrink."

"I'm sorry. I shouldn't ask. We agreed we wouldn't talk about her."

"Explosions, out of nowhere. I think everything's fine, and then..."

He felt himself starting to get anxious, and looked away, getting control and hoping she hadn't noticed. He held out his arms and she came into them. They lay together silently.

"You never had kids. How come? I've wondered that."

He ran his hand through her hair, played with the strands.

She watched him.

"It was a really critical time at her job; she was going in at five and not coming home till eight or nine. No rush. We have time. Then later she got a big promotion and it was the wrong time.

Then..." He shrugged and fell silent. He continued to stroke her head.

"What I said to her is true. Everything about you gets me hot. I adore you."

"Me too." She said it almost reluctantly; something she just could not deny.

"It's as if our bodies and our minds know everything about each other. I don't feel any separation when I am with you. No self-consciousness." He kissed her cheek. "No anxiety," he added. "Do you feel that?"

"I do. I haven't exactly been with that many people, but it's never been like this."

"It's not about sex."

She nodded. "I don't want to say the cliché. It sounds stupid. But it fits. It's really true. *I* think, anyway."

"I don't think," he said. "I know. Go ahead and say it. First word starts with an S? Second word..."

"With an M." She laughed, realizing what the letters also meant. "S & M, that's us."

"You'd look hot in leather."

"But you're married. To someone else. And twice my age. And now I heard her, how vulnerable she sounded. I never thought about her that way before. I guess I never really thought about her. I mean, I knew what we're doing, but.... How many times have you done this before?"

"Never."

"Yeah, right. See, now I can't believe you."

"It doesn't really matter, does it? But the truth is, never. I've fantasized about it. But I never did anything, ever."

"Has she?"

He was silent.

"Are you going to tell me she cheated on you. Really?"

"I don't know. One guy she worked for, they were very close, really close. And I just don't know. She was very distant from me for a long period. It was three years ago. I didn't let myself focus on it. but I don't know."

"What happened?"

"He left the company. And moved. And by the way divorced his wife. Or she divorced him. I just don't know."

"Didn't you want to know? Didn't you care?"

"Yes to both, of course. I guess I was too scared to know."

"Then you love her?"

He didn't respond. She stared at him for a time, then sat up and pulled a pillow into her lap and hugged it. "No," he said then. "No. I don't. Not like you."

"Talk about clichés," she said. "I can't believe I got myself into the oldest cliché of all. Being with you doesn't feel like a cliché though. Didn't until today, I guess. So do we have a cliché ending?"

Josh sat up. "Which cliché ending do you want? There are several."

They sat staring into space for a time, she hugging her pillow, Josh hugging his knees. Then Josh whispered, "Let's go to sleep."

She nodded, and they got ready for bed, not speaking very much.

In bed again, she lay on her back and he pulled her toward him, kissing her gently. She smiled and then kissed him, not very passionately. "Where are you?" he said quietly.

"Nowhere," she said automatically. Then she laughed. "Actually, that's where I am, isn't it?"

"No. It's not. Not At All." He hugged her, and clung. She didn't pull away and she didn't hug back. She let him hold her. Soon she was asleep against him. And after a while he fell asleep too.

In the morning of a bright sunny day, he lay listening to her breathing, and the distant sound of shovels and blowers on sidewalks. He squinted until his eyes adjusted to the brightness. He gently stroked her forehead as she slept. He leaned over and kissed her lips, dry and with the scent of sleep. Then he lay back, staring at the dancing patterns of light on the ceiling. Anxious, knowing they had to talk through last night, not let its unsettling tension linger.

When she awoke, she reached over for the glass of water on the bed table and took a sip, then lay back down, also staring at the ceiling. She didn't turn his way, which made his stomach muscles knot. He wondered how to start, what to say. He watched her not looking at him, and he felt his palms start to sweat. He was about to say something, anything, when she yawned.

She rubbed her eyes. "It's bright," she said.

He reached over and stroked her hair. "Ummm, that feels good," she said. Her words let him relax a little. They lay together silently for a time.

Then abruptly she turned to him and said, "'Happily ever after' isn't going to be the one, is it?"

"What? You mean the cliché ending?" Josh felt an enormous chill run through him. His hand clenched closed on a clump of her disheveled hair.

"Is it ever?" she whispered as a tear welled up in an eye, and she sank back in her pillow, staring up. The tear made its way around her nose.

His clenched fist remained in her hair. He wanted to say yes, "Yes, Yes, Yes." But no words came out. He nodded. Maybe she saw. He reached out and wiped the tear, now clinging to her upper lip. She continued to watch the ceiling, and he watched her with dread. The seconds became minutes.

"I don't know," she finally said, "how I'm going to survive without you." Her voice broke. Her face twitched as two agonized sobs shook her before she regained control.

Josh didn't try to stop the tears that were now sliding down his face. But he forced himself to respond to her words. "Cliché," he said.

She let out a laugh that turned into a choking sound. She started to shake and cry. She slipped her arms around him and pulled him tight. He could feel her ribs heaving and her delicate body trembling as they clung to each other.

A Degenerate On A Darkling Plain

HE THOUGHT ABOUT GOING to Washington for the Vietnam march, but it was only a halfhearted reaction to his shock over the election. He did not care enough any longer to make the effort. For that matter, he did not much care about anything right now. All he wanted to do was ride his Honda 160 motorcycle and sleep.

But he did have to make a decision about showing up at Diane's party tonight. The party would probably be half Ted's Economics people. The thought of making conversation with Economics strangers exhausted him. Besides, he would feel so awkward in a room full of couples – diminished, a loser.

He told himself he had piles of reading to do, and he moved himself to wade into a scholarly journal for a while. Not for very long. He had a black and white TV, which he flipped on to watch *All In The Family* at eight, *Bridget Loves Bernie* at eight-thirty, and *Mary Tyler Moore* at nine. He thought about going to sleep. He was already drifting off.

He had not been with someone for a long time. One of those inexplicable barren periods that starts seeming as if it is not an inexplicable interlude but the new permanent reality, his lonely future. Not sure if he was depressed or angry, he forced himself to confront the party decision. Maybe someone unexpected would be there. Maybe the girl who thought he was cute. Diane had tantalized him with that bit of information. He could not picture who she might be.

So, curious, he put on his black jeans, a denim shirt, his bomber jacket, hopped on his bike and cruised over. It was just after 10:30 when he pulled open the screen door and reluctantly inched his way in. His hands were sweaty. From the entry foyer he could hear the laughing party voices. He almost turned around. A few steps more, and he saw at a glance that he knew everyone in the living room. In a way that relaxed him somewhat, but at the same time it made him more anxious about being conspicuously solo.

Diane's house was comforting in its familiarity and funkiness. Diane and Ted rented half an old Tudor, and had filled it with a mishmash of Salvation Army and parents' former furniture. Frayed couches and chairs with sagging cushions, those old pole lamps with wide-based bulbs, a scratched-up coffee table anyone could rest his shoes on without giving it a thought.

A dozen or more candles in unpolished, old brass candle holders cast flickering light and made dancing shadows on the walls. Twenty or so people from the department were sitting or standing around in the dim light and fog of cigarette smoke, with bottles of beer or glasses of wine in their hands. Looked like the Economics people had segregated themselves in the dining room.

Almost all couples, as he had suspected. Mary Lou was alone, and walking toward him.

"Hey Robby. We were wondering where you were. Come in the kitchen, I'll get you some wine." She had her arm on his shoulder and was shepherding him in.

"Hi Diane," he said. She was cooking something that smelled like barbecue.

She looked up and mouthed, "She's here." Mary Lou saw the communication and frowned, though she was not in a position to make out the words.

Back in the living room, Robby sat down on a threadbare but very comfortable upholstered rocker. He had no inclination to mingle. He settled in for the night. He lit a cigarette, took a deep drag, and sipped his wine. People drifted over to him, sat on the nearby sofa or stood, and chatted.

It was sounding like a McGovern wake. No one could believe he had not won. But it was simply incomprehensible to them that he had managed only one state. How could he have possibly lost forty-nine? What was wrong with the people of this country?

Robby caught sight of a cute girl walking out of the dining room toward the bathroom. At least in the dark and distance she seemed cute. He did not know if she was the one Diane had mentioned. Probably so. Still, he was not one to be optimistic; most likely a wasted night, girl-wise. But he was content sitting there, smoking, drinking; relaxed now in the hum of voices.

Mary Lou hovered. She sat down on the floor in front of his rocker and was giving him a recipe for cherry pie with her hand resting on his knee. He was asking her where he could get sour cherries at this time of year. Her arm pumped up and down as he rocked. Diane strode in with the barbecued bits, offered them around, shouted "Fuck Nixon," to general agreement, then plopped down on the floor next to Mary Lou, who let that outburst pass though Robby could see it offended her. They hung out like that for a while, exchanging department gossip.

"Janice not here?" Robby asked.

"No, I haven't seen her," Mary Lou said.

"I don't think they're coming," Diane added.

Diane got called away, but Mary Lou was not going to budge; that was apparent. She was very obvious, but he had no interest. Aside from the fact that he did not find her attractive, she was from a military family, gung-ho Vietnam, had voted for Nixon, and so forth and so on. She was nice enough, but why was she interested in him?

The only person who intrigued him was that one maybe-cute girl. She was walking around the living room now, flirting with safe people, married guys she clearly knew. She had responded to Diane's outburst with a loud, slightly drunken whoop. Maybe she was showing him how cool she was. She was short, which he liked, with short-cut dark hair, which he did not especially like. A little chunky. Her face soft and rounded. She was OK. Diane was back. She pointed with her head to indicate the girl. Robby nodded that he understood.

Soon enough the girl came by, barely looked at him, talked to Diane and Mary Lou. "You're the girl with the cats," Robby interjected. Very clumsy, he realized. She *was* the girl with the cats, she agreed. She had two of them. They exchanged a few words. She drifted off. Nobody would suspect they had each been told about the other.

Next thing Robby knew, she was sitting across the room talking to Dean, who was the only other unattached guy at the party. The two of them were having that kind of intense conversation that excludes all others. It was going on twenty minutes and they were still huddled together. So much for her as a prospect.

As he watched them, Robby felt himself growing morose. He had no chance. Dean had the kind of good looks he could never compete with. He decided it was time to leave. Fuck parties. He could pick up a girl in the supermarket or the campus library, but at a bar or at a party where it was direct competition, a meat market competition, he had no chance. And no confidence.

To make it worse, Mary Lou, sitting on the floor with her hand again on Robby's leg, and Diane, sitting on the sofa now, were offering a running commentary across him. "If Mara hustles Dean that will be a real coup," Mary Lou said. "And she would be good for him."

"She'll shake up his orderly little world, that's for sure."

"Indeed."

"Not sure her looks are striking enough, eye-catching enough for Dean."

"Not model looks. She's cute though."

"I just can't picture Dean fucking her," Diane said. "I mean, literally, I have no image of how it would look."

"He would do it just right, he is such a perfectionist."

"I would rather someone did it wrong than perfectly."

"What do you think the odds are they leave together?"

"They're very cozy."

This went on for five minutes and Robby sank deeper into despair. Self-loathing oozed through his body.

Several others joined them, and the topic changed, to his relief. He looked at his watch and was just about to stand up and get his jacket, go for a long, high-speed ride on the Interstate, when he stopped himself. Mara was walking toward them. She plopped down on the sofa. "I know you're Robby. I'm Mara."

The abrupt shift in circumstances awoke Robby's never-far-from-the-surface sense of the absurd.

"Should we shake hands or what?" he asked.

"No, my hands are sweaty."

"Why? Do I make you nervous?"

"I'm shaking." She held up her hand and wiggled it.

"Tell me about the cats. I'm thinking of getting one."

And so they talked. Nothing like the intense conversation he had watched her engage in with Dean. There was no thrill of anxiety, no heightening of the senses, no rising heart rate. It was casual, relaxed, as if they knew each other. People drifted in and out of the conversation. No palpable wall of exclusiveness surrounded them. But she never stirred. He felt as if he had her; he was not sure why.

Diane was passing around a rather explicit book of 200 sexual positions, which was amusing everyone. Robby took out a joint and offered it. "I have asthma," Mara said, shaking her head. Mary Lou said she never had smoked, and Robby said he didn't want to start her. Diane and Ted shared it with him.

As Robby grew more effusive, a small crowd gathered around his rocker. "This is a true story," he said. "This afternoon, I was walking down Maple Street some distance behind these two girls. One of them was not paying attention to her surroundings; too busy making a point to her friend, her hands flying. She walked smack into a parking meter. Direct hit."

"Ouch," someone said.

"I called out, 'You don't take Dylan's advice regarding leaders and parking meters?' She, you won't be surprised to hear, did not find that funny. I thought it was pretty amusing myself."

"That was very quick of you," Mara said. "'Subterranean Homesick Blues', right?"

"Yes."

"Robby has a fan," Diane said. Mara glared at her.

"The klutz was pulling herself together, feeling around for bodily damage, while her friend tried to keep a straight face. So embarrassing.

"As they started walking again, the klutz turned her head back toward me and shouted, 'You saw me and you didn't say anything. Didn't warn me.'

"I said, 'I assumed you knew what you were doing. Some people get off on banging into parking meters.' Her girlfriend thought that was pretty funny."

"Were they cute?"

"Yeah, actually they both were. Very cute. But I was a little too far behind to catch up to them. Anyway, I don't think the klutz was in any mood."

"A shame. The other one thought you were funny."

"Sometimes a story does not have a satisfying ending," Robby said.

"Well," Mara put in, "you have the story you can tell at parties for the next year, next five years for that matter."

"He'll probably still be telling the story when he's 75," Ted said.

"Wow, fifty years from now. I wonder where we'll all be. If the world will be any different."

"I think he would rather have gotten fucked than have the story." That was Diane.

"He would have missed the party," Mara said.

"No offense, Diane, but I think he'd have happily blown off your party," someone said.

"I don't know. I'd go with the story over a one-night stand," one of the Economics people said. The two groups had been intermingling for a while. It occurred to Robby that he would have the story whether or not he picked up one of the girls.

"How do you know it would be a one-night stand? She might have been his forever soul mate." That was Dean, who had wandered over.

"The klutz?"

"I don't know. You can't love a klutz? Maybe the klutz. Maybe the other one."

"Ah, now the story is taking on a life of its own."

The crowd slowly dispersed, but Mara did not go far. Robby wanted to make a move, but she was never quite alone. He was afraid she might leave, or reconsider Dean. Finally he thought, fuck it, who cares if people hear her turn him down. He stood up for the first time since he arrived, and walked over to Mara. "Want to go for a motorcycle ride? It's a fairly small bike, not scary." Half a dozen people watched to see her reply. She did not exactly answer for that audience, but wandered off and came back with her sweater.

"Can I ask you a question?" she said as she squirmed into the sweater. It emphasized her breasts nicely. "Are we coming back?"

Robby shrugged. "Up to you." He snubbed out his cigarette in an ashtray.

"The thing is, long story short, I have to drive my roommate's car home."

"Don't worry about the car," Diane swooped in to say. "Really. It's OK here." And in a whisper that was not much of a whisper, "Stay with him."

As they left, Robby said to Mara, "We'll come back."

She nodded with a look of relief.

"I never did this before," she said as she sat down behind him.

"Just put your arms around me, and don't fight me. If I dip to one side, don't lean the other way; go with me."

"Sounds very sexual."

"Well if you come, just be sure you don't let go of me in your ecstasy."

"You're a riot."

They had to ride over to Robby's house to get a second helmet. He lived in a big, old house that had been carved up into five apartments by a sour guy who owned a dozen houses close to the university. The old man rented only by word of mouth to graduate students, so it was quiet.

Mara gave the place a once over. The wood floors creaked as she roamed. The bedroom and living room were wood paneled, with high ceilings. Nothing was new. Windows were warped and quirky. Bathroom fixtures had probably not been changed since the 1950s. The kitchen was a converted porch with linoleum floor. It sloped noticeably.

Mara sank into the old couch and asked for a glass of water. He brought the water and sat beside her. Now that they were there, Robby had no desire to leave. He felt awkward though, like the motorcycle ride had been a ploy.

She studied the room. "This is very nice. Not what I expected. I thought you would be a slob, but it's all so neat and tidy. Myself, I'm a slob. I like that you didn't just go and buy wall decorations. Looks to me like the posters are all from places you went, right?"

He nodded.

"I love that Istanbul one."

"That carpet by the desk is from Turkey too."

"The colors are so vibrant."

He took the glass from her and sipped himself. Still feeling like he had lured her there dishonestly, he asked, "Do you prefer to go for a ride or stay?"

"I like going for a motorcycle ride, but I also like staying." She took back her water and sipped, as he watched her. She was not beautiful, but she was really sexy.

"But I like going for a motorcycle ride more," she said. At which point he kissed her, and they ended up lying on the couch snuggling.

She sat up. "I'm afraid my roommate will worry if I don't come back soon."

"So talk to her. Call the party." She thought about it, and nodded.

She walked over to the speaker phone on his desk and dialed. While the phone rang, she flipped through his handwritten notes for a paper for Durkow's seminar.

"Nosy," he said.

"Curious," she replied. She pulled a page out of his typewriter and read that too.

Diane answered, and told Mara her roommate had already left with her boyfriend. "She doesn't expect you home tonight."

"Diane, I'm on a speaker phone."

Robby laughed.

Diane did not seem to get the point. She kept on talking. "Pat does not expect you to get the car. It's fine here overnight. Are you staying at Robby's? Stay with him. Go for it. Word is he's really good. She won't be worried if you don't come home tonight."

"Diane!"

Meanwhile, Ted, shamelessly listening on the extension, said, "Fuck it, stay."

"I don't know if I'm staying. He hasn't asked me and I have not said yes. I'm hanging up now. Thanks for that."

They looked at each other and broke out laughing.

"She's correct, by the way," Robby said.

"You have testimonials to provide me?"

"Notarized."

She said, "I realized while we were talking, I left my purse too."

"You left your purse on purpose."

She smiled. "Maybe."

"All right, let's go back, get your purse, get the car, drop the car off, then come back."

She nodded.

"What are you doing here?" Diane asked in a chiding tone as they burst in the door laughing together. A handful of people remained at the party.

"Just stopped in," said Mara, scooping up her purse. She waved as she turned and walked out the door with Robby.

Robby followed the car. They stopped in briefly for her to get warm pants and a jacket. The cats were curious. Robby picked up the calico and gently pulled its whiskers. It purred.

"I can't believe she's letting you do that. It's unusual for her to even let a stranger pick her up." The cat was not budging. Robby scratched its chin. Mara took the cat from him and put it down. "I want to ride," she said. "You can play with the cats another time."

And they rode. It was a glorious night barely lit by a sliver of moon. They rode along the river, stopped every so often to listen to the invisible water lapping. Then took off on the highway so they could speed. Robby heard Mara laughing as the breeze grew into wind in their faces and the wail grew too loud to talk over. They took a side road into a park to crawl along the wooded paths. Probably illegal, but they were entirely alone with the trees at three in the morning. They rode through a tunnel of gangly branches, tangled shapes illuminated only by his headlight.

"Back?" he asked.

"This is wonderful, but yeah, my butt is getting sore."

He did not ask the destination. He simply drove to his house. They were soon on the bed, kissing.

"It's hot in here," she said. As she pulled her sweater over her head, she surprised him by saying that Diane and Ted were seriously on the rocks. "Diane just does not care about him any more. The poor guy wants her so badly. Two weeks ago, he left out of desperation. He came back for the party. It will be interesting to see if he stays."

"That is so depressing," Robby said, unbuttoning her blouse. "I thought they were really tight. You just never know, do you?" He removed her bra and was kissing her breasts.

Mara ran her hands through his hair. "She's asexual. It is so hard on Ted."

"Diane? All she ever talks about is sex." He unbuckled her belt and pulled her pants off.

Mara shrugged. "That is certainly true." She helped Robby remove his clothes.

As he went for her panties, she pushed his hand away.

"I think it is time for the speech."

"Speech?"

"You know, the classic speech. I'm sure you've heard it before. You ready?"

"I'm all ears. Not sure I expect to find it stimulating though."

"No, you won't. OK, here goes." She recited in a monotone. "I'm not a virgin. I've been around. In fact last year I went on a real sex spree, was screwing four or five guys a week, sometimes two in one day. And then I actually got to know one guy and started to feel something for him. After that, it repulsed me to have strangers inside me. So now I don't do it with people I don't know."

She looked him up and down, from his long curly brown hair to his thin not particularly muscular body to his erect penis. "And I don't know you." She waited for him to say something.

He didn't.

"I trust you. I'm sure you don't have to stoop to pressing girls to get sex."

"Flattery, huh?"

"I'm just saying. I trust that you will respect me. Come get under the covers and kiss me."

They played for a while, more and more intensely. He made an attempt at the panties, to see if she had changed her mind. She had not. A half hour more of intense stimulation and Mara said, "You poor baby; is baby ready to explode?

Robby nodded.

Mara took his cock in her hand and jerked him off. She leaned down and took a quick lick, then wiped his stomach off with a tissue. "Feel better now?"

He snuggled up against her. They lay with her head on his shoulder, silent for a while. Then talked and dozed till the sun started brightening the sky. "I was watching you all night at the party," she was saying.

"You were oblivious to me. Or is it 'of me'?"

"Uh, uh. I saw. You did not move your butt, just sat there rocking, like you were some kind of prince, as everyone else shuffled over to pay their respects. I'm thinking, what an ego. And girls sitting on the floor at your feet. My God, Robby."

He felt embarrassed and gave a little laugh. That was not exactly how it had felt to him.

"Do you even realize how you dominate a room without doing a damned thing?"

He looked at her.

"I kept waiting for you to fucking get off your ass and come and flirt with me, try to pick me up. Finally a little light went off in my head; I realized, that ain't happening, girl. I was going to have to come to you." She slapped his arm.

"Women's Lib and all that."

"Yeah, right."

He said, "I was really surprised when you came over to me. You seemed so cozy with Dean. I was ready to leave."

"Oh God, he was so boring. I couldn't wait to get away. He was lecturing me on 18th century philosophy. The only other thing we talked about was you. That was more interesting."

"Me? Why?"

"I'm curious to hear your side of why you and a guy named Richard hate each other?"

Robby stared at her. "Excuse me?" At first he thought he had dozed off and was dreaming; the statement had the disconnection from reality of a dream. "Where did you get that?"

"Dean, obviously. He says he feels very awkward. He likes you both and he does not know quite how to negotiate this intense hostility. He is closer to Richard socially but he likes you a lot and he feels like he can't be friends with both of you; your hatred is so intense."

"Our hatred is so intense? This is crazy. I don't hate Richard. Where is this coming from? I don't really give Richard a thought. He is not my favorite person in the department, but I don't even have enough interaction with him to have any feelings about him. Is this a joke?'

"No, Dean was very serious. It bothers him. He said Richard is obsessed with you."

"Come on. You're pulling my leg."

"I don't know if I should tell you this."

"What?"

"Forget it."

"Apparently half the department must know whatever it is. Fucking tell me."

"He fantasizes about you."

"Oh God."

"Not like that. You know he is a karate something belt?"

"Yeah, I know. Green I think."

"He fantasizes about snapping your neck."

"Really nice. A fucking psycho." He was trying to process that piece of information, as he watched her. He pictured Richard with his square jaw, tiny eyes, and short, curly, reddish brown hair. She started to say something else, hesitating as she carefully formulated words.

"What?"

"Again, I don't know if it's my place to tell you this, but someone sure should, so I'm going to. He told Dean that if you ever so much as touch Janice... His girlfriend?"

"Yes."

"He will crush your jaw. He lies in bed imagining the sound of your jaw shattering." She smiled and caressed his jaw. "Such a nice jaw too."

"You're making this up."

She lay on her side, propped up on pillows, shaking her head. "I wish."

"Honey Grits and I have been friends since first year. But come to think of it, she has been kind of distant since she took up with him."

"Honey Grits?"

"That's what I call her. She's from Georgia. Big draaaaawl."

"He knows what you call her?"

"I'm sure he does. I've been calling her that for three years."

"Well that explains his feelings."

"Ha ha. I thought they would be at Diane's party."

"I asked. I was curious to see what they look like. Dean said Janice was swamped with papers and Richard could not stomach the thought of coming alone and having to sit and watch you perform."

"Perform?"

"That's what he said."

Robby shook his head, feeling bewildered.

"Oh and here is a tidbit you'll like. Richard was a virgin until Janice."

"Jesus, you sucked everything out of Dean."

"Yeah, I'm really good at sucking." She took hold of his penis.

Robby eagerly abandoned thoughts of Richard, but she just kissed his mouth.

He lay down on his back, returning to consideration of this bizarre information overload.

"You think you should talk to the campus police, see what they think? He sounds really on the edge."

"I'm not going to do that. I don't even know if you're putting me on. As you said, we don't know each other." Robby was shaking his head back and forth once again. "If anything, I would have thought Dean was the one who did not like me much. You just can never tell about anything. According to you, I'm in a war I did not know had been declared?"

"Yup."

"What is it about? If I may be so bold as to ask why I hate Richard. Is it some kind of department rivalry? Or is he jealous of Janice? We're just friends."

"No and no. He isn't jealous. It's not that. He's confident of Janice."

"What then?"

"He thinks you're a degenerate."

"A what?"

"You heard me."

"Yeah, I did. That's why you came running to me. Soon as Dean told you that, you sprang out of that seat, made a bee-line for me."

"You're probably right about that." She threw the cover over their heads and kissed him. He started to explore degeneracy, but she said, "Uh uh, the speech. Remember the speech."

"Tease."

She crawled out from under the covers for air. "It's a philosophical distaste; a physical revulsion."

"Well those are two very different things."

"It's both. It's everything about you." She stopped abruptly, a look on her face that said maybe she had expressed her thought too enthusiastically. She started again. "It's a morality issue for Richard, according to Dean."

"What does he even know about my 'morals?'"

"Pretty judgmental guy. Pretty extreme reaction to a colleague, wouldn't you say? Sure you don't want to alert someone?"

"You mean in case I turn up dead?"

"Don't say that."

"I don't buy the morality crap. If his feeling is that intense, it's Janice; it's Honey Grits."

They finally fell asleep around six. But by nine they were awake and playing. He slid her panties off.

"You're so impatient."

"A new day. You know me now." he said.

"Uh uh uh."

He shrugged and lay back down.

Then she said, "My turn," and pushed his face down between her legs.

❖

Monday morning, late for Durkow's class, Robby bypassed the agonizingly slow elevator. He bounded the stairs two at a time to the third floor where most of the graduate seminar rooms were located. Stopping in front of the classroom door long enough to catch his breath, he then pulled it open very gently. This door had a loud annoying squeak, and in spite of his efforts everyone looked up.

"So good of you to join us, Mr. Rivlin," Durkow said.

"My pleasure, Professor."

Laughter bubbled up around the room. Durkow gave a dramatic sigh.

Robby's eyes focused on Janice right off. A picture of stocky, beefy Richard loomed in his mind. He hesitated for just a moment, then angry at himself for hesitating, he took a seat directly behind Janice, only because the one next to her was occupied. She turned, still smiling over his exchange with Durkow, and shook her head at him, as if to say, "incorrigible."

As the discussion of Matthew Arnold began and ceased, and then again began, with tremulous cadence slow, Robby's mind wandered to Richard. The guy seemed so mild mannered. Had they had a fight he did not remember? He stared at the back of Janice's head, her long brown hair rippling as she wrote carefully-formed words in her notebook. He was having difficulty understanding how Janice could be in a relationship with this person, this rigid, recently-virgin psycho.

The class ended. Books closed; papers riffled. Several students sat, perhaps thinking a last thought about *Dover Beach*, perhaps simply numb. Robby stepped around a chair and plunked down in the now-empty seat next to Janice, placing his hand on her shoulder, feeling the warmth of her body.

"How you, Honey Grits?"

"I'm good."

In his newly awakened state, Robby noticed alert eyes on them. "I haven't seen much of you lately."

"Yeah, I've been in seclusion. Two papers."

If Dean found himself in an awkward position, how did Janice feel?

"So let me ask you something, Honey Grits," Robby said, the thought coming to him on the spur of the moment.

"Yes dear?"

"What do you think of me? Really, deep down. How would you sum me up?" Degenerate, he thought, go ahead and say it. He smiled.

Janice gazed at him with those big gray eyes of hers. She was probably good looking, but he just did not find her so. He was not sure why. Her face was long and gaunt, but it was mostly something about her mouth or maybe the shape of her fixed nose. He liked her quite a lot, but he could not imagine making love to her.

"Why?" she asked.

He did not know what to say so he just shrugged.

When she opened her mouth to respond, without much hesitation, she said in her southern drawl and deep voice, "Robby, you have an infinite capacity for cynicism."

He contemplated that. Nodded after a few seconds. "That's probably right. You're very perceptive."

She continued to scrutinize his face. "I'd like to think so."

And yet you're with Richard, he thought.

She added, "It's not healthy."

"No, it's not. I'll call you. We haven't talked in too long. Gotta run now. Bento's class."

She nodded.

And then he did something else on the spur of the moment, aware as he was of the eyes on them. He leaned forward and kissed her lightly on the lips. He had never done that. "Bye," he said.

She took it in her laconic fashion. Simply said, "Bye." More like "Baahh."

He stood up. Among the classmates taking note, he especially saw Dean looking their way with concern etched on his face.

Just As I'm Going

I AM SITTING AT Cindy's kitchen table, swatting flies. The day is bright and hot outside, but in the house it is cool, dusky. The flies lie among the crumbs left from breakfast, crumbs that will still be there when Cindy is cooking dinner. I've become attuned to the pace in my year here. I've grown so mellow I'll probably leave the table just as it is.

Cindy walks into the kitchen, letting the screen door swing half closed. Even with a hitch she has in her step, she moves with an ease that I find soothing to watch. She is short and slim. Her face is full. She carries a bowl of plums to the kitchen counter and sets it down as if the plums were eggs. In her faded blue jeans and white flowered blouse she looks cool, but she wipes her forehead with a napkin and pushes her short curly hair off her neck.

She begins to pit the plums, gazing out the window at the shimmering green of the sun-drenched fir trees. In her hair as she stands at the sink, burrs glint against the black that is streaked prematurely with gray. She doesn't notice a burr fall from her hair, whirling to the floor.

"Where's Mitch?" She turns with sudden attention, looking, squinting out the front window into the clearing.

"Mitch?" Her voice has always been weak. It cracks when, as now, she speaks with intensity.

Nothing.

She starts to walk, the hitch in her step more pronounced, more jerky. "Mitch."

"Kihin," from a distance.

Her muscles relax. Half to herself as she turns back to the sink, she says, "Don't hurt the kittens, Mitch. Be gentle, or Ginger will get angry."

"Kihins."

"Yes, Mitch, kittens."

Mitch loves Ginger. He can sit for a long while watching the babies lie at her side sucking, restraining himself from touching, whimpering from time to time, "Kihins." In the end, he is unable to contain himself and reaches for one squealing twisting bit of fur to press to his bare belly.

The door bangs open and stays wide. "Hi, I'm back." The face is a smile of energy, the presence a cliché of freshness. In the room, the tranquil atmosphere evaporates. "What a night, we practically froze." The voice is soft, brittle, lilting. "Geeze, I'm glad I brought that extra sweater. I wish this were over, I feel so filthy."

"Mehdy." The little body waddles in, no pants, shirt reaching nearly to belly button, little penis leading the way.

"Hi Mitch." Melody picks him up, swinging him around.

"Kihins," pointing to the cramped room used as a study.

"Yes, Mitch, kittens. Have you been gentle with the kittens?"

"Gen-tal."

"Is Lionel back yet?" This Melody directs to Mitch's mother at the sink.

"Linonel," Mitch repeats.

Not turning from her pitting, but her face showing a sudden flush of energy, Cindy responds. "No, of course not. Ethan and I are going to the inn tonight and Nell said she would come. So

I'm sure he'll arrive just as I'm going, to make me feel guilty. He *always* does."

"Oh, now Cindy." Melody pauses, takes a plum from the bowl and pops it into her mouth. "When does the plane land?"

"It doesn't matter," Cindy insists. "He'll get here just as we're going out. I know it. He plans it that way."

"Ohhh, now you're being silly. What are you making?"

"The plums are all overripe. I thought I'd better pick them." She wrinkles her nose at a rotten one and tosses it in the garbage bag, disturbing some resting flies. The bag is too full and the plum bounces out. Melody deposits it. "Ethan promised to make a crust if I picked and pitted. So we'll have plum pies any hour now."

"Ethan," Melody gushes, "that's nifty." Her smile of sunshine broadens. "You're so talented." She bites into a second plum. "Um, sweet. What's that in your hair, Cindy?"

She shrugs, still pitting, and Melody picks the burrs out of her hair. "You really attacked that tree, didn't you?"

⸻◆⸻

The crust has been baked and the pies are in the refrigerator setting. Time has slipped away as it always does here. Cindy sits now in front of the house on the patchy grass in the cleared space as the sun, beginning to sink, streaks through the Douglas firs all around, yellowing the near ones as the distant ones recede into deeper purple. Mitch rides his fire engine. Melody has long ago gone off to bed and in the welcome coolness of the late afternoon I walk up the hill to the house where I am staying to get my wallet for the trip to the inn.

When I return, Nell has joined Cindy and Mitch. She sits cross-legged and erect in cut-off jeans, facing the lowering sun, with her large uncovered breasts drooping. Her face is firm, her expression strong. Her hair is in pigtails. She does not pull her halter on as I approach. After smiling hello to me, she says to Cindy, "I think we should go." As always she speaks in a clipped assured voice.

Cindy waffles.

It is Cindy though who makes the move at last. When she has stood and walked toward the car, Nell puts her halter on, pulls her long wavy brown hair out of the rubber bands and gathers it, running her hand down the waves and swinging her head till the hair falls right. She follows Cindy toward the car.

"Come on, Mitch," she says, taking charge of him as the fire engine jingles by.

"Nooo," he screams and starts to cry. His round face contorts into furrows and creases with his mouth a great round hole in the center as Nell lifts him up kicking, and carries him to the car. Cindy, ever at half-speed, has still to get the car keys from her purse when Mitch is settled, still crying, on Nell's lap next to her. I get in the back and make faces at Mitch. The eyes become larger than the mouth again and a smile curls up the lips. "Oh fun-ny," he says. As both arms reach out to the rear seat, Nell pulls back her chin, but too late.

"Ouch, Mitch. Sit still," she says. He has by then wriggled free and is in the back seat, where I entertain him.

The car crunches down the dirt path, bouncing when it hits the bumps and ruts. As we approach the wooden bridge over the narrow creek, Cindy gives out a loud sigh of frustration and bangs her open hands against the steering wheel. "I told you," she yells.

There on the bridge is Lionel, tall, unshaven, hair blowing. He has parked the truck at his house. His inevitable grin greets us. "Hi," he says amiably. "Where you going?"

Cindy's voice comes out fast and sharp. "We're on our way to the inn. How long have you been back? We expected you ages ago and were waiting, but we have to go now or it'll be closed. Bye."

"See you all later," Lionel says, bemused, amused, I am not able to tell which. "The plane landed late," he adds as she starts to drive.

"You could have called," Cindy says.

Lionel crouches and peers in the back window "Hi, Mitch. Hi, Ethan."

Mitch flaps his hand at Lionel, mouthing "Linonel."

"I'll see you later, Mitch. Bye, bye. Bye, bye."

"Bye, bye."

As we drive off, Mitch is flapping his arm out the back window.

Cindy pounds on the steering wheel again. "I told you. Did I say it? No matter when we left, he would have come then. I hate him."

I am laughing at her and she starts to laugh too. "Well, I do hate him."

"He didn't seem to mind," Nell says.

"No, he never minds anything. Oh, I can't stand him." She laughs again.

We ride in silence most of the way. Twilight rustles in the deepening green and the scent of the forest blows over us. A car shoots by. Otherwise we are alone on the still, shadowed road.

At the inn, we are put at a table by the kitchen. They know Mitch well. But Nell says, "Wait, don't sit down." She walks after the matronly hostess. After an exchange of words, she waves to us and we sit down at a table in the center of the dining room. When the waitress comes to take our drinks order, we all have beer.

The waitress returns and Nell tells her we need more time. Mitch, who has loved beer since he was six months old, is reaching for Cindy's beer. "Bur," he calls it. The matronly woman comes over and asks us not to let the baby drink the beer. "We'll lose our license if someone says something," she whispers. Nell nods OK. Cindy is muttering to me that they can't lose their license if the state already owns the place. On her face is a frown bordering on a glare. Cindy does not like strangers interfering with Mitch.

Cindy gripes about Melody. "I'm really tired of it. Her house is almost finished. Why doesn't she go and live in it? Or why doesn't she stop working in the hops fields all night and spend time finishing her house?" House is something of an enthusiastic description of the four dwellings erected by the four inhabitants with help from a few friends. Lionel and Cindy own the property. Melody's house is a work in progress.

"She needs money to pay you rent."

"Ron would stay there now on sleeping bags. He told me so. It's still summer. Or why don't they live at Lionel's house while he's in Eugene?" She is angry now. "Since Ron and Lionel are such good friends."

"Ask them to. Anyway, Ron should pay rent," Nell asserts. "He's living off you. There's no reason he should live here free. He's just using Melody; everyone can see that, but that is no reason you should let him use you. Cindy, take the beer away from Mitch."

Cindy makes a halfhearted grab and comes up with the can. She is enthusiastic. "That's right. I'm going to tell Melody she can pay for him if she wants him to stay in my space. Or they can go and live in her house in sleeping bags. She can tack up plastic for windows and a door for now. And they could dig a latrine in a day. Why don't they do that? Ron said he would. I'm really tired of it. What is it, Mitch?" she says distracted by his reaching. "Here. Now sit still."

"Cindy, don't give him the beer can. Would you keep it away from him."

"Why? It's empty."

Nell looks at her. "It doesn't matter. Mitch," she erupts. She reaches and yanks it out of his hand.

"Bur," he says.

"No bur, Mitch."

"I have no privacy in that house," Cindy fumes. "And I don't see why I should have to be quiet in my own space all day because they're working in the hops harvest at night. I won't."

"Did they say something to you?" Nell asks.

"No." The waitress is stepping toward us. "I just want a little privacy."

When the meal arrives, Mitch takes our attention first with his table manners and then with his decision to socialize with the other diners. I see the matronly woman's eyes following him. Cindy is uninterested. It is left to Nell to collect him or be embarrassed.

Watching her son across the room holding onto a chair and starting to bawl as Nell pulls him by his other hand, Cindy turns to me abruptly, still annoyed about Lionel's appearance on the bridge. "I don't know why I stay here," she tells me. "I think I'm going to take Mitch and move to Eugene. I could get a job teaching composition. It would be good." Cindy taught English in Grants Pass until Mitch was born. "I should move back to the City." New York is still the City. "It's dead here. I haven't seen a play in ages. Never any good movies. Kung Fu, Kung Fu, Kung Fu. And, God, I miss the seasons."

"What about Lionel?"

"Oh, he'll never leave here." She waves it off, sips her beer, a pensive look on her face. She fingers the frost on the can. "When Mitch starts school, I'll leave for sure. There is no school worth anything here."

Her eyes flash with an idea. "Maybe you and I should drive to San Francisco next week. Nell said she would take care of Mitch if I need to get away. I hate to impose though. It's a lot to ask of her." She is quiet for a minute then, but the enthusiasm bubbles back up. "We could go down the coast highway. So beautiful along the ocean."

I say I would love to.

"You'll be gone just when Lionel gets back from his next trip."

"Even more perfect," she says. "It serves him right for scabbing."

Lionel is heading to Eugene. A teacher strike has started and he is going to scab. Cindy was furious last week before he left for his speed reading trainer course when he mentioned that he might scab. He had taken the course on a lark. Maybe he would teach a few speed reading classes, make a little money. But the scabbing would be sure money.

⸺◆⸺

Lionel is sitting in a rocker in Cindy's living room when we return from the inn. He has showered and shaved and is reading the Grants Pass *Courier*.

"Ethan and I are driving to San Francisco. We'll stay with Claudia for a while," Cindy announces when we walk in. "Don't you think that's a good idea? I need a dose of civilization."

I say, "Unless you would rather we not."

"It sounds like an excellent idea," Lionel says. "Cindy is restless." He closes the paper and sets it down on the floor. "When are you going?"

"In about two weeks, right?"

I shrug.

"I guess I'll miss you then. Ethan, we haven't gotten to see that much of each other lately. I'm sorry."

"So am I, but your son filled your space quite..." I search for words. "dynamically."

Lionel smiles.

"We won't be away long," I say.

Cindy says, "Not if you don't scab, you won't miss us. You could come."

Lionel shrugs. He is clearly not willing to have that discussion again. He starts to tell us the techniques he has just learned for speed reading.

"I'm more interested in what you are about to do to people trying to earn a living wage," Cindy says.

"Lionel must be really glad he came home," Nell comments.

Lionel peers at Cindy with supreme self-assurance. "If I were offered a fifteen percent raise, I wouldn't strike. I would say the teachers in Eugene are quite well paid for nine months of work a year. Lots of vacation. Benefits. Home from work early."

"Paid worse than garbage men."

"And so they should be."

"Funny Mitch, your father is oh fun-ny."

Mitch looks up from his coloring book. "Oh fun-ny."

"Cindy, no one is asking you to compromise your sacred moral values." Lionel's mouth breaks into a wider grin than his usual one. "If I am there for three days, not even to mention the possibility of two weeks, you know, that is a washing machine."

"Scab money. Dried bloody scab money. I don't want it."

"Now Cindy, let's not say things we know we don't mean. You have been telling me almost daily that you need a washer. Let's not deny that."

"I deny it. I don't want a washer. Everybody in the area will bring their dirty laundry in. There's no privacy here as it is."

Ignoring that stab, Melody asks Lionel, "Is it going to really last two weeks?" She is bending over the table rolling a joint.

He nods. "I have no reason to think rationality will prevail."

"How much do they pay?"

"Melody!" Cindy says.

Lionel tells her the number. The room becomes still. Lionel grins, rocking gently in the chair.

"Oh boy, she's gone," Cindy says.

We are silent again for a time. Mitch is humming to himself. The sound of Lionel's rocking chair legs hitting the floor fills the space.

Melody tips her head up, inhaling, holds the smoke in long. She offers the joint. No one responds. She lets the smoke drift out of her mouth. "Geeze, I could sure use money like that," she says finally.

Cindy starts speaking. When she assaults, she speaks very fast, not loud. "Melody, you don't want scab money. You don't want to be a strike breaker. Think about it." Her voice, still fast, takes on the sparkle of satire in mid-course. "A tool of the capitalists. A stealer of the food of hungry children. An evil person, Melody, you don't want to be an evil person, do you? Think of the sad, hungry children of teachers, Melody."

"They might take you without a teaching license; it all depends on how many open spots they have. There's plenty of room in the truck."

"What should I do, Cindy?"

"I think you should go. Do it. Be decisive. You need the money." The mockery in this turnabout is lost on Melody.

"Geeze, but is it wrong, do you think?"

"No, I think you should definitely go. Think of the children being deprived of learning. They will never make up this deficit. You can save them, Melody. Maybe we should all go. Then I won't be able to be angry at Lionel."

Melody wavers on through the evening. When Lionel is ready for bed, I leave with him. He says to Cindy, "I guess I'll see you when you get back from the coast." He kisses her unresponsive lips and tousles Mitch's hair. Cindy doesn't speak except to say goodbye.

Lionel and I walk up the dirt road together. I carry my flashlight which makes a darting beacon as we walk through a darkness I have never seen anywhere else. The night sounds are abrupt in the blackness. We feel or hear more than see a bat swoop down low and shoot off. I hate the bats. When I am walking alone I think of rabies.

Lionel is telling me about the new tubing system he has rigged to provide hot water for showers. "It works," he says with pride. "If I start the fire when I wake up, I can take a hot shower by the time the 8:20 freight train goes by." The little used railroad tracks cut through the property. Lionel's shower is outdoors and he looks amused when he talks about the train. No doubt the engineer has shouted interesting comments across the distance.

"Cindy wouldn't be able to shower till dinner time," I joke.

"Cindy manages just fine," he is quick to say. "She's on her schedule and I'm on mine, but that's OK."

We are at the point where we separate and Lionel says good night. I switch off my flashlight to feel the darkness of the moonless night for a moment. Stars spring out above, but around me the black is impenetrable. Lionel, who needs no flashlight, disappears as soon as he moves from my side. I listen to his steps fade into the cricket noises and then sit for a moment on a rock, staring up at the vast dome of twinkling dots.

The one-room house in which I am staying was built by a woman named Sunflower. Cindy told me in confidence that her name had been Susan Hoffzinger from Woodmere, Long Island, but now her legal name is Sunflower. I have cold running water in the sink, electric lights, a stall down a path that has gotten narrower each week as the poison oak flourished and encroached. I had been warned of the poison oak, and when I asked Cindy to describe it she had to send Nell to point it out to me. I am renting for a more or less open-ended period. Last we heard, Sunflower was at a silence retreat in the Himalayas. When I first arrived, Cindy was sure Nell and I were going to get it on. No sparks though.

⟞⟝

The next evening, Lionel has left for Eugene, and no one is around but Cindy and I, and of course Mitch. Cindy planned to cook me dinner, but she never got to it. We remember the two plum pies and sit down to a delicious but not very healthful dinner in the twilight kitchen. The house, as usual by this hour, looks a wreck. We cannot stop eating, and before we know it, one huge pie is gone We have started on the second when in mid-bite I have a thought. "I wonder," I ask, ever so slowly, "do plums have the same effect as dried plums – or, as they are more commonly known..."

"Prunes, oh my God." Cindy is bending over a forkful, but her eyes rise to meet mine and she declines to put the fork in her mouth. We start to laugh, and then are shaking so hard I fear the plums may not get far enough down to cause the effect we anticipate. From the floor strewn with toys, where he is eating, Mitch stares at us. Then he starts to laugh, dribbling dissolving plum out of his mouth, onto his clothing, the toys, the floor.

"Oh Mitch, Mitch, Mitch," Cindy starts to yell, her voice cracking; then she collapses in laughter again.

"I have a suggestion," I say. "Chocolate for an antidote. How about a big pot of cocoa for dessert. Balance our – karma, as Melody might say."

"Co-co, co-co," Mitch sings with delight, sputtering out the last of the plum.

After this dessert, we sit in the living room watching Mitch empty his chest full of toys onto the floor. He is bending into the chest, backhanding toys as far as his chubby arms can toss them.

"I definitely need a vacation," Cindy says. "God it would be easier if Lionel would take care of Mitch just sometimes."

"Why don't you tell him he has to? It isn't as though he's not around."

She waves her hand. "He does volunteer every so often, but he's irresponsible. I walk out and find Mitch wandering across the bridge. It doesn't even have sides, rails, barriers. He could fall off. Lionel says he was busy with the fuses or something. 'You want your lights to work, don't you, Cindy?' he says."

We hear Melody and Ron stirring and soon Melody appears. Ron calls something to her from the bedroom.

"Just a minute," she says.

Cindy says, "We saved you some pie."

"Oh great." She finds her watch on a bookcase. "I've got to get moving. Can Ron have some too, I mean, I don't want to be accused."

"Of course Ron can have some."

Cindy and I look at each other and start to smirk. "Take a couple of pieces for later in the hops field." Melody squints at the two of us, both now with our heads on the table, shaking with laughter.

When Melody and Ron have gone, Cindy is thoughtful. She says, "I really should leave, shouldn't I?"

"How can I know that? Not for me to say."

"You think I should, I know. I should."

"But?"

She shrugs. "Inertia?" She sits for a while, twisting the cocoa cup around with the tip of her finger. "Maybe I'll go to law school. I've been thinking about that."

Mitch crawls over saying, "Mihk."

Cindy sighs. "OK Mitch."

He climbs up on her lap and she tiredly opens her blouse, twisting out her breast. The nipple springs up large and firm, and Mitch has his little hand on the side of her breast, guiding the nipple to his mouth. His other hand is around her neck. His wavy hair is long and rumpled. Nell has said the only way they will break him of this is for Cindy to go away for a month. Cindy doesn't have the disciple to deny him. She sits with a pensive look on her face. "It'll be good for me to go to San Francisco. Nell thinks now would a good time to –" She nods her head at Mitch. "She says she isn't too busy with her pottery right now." It won't be a month, but it will be something.

Cindy walks around turning on lights. Mitch has now begun to collect the strewn toys and repack them into his chest. He does this so he can throw them around again. He goes through the routine twice more before I finally walk home around midnight.

In the morning it is pouring rain. I stumble down the poison oak path to the stall, which has a plastic roof over the seat, but no awning that would serve for the legs of someone sitting. Water splashes on my legs. I discover that cocoa was indeed a good choice. I sit for longer than I have to. The whoosh of the rain in the trees, the steady beating on the plastic, the wet pricking drops on my bare legs are soothing. The musky scent of the waterlogged woods is comforting. Sitting there, exposed to the wet glistening forest, I understand why Lionel will never leave.

The days pass by and the strike continues. At first, Cindy hoped it would end soon. Now she is hoping it will not end before we leave. She again envisions Lionel appearing just as we are going. She is quite serious about the trip. She has even brought the car in to be checked. Nell approves wholeheartedly and tells me she has not seen Cindy so decisive in the two years since Mitch was born.

Lionel calls every now and then with reports and Melody again thinks about going to Eugene. The talk is incessant, repetitive. On the phone Lionel asks Cindy to come. She refuses, using Mitch as her excuse. When Lionel reminds her she is going to San Francisco, she uses me for her excuse. Afterwards she wonders to me and then to Melody and then to Nell whether she is doing the right thing.

We are to leave on Thursday. On Tuesday afternoon, Lionel's truck bounces down the dirt road and stops at Cindy's house. Mitch hops off his fire engine and Lionel scoops him up, tousling his hair. Mitch is telling him a story that is more or less incoherent when Cindy hears the commotion and walks to the half-open door, drying her hands on a towel. She drops the towel to catch what Lionel flings at her. It is a bag of bagels. "And one for Ethan," he says, flinging it at me. "And Melody and Ron. Where's Nell? Oh well, keep them for her." He tosses the last bag to Cindy, who is laughing. "How's the boy, Mitch? Have you been good? Not causing any trouble? Picking up your toys? Drinking out of the bottle." Mitch is nodding his head to everything, laughing. "That's wonderful."

"He's been terrible. I need a vacation." Cindy first sees the truck then. She stands in the doorway with her hands on her hips, shaking her head. "You did it, did you?" She tiptoes toward the truck and looks at the gleaming white washing machine strapped down in the back. She walks around the truck, examining, not speaking.

"Where do you want it?"

"How much was it?"

"What's the difference? Did it cost you anything?"

"Put it at your house. *You* can have the people coming over all the time to do their wash." She pauses then. "I guess I should be grateful, shouldn't I?"

"At least polite."

"Thank you, Lionel."

"You're welcome."

"It is good you got back today. You know we are leaving on Thursday."

For an instant I think I see a tightness in Lionel's mouth. He nods. "What's the itinerary?"

"We're going down the coast, slowly, take the weekend. We can stay at Linda's for a couple of days. Then Ethan wants to see the aquarium. We'll stay with Claudia in San Francisco. Nell is going to take Mitch. Unless you want to."

"I'll help Nell out."

"I'm sure."

"You know I have been away for most of the last month. There are a number of things that have to get done. I know you want that new oil burner set up before winter comes, don't you?"

"Yes, Lionel," she says. "I wouldn't dream of burdening you with your child. Nell doesn't expect much help from you."

Cindy keeps busy in the vegetable garden for the rest of the afternoon. When Lionel has gotten around to unloading the washer, he waits with infinite patience while Cindy tries to decide where she wants it. They commune in a row of gargantuan yellow squash, while Cindy crouches with a spade in one hand and a clump of weed in the other. He explains how inconvenient most of the places she suggests will be for hooking up the machine. "Near a water connection please, Cindy."

When, with all our help, she decides finally where she would find it least objectionable, Lionel and Ron get it moved and spend the twilight hours hooking it up. Cindy hovers, and leaves, and hovers again. Melody and I walk into town to the general store to buy cream cheese for the bagels. When we return, Ron is testing the washer.

"I thought I would be the guinea pig," he says.

"Cindy will have a fit; she hasn't even tried her machine and already the hordes have descended," Melody says, munching bagel and cream cheese. "Where are they, by the way?"

Ron nods toward the bedroom. "Nooky nooky."

⸎

On Thursday, Cindy and I do not drive to San Francisco. She decides she cannot leave Mitch. It would be the first time she has ever been away from him, and she doesn't think he is ready yet. Nell is angry. "A two-year-old boy should not be breast feeding. We'll all go through hell if you try to break him yourself."

Cindy says it will happen when the time is right.

Nicole

R AIN THUMPED ON MY umbrella as I stepped out of the deli. I trudged along, carrying the bagels and stuff Lavender wanted before the grandkids arrived. A reflection in a store window caught my attention. A stance. A gesture. Waist-length hair pulled over the shoulder and matted from the downpour. The face in the glass dripped tears of rain.

I called her name before I caught myself. If I had been sitting at home trying to recall her name, I would not have been able to. I had not thought about her in four decades. Even then I barely knew her. I stood on the sidewalk as rivulets rushed toward me and pooled around my shoes. The girl reflected in the glass, for she was barely a woman, walked off, and I just stood in the rain thinking about Nicole as people detoured around me. Who had she become? Forty-five years. Forty-five years had slid away so unexpectedly.

Time felt as if it were already sliding away from us in those days. I remember Ned had a poster from five or so years before still on the wall over his desk, the picture of the girl kneeling with her arms spread above the dead student. The scotch tape was peeling away and the picture was wrinkled and cracked. That's what stands out now; then the picture itself still seemed important. Ned had just added an "Impeach Nixon" sticker to his wall.

I sat swiveling restlessly in my chair. It was Saturday at Football U. and from our cavernous office, which was on the fifth floor of the English Department Building, we could hear the roar from the stadium roll across campus every few minutes. I sat at one of the eight wooden desks lined up around the walls. The desks were pitted; the walls smudged with the unconcern of years. Our bookcases, ill-matched to say the least, were crammed with odd, outdated texts and yellowing piles of freshman themes abandoned by generations of TAs. We kept saying we were going to clean house, but there it all still was. And one day, we'd be gone too.

Lavender sat erect at her desk off to the side of me, her arm vibrating at the elbow, her pale eyelashes fanning, her thin lips pressed tight. She was scribbling madly. Dissertation topic research. In between roars from the stadium, and when the heat wasn't rumbling through the vents, I could hear Lavender's fountain pen scraping away. Her desk was strewn with books, open and turned downward and piled on top of each other in ways that would make a librarian's spine snap.

Ned was methodically propelling himself back and forth in his chair. The linoleum floor had been mysteriously waxed during the night, something that hadn't occurred in any of our memory. For Ned it was an irresistible shiny object. He was facing his desk and the girl in the picture, his arms reaching forward as if to meet hers, as he prepared to fling himself backward across the room toward me yet again. Last time he pushed off with his feet. His feet seemed to get him farther than his arms. Once so far, he had made it all the way, his chair just clinking against mine with the extra body English he gave it at the last moment.

Lavender was not amused. "Come on, Ned. I can't think with this flying blob of fat in my peripheral vision." Lavender was habitually cruel to Ned, so her words didn't penetrate too often.

I was waiting for my heating element to boil the water in my cup. When little bubbles just began to appear, I unplugged the heating element, pulled it out of the cup, and spooned in the Tasters' Choice. I yanked a ditto sheet out of my typewriter and pushed the typewriter away. I would go to the ditto machine and make copies of the week's assignment for my freshman English class eventually. Now I reluctantly faced the pile of themes.

"Throw me a sugar, Lavender," I said.

Lavender took a sugar from her cupful without breaking her fountain pen stroke, but then decided to have a cigarette. A moonstruck freshman who thought he had a chance with her had given her the lavender cup that held the sugars. When she ended up giving him a D, she had to call the campus police. Ah the pain of love. She did once have an affair with a student. He was older, she had told us defensively, long after. I didn't know her well at the time it happened, and of course she didn't exactly advertise it.

Ned, just taking off, added pressure on his right arm that veered him into Lavender's desk. Harder than he intended. She gave him eyelids of contempt as he lit one of her cigarettes and pushed off, letting out a choppy stream of smoke across the room and reciting several lines from a Dylan Thomas poem, ending with the enthusiastically emphasized word "bitches."

"You conflated two verses, idiot," said Lavender as she blew out smoke.

It was raining hard outside, at least it had been when I arrived in our windowless office. The heat was on high and I was becoming drowsy. I picked up my red felt-tip and returned to the freshman theme in front of me, read a sentence, and groaned.

We were all more or less in the same place: finished with coursework, studying for our Ph.D. qualifying exams, and pushing the date off into the future. We obsessed on the passed-down stories of sixty-year-olds still reading for exams, swearing that next year they would be ready. Ned set a date he was not going to push back, a firm date in January. So close. It gave me chills just to think about it.

There was a timid knock on the door. Unusual to have a knock on a Saturday, when the fifth floor was our private sanctuary. No student conferences; no office hours. None of *us* ever knocked.

Ned called, "Come in."

No response.

I yelled, "Come in, come in." The door opened a crack. A head peeked in. "Entre vous," Ned said to the long wet hair hanging in the doorway.

She opened the door and stood self-consciously half in, half out, looking from one of us to the other. From Ned to me, that is. She was not looking for Lavender.

She stepped in, bedraggled. The waist-length brown hair was soaked and tangled; her tight jeans with the elephant bells were dark from the knees down with rain. She wore a black bomber jacket and looked at us through small, practically iridescent eyes. She shifted her weight from one foot to the other as we stared back at her. Lavender smirked obnoxiously at Ned and me.

I broke the awkward silence. "Me," I said. Her eyes came to rest on me.

How did I know that so surely? So absolutely? There was no way I could know, but I did. I knew instantly who she was, and my heart leapt nearly to the fifty yard line of the stadium.

"Nicole, right?"

She nodded. "How did you know?" "Niyw" is how it came out.

"Come on in," I said. Ned walked out, saying he was going for coffee. Lavender was staring down at her page, but from the side

I could see her face spread in a tight-lipped, smothered grin. "I'm not leaving," she said to her books.

Nicole looked over, squinting, flicking at her hair "Um, is it OK? For me to come? You said…"

"It's fine. I'm really glad you did." Lavender let out what she probably thought could pass for a cough, but Nicole looked over at her.

"Come on, " I said. "I'll buy you coffee, or something." She looked relieved as I went for my coat. I gave Lavender the finger as I left the room and she broke out in her derisive laugh, which sounded through the closed door like a train chugging in the distance as we walked down the empty hallway to the elevator.

"You sure this is OK?"

"Absolutely."

"You do look like Paul a little," she said. Her voice was soft with just a hint of gravel, and that twang. The eyes had settled on shades of blue. We walked down Dike Street, the main campus drag. I could see that she was nervous, uncertain. Wondering if it had been a mistake to come. I handed her a piece of bubble gum. She looked at it with surprise, then smiled. We walked along in the rain, chewing and blowing bubbles. She grew more relaxed now as we competed over the size of our bubbles. I had my umbrella over both of us, and my arm lightly around her shoulder to keep us close. I couldn't take my eyes from her face. Her full lips, the upper one slightly protruding, so inviting. We hadn't spoken half a dozen sentences, just chewing and blowing, snapping the bubbles loudly. I blew a large bubble and leaned closer to her. She responded with a bubble of her own. They touched and burst. We both laughed. Our eyes met, and we paused, mid-step. In a motion at first hesitant, then sure, she raised her mouth to mine. The pull of her sensuality – I would probably have told my students they meant sensuousness, but it was sensuality all right – was so intoxicating, so utterly irresistible. She pressed her body up against me as I slid my tongue into her unfamiliar mouth, thrilling to her taste mixed with bubble gum in that noisy street; the shock of intimacy so unexpected, so intense. She pushed her gum into my mouth. We stood embracing and kissing under the umbrella as people hurried by us in the rain.

———◄O►———

Lavender and I were alone at Andy's house that night. Andy was out in the rain jogging with his dog. Lavender was at the sink doing the last two days' dishes. I was drying, at least when she kept after me.

"He's such a slob," she said of Andy. I watched her scrape some crusted cheese off the dish with her fingernail. She laughed her deep chesty laugh. "So why aren't you out with this new fluffy?" she taunted me. "Your charms not equal to the task?"

"Isn't she absolutely exquisite?" I asked.

"She looked just like all your balls of fluff." Lavender turned to me, putting the dish in the drain. "Just a little younger."

"Give me a break."

"So what happened? Who the hell is she?"

I walked over to the dartboard and pulled out the darts. "She had to babysit for her friend," I said. "We had a quick coffee is all."

"Good God," Lavender said; then turned her attention to the charcoaled bottom of a pot. She had the pot in the sink and was scrubbing away with a Brillo pad. She looked up, breathless.

I ignored the query of her eyes and threw a dart.

"Why didn't you go with her? That sounds like a fun high school night."

"She is not in high school. Give me a break."

"How old *is* she?"

I collected the darts, and concentrated this time. Two twenties and one off the board.

"You're getting as bad as Andy," she observed.

"I got two twenties for Christ sake," I said

"And the wall." She put the pot in the dish drain. "I thought you were drying?"

I came back and picked up the pot. "Pretty spotty job."

"Andy won't even notice they're done Why waste perfection?"

Andy and Lavender. They were becoming a long-term couple, at least by department standards. It was the previous Spring that I sat with Andy in Mr. F.'s Aunt, the local gay bar that doubled as a grad student bar because they played classical music and jazz on the jukebox and few undergrads intruded. Andy, having recently severed a connection, was making out a list of available women. He was very methodical even drunk. Perhaps that was what he and Lavender were to find in common. It was only after four or five Rolling Rocks that I suggested he add Lavender to the list.

She had just disengaged herself from Arthur Yikes, the Milton specialist who had arrived as an assistant prof at about the same time Lavender had arrived as a graduate student, and, as I heard it, won her after some months of a much bruited contest with the Dryden specialist.

I didn't tell Andy that a while before, after a Milton seminar, having coffee with her, lighting cigarette after cigarette, talking relentlessly and restlessly about *Areopagitica* which seemed to be what she wanted me to do, our eyes were speaking on a nonacademic subject. She sighed finally and said, "You've always intrigued me." Her curiosity was explored forthwith. As we lay on my bed, her hand caressing my chest afterward, she said, with a tight smile, "I still can't figure out what makes you tick."

"You could keep researching."

She gave me a look.

Eventually she and Arthur broke up, and in Mr. F.'s Aunt that night, I suggested her to Andy. I did like, as Lavender put it to me some time later, the thought of his following in my footsteps.

"Jail bait," Lavender was saying as she wiped her hands on the dish towel and surveyed the kitchen with approval. "And hillbilly fathers carry shotguns." She laughed at my discomfort.

"She's legal, damn it. That face, that fabulous, perfect face." I lit a cigarette with a wooden kitchen match.

"So what are you going to do about it?"

"I'm seeing her tomorrow; she's coming over." I stared defiantly at Lavender, who was dragging on my cigarette and not saying anything about her friend Jody, whom I had recently started seeing.

At that point the door banged and a very wet Weimaraner hurled himself into the kitchen, wagging his entire rear end. Andy came up behind, his short blond hair and close-clipped beard glittering with rain droplets.

"Hey, Jord," he greeted me with that smile that put the world at ease.

We had discovered cribbage recently, and spent the night pegging away madly, smoking cigarettes – Andy would go through a pack and a half at least – and downing cheap Gallo wine.

"I wish we still smoked dope," Lavender said. "This wine makes me foggy." But except for Marian we had all grown bored with drugs of any kind.

By midnight we were pegged out, and glowed in the mellowness of Ernest and Julio's elixir. The dog whimpered in his sleep now and then. No one had put a new record on the stereo for a while, since Leon Redbone finished.

Andy chuckled.

"What," Lavender said.

"Ned," Andy said, chuckling again. "I don't know where he comes up with them." He looked at me. "Who was the only hermaphroditic incestuous poet in the English language?"

I smiled. Ned had told me.

"Emily Dick-in-son," Andy said.

"Tell that to your chippie," Lavender said. "See if she gets it."

"What chippie?" Andy asked, standing up. "How about some Steel Eye Span?"

"As opposed to Steely Dan," I said.

"Jordan is cradle-robbing."

"That is not news," Andy said cheerfully.

"No, really, this time, really."

"An actual infant?"

"All but."

"Lavender, you tell him what she looked like."

"Fluff. This one is a twit and a hick to boot."

Andy laughed. "Have you come up with ideas for a topic yet?" he asked me, diplomatically changing the subject. "I had this great idea while I was running, and even a title, 'Urizon Resartis: Revolution, Carlyle and the Blakian Mythology.'"

"Has a nice ring."

"But the only one who would do it is Yaslow and his reputation is four-year dissertations. He's the one who failed Tom Jenson last year in his orals."

"That's been last year for five years now," I said. Poor Tom had become mythic in his misfortune. Failed orals were a rarity.

"You heard the latest about Yaslow? He's going out with some undergrad. Supposedly really smart and hot."

"There should be rules against fucking students. It puts the girl in a position where she doesn't know if she is really good or is just treated like she's good to get into her pants. I have my own rule." I said.

"You rules?" Lavender said. "Ha."

"Yes. I won't go out with a student until she is no longer my student."

"Forget about rules anytime soon. The department head and his wife are in a menage with Jessica."

"Marston? With Jessica Waters? You're shitting me."

"You didn't know that? It is hardly secret."

"No. This place is a fucking hothouse," Lavender said.

We avoided looking at Lavender, what with her own past adventures with faculty.

I added, "And don't forget Professor Kitney and his problem. He had to turn down an offer at some Ivy League school, I forget which, full professor, because after that wife swap thing went bad, and the breakup, he would not be able to see his kids if he left town. Carla was really vindictive."

"I want to know about this twit," Lavender returned the focus to me. "Where did you meet her? She wasn't a student here. And she hardly seemed to know who you were."

I sighed.

"Give."

"If you must know, she was a wrong telephone number."

"You're kidding."

"I picked up the phone and heard that voice. That voice," I said dreamily, "that languid, molasses voice." I closed my eyes. "She talks soft, real soft, and slow."

Lavender turned to Andy. "And with a definite hillbilly twang!" She turned back and gave me a look. "How did you know she wouldn't be a dog? How did you talk to her long enough to even get there. Could she put a sentence together? She seemed so mindless."

We had talked for two hours. I thought back: "Are you as sexy as you sound?" I had asked her. I could hear her lighting a cigarette and she replied, "Some says I'm real foxy, you niyw, and some says I'm just plain." There was quiet on the line then. "How's about you?" she asked after a time. "What do you look like?"

"I'm OK looking," I said, not at all comfortable doing the evaluation.

"Niyw, but like who do you look like? Tell me a movie star or something."

I told her people said I looked sort of like Paul.

"Well, that's OK," she said comfortingly, "John's the cutest, you niyw, but Paul's cute too."

We left it that she would come by the office; she could look me over without committing herself, in case I was too watered down a Paul.

"This'll rile Jody if she finds out," Lavender finally said what I knew she had been thinking.

Andy chuckled and said "Outfoxed by a mindless teenager. Where is Jody tonight?"

"She has that Austen paper due," I said.

"How *can* you prefer her to Jody?" Lavender persisted, with exasperation in her voice.

The truth was nothing ever matched that rush of newness: that first intimacy exploding out of separateness, that sudden unearned, unreasonable knowledge of exquisite difference. And my God, this was different. If I could only hold on to that moment once. I reached out my hands toward Lavender. "Verveile doch, du bist so schön."

"Hey," Andy said, "not this one, she's mine."

"Property, chattel," Lavender said.

Evanescent, always. Always not enough. Wistfully so, like the still twilight on an early Spring day. Lavender told me once I would never find a woman until I stopped thinking of them as little perfections of fluffhood.

The bell rang. Andy mumbled as he sipped his drink, "That'll be Ned. He was going to see *Casablanca*." He laughed. "For about the twenty-seventh time."

"I think I've seen it more than that," I said.

"Andy, God damn it, did you ask him over?" She stood up in a barely suppressed fury. "I can't believe you. Monday night for football is the limit. I get enough of him all day, every day. Damn it," she spit out, turning away from him.

Andy passed it off. "He said they'd stop by, that's all…It's open," he yelled, downing what was left in his wine glass. "Throw your coats in the bedroom."

Ned's and Marian's footsteps sounded in the hallway, the bedroom, and into the kitchen.

"Hi, hi," Marian said. "Oh, hi Jord. Where's Jody?"

"Excuse me," Lavender said, and left the room.

"She's tired, drank too much," Andy explained.

"Hah," came from down the hallway.

After a while when Lavender didn't return, I went looking for her. She was in the bedroom, crying among the coats. I sat down beside her on the bed and asked, "Should I go?" She gave me a quick jerk of her head, so I stroked her hair and told her not to let it get to her.

"Why does he do that? He knows I don't like Ned."

I didn't answer. I sat with her in the quiet for some minutes. We could hear the hum of their chatter over the music and occasionally Andy's cackling laugh. I looked at Lavender lying on her back. When she first started seeing Andy she said to me, "You know I'm seeing Andy?"

"I do," I said. She looked at me then quizzically, but said no more.

Now, as I watched her fine, sculpted face, her tears were pooling up between the well of her eye and the bridge of her nose. I found myself leaning over and flicking them away, well, actually licking them away.

She let out a grunt of annoyance. "Damn it, you're not supposed to be licking my tears and thinking about fucking me. You're supposed to be comforting me in my great distress."

She was lying on the pile of coats, mostly on Ned's. "We *should* do it," she said, biting off the words. "I'd like to come all over Ned's coat."

I raised my eyebrows.

"But we're not."

We could hear the background sound of banter from the kitchen.

I made a pouting face.

"Idiot."

The phone rang eventually, and Andy yelled that it was Jody. Lavender laughed derisively and stood to go. I picked up the extension.

Lavender waved her hand at me as she closed the door behind her. I talked to Jody about *Mansfield Park*.

Next day, Sunday, I was standing in the kitchen of my apartment – the top floor of an old house – looking out over the puddled backyard and having second thoughts about this girl, Nicole. I considered calling the whole thing off, but even the idea of trying to reach her made me uncomfortable. What had I been thinking? She was already two hours late and I was just happily convincing myself that she was not coming, when I heard her rattling up the metal stairway.

"Hi," she said. She had her hands in the pockets of her bomber jacket as she stood awkwardly before me.

I waited for her to explain why she was late, but she didn't speak. She walked on in, looking around her, and disappeared from view. I heard her voice through the long corridor between the kitchen and living room. "Wow, look at all these books. Did you really read all these?"

I walked in after her. "It's four o'clock," I said.

She looked back at me, not comprehending my meaning.

"You were supposed to be here at two."

She squinted. "Well, what's the difference?" she asked softly, "I'm here."

I felt more uncomfortable than I had before she arrived. "Come on inside, take off your coat," I said abruptly.

"Are you sure?" she asked, catching the edge in my voice, and stopping in the corridor.

"Why? What do you mean?"

"I don't niyw, do you want me to stay? I could go; it's OK."

I missed that chance; I knew I would, even as I walked up to her. "I don't want you to go," I said. I took her coat and she commented again on the books.

"I really like to read," she said. "My mom says I'm the reader in the family. My stepfather – they're not really married, you niyw – says I'm just ruinin' my eyes. I'll tell you the truth though, I couldn't get into most of the stuff they gave us in school. They made us read this one called *Portrait Of A Artist.*" She sat down, sprawled out on my old couch with the sagging springs. "It was real dumb, all about this little kid. And hard to follow. I couldn't get through it."

She propped herself up with her elbow on the cushion, her head resting on her palm. "There was one though I really liked. I can't remember the name. All about this woman as loves this dude, you niyw, but he's like so much above her. He's got this crazy wife locked up in the attic. In the end she gets to marry him. I was like crying all through it. It was real good."

"*Jane Eyre?*"

"Yeah, that was it. You niyw all that stuff, huh?"

"Well, that's my field."

She was warming up as she felt more comfortable, sitting cross-legged on the couch now, and I, torn between my nervous doubt, which she drove home with every word, and the inexplicable enchantment of her, just kept drifting along.

Once she got talking, she didn't stop. "Lu Ann was going to take me," she said, lighting a cigarette, "but her car wouldn't start."

"You told her about me?"

"A'course. Lu Ann and me, we don't hold nothin' back. We're like this close." She held up two fingers. "Anyways, her old man banged her around some, said she flooded the engine. He got the car going, but she was hurtin' then and didn't want to drive after that. Anyways, I got out of there. I don't need none of their shit. So I hitched. Only I got dropped in Quinterville and couldn't get a ride for ever and a day."

"So that's why you were late," I said, angry at myself for being curt with her when she walked in. "Why didn't you call? I could have gotten you."

"It's all right."

"So Lu Ann is married to this guy?"

"Tom. He gets impatient when she's stupid. Wasn't anything."

"Lu Ann's the one who wants to go to beautician school?"

She nodded.

I remembered now. Dropped out of high school when she married this mechanic last year. Now she was pregnant. Rosalie was her other friend; had two kids. She was eighteen years old.

I got us beers from the kitchen. Nicole leaned her head against my shoulder. "Givin' liquor to a minor," she said.

I looked at her.

She laughed suddenly as the realization hit her. "It's still so new to me, I forget. I'm still not used to not being a minor. I can just waltz into a bar and order a drink. It's like wow." She rubbed her hand lightly along my arm. She sighed contentedly.

"Yeah, like wow," I said, having third thoughts. Maybe Lavender's barbs were making me paranoid, or maybe I should not be doing this. How about that idea.

Nicole was happy. She kissed my cheek and nuzzled up against my face. "You're so different, you niyw?"

I put my arms around her and into her back pockets as I kissed her. My hand was crumpling a paper and I pulled it out curiously. She looked up to see.

"What is it?" I asked.

"Oh, nothin'. It's dumb." She took it from me.

"Can I see?"

"No, you don't want to."

"Yes I do." She let me take it and I started to read.

"It's just dumb. They're little girls. Don't read it."

I read. It was in blue and purple and yellow crayon: "This is for Nicole, who is eighteen today and now has no excuse not to be a mommy like our mommy. We love you Nicole. You are our most favorite aunt and babysitter, even if sometimes you get mad when we are silly and have pillow fights. Happy Birthday. Love, Mary Ellen and Joanne Brewster, your nieces."

"It's sweet, " I said. "They love you."

"It's dumb. I'm not *even* their aunt. And their mother mostly wrote it, anyways. She wants me to hurry up and have a baby so we can have them together."

"It's still very sweet." I brushed a strand of hair from her forehead. "I'm glad you finished high school," I said, and realized I was feeling paternal. This was getting confusing. "Do you want to be a mommy?"

"Yeah, I guess."

"When *was* your birthday?"

"Last week."

"Happy birthday," I said and kissed her. Her heat was exciting against me. And thinking about making a baby in her was so crazy it turned me on. I stroked her hair. "What do you want to do now that you're out of high school all these months."

"Maybe go to beautician school. Have kids. I feel like a old maid already. Lu Ann's having a kid. Roselie'll be having her third one 'fore long."

Her mouth, making words about babies, was very close to mine, tempting and warm-breathed. I drifted into her being, mindlessly letting the passion take me. The moves were all automatic then, going for the shirt buttons, flicking the bra hooks. We were naked to our waists, merging in heat and moistness. Her body was perfect, her breasts small and firm. I undid her jeans, slowly pulled them down over her knees. She arched them over her last ankle. Her scent richer, fuller now. I was bursting with her.

And then...

She looked up at me expectantly. I looked into those eyes, those amazing iridescent eyes, the delicate lashes. The sensuous nose. That luscious mouth. That fabulous face.

"I can't," I said.

We looked at each other. I could hear the faint sounds of the neighbor downstairs talking on the telephone. I was half kneeling, half crouching at her knee, where I had let the pants go. She looked at me. "Why not?" she asked softly. "What's wrong with you?"

She looked concerned.

"I don't mean I can't."

She stared at me, uncomprehending. "What, then?"

"I mean I shouldn't."

"Why?"

"You know."

"I don't either." She was quiet for a minute. "It's safe. A safe time."

"Your age."

"I've done it."

"I know, but you're very young."

"Eighteen's like way legal. The age is sixteen. I'm an adult now." She said it softly, but with intensity.

"I know sixteen's the law. But it doesn't matter. It was really wrong of me to start this."

"But why?"

"I can't."

"You scared of my stepfather?" she asked, grinning. "I ain't telling him."

"I know you're not."

"Well, then?"

We sat like that, with me half crouching, half sitting for a long several minutes. She looked so hurt, so beautiful. The pout of her full lips; the soft flair of her nose; the perspiration curling the downy hairs of her temple; her hard, pointy pink nipples.

A tear, I abruptly became aware, was flooding over her eyelid. It formed and rolled down her cheek. She was staring straight ahead at the wall. A second tear which had been welling in the other eye, overflowed finally and joined the first one at her chin. She didn't look at me, but she mumbled softly, "OK," and started to dress.

"Don't cry," I said.

"I'm not," she snapped, buttoning her shirt and rising to pull on her jeans.

I took hold of her shoulders and tried to hug her. She twisted away, leaving me feeling suddenly lecherous.

"Nicole, don't you see why?"

"No," she said. She looked down at the sofa cushion, picking at a frayed spot with her fingers. After a while she said in a whisper, "I thought you liked me."

"I do like you," I said. "I like you a lot."

My doorbell rang. It stunned us both into an instant of suspended motion. I grinned. "Your stepfather didn't waste any time."

"It's not."

"I know. It's probably a package or something. I'll just let it ring."

"It's OK. Go see. Maybe it's someone as wants to give you money." She smiled.

I looked at her questioningly.

She nodded.

I got up and walked to the door.

As soon as I opened it a crack, Jody was on her way in, with a big smile and talking a mile a minute. "Oh God, it was awful. Turned out to be thirty pages, but it's done. I dropped it off and now I am free... Hello?"

Nicole had come up behind. "One of your students?" Jody asked me, suspecting nothing, but instinctively proprietary, placing her arm on my shoulder. "I'm Jody," she said to Nicole.

Nicole stood with her mouth quivering as she tried not to cry. I stared back at her; her pain twisted through me like a driven screw. My eyes started to tear. She turned abruptly on her heels, and strode inside, then reappeared with her jacket in her hand, the sleeves dragging on the floor. She brushed by me, her cheeks glinting with wet. "Nice to meet you," she said to Jody and was bouncing down the metal stairway.

"Nicole," I called after her, and crashed loudly down the metal steps. I reached for her coat sleeve as she strode ahead of me. She tried to pull it out of my grip. She stopped and we faced each other across the coat, holding it taut between us. She was composed as she looked at me, but her eyes kept running tears.

"It's all right," she said. "I knew it wouldn't be. It wasn't really possible. I just thought, I don't niyw, you were so different, so – different. I'll never meet anyone like you again. A professor and all."

"Nicole – " I wanted to say so many things. The truth is, I wanted her to see me for the not-so-great person I felt like. More, I wanted her to have a different life. I wanted to remake her world. Wave a wand.

I walked up to her as the coat relaxed between us. I brushed away her tears. "You're foxy as hell. Anyone who says you aren't is a moron." She sniffed out an inadvertent titter. I ran my fingers along her cheek. "Nicole, you are as beautiful as any movie star that ever was."

She smiled, choking over her tears, and started to laugh just a little. Then she was gone.

The Life That Late He Led

I T WAS AN EARLY Spring day in 1988 – before we knew whether George Bush or one of those seven or eight unknown Democrats scrambling around the country that Spring would be our leader; before we knew the Cold War would abruptly end; before we knew we'd have a rousing war with Iraq: befores; they seem so unfathomably remote after.

On that day, I was at Victor's twentieth floor Manhattan apartment. We had crawled through his window onto the narrow ledge that served as his terrace, a tranquil citadel, protected by a low granite parapet. The view from that terrace on a cool, clear Spring day like this one was nothing short of spectacular. He had just been treating me and the white puffs in the clear blue sky to a Cole Porter song: that rich baritone voice of his pouring out the words about a man who since youth had enjoyed an endless succession of conquests. This verse, which he loved to sing with every bit of gusto he could muster, I do believe he thought of as his anthem, and rightly so. Victor breaking into Cole Porter brought me back indubitably to our college days together – a before fragrant with imagined afters, and now itself a scent unbearably faint.

I was on the terrace still; Victor had gone inside. Sitting there in the bright sun and cool breeze, above the traffic, above the world, looking downtown toward the metal stalks scraping the sky, you couldn't help feeling like you owned the whole forest. I didn't, of course: I was just in from New Jersey where I rented a room, but Victor sure did, at least at that precise moment he did. A few moments later he didn't. It was that quick.

I crawled back in through the window, my joints cracking, my stiff, overweight torso refusing to bend enough for me to negotiate the passage with any modicum of grace. I stumbled into the room like some drunken buffoon. Victor was sitting reading, working. He glanced up as I made my awkward entrance.

Collecting myself, I wandered around the large room, squinted up at the loft with that bed that saw so much activity. I gazed at my flabby body and my graying hair in the mirrored walls at either end of the room. I disliked this excess of mirror.

All at once, Victor's head jerked up from his reading. This was the moment, the turning of before into after.

"What is it," I asked.

His green eyes that had charmed so many young ladies were dull and cloudy. His always perfect face now showed crow's feet around the eyes and a certain sagging below the chin that I had never seen before. His expression radiated a combination of fear, shock, and outrage.

"Are you OK?" I asked.

He licked his lips.

"What?" I urged in a whisper.

"I'm going to kill myself tomorrow," he said. He said it with a resigned finality in his voice that left no room for doubt. No room for the possibility of persuasion, negotiation.

"The airline found out about the drugs I carried into the country that time, when Ellen was in the hospital and needed the transplant, and I had to get the money right away. They're taking away my pilot's license. Flying is everything to me. If I can't fly – ." He looked back down at the pages crumpled in his hand. "And Ellen just announced that she is leaving me – for the doctor who gave her the new liver. After all I did for her. I mean, he just stitched someone's organ into her. What does that make him, God?"

I felt awkward being there. He was sitting, numb, not moving. I could feel his despair turning bitter, welling into anger. "It's Fraska. It's all goddamned Fraska!" he screamed, fairly bursting, and then deflating into his chair. As the minutes and then hours passed, he sat. The sun traversed the heavens. It lighted his face through the ten-foot-high windows of his apartment, and then left him in shadow. The day grew dark, and I was still there, staring out his wall of windows. In the evening, when the millions of candles out there twinkle, melt into a milky way of light, you feel, as Victor often said, almost as if you are living in a Fred Astaire musical.

"Let's go out," I finally said. Out on the town, that's what they would do in a musical, isn't it? Well, *we'd* go for a walk at least.

He picked himself up as if every limb weighed as much as his whole body.

When we graduated college in 1970, and I began my brief debacle of a career as a graduate student, Victor was already living a celebrity life in a small way. He had starred in the major campus production of *Kiss Me Kate* (while I was dodging teargas). He was swooningly good looking. He came to New York charmed. After not even a year of off-off-off-Broadway dish washing and table waiting, he managed to get himself into the Broadway production of another Cole Porter musical revival, *The Nymph Errant*, with such top stars as Carole Channing and Robert Kiley. He had a small role, but he had songs and he was noted in the *Times* review. The guy had made it to Broadway at 22! He went on to several off-Broadway musicals, some serious drama, *Twelfth Night* in the Park, then more Broadway.

By 1980 when he landed the soap part, he felt as if he were on an express train. But with that kind of money pouring in for the next eight years, he started pouring powder up his nose, and forgot about serious work. He got comfortable. He bought the Jaguar, had every woman he wanted (and he only wanted perfectly formed beauties), had them in every position, doing every bizarre thing I had ever even momentarily fantasized, and made sure to tell me the details.

Meanwhile, I was out in Wisconsin, the cows looking more and more within the realm of possibility. I had been in graduate school there, and then wasn't. Terminal M.A. they called it, meaning: "No doctorate for you, but here's a certificate with Latin on it entitling the bearer to teach writing to future plumbers and farmers, part-time, non-tenure." Terminal it was – a lingering death, and then when Wisconsin's education budget dried up in '84, the corpse came East.

I read about the exuberant 80s, the wild Reagan years, and I wonder where I was. I didn't make and lose millions. I sometimes feel as if I have drifted through some retro fantasy world, inhabiting nooks and crannies abandoned in about 1972 by all the real people, the people who live in corporations now. Something happened that I missed. I still use a ditto machine with that solvent-smelling blue ink for my class assignments. I have no intercourse with computers or fax machines.

For that matter, I have no intercourse at all anymore. Unlike Victor, I was never any good in bars. I mean, "What do you think of Cowper's odes" was never a line that got anyone laid. But it used to be I'd find a young impressionable girl in one of my classes who had half a brain, or who thought I did – or even both. Flat-chested, long-nosed, stove-pipe legs, I didn't care, anything warm. I didn't even care about all the new diseases that had been invented all of a sudden. But then one semester maybe five years ago I realized it had been quite a few classes since anyone had taken an interest in me.

My only social activity now was a Marxist group in Montclair, New Jersey, and even that may be a relic of memory before long, what with the abrupt disappearance of communism all across Eastern Europe, and the evaporation of the USSR. I always vote Democratic, but since the old days, I have found these groups, which existed on every campus, fertile ground. Marxist women never thought I was quite as strange as others did. They gave me the chance no capitalist daddy's girl would. After all, a good Marxist could hardly dismiss me because I had no money. At the time of Victor's impending suicide, in 1988, I thought I was getting somewhere with this one black-haired woman; surprisingly cute she was to be with me. We'd gone out after a meeting on solidarity with the Sandinistas. I had suggested Dunkin' Donuts right off so I wouldn't have to decline something more pricey, and I let her pay when she insisted on not being patronized as a woman. But the next month, she wasn't at the meeting and I learned she had gotten married to a meat butcher from the Grand Union, a union shop steward.

I was sure Victor's friends didn't understand what he was doing with me. Deep in my heart, I believe he kept up with me all these years to measure himself, to confirm his attractiveness and success against my failure. The thing is, it didn't seem like it would be this way at all when we started out in college. It's true he was always better looking and really talented, but I was pretty bright, and we were both headed for success. Everyone said so.

"How are you going to do it?" I asked. Methods of suicide were beginning to interest me. We had emerged onto the bustling street, to crystal clear air; one of those rare Spring evenings in New York, when everything is vivid, the colors and shadows beneath the street lights are vibrant; this is before the insufferable stinking heat mars everything. Today the array of life that rushed by felt energizing, not, as it would when the humidity rose, like a frightening infestation.

"Jump out of the plane over the ocean," Victor said. His eyes were blank. "I think I tell the co-pilot I have to relieve myself, pat him on the shoulder, give him a last lingering look, and stride back up the aisle. And while the shocked passengers watch in horror, I open the cabin door and step out. Janice, the stewardess who has had a crush on me all the time I was faithful to the ungrateful Ellen comes rushing up, stands horror-struck, index finger over mouth. Fade to credits.

"So much for Captain Richard McCulluch. The dashing Captain Richard McCulluch. So much for my fat fat paycheck per show. Hank, what am I going to do? Fucking Fraska. He wrote me out because I contradicted him on the set. Just like that. The guy is a producer, not an actor. Not even a director! He has no dramatic sense and he thinks he's Lee Strasberg. How can he have that much power? Can you believe the way I find out? No one even tells me. Just give me the script. I think they'll have to pay me for a while. I don't even remember what my contract says. I have to call my agent. I am just stunned. I had good fan response every rating period. I can't get used to this being real."

"You'll get picked up by another show."

"I can't face going back to waiting tables. You don't know."

Right, I don't know. Me. My life hasn't been exactly limousines picking me up and dropping me home after a day of shoots.

We were standing at the counter in the bakery on the corner and I noticed a woman who kept turning our way. She hesitated, then started walking in our direction. Ah yes. I recalled who I was with, the dashing, soon-to-be-deceased, Captain Richard McCulluch.

"Captain?" she probed, not certain. Victor was lost in his misery. "Captain McCulluch?" she repeated. "I knew it was you. I just want to say, as gorgeous a guy as you are, you are so stupid to stay with that bitch Ellen. Don't you realize she is cheating on you with that fairy of a liver doctor?"

"No?" Victor said, sweeping backward, arm across his chest, bumping me out of the way as if I didn't exist; ever the dashing captain.

"Yes. I saw it," she said, her enthusiasm feeding off Victor's. "I-saw-it! They met just this Tuesday. While you were over the Atlantic. They did it at the Meadows Motel. You should have seen them going at each other. Frankly it was disgusting. I'm sorry to have to tell you, but you have to wise up. Excuse me, ten poppy seed, five sesame and three whole wheat. Yes thanks. Wise up, really. You're too good for her."

"The good and the dead," Victor said when she was gone. He sagged against the counter.

<hr>

That was in 1988. The next year it was Bye Bye Reagan and Hello Bushy. Victor was in a couple of off-Broadway non-starters that year. Then nothing. It was as if he had played all the cards in the deck; lady luck had fled him; the worm turned; the fates abandoned him.

I can hear another Cole Porter tune filling the air: "Get Out Of Town." Victor used his current flame, Mimi, as his excuse. She got her shot in a regional theater in Minneapolis and he went with her – just for the season. They had a role for him in the play they were doing. He started talking about marriage.

Mimi didn't last, but the job did. He stayed on with the company as a stagehand after the run of the play he was in, waiting for the next role he could play. When it didn't come, he drifted into being the company's set manager. "You have to eat, Hank, and I can't go back to waiting tables." The years kept passing, and Victor was still temporarily out of town. He held onto his apartment in New York of course; you don't let a rent-stabilized studio in the heart of the Upper West Side go. It was nigh on three years now, but who's counting.

I talked to Victor every so often, and at some point it occurred to us both that I ought to move into his place. "Maybe you'll get lucky," Victor said. "That bed is charmed." So last year, after Victor's last sublessee neglected to inform Victor that he had quit the scene two months earlier, I did. (Move in, that is; I didn't get lucky).

The building suited me. Old and dilapidated, with a dark cavernous lobby of bare walls and concrete floor, it was one of the few buildings in the neighborhood yet to be spruced up and co-oped. Now that the frenzy of the 80s had gone bust, its time probably had passed. It wouldn't change. As I say, it fit me.

The walls were recently painted, but in that shiny yellow tenement paint that leaves the lobby still looking sleazy. A sign just inside the door warned that Visitors Must Be Announced, but there was no one immediately apparent to make the announcement. Most visitors headed directly to the elevators, only to be halted by the irascible voice of Raj, the concierge whose ill-placed desk, recessed in an alcove to the right of the door, was out of the sight of someone entering.

I fell victim to Raj the first day. And after that, any developing sense of this being my home, a place where I belonged, was crushed by his stubborn unwillingness to remember me. In a way, this may have been my fault. Each time that he halted me in my tracks and I told him where I was staying, and he reluctantly allowed me to proceed, I raised his suspicions anew by stepping into the wrong elevator. There were two. Invariably I took the one that went up only nineteen floors. Victor was on the 20th, the "P" floor, which I assumed stood for penthouse, a name I found quite irreconcilable with the inhabitants of the floor. Happening upon any of these denizens in the hallway led me to check the water when I entered the apartment, thinking I had missed a sign in the elevator that the plumbing was not working this week. Moreover, the floor was a musical cacophony that drove me to Hammacher-Schlemmer for a white noise machine. The opera diva thought if she just did her scales one more time and just a little louder, someone from the Met a few blocks south might happen up and listen. The two pianos across the hall from each other seemed always to be involved in a heated competition between Ludwig Beethoven and Bela Bartok. Ludwig seemed definitely to have the edge in the stamina category. At least the brief but extremely unpleasant trombone period Victor had complained of was history, as was the rather bizarre triangle period. Or was that a joke we made up? Reality and fiction start to blend as the years pass and our memories intertwine.

My habit was to turn off the phone when I went to sleep. I left the answering machine to deal with any late night breathy women thinking Victor was still available for a little last minute tumble between the sheets. I swear, after all the years he was away, I still got two or three calls like that a month.

I woke up one morning to a thump below me that I realized was not the crescendo of a Beethoven piano concerto. I looked down from the loft bed. There stood Victor looking at himself in the mirrored wall. He saw me in the mirror, up there above, hanging my head over the edge, too sleepy to have any idea what was going on and said, "Hi, Hank, did you get my message?"

Apparently, he'd left it sometime around 4 A.M. Now it seemed to be almost noon.

"What message?" I mumbled.

He turned on the tape machine and played it for me. He sounded really down on the crackling tape. Said he had been working too hard, had been having chest pains that scared the shit out of him, finally went to the doctor who told him he was stressed out and had developed a possibly serious heart murmur, he was too old for this kind of heavy work. Told him he had to take a break. Victor said he was coming back at least for a while. Said I could stay. He didn't want to kick me out before he knew what he was doing. He had just decided that minute he was coming. He wanted to give me some warning.

"Thanks," I said.

"Guess you weren't expecting me then. Sorry."

I certainly wasn't expecting what I saw. I hadn't seen him in three years. Victor was not young anymore. Neither was I, of course, but that had crept up on me so I didn't have to confront it. Victor had been youth personified. Victor was a shock that announced to me that I was middle aged for real now.

I couldn't get Victor to do anything, go anywhere in the days that followed. He mostly lay in bed or sat out on his terrace listening, either with or without headphones, to Cole Porter songs – Frank Sinatra, Fred Astaire, Julie Wilson, Julie London,

Bobby Short, it didn't matter. He had them all and he listened virtually every waking moment. It was some kind of strange narcotic.

I could no longer walk down the street, brush my teeth, eat a meal, fall asleep without one or another Cole Porter tune running through my head. Today it was "You've Got That Thing."

I was now spending my days apartment hunting. I'd walked the pavement enough already to realize that with my meager income I'd have to go back to New Jersey. It was an unremittingly hot June. This day, a couple of weeks after Victor's return, I'd walked myself into exhaustion. I returned sweaty and thirsty, to hear Victor singing a cappella in the distance: the Cole Porter song with the line about endless girls. "The Life That Late I Led," I think it was called.

Victor was out on the ledge, singing into the breeze, into the tops of water towers, into the distant skyscrapers to the south; his voice wafting soundlessly down Broadway far below.

Up here, his melody filled our private theater: I stood and listened for a while. He was still captivating. He was singing Cole Porter's song in which daddy spanked.

"Ah Hank," he said, spying me. "Come on out. I've been sitting here – recherching temps perdu – chickens perdu, as it were. You remember that sweet thing who sat in front of us in Modern Literature? What was her name?"

"Sweet thing of 1967 you mean? Who, Miss Villey? Did she like to be spanked? Good Catholic-school girl that she was?"

"Of course, that's it, Miss Villey. The days when there were still "Misses." The good old days, Hank. Sweet Miss Villey. That, Hank, whether she did or didn't, neither you nor I will ever know. Miss Villey's rosy behind eluded us both, though mightily we lusted. Where is she now, Hank? Our sweet Miss Villey of yore. Four kids in college? A balding husband, properly Catholic.

You think she puts out for him Hank? Don't you wonder what married people do behind those conjugal doors?"

"Victor, do you realize that we are not normal? Most people our age have been married for 20 years, some have even tried it twice or more."

He answered me by singing several lines in which a stork appears with a baby.

"Yes, from 'It's Delovely.'" He'd been playing the damned stuff so much I knew all the lyrics as well as he did.

"Is that what you want, Hank? Do you want to be normal?"

"Yes," I said, looking off at the city below. It had struck me that that was all I wanted anymore. I glanced at Victor. He had a far-off look in his eyes. Then he peered directly at me and said, "You never will be."

I turned to face him and belted out Gershwin's "But Not For Me" in a full-throated voice. He grimaced. I'm not entirely certain if it was my truly awful voice or the sentiment.

"I'm a middle aged guy with no money, no place to live, no one to live with," I said.

"Middle aged?"

"Yeah, what do you think. It's going to be 25 years since we graduated!"

"You're very depressing." He had a dismissive smile on his face, but then he said, "Do you know I haven't gotten laid in almost nine months? Me. We're talking me, not you."

"Thanks a lot."

"Sorry, I just meant – "

I knew what he meant. It had always been this way. Victor was the success. I was the failure. Only now here we both were and there was no longer much difference. This shocked me, now that I thought of it.

"This is depressing," Victor said. He climbed in through the window and flicked on the television. Some soap; a pretty boy, more or less a clone of Victor, was acting shock in someone's kitchen.

"Fuck this," Victor said. "That exquisitely pompous fluff ball thinks he's reached a pinnacle of success."

"You're a successful actor."

"Successful? Who knows my name? De Niro and Pacino made it. What, I'm serious. They may have been a few years older, but we were up for the same parts. I was in their league. You don't think so? I was. They made it. I didn't. I got fucked. It's nasty to get set up for a fall, Hank. I was a success at twenty. Now I'm a failure at forty."

"Five," I said.

"What?"

"Five, forty-five." You have to keep it honest.

"Who ever heard of me?"

"I remember a lady in a deli three years ago, a bakery. Remember?"

Victor waved his hand dismissing me. "Not me, Hank, not me. She knew the captain. Captain McCulluch, Hank!" That was true, I had to admit.

"I could taste it. Even now it seems like it was so close. I had the looks, I was good. I *was* good. I got the notices, damn it. I got good reviews. I should be where De Niro is. Look at me, 45 and a stage hand. And now not even. That fucking Fraska."

I was silent.

"Look at that fellow, for all his strutting, has got pimples. They didn't quite do the make-up well enough to hide it for the tight shots. Did we have such awful pimples, Hank, in our lost and wanton youth?"

"I did; you didn't. And I didn't have a wanton youth; you did."

"What time is it?" Victor asked, suddenly, looking at his watch and flipping the channel. "You know, I haven't seen this since the day I died. It's Edgar," he said grinning, walking up close to the television to study the man speaking passionately to the pretty young woman in the wheel chair. "Still there. Look at that – he's gotten thick in the middle. I have not looked at this show in three years, and there they all are. Poor Mary, looks like she met with tragedy, poor dear."

"Yeah, they're still drinking the same cup of coffee."

"Not Captain McCulluch. Captain McCulluch isn't there drinking his coffee, is he? His coffee has gotten cold, cold and bitter, the milk gone sour. *He* was snuffed out, stricken, by fucking Fraska for deigning to make a few suggestions on the finer points of acting."

The tense faces on the screen stopped talking. Stared significantly at each other. Anxious looks in their eyes. A last sip of coffee, eyebrows raised. Fade to commercial.

"Damn Fraska," he exploded. That asshole is probably still pontificating, ruling the roost."

"Don't obsess. It was just a soap opera; it isn't as if it was a Broadway show you were supposed to star in. Come on, it's three years ago. You've got a heart problem, that's what you should be worrying about."

"He fucked up my whole life." Victor was up and pacing his narrow apartment, rage in his eyes. "He ruined me."

"Why are you torturing yourself?" I asked. "Turn it off."

"I want to stare at his name. I want to see the credits. Let's rot our minds for the rest of the hour, Hank, have a beer, sit back. Watch the tired little beggars fulfill the great maestro's master plan. You know they have all been up since five this morning doing and redoing this. While we relax. You see Edgar there, he can't remember a line, and he's too damned nearsighted to read the monitor. Look there, see his eyes, see the way he hesitates; Justine is telling him his lines. She is fucking reading him his lines half a sentence ahead of him. He can't listen and talk at the same time. And I am sitting here and he is standing there. What kind of world is this?

"What's this? I don't know this guy." Victor fell silent and we both stared at the character who had just walked into the kitchen set. He was extremely handsome in his uniform, and took off his hat as he smiled at the woman brewing coffee.

"Hello Doris," he said, with tentative written all over his face and carved in his posture.

"What the hell is this?" Victor screamed.

Doris stared and frowned at the man. Slowly recognition spread across the wrinkles of her face.

"I've been in town for several months now, been staying with Mr. Jenkins, but I've hesitated to see you, I've – How is Ellen?" the man blurted out.

"Ellen – " the woman Doris was fumbling, not knowing what to say. Ellen had probably been remarried twice, had 10 affairs, three kidney transplants, and two livers removed in the last three years, but who's counting. "We thought you were dead," Doris said. "Why it's been years. Years and years. They said you drowned in a plane crash. You are Captain Richard McCulluch aren't you?"

"Yes of course I am."

"No of course you're not," Victor exploded. "You're dead, you fucking idiot. You didn't die in a plane crash, you killed yourself. I'm you. And I'm dead, dead. I killed myself, you moron. Three years ago. Hank, he's me. Why is he alive, Hank. He's dead; I killed myself."

He was silent then. I sat watching my old friend, a graying man of middle age standing stock still over a TV set in his studio apartment that was mirrored from wall to wall, as his words reverberated in the stillness.

Namby-Pamby

T HEY LUCKED OUT. THEY chose an April date, it rained all week, was predicted to rain all the next week, but their whole weekend was sunny, cloudless and warm. Brandy had always told me she *must* have an outdoor wedding. It was one of those things we used to lie in bed fantasizing, after, when we were all blissful and smelly with each other. My reveries always went toward the exotic. One of my favorites was tails for men, long dresses for women, on a jetty into a sea of emerald green water, with a string quartet on a barge just off the jetty. With the sun setting – rising would be better, more symbolic, but hardly practical. As if the rest of it were practical, Brandy was always quick to point out. Brandy got exactly what her reverie had called for: a cozy backyard wedding, with family and, and close friends.

She looked exquisite in white. Truly, she was made for the role of bride. I could see how she was basking in it. I sat down at one of the round tables in the sunny part of the yard. By now, people had started moving out of the hot sun into the shaded area, so I was somewhat distanced from everything for the first time. I sat with my head propped up on my palm, making clouds of smoke with my wedding cigar, and watched Brandy circulate.

"Oh Brenda, dear, you look the perfect bride." An elderly hand reached up to Brandy's extended one. Brandy bent forward, careful of her gown, touching cheeks. Words of thanks. Big smile, eyes rolling up at how happy she was, what a whirlwind it had been, what a relief to finally relax. Then a self-conscious moment, a "Thanks again," and off to the next one.

How she'd wanted this day, how important it had always been to her. Her little girl dreams all come true. I puffed my cigar. To be a bride. To walk down the aisle to ooohs and ahhhs at how pretty she was. To be adored by everyone. It was about neediness, about a lifetime of deprivation by her critical, withholding mother. Well, that was just me talking to myself, playing with psychobabble. But what about the marriage? How would that go, I wondered, really. I had been thinking about it, on and off all week. Am I kidding myself? There was no off.

These festivities surely weren't the aspiration she shared with her activist friends. The lesbians and crusaders, as I amused myself by calling them, were not here of course. I knew she wouldn't invite them into her dream world. They would have been polite enough. But their faces, however unaccusatory, would have compelled her to face her contradictions. I think I originally dubbed them the L's and C's to celebrate the preposterousness of their being Brandy's friends. We had spent a lot of time with the L's and C's. I was quite comfortable in their world though it was not really mine. I was not a committed kind of person, sad to say. I was astonished the first time she dragged me to one of their meetings. I never ceased to be awed at how completely she fit in, even as she so flagrantly stood out in her uncompromising standards of dress and "finished" demeanor – this woman that I knew so well craved an Ozzie and Harriet world, inexplicably a crusader for justice. But the little girl with the dream was the realest part of her. I knew that, oh so well. And today was Brandy's wedding day.

I guess I should not have been surprised about the incongruity of Brandy and the L's and C's. After all, no one could fathom *us*. My good friend Darla, after hearing for months about my new love, had been flabbergasted when she finally met us for drinks one evening. Darla was very protective of me, and never one to couch her thoughts. "What could you possibly see in such a superficial airhead?" was how she put it. Brandy had been in social banter mode. Some fashion model had captured her fancy. Darla was brutal. "That over-done makeup, her teenager hair, and she's dressed like a secretary who thinks she's being sophisticated." None of it was fair. I was especially offended by the airhead comment. Brandy was at least as smart as I was, probably smarter.

My friend Tom, on the other hand, inhibitions loosened up by several beers one night, gave vent to his suppressed envy, waxing eloquent on his inability to understand how such a stunningly beautiful and sophisticated woman could see anything in me. "And she's a math genius, to boot. A fucking quant! Where the hell did you meet her?"

Where indeed. I couldn't help my smirk. Tom, Tom, you would have a whoooole different view of her if you knew the answer to that question.

Anyway, I get it. We didn't match. The connection was at a level so beyond all that stuff. We clung to each other where Freud and Jung lived.

Harvey came up behind her and smiled at the relative she was working. He rested his arm lightly on Brandy's hip. *Harvey*. It was almost too deliciously perfect a name to believe. He was not a dentist or an accountant, but he might as well have been; as far from the L's and C's – and me – as you could get. The essence of steady and trustworthy and – normal. She had done exactly what I had told her she would do. Screamed it at her in a spasm of hatred and despair.

I sat puffing on the cigar. I didn't even know Harvey. But still. I knew he was the better choice.

Brandy was straightening up from another greeting and taking a deep breath when she spied me across the yard. She pointed to me, took Harvey's hand with one of hers, lifted her gown with the other, and started toward me across the lawn, smiling with pride to either side as she wobbled past tables of admiring guests on the irregular grass surface in her high heels.

"I want you to meet my friend Steven," she told Harvey. He was trim and fit, a runner. She had met him at her health club. He stuck out a hand, smiling. I stood up, still puffing, and shook his hand. I took the cigar out of my mouth and congratulated him.

There was something about his smile. Was he patronizing me, I wondered. Did he think I was the pathetic loser I knew I was? His hair was cut short and his neck was shaved. Did he think my ponytail was absurd?

I was in the only suit I owned, blue with a faint stain on the lapel that would not come out. My white shirt was not exactly bright white anymore. I had bought a new tie though.

He thanked me for my good wishes and said, "Brenda's told me a lot about you. I'm glad you could come."

Brenda? I thought, and glanced at her. She made a surreptitious, amused twitch with her face.

"I wouldn't have missed it," I said. "I hope you make her very happy."

Brandy took a step forward. "Brenda," I said, and kissed her, my lips just brushing hers, and my hand squeezing hers.

I smiled the smile of the lost. It hadn't died. It never would. For either of us. And all of a sudden I could not stand to be there.

Why had I come, to prove to myself that I could? Where the hell had Laura gone anyway?

I was sitting down at the table chugging on the cigar like a locomotive and gulping my scotch and water when Laura rustled up, smiling. "How you doing?" she asked, sitting down and running her hand through my hair.

"I'll make it," I said.

She kissed me on the cheek. "Good boy," she said.

"You really are incredibly – something."

"Warm, wonderful, understanding."

"And a lot more."

She smiled.

———◦◦———

"Then buy the ring, just buy me the ring." Brandy was screaming at me. Her thin, naked body pulled tight, all the ribs countable. It was ludicrous. Our hopeless, frustrating soap opera. We had broken up yet again and hadn't seen each other in over a month, when we ran into each other by accident and stood groping for words, until my hands drifted over her and she whispered, "We could go and have that wine I bought you for our anniversary. If it's still there," she said. Her eyes flashed a moment of alarm. Of course it was still there. I never believed, really believed, it was over. It would never be over until both of us were over. Dead. We went back all right, but we never got to the wine. The only thing I did before I pushed her toward the bed was lock the front door. It was like coming home. Afterward, still lying on top of her, stroking her forehead, seeing again how her little ears stuck out when her curls were pushed away; smelling her breath, her shampoo, feeling sweaty in her heat, all I could say over and over was "You're mine; you're mine. All mine."

"I guess I am," she mused.

But then we were sitting up, sharing a pint of Haagen-Dazs and for the first time actually thinking since the sudden shock of stumbling upon each other. I was holding the pint and my hand was getting numb with the cold. I didn't want to ask, "What happens now?" But I knew she was thinking it just as I was. She was incapable of letting anything lie. She didn't then. "Does this mean we are seeing each other again?" she said.

I replied without hesitation, "Yes."

"I'm not sure it's a good idea," she said.

If I had said no, that would have been the wrong answer too.

"We can't be friends," I declared, anticipating. "Ever."

"I don't know what you want. Do you finally want to marry me?"

"Shouldn't we see if we can get it back together first?"

"No. No. That's always your story. Two years is a long enough time for you to know."

"But we didn't have two years. We haven't been able to go a month at a time without a major catastrophe. I'd like to do that. Manage one utterly good month."

"No, you have to commit yourself. I'm not going to sit around while you namby-pamby again."

"This is crazy" I said, shaking my head. "We're already at loggerheads. It's been one hour."

And that is when she screamed, "Buy the ring, just buy me the ring. Just give me the ring."

———— ◆ ————

We had met when she was a college freshman and I was a graduate student. It was a brief meeting.

I was in her dorm with a woman I can't even picture now, when there was a staccato banging noise down the hall. That was followed by frenzied beating on doors along the hallway and then my friend's door. We opened it to a woman who, I later learned, was Brandy's best friend, Stephanie. She was drained of color. She screamed a jumble of words, and grabbed at our arms, pulling us, running us down the hall into a room that was, I saw as I glanced around, covered, walls and ceiling, with posters of ballet dancers and fashion models.

Then I focused on the long curly brown hair, a thick pool of it against the white linoleum. The face, pretty, delicate – damn, it was so striking I was distracted for just a moment from the predicament – lay with one cheek on the cold floor. The mouth was open and saliva trailed out into a little pool.

"Is she dead?" her friend shrieked. She was shaking. My friend held her and tried to calm her.

I didn't think the woman on the floor was dead. I first called the ambulance. My friend said, "I'll see if I can find the pill bottle. She must have changed her mind and gotten out of bed." Then I felt her pulse. I lifted her warm wrist, pressed my finger against the faint blue line, not having any idea what it would tell me. I felt something. Her eyes were now open but not seeing. They were a stunning emerald green, and very glassy.

"Make her vomit," my friend said. I stuck my fingers into her mouth, against her soft tongue, into her slippery throat. Her head shook; her hands flailed at me. But she did start to gag before she could break loose. My hand emerged from her mouth slimy with the film of her saliva and it was imprinted with her teeth marks. She bolted into a half-sitting position and threw up on me. Something wretched, stinking. Sour death.

The EMTs asked her friend Stephanie and me to go in the ambulance with her. I protested that I didn't even know her, but to no avail. I took off my shirt and they gave me a gown. Brandy, semi-stuporous, was dressed in her funeral suit, a pink ruffled blouse, a long flowing peasant dress, a pink ribbon in her hair, now half slipped out and dangling.

"What did you take," the attendant kept asking, trying to pry words out of her. We had found no bottle.

She focused her eyes for just a moment. "You're beautiful," she murmured at me, the words slurring together. "I feel so dizzy," she added. I stared back at her. Those pools of green pulled me, held me, and I had a fleeting sense that we shared a vast ocean of pain.

As she was carried into the emergency room on a stretcher, she peered around bleary-eyed, then faded from consciousness. A doctor went about preparing to pump her stomach and work whatever other magic would restore her to this world, while we were hustled out.

Stephanie and I alternated between waiting together on the bench in the outer room and standing outside. Stephanie sucked in Marlboro smoke and seemed oblivious of it after it went in, as it drifted out of her mouth and nose while we spoke.

"I don't get it," Stephanie said. "She was as cheerful and normal as ever last night. And look at her, all dressed up and her makeup just perfect and her hair all combed. I kidded her about that once. She said her mother trained her well. Demanded she look perfect in every situation. Punished her for the slightest flaw in her image, even for zits. How was she supposed to control zits? It takes her a half hour of brushing and curling to get her hair like that.

I nodded, for lack of anything meaningful to say.

"She called me and said she wanted to tell me goodbye." Stephanie started to cry and I placed my arm on her shoulder. "She was packing it in, she said. She told me she loved me. She said I was a true friend. Good luck with my life. And then she hung up. At first, I thought for sure she was joking, but it didn't sound like a joke. Packing it in? Why Brandy? Why? Why? Why? I got really scared. I realized I had no idea where she was. I prayed she was in her room. I raced over." She started to cry again. "What if I hadn't answered when she called me? She had already taken the stuff. She would be dead. DEAD! Oh my God." She began to sob. Her shoulders shook and heaved.

I was invited to the party her friends threw for Brandy when she was released from the hospital, the night before she left school. At the last minute, her parents hadn't been able to come for her until the next morning. Just the excuse for a post-stomach-pumping party. It was very boisterous. Very drunken. Very stoned. Brandy looked for all the world as if she were having the time of her life. Why not? She was alive.

I happened to see her parents in the distance when they were carrying out her suitcases that next morning. Her father seemed relaxed with a suitcase in each hand and several bags dangling. Her mother was decked out to the nines and smiling like a hostess at a party, carrying nothing, charming Stephanie and another of Brandy's friends as they all walked to the car. Brandy, weighed down with a hefty suitcase, was the only one who looked as if they were taking this walk because she had just tried to kill herself, had come very close to succeeding.

⸺◆⸺

I don't believe I even thought about Brandy for eight years after that, except maybe once. I had only been involved in Brandy's sudden departure from school by the most attenuated coincidence of being in a room several doors away. I hadn't known her at all before that. I was having my own future pulled out from under me over those next years. There were not any jobs for English Literature Ph.D.s anymore. My smarter graduate-student friends were now in law or business school. My smarter undergraduate friends were already wealthy, by my standards, entrepreneurs and corporate whatevers. I had waited too long. I should have dropped out. I was working at a photocopying place and teaching a couple of classes at a junior college for a pittance a semester. I was surviving, if you could call it that. My life felt bleak.

But some things are just fated. I can't think of any other explanation. I was in New York now. One fine bright day, I was walking up Lexington Avenue in front of Bloomingdale's when my eyes caught a rather attractive form in front of me. No suspense here. Obviously it was her, though I didn't know that when I spied her. I sped up. It was a reflex. Not that I had any expectation of an on-street pickup. I had once been confident about things like that. But what chance would a photocopy guy have in front of Bloomy's, or anywhere for that matter. Certain things, though, are just automatic. Maybe I was only curious whether the front was as nice a view as the back. All about aesthetics.

But my catching sight of her on the street would not have been enough for fate to have its way. The scenario would have played out with nothing more than a momentary twinge of sadness. I would have caught up to her, quickly glanced over, confirmed that she was indeed a knockout, and continued on my way feeling dejected that I would never know this woman. I wouldn't have recognized her in that momentary glance. In actual fact, I didn't. Maybe an hour afterward I would have realized who she was, too late.

Fate needed more, and got it. I came within a couple of feet of her. Hoop earrings peaked out from under a lot of meticulously curled hair. She was all decked out in boots and designer jeans, well-fitted to her form. A cashmere sweater, a vest and an expensive bag slung over her shoulder completed the outfit.

I was taken by surprise when this fashionable woman's head jerked to the left. A phlegmy rattle issued from the throat, worthy of a fifty-year-old boozed up street bum. Then her mouth opened and she expelled a monster glob of phlegm. An amazing feat of propulsion sent the glob flying practically in a line for eight feet before it splashed on the pavement with a splat. A slight breeze was blowing, and I was so close by then that I was showered with a fine mist of spray.

Only then did she notice I was there. She stopped in her tracks, her eyes darting with concern over my clothes. She turned fully to face me, looking embarrassed. She opened her mouth, and effusive words of apology flowed out. She ran on about spring pollen. Then she stopped talking. A frown came over her face.

It took me the same couple of moments to place her. "Isn't your name White Wine Spritzer or something?" I asked. Not very amusing, I suppose, but neither was depositing humongous globules of phlegm on the sidewalk.

"Funny," she said. "It's Brandy."

"I knew it was something alcoholic," I replied.

"Where do I know you from?" she asked somewhat cautiously. I could see, through those emerald eyes I so vividly recalled, her mind working away. Was I someone she had slept with and didn't even remember?

I gave her time, but she failed to place me. "I was at your farewell party freshman year in college," I said, putting it as diplomatically as I could.

I saw her remembering. Her face took on an intimate air. "Now I recall," she said in a soft voice. "You were the one who made the party possible, weren't you?"

I didn't know quite how to answer. I had my mouth open to speak, when all at once she started fumbling and rooting around in her bag. "Shit," she said, and looked up at me in a panic. "Do you have a tissue?"

"No," I said. "Just a not-so-clean handkerchief."

"Uhhhh," she said like a baby's demand, wiggling her fingers at me. Her nose was doing a rabbit twitch. I reached in my pocket and she wiggled her hand faster for me to hurry. She snatched the handkerchief from my hand the instant it appeared, and sneezed repeatedly into it. I stopped counting after the seventh. When that spasm came to an end, she blew her nose into it several times and handed the soggy cloth back to me, with a perfunctory thank you. "I never bring enough tissues," she said. It seemed to me that I might possibly never encounter this woman that we would not be intimate with regard to one or another of her bodily fluids.

"I hate this time of year," she said. "I'd like to cut down every tree in sight."

I scanned the asphalt; it was really just a reaction. I didn't mean to be snide or smart.

She shrugged. "The Park's not that far."

True enough.

Her life was going well, she told me. She had a job in finance, was on the fast track, working hard. "What's your name again?" she asked. "I'm sorry."

I told her.

She nodded, as the memory of it came back. "Can I buy you a drr..." she started to say, and then changed her mind with a smirk. "A white wine spritzer?"

"Sure," I said. "Should we buy some tissues first?"

It seemed to me that all Brandy and I did for the next number of months was exchange bodily fluids of a preferable kind day and night. The intimacy I felt with Brandy was like nothing I had ever experienced before. I could go into all the psychiatric mumbo jumbo. We were both damaged, irreparably damaged, in childhood, under somewhat different circumstances. But we were both left desperate with the same need. Three shrinks over the years had gotten me nowhere. My future friend, Laura, did not tolerate it. She just didn't understand. You are 34 years old, she would say with impatience. You are an adult now. Act like one. You aren't a prisoner of things that happened when you were an infant. You have will power. You need to pull yourself together and live a life.

I never argued with Laura. She would never understand. Brandy understood though; really understood.

Eventually, after those first incredible months with Brandy, it is not so much that it burned out. It definitely did not burn out. It never would. It is more that the intensity became all need and demands on both sides. Demands so intrusive and overwhelming that no human being could meet them. Neither of us knew how to negotiate a safe path through all the mines and trip wires. Our battles were monumental, over things small and large, followed by one of us storming out, in a deluge of tears and desperation and complete frustration. It never became physical; we loved each other way too much for any provocation to end in that, but we hurt each other so badly. It was not even intentional. I think the walk-outs were a contest of pleas. Show that you love me. Prove that you can't stand being away from me. I willed her to call me. And then one of us would prove more needy. But the more those jarring breaks happened, the more a terror rose in me that the whole ritual, if that is what it was, would lose its potency.

For a while, though, the high when we came back together was beyond any drug. What we craved was a closeness that obliterated separate identities. In those first moments back, it felt as if we were achieving that. But we were separate people and so we would always be disappointed. And then angry.

I had myself entertained thoughts of suicide before I met her the second time, but they were just thoughts. Everybody does, from time to time, right? It was the drugs, I know. I'd gotten into stuff, and some days I just floated off into another world. Some days I loathed myself for working at the copy shop. I felt so numb, I was barely able to get up in the morning. I was close to getting fired from that pathetic job for not showing up. The woman who had to fill in for me already hated me. My career plans had been thwarted. I saw nothing ahead but dreariness. I had few friends anymore. Even the old friend I was getting my drugs from didn't want to see me except to sell me drugs. Turns out status matters. You don't understand that until you have none. I had not been with a woman in a long time. Who would want me. I found myself reciting the M*A*S*H song in my head at odd moments. Once, I think, I recalled Brandy. I thought about how easy it had been for her to make her very serious attempt, and I couldn't even accomplish that.

One night we were taking a bath together, which brought the subject to mind, and I told her about my thoughts. "How were you going to do it?" she asked. She perked up with curiosity.

"I got into the bathtub with a razor. More than once."

"That's the wrong way."

"Why?"

"Because there is a good chance when you see all the blood you will panic. Drugs are surer."

I thought about that, looking at her. Her face was flushed from the heat of the bath. And then she said, trailing her finger through the water and watching the ripples, "When you're ready," and she paused.

"What."

"When you're ready, I'll do it with you." She looked up at me. "If you're serious. I've actually given it thought," she said, as if she were talking about buying a house instead of renting. "It's best for us."

I spluttered out a laugh.

She just nodded. But I knew she couldn't mean it. Not the way things were falling in place for her now.

Then she thought for a minute and said, "This offer doesn't *expire*." She was very pleased with herself and started to laugh.

"At least, good until *cancelled*," I said back.

We laughed until our stomachs hurt. It wasn't that funny.

And so we would go on until the next time one of us failed to fill an unfillable need. And then that time I feared came, the time when she did not come back. I tried to pick up the phone several times a day, as one, then two, then three weeks went by. I finally caved and left a message, a couple of words. But I hadn't realized the game had changed. I was now playing solitaire. She did not call back. Funny, it never occurred to me that she might be dead. I didn't have even enough faith in myself to believe I could cause that.

One day the next week, I found a terse, handwritten, unsigned note shoved into the jamb of my door. "I'll be coming to get my stuff." I ran into the bathroom and threw up. I suppose I could have called her, but I knew this was different and it would be pointless. She had moved on. She had really done it. I lay in bed trembling for a long time. When I somehow managed to calm myself, I put her things all in a trash bag so when she came it would be quick. I hid one stuffed animal. It was a large white monkey she had won when we went to an amusement park once. First though, I cried myself to sleep hugging it, and was useless for days after. Actually, I lost the job.

I found myself holding my breath coming back to my apartment any time I went out. I felt relief when the bag was still there. I was like someone who had fallen out of an airplane and kept clinging to wisps of cloud. Then one day the bag was gone and my extra key was on a table. A chill like I had never felt shot through me. My knees buckled and I had to rush to get to the bed before I gave out. I may have lost consciousness. Probably not. I put my head under the covers and cried. I cried out for my daddy until the darkness finally took me.

———◆○◆———

The wedding party was winding down. I had not been able to leave. I'm not sure why. I am sure. I knew that probably, hell, I knew to a certainty, that I would never see Brandy again, at least if this marriage took. And I was sure it would. I wandered through rooms, wanting to be alone, but wanting to be in the house she was in. I guess I knew this was the last moment she could be mine even in my illusions.

I stepped into a small study. The lowering sun streamed through the lace curtains in a beam of light that fell on Brandy. Rembrandt lighting that, in the moment before she knew I was there, highlighted the crash from the exciting day in her fallen face, her blank stare. The inevitable crash from this once-in-a-lifetime high that had been in her mind for most of her 28 years on earth, the day that would make everything better, at last. The emptiness was flooding back in. The doubt that the marriage that followed the day would make anything different. More complicated, yes. But different? It was all there in her face.

"Brenda," I said softly. Her white gown rustled. I stood there in my yellowed white shirt and pressed suit with the stained lapel.

She looked up at me, and her game face was back on. "Oh, stop," she said.

I shrugged, with a little grin on my face. "Does he even know people call you Brandy?"

"It's not a secret," she said with a little smile.

"I guess I should be going now," I said, and walked closer to say goodbye.

"You startled me," she said. Her skin was pale and a tiny pimple sat in the crack of a nostril, waiting to be squeezed. I could imagine what her analysis must have been that morning. Would it look worse to have this little pimple or a raw spot where it had been squeezed. Which would makeup cover more completely?

Was her mother still punishing her? Easy to do with a harsh word on her wedding day. It was the only imperfection in her perfect marriage portrait. She blinked at me. An eye lash fell on her cheek. I held myself back from flicking it away. Her emerald eyes were stormy. Those oceans that I had first seen smooth and tranquil, or rather, glazed and uninhabited, pulled me into her turbulence, as I was always her captive.

"Why couldn't we be?" Her words came out softly, but vibrated with a tantrum of frustration.

"We're too fucked up," I said after a moment. We're both – too fucked up." I could feel my voice quavering. My eyes, though, were dry. I slowly shook my head back and forth. "We tried," I said. "We tried and tried."

One little tear sat in a corner of her eye; just rested there, as if it knew not to run her makeup.

"I'm glad you invited me. It was a shock out of the blue to get the invitation."

"I hoped you hadn't moved."

"I see you didn't invite the lesbians and the crusaders for justice."

She shrugged. "A different life."

"But you invited me."

She gave a brief smile. "I did."

We were silent then. Took each other in.

"I didn't expect you to come."

"Really? You knew I would come."

"I did." Her body was shaking almost imperceptibly. It was not cold in the room.

"This is the right thing for you, Brandy. I know it is. This is what you have always wanted. You're just crashing from all the excitement. He'll be good for you. Really good. He'll center you."

She nodded, without much enthusiasm. He would, I thought. He would save her, but who would save me.

As if reading my thoughts, she asked, "What about Laura? Is she the one?" Or maybe she needed to confirm that the answer was no.

I looked down at the floor, then back up at Brandy. I studied her for a long moment, from her perfect hair to her beautiful if drawn face, to her thin vulnerable body, her little feet that she so loved me to rub. "You know the answer to that," I said.

For a moment she just stared back. Then she gave a slight nod. "I'm sorry," she mouthed.

Neither of us knew what to say after that. I had not meant to let myself say anything at all. The moment was too fraught with unknown perils. Just say goodbye and leave. Make the break. Oh, God, the final...

"Well, then," she said. And left a yawning gap of silence that punctuated the chill of finality.

Into the horror her words triggered in me, I just blurted out, "How come I can't do it? How come?" As soon as I said it, I wished I could take it back.

She looked at me for a long time. My fists clenched, I whispered, "Why – can't – I – do – it!"

"Namby-pamby," she said softly.

I wanted to cry but there were just no tears.

She stared. She didn't come and hug me to comfort me. I knew she wouldn't. That would be way too dangerous.

"You should have made us work," she said with rage in her voice. "Why didn't you make us!"

I looked at her, at her contorted face. I said, "Did you ever stop and ponder a jar of vinegar and oil?" Her mouth twisted with the venom she was about to spew. "No, I'm serious," I said. "You can stir it and shake it and it turns into a lovely mix, for a moment. But that's it. You have to keep stirring and shaking forever to get the moments."

"Yeah, so which one of us is the vinegar and which one the oil?"

"Don't you get it yet? The question is meaningless."

Our eyes were locked for a long long time. My head was empty. Finally she opened her mouth. It was several seconds before any words came out. "So you know what it means if there is only the moment?" she said.

"What?"

"One thing. One thing only. It's reductive. It's irreducible. QED."

I looked at her, waiting.

"After we stir – stir gently, not a violent shake, I cannot take even one more episode of shaking – nothing else can happen. That moment has to last forever. It has to be the final thing that happens."

I heard one of her mother's antique clocks ticking away seconds. Then she said, in a voice barely audible, "My offer is still good." Her head was bent to my shoes. Then she raised those limpid green eyes that revealed her soul. Her mouth, set tight, twitched. She whispered, "I'll do it with you right now. Upstairs. There is a beautiful little room, with a small bed, very very peaceful, and intimate. Perfect for us."

"You have something with you now? Here? Today? On your wedding day?" I whispered.

"I always have something with me." Her voice was defiant. "Always. It makes me feel protected." Her head motioned out the door, in the direction of the stairs. "Go up with me," she said. She lowered her voice. "Go out with me."

She stepped close to me and touched me, one hand pressed tight to each of my hips. "It is a perfect restful room. I used to hide there when my mother made me feel small. It's where I want to be. With you. We'll hide. We'll bring each other a last moment of ecstasy, a lasting moment. We'll sleep forever, our bodies entwined, our mouths pressed together." I felt the warmth of her moist hands. She was looking deep into my eyes. "Just say the word," she said. I took her hands in mine, and squeezed them, held them tight. We both turned our heads toward the staircase. And then I looked back into those bottomless emerald green depths.

Two Sleepy People

THE SATURDAY NIGHT UPPER West Side crowd swarmed the street as Graciela Shaw and Jake Simon walked north toward his apartment in the lingering daylight. They'd been chattering since the sun was high and the car exhaust shimmered over the seemingly molten asphalt. Her white, western-style blouse with Navajo motifs was soggy with sweat, as was his gray Henley tee shirt, no longer tucked into his jeans. She wore a tutu-like white skirt below her blouse, ballet slippers on her feet, and a long red bandanna around her neck that she was using regularly to wipe beads of perspiration from her forehead and upper lip.

Just now, he was bending over her and wiping his neck with the end of her bandanna. She took the opportunity to slide her tongue, snakelike, into his mouth and out before he could react.

She was five feet tall, waifish, with short spikes of black hair standing more or less straight up, less right now because of the humidity; he six feet, with long, brown, curly hair on his head and none on his face. He was old enough to be pleased, if not self-satisfied, to see that thick head of hair when he looked in the mirror in the morning. She was young enough to feel at ease in her attire, which attracted glances as they strolled. They carried a bag of bagels for the morning, and the early edition of the Sunday *Times*. As they opened the door to his apartment, the July twilight had all but faded. They fell into the easy chair in the living room yawning.

"This heat really takes it out of you," he said.

She sighed agreement.

"Is it still turned off?" she asked. He knew it was, but he checked his cell phone and nodded. It was their rule.

"Damn," she said.

"What?"

"I forgot to get cigarettes. I'm out."

"I'm glad," he said.

"I'm too tired to go back out."

He looked at her, reluctant to separate from her. But he said, "I'll go."

She thought for a moment and then shook her head. "No, I don't want you to leave."

They sat scrunched together and began reading the *Times*. The chair was a bulky, very odd piece that Jake had acquired in his hodgepodge law student days. It was almost big enough for two people smaller than they were, though neither of them was large, or, more to the point, wide. It had brightly-patterned upholstery in yellows and greens that went with nothing, but the chair was obscenely comfortable.

They exchanged newspaper sections without speaking. Occasionally their sections collided as they turned pages, and they frowned at each other with annoyance. Abandoned pages lay scattered on the floor around the chair. They could have moved to the sofa, of course, and spread out, but they preferred to share each other's space.

"I brought your fortune," she said. You forgot to read it."

He put down the newspaper and cracked open his fortune cookie. He read the fortune and smiled.

"Well, tell me."

He read, "'You will meet that special someone next month.'"

She snatched the little strip of paper from him and read it herself. "Hummm!"

"What?"

"Not exactly what I see here."

"You don't know Chinese."

"Neither do you."

"Oh."

She gave him a dismissive look with those black penetrating eyes of hers.

Music played for a while. But eventually neither of them got up to change it and the room fell silent. Jake yawned. "We should go to bed early," he said.

"Good idea," she agreed. "I'm beat."

They had tumbled into the chair fully dressed, but it was warm in the apartment. The air conditioner was still straining to keep up with the steamy day. After reading the paper for a while, they felt too sticky in their clothes, so they began undressing each other without leaving the chair. It was a slow process without a plan. He complained one too many times about sweltering, so she pulled his shirt up over his head, and tossed it on the floor. Gave him a look. He unbuttoned her blouse, and removed it. Some number of newspaper articles later, she yanked off his socks, and he responded by pulling down her skirt, struggling with it in the cramped space. Quite a while later, his pants and her bra landed on the floor. Clothes were now intermingled helter-skelter with pages of the *Times*.

For several hours they remained in underpants and panties, and the red bandanna, reading the Times, sharing the odd desultory comment about the outrages found within its pages. When they lost interest in that, they caressed, kissed occasionally, mostly just clung to each other, with nothing left to say, nothing that needed to be said. They yawned more and more frequently, her yawn spurring his, his spurring hers.

"Do you have any toothpicks?" she asked.

"Why?"

"My eyes won't stay open."

"Let's go to bed."

"OK."

But instead she collapsed against his chest.

"I'm listening to you breathing," she said.

"So I'm still alive?"

"Apparently."

They remained like that for several minutes. A car stereo blasted. Drunken voices moved down the street. Those were the only things that kept them from dozing off as they were. Soon enough, the voices disappeared in the direction of Riverside Park. The only sounds were the air conditioner and the humming of the refrigerator. Her voice broke the stillness. "We should go to bed," she said softly into his chest. He mumbled assent, but neither of them moved.

When she eventually picked up her head, she gave him an amused smile.

He raised his eyebrows in question.

"You know, we wouldn't have to breathe all that car exhaust you were complaining about if we could just breath each other."

He absently untied her bandanna and threw it on the floor. He was trying to come up with a worthy response when she pressed her lips to his and breathed into his mouth. It took a second for his eyes to focus on her face up so close. Then he breathed back into her mouth. They began to experiment, mouths sealed together, one breathing in, the other out, alternating in and out. It took them a few tries to get the pace right, and to remember to breathe only through their mouths, and for one of them to swallow their pool of saliva every so often. Soon enough they were in a rhythm, but as five minutes became ten and ten became fifteen, it got harder and harder to stay focused. Their hearts thumped and their breathing became quicker as they felt each other's warm breath – repeatedly, insistently – surge through them. With great effort, they restrained themselves – they were both compulsive enough that they wanted to see how long they could keep it going. For almost a full twenty minutes, they breathed each other's breath while her black eyes and his brown ones locked on each other. Then he fell out of sync when he tried at the wrong instant to swallow. It caused her to drool on her breasts.

She never had a chance to wipe herself off. He was ripping at her panties and she was yanking off his boxers. They clawed at each other, frantic, gasping; smashed into each other again and again with such ferocity that the venerable tank of a chair tottered precariously for an instant on two legs.

"Oh God," she said as they clung, limp and panting, afterwards. All Jake could do was let out a weak moan.

Eventually they stood up, tentatively, on shaky legs; got drinks of water. Graciela picked up the newspaper sections while Jake sorted the clothes.

She turned on her phone.

"What are you doing?"

"I'm sorry, I have to call my mother."

"At three in the morning!"

"They won't pick up. They turn their land line off at night. I just have to leave a message."

"You can't just text?"

"My mother? Right. Why didn't I think of that?"

"What could be so important now?"

She studied him. The hint of a smile creased her lips. "My mother will want to know without delay that you just fucked my brains out. That I came like I never came before."

"Yes, I can see the urgency of that. Do give her my best."

"Ha, I don't think so."

The phone beeped and Graciela left her message. She turned the phone back off.

"I don't know about 'like never before,'" Jake said. He looked at her skeptically. "What about last Tuesday, and the Sunday morning two weeks ago when we first woke up, and that night last month? And –"

She rolled her eyes. "You should graph it."

"Maybe I will."

"I wouldn't mind taking a shower," she said. "I feel grungy from this heat...and everything. Do I stink?"

"Sort of," Jake said. "Do I?"

"A bit."

Graciela ran the water. They stepped in and soaped each other, lingered, in no hurry to come out. When they had dried off, the chair drew them back. Once there, they soon found themselves with their mouths again locked together, but they stopped themselves. "Another episode like that, they'll find us dead in the chair," Jake said.

She considered his words. "Who would find us?"

"Good question."

"That's an unpleasant thought. How long do you think it would be before..."

"The fragrant bouquet seeps through the door?"

She nodded with a shudder, and he shrugged. "No idea. I can just picture Susan from up above, climbing the stairs, her nose wrinkling up as she passes my door, wrinkling more each day."

"So gross."

"'Suicide tryst baffles coroner.' Daily News."

"Funny."

"I'm beyond tired," he added.

"Bed," she said, definitively.

"Four fucking thirty in the morning," Jake cried out with indignation. A car alarm on the street below them had begun to wail, shattering the stillness.

Graciela stood up, stretched away a crick in her back from her awkward position in the chair, and walked to the kitchen. He watched her as she returned with the carcass of a rotisserie chicken. Her little breasts bounced ever so slightly. He loved how she glided along; her graceful walk. She squeezed into the chair, balancing the plate of chicken, using her hips to shove him, reposition him.

"What?" she said. He was looking at her with amusement.

"I thought you would come back with the bagels."

"They're for the morning," she said, stuffing a piece of chicken into his mouth.

"It is morning," he said as he chewed.

They sat picking at the chicken, feeding each other.

"Dark," he said.

"There is no more dark." The car alarm ceased as abruptly as it had begun.

She yawned a big yawn. "I'm so tired," she said.

"We should go to sleep," he said.

"Umm," she grunted agreement, wiping her chickeny hand on his thigh, laying her head against his cheek. He smelled her fresh, shampooed hair. It was still damp, cool against him.

They hadn't closed the curtains. The faint pink light of dawn soon appeared. They both yawned at the same time, which made them laugh.

"Don't make me laugh in the middle of a yawn. It's so frustrating," she said.

"We should have gone to bed hours ago," he said.

"We should have."

She yawned again, a big, wide, open-mouthed yawn with her head thrown back, to make up for the aborted one. He gazed at her perfect little teeth, her tongue, the roof of her mouth, and then he looked over at the window, where the day was breaking.

"What are you thinking?" she asked.

He smiled. "Just a thought that came to me."

"What?"

"Yawny laddie; dozy little lass."

"That's an odd thought."

They fell silent again. She stifled a yawn and played idly with his penis, swinging it back and forth and in circles. After five minutes or so had passed, she asked, "Well are you going to tell me what that is?"

"Some people call it a wiener; others call it a cohhh –"

She gave him a push. "You idiot. What you said."

"Oh."

She peered at him.

"I just made it up."

"Why?"

"Hoagy Carmichael."

She stared at him blankly. After a moment's thought she said, "That's a funny name for a sandwich."

"Good one. I was thinking of a 1930s song by the song writer Funny Kind of Sandwich and I made up my own line. I only first heard the song a year or so ago. I thought it was just about the most romantic song I ever heard."

He looked at her naked body, her jutting black hair, her India ink eyes watching him. "What I was thinking is that when I first heard the song I never for a moment imagined –" He hesitated.

"Imagined what?" she asked softly.

He saw that she understood and he felt himself blush. But he went ahead and answered, in a bare whisper, "You."

It took a moment for the word to resonate in the stillness. Then Graciela beamed for just a flash of a second, before they both looked down. When they looked at each other again, she said, "Let's go for a walk by the river."

"We've been up all night."

She kissed his cheek. "It will be beautiful now. Walk with me, my darling."

She rummaged in his dresser and threw on one of his tee shirts, way too spacious for her little body, and a pair of his sweat pants. She rolled up the legs and pulled the waist string tight and knotted it.

He inspected her. "Ragamuffin," he said.

She squinted up at him. "Stubble face," she responded.

They traipsed down the stairs, eyes red and puffy.

"The air's so fresh," she said.

"For another hour maybe."

They walked along the Hudson arm in arm, in the dawn's now golden light, the tangy smell of the river to one side, the already building traffic on the Henry Hudson to the other.

"You never told me the name of the Sandwich's song," Graciela said, turning to him.

"Oh. 'Two Sleepy People.'"

"Not a very romantic title."

"No, I guess not."

"I would love some coffee," Graciela said. "I feel like I'm dreaming of it rather than thinking of it. I can actually smell it, it's so real."

She stepped away from him as a miniature labradoodle on a leash came between them briefly.

"I know, but coffee would be a big mistake now."

She made a soft sound of agreement and they fell silent. She reached out, feeling for his hand, as he was reaching for hers. They walked, holding hands.

When they were no longer able to put one foot in front of the other, they sank to the soft grass and lay side by side. Jake kissed her lightly on the lips. Graciela mouthed two soundless words. "My love." They looked into each other's eyes until their lids flickered shut, and they reluctantly parted. They slept until well past noon, as Sunday picnickers and sunbathers came and went around them.

About The Author

Lewis Bogaty is a writer and photographer living in New York.

His fiction has appeared in *Virginia Quarterly Review, Mississippi Review, Descant, Sou'Wester, Another Chicago Magazine, Confrontation, and others.* His non-fiction has appeared in *Virginia Quarterly Review, Columbia Law Review, and various other magazines and newspapers.*

His short story in *Kansas Quarterly* received a Kansas Arts Commission/*Kansas Quarterly* Fiction Award. He has also received a BRIO fiction award from the Bronx Council On The Arts. This collection, in an earlier version, was a semi-finalist in the 2021 Elixir Press Fiction Award competition.

His photographs have been exhibited in solo and group shows, most recently in Upstream Gallery's 2024 juried photography show. His images have appeared in the *New York Times* and other newspapers, magazines and corporate publications. His prints are owned by institutions and private collectors.

He holds a Ph.D. in English and a law degree, and was an editor on the *Columbia Law Review.*

www.LewisBogaty.com

www.LewisBogatyPhotography.com

Instagram: @lewisbogaty

Also By Lewis Bogaty

Coming Soon:

When Elsa Sang The Blues, a new collection of short stories by Lewis Bogaty

www.ingramcontent.com/pod-product-compliance
Lightning Source LLC
Chambersburg PA
CBHW021158310726
48971CB00002B/688

my soft legs. I don't think soft is bad, but what do the Liams of the gym think when they look at me?

"That's no problem at all! Follow me, and we'll get you sorted with an available trainer," Liam says.

With a nod, I follow Liam through automatic sliding doors. A fan blasts my hair into my face as we pass the gym's threshold, leaving me to frantically swipe my thin, black bangs out of my eyes.

"Hey, Josh! You available?" Liam raises his hand, and a large man with a military shave looks up from his phone.

"Yeah, what's up?"

Liam stops, so I come to an abrupt halt behind him.

Josh eyes me over Liam's shoulder. "You got a new client for me?"

"Yep, this is Lily. Lily, Josh. He's one of our best trainers, so you're in luck today."

"Oh, thank you," I mutter. I don't know what else to say, so I smile.

Josh holds out his hand. Secretly wiping my palm on my tote, I can only pray I'm not about to give Josh a sweaty, feeble hand to shake.

But when Josh grips me, he crushes my bones together with his force. I wince, and he jerks my whole arm. Josh frowns. "We need to work on that grip strength."

I drop my hand the second he releases it, thankful to have some space between us again. My heart hurts, and I hate it. I feel so foolish for letting myself feel humiliated over something so small. Of course he thinks I need more grip strength; I didn't know people worked on grip strength at the gym, let alone had time to work on it at home.

Josh takes off to our left, checking over his shoulder. "Well, come on."

With Josh's placating nod at Liam, I'm left alone with my new trainer. Chasing after his wide strides through a row of treadmills, I meet eyes with another woman. She politely smiles at my weak grin, her brisk jog swishing her blonde ponytail from side to side with every muscled step. I look nothing like her.

"You've never been to the gym before, have you?" Josh doesn't turn around, but of course he's talking to me. He's so loud about it that a man loading ginormous weights onto a bar glances at us.

I drop my stare to my feet. "No, I haven't."

Josh stops. I almost crash into his back, side-stepping just in time for him to turn and face me.

He crosses one arm, leaving the other free to give my body a sweeping gesture. "You can't wear that to a gym. It's way too baggy."

My heart stings. Why did Gabby say it was fine to dress however I wanted? Josh is right; there are only silent, focused people working out in tight-fitted outfits all around me.

I swallow hard, doing my best to soften my quivering lungs. "Okay. Sorry."

Josh steps behind a long row of dumbbell weights. I've at least used those before, so my shoulders relax. But then he looks at me straight on. My stomach plummets. I don't know why I'm so sensitive, but I can't stop feeling like he's judging everything about me.

"Are you a beginner?" He asks in a low voice.

I don't like how closely he's looking at me. I drop my eyes again, unable to stop a defensive quip from escaping my lips. "I-I've used those types of weights before."

"I meant at working out. You probably haven't made any goals for what you'd like to accomplish here, right?"

Shame prickles my hot cheeks. All I can do is shake my head.

Josh drops a wide dumbbell back onto the rack with a loud *clang*, and I jump. He turns to the mirror, and I dare to peek at him. But we meet eyes in the reflection. I've never felt so small beside anyone - other than my dad.

Josh turns to me, but I keep staring into the mirror. I didn't realize how many people could see me, but with every wall covered by mirrors or windows, all sides of my body are plastered across the room. There's nowhere to look that won't meet someone's focus, and I can see my own ass on display for everyone behind me in these see-through, old leggings. What the hell was I thinking, wearing this? Tugging the back of my baggy jacket, I bite my lips, struggling to still my short, rapid breath.

"Alright, so here's the plan then. Women like you usually want a slimmer waist and thighs and to boost their backside." Josh vaguely gestures to my ass, and a sharp, painful sting wracks my heart.

As Josh launches into an explanation about what exercises will help me achieve "my goals," I tuck tighter into myself. Maybe I do want a perkier butt, but I didn't think anything was wrong with my waist or thighs. Actually, I worked hard not to hate them my whole life, even though I have other issues with my body. Can people really see how weak I am with one look at me?

Josh checks his watch. "We've already used up five minutes. Let's start with a warm-up."

Following Josh through simple stretches, jumping jacks, and short jogs in place to get my heart racing, my nerves settle. I can do this. It's not as taxing as expected, so maybe my job has helped me retain my endurance better than I hoped. I almost forget we're not alone.

Until I happen to make eye contact with the man loading yet another set of weights on the machine behind us. He isn't jacked the same way as Josh, but he's broad. Sturdy and solemn. Tattoos coat his light olive skin, peeking from his sweaty t-shirt to trace down his arms and up his Adam's apple. Some people are afraid of people with tattoos, but as someone who took refuge among alternative-dressed teens growing up, I feel safer just looking at him. When he turns his back to me to sit on his machine, he lifts his eyes to meet mine a second time in the mirror. My heart flips.

"Are you paying attention?" Josh snaps.

I jolt, wobbling through a lunge now that we've added dumbbells. Josh catches me, righting me by the shoulder.

"Sorry, can you repeat that?" I ask.

"Turn around. Stop looking at other things," he says. I quickly spin, facing Josh's glare in the mirror closest to us. "I said you're losing focus and losing your balance because of it. Start over, and get your head straight. *Focus.*" His voice raises into a yell, and adrenaline bites my core. "You want to get stronger, don't you? I don't see you lunging."

Tightening my sweaty hold on the dumbbells, I huff through my mouth, unable to breathe deeply enough through my nose as I restart my lunges.

Now that Josh analyzes me twice as viciously, every little thing I do feels wrong. Are my feet straight? Using the mirror to check my reflection, I tuck my left heel in to make it parallel to my thigh. It throws my rocky balance off just enough to make me wobble.

"Straighten up, come on," Josh says.

My heart hammers into my throat. I rock between my dumbbells, chasing my uneven weight distribution until each lunge bends into a smooth equilibrium. Finally, I look like I know what I'm doing. Relief floods my chest.

But Josh isn't impressed. "This is what happens when you let yourself go like that. You have no sense of balance. You need to work harder."

Heat flushes my eyes.

Oh, no, no, no. I can't cry.

I need to seem strong.

"Go, lunge deeper!" Josh booms.

But my thighs dissolve into an acidic burn. I bite my lip, unable to focus on staving back tears if I want to keep my balance straight. When I wobble again, Josh claps with every lunge, directing the speed of each rep. Except his pace is far faster than what I could do at my best, and the burning in my legs shifts into a violent stabbing.

"I-I can't," I mutter.

"Ten, nine, eight! Come on, don't give up - unless you're weak!"

Maybe I am weak. Fear strikes my heart when I meet my strained, panicked eyes in the mirror. I can't afford to be weak anymore.

But I'm not strong enough to keep going. A tear slips down my cheek.

"Don't cry. Faster! Five! Four! Three!" Josh claps. But I'm still stuck on the fifth-to-last lunge, unable to keep up anywhere near his rapid pace as my whole body shakes. A vein pops on Josh's temple, restarting my heart. "Don't you dare give up. You just started. Get your ass moving."

This should motivate me, right? Why do I only feel weaker by the second? As a sharp, tight sob chokes from my lips, I'm mortified. People are watching us now, and I can't even do a fucking lunge.

The man with tattoos flips to face us. I duck my head in embarrassment, and Josh yells louder.

"Stop looking down! Head up! You owe me five more–"

A rich, dark voice takes Josh's place. "Just fucking *stop*."

The tattooed man stares down Josh, his breathing labored. I hadn't noticed him coming, but now he's less than a foot from Josh. But Josh escalates beyond what I feel is appropriate: shoving the tattooed man back, he scowls. But the tattooed man doesn't budge more than an inch.

Josh's scowl contorts into a snarl. He hits even harder this time, but his own shove pushes his back into the mirror. The tattooed man grips Josh's shirt to keep him restrained. With how tightly they're pressed against the mirror, away from blaring gym lights, the tattooed man's eyes are shrouded in a dark shadow.

But Josh finally shoves the man's hands off. "The fuck is wrong with you?!"

The tattooed man's deep voice echoes across the tall ceilings despite his tone remaining even. "You have no right treating anyone like this. You're hurting your client - in front of everyone."

Josh opens his mouth to speak, but multiple people have stopped working out to stare, leaving the gym in sharp silence. The only sound is my hard panting between rasping, pathetic tears.

Breaking into a sour grin when he meets my eyes, Josh laughs. "Chill out, man. She's fine; she's just crying."

My heart crunches like Josh smushed it in his beefy palm, forcing me to hold my breath to keep a grip on my tears. The tattooed man's eyes flicker to mine in the mirror. His heavy concern rips a fresh sob out of me. I drop my head to my lap, hiding my ugly crying face. I've created such a humiliating mess, but I can't stop my heart from aching like it's been ripped out. I'm not just disappointed in myself; I'm terrified by what this workout failure means. I really wasn't strong enough.

But Josh's voice tenses, zipping my focus back to him. "What makes you think you can tell me how to work with my client? I don't think you own the place."

The tattooed man glares at Josh, leaving a long, extended pause. Josh tenses, but the tattooed man drops Josh's staredown to fetch the discarded dumbbells at my sides. He's not stooping to Josh's level by laughing or taunting back, and the deepening hatred in Josh's furrowed eyebrows tells me that's an insult to his manhood.

I scramble to my feet, ready to pacify both men and leave the gym as quickly as possible, but my side cramps harder than I've ever felt, forcing a sharp cry from my lips.

My overworked legs threaten to send me to the ground, shaking hard despite how horrendously heavy they feel, but the tattooed man steadies me by the arms. He settles me safely on the floor, propping my back against the nearest workout bench. I whimper as the pain only continues, but he keeps a firm hand on my arm. "You're okay, you're okay. Keep breathing through it. What's hurting?"

I grimace, grabbing my side as it pinches like a piece has been torn out of me. But before I can speak, Josh scoffs.

"Go on, play the hero. She's just whiny. It doesn't make anything happening here illegal. I can make her cry as much as I want to."

Whipping a phone out of his pocket, the tattooed man points his camera at Josh. "Want to repeat that?"

Josh's jaw tightens.

The tattooed man shakes his head. "I don't remember the part in Psychology for Sport and Physical Activity that taught us how important it was to make our clients cry as Kinesiologists. Care to jog my memory?"

Josh grabs his water bottle and keys, but not after slamming down a heavy weight with a resounding *bang*. I shriek, gripping the stranger beside me. The tattooed man's arms tense beneath my grasp, ready to lurch into action. My heart hurts for him too; his wide, clenched stare tells me he's just as terrified of what Josh might do next. But thankfully, Josh storms out, leaving us all in silence.

With his jaw tensed, the tattooed man closes his eyes. He hisses out a deep, growling exhale. "Gym bro motherfuckers thinking they own the fucking world, I swear. He better not have a girlfriend–"

But as I meet the worried eyes of everyone else in the gym, I dissolve into hitching, weepy tears. Burying my face in my hands, my strained voice comes out choppy. "I'm sorry–"

The tattooed man softens his hold on me, gently stroking my upper arm. "Hey, hey, it's all good now. You're safe."

I let out a deeper, harder sob, leaning into his touch. My whole body shakes through violent tears, but his melodic, even tone remains gentle.

"There you go. You're doing such a good job. You're safe now. You're safe." His words leave a light fluttering in my stomach.

But I shake my head. "Everyone's so upset, and you got harassed and shoved by him. I'm so sorry he pushed you."

The man is silent for a while. I peek from my hands to find

him looking straight at me. I hadn't realized how dark his irises were, an endless pool of black staring back.

He sighs. "You're so sweet to think of me, but I'm okay. I chose to step in because I care about protecting my community, and I hate that you were treated like this. He's the one who chose to behave like a caveman, not you."

Dropping his stare, I bite my quivering lip. Hotter tears shudder from me, but this time, they're slow-rolling. Aching and silent.

He hums, shuffling to squat in front of me. With his wide shoulders blocking me from everyone's view, I sigh.

"Thanks," I whisper.

"When you think you can stand, let's take a breather somewhere less busy, yeah?"

"Okay."

Taking his hand, I try my best to stand but collapse onto the bench behind me with a sharp hiss.

"My legs," I whimper. I feel so pathetic.

"You can't stand, can you? Shit, that pisses me off so much," the man growls. "Change of plans - stay right here." Dashing to the exercise machine he was using before Josh's outburst, the tattooed man digs through his gym bag. I glance at the other gym-goers in my peripherals, but thankfully, they've stopped staring. Either way, I have an unavoidable need to hide. I hunch over myself, wrapping my arms around my waist.

The tattooed man returns with furrowed brows. "Does your stomach hurt?"

"N-no, sorry, I–" I shake my head, deciding there's too much to explain that won't make sense to anyone else. He doesn't need to know about my crippling, residual anxiety or how Josh reminded me of my father in his worst outbursts.

Maybe the man understands, or maybe he has no idea I'm struggling to speak, and he's simply a patient person. He squats, balancing a plushy stick over his knees. "Have you seen one of these before?"

He offers the padded stick to me. As I grasp it, I'm surprised the plushy portion spins.

"Let's try to lessen the damage so you're not suffering as much later. Roll this over your leg muscles where it hurts. If your arms feel too tired and you'd like some help, let me know." He nods as I roll the stick over my thighs. "There you go. Good job."

I don't know what it is about him - maybe the way he softens his voice when he says encouraging things, or maybe the stark contrast of his sweetness against the sharp tattoo designs clawing over every inch of his arms and legs - but a thrilling warmth builds in my core. I want to know more about him.

"What's your name? I'm Lilibet– Lily," I blurt out.

He peeks at me from tying his shoes, moving just his dark, steady gaze. "What was that first name you said?"

My stomach flips. "Oh, um– Lilibeth. It's just my full name, but everyone gets it wrong."

"Ah, yes. I know a lot about that, Lilibeth." He relaxes into his casual crouch like he didn't set off a tingling avalanche of nerves in my chest by saying my full name. "My name's Remington, but people just call me Rem, or Remi."

Wiping the last tears from my eyes, I smile. "Oh. What do you like better?"

He doesn't exactly smile, only quirking up one side of his mouth. "Depends on the person. Maybe you'll have to try them all."

My breath hastens the longer we look into each other's eyes. I giggle without meaning to, dropping my head. Is he flirting with me, or am I just an emotional wreck today?

"How about you?" He asks.

"I'm fine with either," I mutter.

"Yeah? Good to know."

A heavy silence stretches between us, but I'm left to bite my swollen lips, trying not to laugh again. Unfortunately, my muscles feel like goo, and I've only rolled out my thighs for one minute.

I stop rolling, instead rubbing my burning arms. Remington

said he'd help me if I needed it, but do I really want a strange man rolling out my muscles? A deep, rising warmth in my belly tells me I do.

When we meet eyes, Remington's eyebrows soften with his lips. "Do you need help?"

My shoulders rise. "Um– If that's okay."

"Of course. As long as you're comfortable with me doing it for you?"

I laugh. "I-I mean, I don't really have a choice."

Remington pulls back. "Yes, you do. You always do, with the right people."

My heart flips. He's starkly serious, but I feel safer than I have all day.

"T-thank you. But I'd actually like some help still, so I'm okay with it."

With my permission, Remington gets to work rolling out my legs. "Okay. But it's your body, okay? You can be honest with me or that other trainer. Has he treated you harshly before?"

I shrink into myself. Remington's scowl is tense, but he's intensely gentle with my sore thighs. His soft rolling over them feels startlingly intimate, but I don't want him to stop.

And I don't think he'll like the truth. My heart throbs into my throat. "I've never been here before."

"To this gym?"

"Um— to a-any gym."

Remington stops rolling, arching his tense eyebrows in sorrow. "Fuck, and this is your first day? God, I'm *so* sorry it turned out like this. There's no need for you to be yelled at or shamed at the gym."

Oh, God. Here comes my ugly crying face in the mirror. I press my chin to my chest to hide myself, begging my tears to evaporate, but Remington softens his voice.

"Hey, it's okay to cry. You're doing so great letting it out. That was traumatizing."

Fluttery nerves swirl in my stomach, tempting me to duck my

head again. But a pull in my heart towards Remington wins over my senses, and the truth comes pouring out.

"I need to carry my mom," I say.

I clear my throat, startled by my confession. I haven't voiced it aloud a single time in my life. Remington stares, brows furrowed. He opens his mouth to speak, but judging by how confused he looks, I sputter as many explanations as possible before he asks too much.

"Sorry, just— I said that wrong. It was traumatizing, probably, but I'm more upset that I couldn't finish my lunges either. I need to be stronger to carry a lot of things, like at work."

Remington hums, returning his focus to my legs. "I don't really agree that you couldn't do the exercise. More like he was pressuring you past your limits. But what do you mean by 'a lot of things?' Does your job involve manual labor, or is it something back at home?"

My heart flips. I blink a few times, wishing I kept my mouth shut as usual about Mom. "I can't carry the big bags of flour or heavy pots of soup as easily as everyone else at work, and it's really embarrassing. I've always wanted to go to the gym, but I– I'm embarrassed by how I look, and how weak I am–" My heart stings, and Remington's eyebrows draw together. I laugh. "Sorry, you didn't ask to hear all this."

Remington shrugs. "I didn't ask for an apology either."

His straightforward, flat tone takes me back. Is this his version of being snappy with me? But looking into his eyes, I'm confused; his expression hasn't changed. He looks genuinely concerned.

"If you're apologizing because you're feeling emotional, or because you're believing that dickhead trainer that you're weak, then I can't accept your apology. You coming to the gym to work out despite everything you told me, and still not giving up on your workout goals now, even when faced with confrontation, was not weak. That's fucking badass, to be honest."

My stomach flips. "O-oh. Thank you. I mean– It's just, either way, I really am sorry. I've been a mess since the second we met. I feel pretty weak and embarrassed."

But Remington softens his voice. "Do you mean then that you think crying is weak?"

"I don't know. Not when I see other people cry. But with me, it feels like everyone else thinks I'm weak, so I'll only seem weaker if I cry."

"I hear you on that. But crying isn't weakness. It's information. Your body is informing us that you're feeling a lot right now and that what you're feeling a lot about is something important to you. That's not good or bad. It's just okay. You're okay."

His words swirl to the scarred depths of my soul. Dropping my head, I let myself cry, sitting on the floor beside Remington.

Digging back into his gym bag, Remington hands me a tissue packet. "Don't hold it in for me. Even if it takes an hour to let it out, keep crying."

I want to laugh, but he's dead-serious. As my smile fades, my tears burn hotter. I've never been told to keep crying in a non-threatening way. It feels like he's holding space for me. It's so kind. So gentle.

When my floodgates open, he hums. "Good. Keep taking deep breaths."

He's right: I'm holding my breath to stifle myself. But when I exhale, a whimper escapes with my air. I duck my head, wishing I could just stop.

But he continues to sit with me, and within minutes, my heart softens enough to erase nearly all the panic Josh created. I suddenly feel so light that I laugh.

Remington perks up. "What's up?"

Digging through my jacket pocket, I fetch my gym membership gift card. Remington takes it from me with furrowed brows, and I groan. "I still have 9 slots left for this gym."

I have to softly chuckle at the irony, but Remington scowls. "For how expensive it is, this place sucks ass anyway. There's a cheaper place five blocks down called Dynamo Fitness Center -

which kind of makes me laugh. But people are nicer there. They don't act like God's favorite gym bros."

His sense of humor hits me by surprise, spurring a rambunctious giggle from my lips. But I sigh. "It doesn't matter, anyway. I can't afford to use extra money on myself, so I'll just go back to exercising in my room."

Remington straightens. "No, I think you deserve a refund. You got straight-up harassed."

Biting my lip, I peek at him. "I-I don't think they'd give it to me."

"Probably not, if this is how they treat women here." Remington stands, holding out his hand. "But you've got a gym buddy now who looks like a scary meathead."

Taking Remington's hand, I laugh as he pulls me to my feet. "Oh. My legs feel way better."

"Good." He gives me another half-up grin before whipping around to shoulder his gym bag. Then he hands me mine, looking into my eyes with a bright stare. "Ready to get that refund?"

I smile. "Yes."

We speed to the front desk, and I let out another giggle at his determined back.

"But you're not a meathead," I mutter.

"Am too," he says, keeping his back to me.

I didn't expect him to hear me, but my smile only widens. As we meet Liam's perplexed stare at the front desk, I remember where I am; thanks to Remington, I forgot how unsafe I felt in this gym only thirty minutes ago.

Remington hands my card over the counter before I can fully catch up to him. He lowers his voice. "I need a refund."

As I come to a stop beside Remington, he loosens his fingers to let go of my hand, but I give him a quick squeeze. He releases me, but shoots me a glance.

"You okay?" He whispers.

I bite my lip, then nod. I hadn't seen how furious Remington suddenly looked, but his scowl is framed by smoky, graphic tattoos up his neck, intensifying his jet-black irises. Maybe he's acting, but the seriousness behind his eyes has an edge I couldn't personally fake. Does he care about everyone like this? With how genuinely kind his heart seems, I wouldn't be surprised.

When Remington turns back to Liam, he gives Liam the dark staredown he gave Josh.

Liam takes my membership card, but it's clear he has the answer before he touches the plastic; after looking between us, the card, and his monitor, Liam swallows hard. "I'm afraid I can't do that, sir. It's company policy. All I could give is store credit - which is basically just another gift card."

Remington gives a sharp *tsk*. "What about if your staff member harassed the gym member with the gift card in front of everyone at the gym?"

As Liam glances at me, my cheeks flame hot.

But Remington stiffens. "No, don't look at her. It's not her fault. You're lucky I'm not plastering this shit all over the internet to shut this place down. Who's your manager?"

Liam clenches his jaw. "He's– He's on a break."

My heart flips. "Josh?"

"Oh fuck, no." Remington leans on the desk, digging into his pocket. Whipping out his wallet, Remington throws his gym card onto the marble with a rattling clatter. "Cancel my membership then."

I gasp.

But Remington turns to me, softening his voice. "How about I pay for your membership to Dynamo to replace this one?"

Shaking my head vigorously, I step closer. "N-no, Rem, I couldn't have you pay for me–"

"Well, that asshole made it impossible for you to feel safe here anymore, so what does that leave you with? That you can never go to the gym again? That's not fair to you at all, Lilibeth."

I drop my chin, tempted to cry again. After sharing with Remington how badly I wanted to become physically stronger, the ache in his eyes tells me he knows how deeply this incident cut my heart.

But before I can speak, Liam huffs. "Fine, fine– I'll refund you in cash. Just– Just don't tell Josh I was the one who gave it to you."

Handing me a wad of cash as he safely escorts me from the gym, Remington waits until we're fully out the gym doors to turn to me, lifting his hand for a high-five. I have to jump to slap it, and Remington bursts into laughter with me.

"I can't believe this shit! You just scored at least 20 gym visits with how ridiculously overpriced this place is."

My jaw drops. "W-what?!"

Remington lets out a sharp, delighted laugh. "Yeah! If they didn't have one stupid machine I can't find at Dynamo, I'd never go here."

My breath catches. If Remington hadn't come for that one machine today, I'd have gone through Josh's harassment all alone. Remington's eyes widen as I clutch my hands to my chest, my eyes warping with emotion.

"Remington, I–" My voice breaks. "C-can I hug you?"

His features soften into a gentle, welcoming warmth. "Thanks for asking first. Come here."

With his big arms outstretched, I can't help but laugh despite the tears pricking my eyes; his vibrant energy makes me want to enjoy life.

Dashing into his chest, I squeeze him hard, my tote bumping his side. Remington tightens our embrace, wrapping his full arms around my shoulders.

"Thank you for today," I whisper.

He softly chuckles. "Even though I'm getting you all sweaty?"

I laugh. "Y-yes. I– I had a good first day now, actually."

It's far past time to let go, but I linger. Well, no, maybe we both are? Am I imagining it, or is his heart beating faster against my cheek too? He's so cozy - a firm plushness to his body that makes me want to snuggle in deeper for a peaceful nap.

The second Remington lightens his hold on me, I hurry back two steps. I haven't hugged a stranger in a long time, but Remington's gaze flips my heart when I look at him again - ten times stronger than the first time we met eyes. It's probably time to leave, isn't it?

But what if I don't want to?

Remington's eyes zip to the cash in my hand. I gasp, hurriedly shoving it into my bag, and Remington laughs.

"I, uh–" He licks his lips, and my stomach tenses. I hadn't realized how full they were until he wet them. He rocks on his feet, and my gut twists even tighter. Is he nervous?

The more he speaks, the faster he talks. "I wasn't kidding about the gym buddy thing. I'd be happy to be a real gym buddy with you. Or just help you settle in at Dynamo, if you'd like. But all of this is only if you'd like–"

"Yes," I blurt out.

My lungs are tight, and I don't know how to stand, where to look, or what else to say, but Remington's half-up grin almost extends into a full smile.

"Alright. Same time next week?"

I grin just as wide. "O-okay."

"Okay."

We stare at each other for the longest second of my life. But after it ticks by, we both let out a laugh.

"Later then, gym buddy," Remington waves.

"Later."

With Remington's final smile, my heart lifts so high into the sky that I don't know if I'll come down from this one without crashing hard. But as we wave goodbye, the tug in my heart tells me I don't care.

CHAPTER TWO

"Hurry the fuck up with that soup! I've got ten on deck!" Our head chef, Giuliano, shouts at Gabby.

She doesn't spare him a glance, stirring faster until her messy, dark brown bun wobbles in her hair net and another bead of sweat trails her neck. "Lily, you didn't tell me how it went at the gym last weekend!"

"O-oh, it–" I bite my lip. I'd rather not tell Gabby how horrendous Josh was at the start of my first day or that I got a refund for her gift card, especially now that I've made a new friend out of it. "I have a gym buddy to go with now."

Her eyebrows jump. "What?! Who? What are they like? Why are you blushing already?" She gasps. "Is it someone cute?"

I sigh, but I'm smiling. "His name is Remington. He's really sweet."

Tossing her spoon in the sink, Gabby yells, "Lily has the order out! It's hot!"

Ready with heat-resistant gloves up to my elbows, I hoist the pot off the stove by the handles. Gabby immediately replaces it with a fresh pot, and Paolo swarms to take my place at the stove. But I hobble, my back straining by the second as I penguin-walk with a vat of boiling soup.

"Jesus, fuck, Lily," Giuliano hisses. He snatches the pot from my arms, effortlessly hoisting it to his waist. "Just say you can't do it and stick to what you're good at. You could burn yourself, and it'd probably be blamed on me. You're lucky you make shit taste better than any of us can. Otherwise, I'd stop fighting for your job."

I swallow hard, left standing empty-handed with a stinging heart. On top of insulted, I feel stupid. I've witnessed how boiling water can rip through skin, and I'm not trying to do anything dangerous. I just want to be helpful.

Throwing my gloves beside Gabby, I speed-walk to the sink. After washing my hands, I hurry back to the clean cutting board table. Fetching vegetables by the armful, I dice 15 onions, skin and chop 12 carrots, and smash as many garlic cloves as possible in under five minutes. Normally, Gabby, Ben, or Paolo would handle smaller tasks like these, but Ben already peeled over fifty Roma tomatoes, and Giuliano swears our menu's "Lily's Hearty Minestrone" tastes better when the Lily-in-writing can get her hands on every ingredient. I love cutting my own vegetables, so I don't mind either way.

"Behind," I say.

Like me, Paolo is quiet despite his Italian roots. He nods, spinning to the fire-brick oven to pull out another pizza. His face flushes dark red from all the steam, just like mine is about to. Entering the stove's wall of heat, I dump seasoning into my fresh broth.

Gabby nudges me with a bright smile. "You said Remington, didn't you? I know a Remington!"

A jolt of fear snaps through my chest. Someone as beautiful as Gabriella Ricchetti - with long, sleek hair, plump curves packed with smooth, muscled power, and captivating brown eyes - would be a far better match for someone as gorgeous as Remington.

I stifle the nerves in my voice, turning back to my soup. "You do?"

"Yeah, I do!" The clanking of pots and bubbling soup drown us out, so Gabby leans in close, adjusting to a regular volume rather than having to shout. "He works at the club I told you about. The one I'm into."

The residual, churning anxiety in my gut explodes like Gabby just threw a match into gasoline. Does that mean Remington is into kink or BDSM? I don't have a problem with it - in fact, I wish I had more courage to explore it - but that would make Remington leagues ahead of me in terms of sexual experience.

A wallowing, throbbing pain breaks my heart. I guess I didn't realize how desperate I was to pursue Remington romantically. He probably thinks of me as a weird, innocent little flower.

"Have you, um– Had a good time with him there?" I ask.

Gabby gasps. "Are you interested in finally experimenting with someone?"

"Shh." I check over my shoulder. "I don't have any experience, either way."

"So? I told you I'd show you the ropes!" She nudges me, softening her voice even further. "Literally."

I shake my head, blushing down my chest. Maybe I shouldn't have told her I'd be open to trying Shibari with the right person.

Gabby sighs. "You still don't realize you're a bombshell, huh?"

I flush hotter, cleaning splotches of soup off the countertops beside the stove as an excuse to turn my back to Gabby. She's really into big breasts, and I know she's trying to compliment me, but in no way is my awkward, uncoordinated self a bombshell supermodel. Every time I've hooked up with someone, they've felt so uncomfortable around my blubbering shyness that they just get off and leave. Attraction to only my boobs doesn't last long.

But Gabby stops me with a gentle tug on my apron. "Did I say something to upset you?"

"I'm fine."

When she doesn't reply, I lift my head to meet her eyes.

She frowns. "You're a bad liar. I was going to say I've never laid a hand on the man, but I think you'd get along well with Remi. He's the Dungeon Monit–" Paolo rushes past, and Gabby returns to the soup. As soon as we're alone again, she softens her voice even further. "Well, in vanilla terms, he's one of the bouncers, so he's usually looking out for us and making sure everything stays safe and consensual."

"Oh," I say. Evidence of Remington's reassuring, protective force flashes through my mind. "No wonder."

Gabby does a double-take at my tiny smile before bursting into laughter. "Oh, I see what's happening. Go for it, Lils. You're right; he's sweet. I can totally see it."

My heart flips. "See what?"

"You two. Duh. Together in general, or at the club."

On the bus home, I can't stop thinking about what Gabby said about Remington. My stomach knots over itself, but I keep having to bite back my smile. Gabby saying she could see us together planted an image of me by Remington's side. I've never imagined myself beside someone so clearly, but if he's into consent enough to mediate between everyone at the club, I find that unbearably attractive. And maybe I might look okay beside him; even if he doesn't dress as alternatively as his tattoos imply, I still wear all black and love my studded jackets.

Tucking my phone close to my chest, I make sure the other bus passengers can't see over my shoulders or in the window's reflection behind me as I open an incognito search tab. I've already researched and asked Gabby plenty of questions, but I can't remember exactly what Dungeon Monitors do.

Within seconds of my search, my stomach plunges. If Remington is the Dungeon Monitor at Club X, he has more experience than I assumed – possibly more than anyone else in the club. And here I am, not only a fresh vanilla bean but also awkward as hell.

Quickly closing the tab, I slump into myself. Why do I care about this so much? We're just friends, if that. "Gym buddies" means nothing more than acquaintances who casually discuss athletics.

The second I enter my dark apartment, I stumble over

Celeste's cat toy in the doorway. She greets me with the tiniest meow, and I laugh.

"Hello, baby." I squat at her side as she runs her sleek, black body against my thigh.

The second her food bowl is full, and I've shoved a microwavable burrito in my mouth, I flop face-first on the couch. It never hits me how exhausted I am after work until I'm safe at home. I reek like garlic, but I can't keep my eyes open. I don't even budge when Celeste's warm body curls over my back, weighing me into the cushions. She must've decided this is where we're sleeping tonight too.

My alarm clock wakes me with soft, quick smacks against my cheek. I erupt into sleepy laughter, stroking Celeste's head. "Okay, okay, I'm up."

She let me sleep in today. Sunlight streams through my sheer black curtains, casting over the cheap TV I won at last year's work holiday party. Dust dances through the sunbeam, settling over my cluttered coffee table of books, candles, and crusty, old plates.

My heart stings. Poor Celeste shouldn't have to live in filth, but I couldn't lift an arm one extra time last night when I got home, let alone do this week's dishes after five days of cooking hell. Maybe I need a new job. Co-workers throughout the years have taken speed to contend with the workload, but I lived 18 years too long witnessing alcohol destroy Dad's mood to want to go down that road, and spent 15 more years rebuilding my life from scratch without his help just to give up on my dreams now. I want to own my own restaurant someday, even if it takes 20 more years.

Once the dishes are done, Celeste follows me into the bathroom. Products I've used throughout the week clutter the small sink, leaving me nowhere to place my phone. I throw my scattered makeup into a bag and the rest into my disastrous top drawer until the counter is finally clean. Celeste springs onto the open countertop, enjoying her newfound perch to watch me in the mirror with a tilted head. I bump my shoulders in my tiny shower as I turn my back to the water.

Then my actual alarm rings.

I gasp, fumbling for my phone with wet fingers. It's already noon. I had no idea Celeste let me sleep in this late, but now I only have 30 minutes to hop on the bus to meet Remington in time.

Celeste meows as I scramble to my bedroom dresser in a towel, throwing almost everything I own onto the floor until I find an old, black sports bra at the bottom.

Grunting, I fight with the elastic pinning my elbows to my sides, leaving my towel to flop on the ground. I yelp, dropping to the floor to hide behind my bed; I just flashed my whole ass to the street window. Celeste tenses, and I wriggle across the carpet to pet her head in reassurance, my arms still trapped against my chest.

Fuck, I'm stuck. An electric thrill shoots up my abdomen as I struggle with the stretchy fabric, except this time, my imagination paints a clear image of Remington tying me up.

"Oh, my God, Lilibeth, stop," I hiss, jerking my hand through one hole just enough to yank the sports bra the rest of the way on.

With my wispy bangs styled neatly over my forehead, I leave the rest of my hair wet, combing it into a high ponytail. Celeste jolts off the counter, just as terrified as ever from the toaster's loud declaration that it has completed its duties. I laugh as I collect my pre-workout carbohydrates. "My poor baby. I'll be back soon, okay?"

Celeste's bright yellow eyes track me as I rush out the door.

Throwing my gym bag over my shoulder, I zip my loose, gray jacket. With it comes the nerves. I'm really doing this - meeting a practical stranger to work out. Except he already knows more about my innermost thoughts than I'd share with most friends, and I know more about him from Gabby than he probably intended.

As I flop onto the bus, my stomach gurgles in complaint. Munching on my toast doesn't help. I'm unsure what to expect or what I'll seem like around Remington today. He was sweet last weekend, but I'm afraid I've built up our agreement in my head all week. We're just gym buddies, I remind myself.

And I'm not sure I'm the best gym buddy - more like an annoying younger sister to babysit on the machines. Josh said I shouldn't wear this jacket while working out, so I put on yoga pants that stretched high enough up my back to cover the mark. I planned to take this baggy jacket off once I warmed up.

But I've never been in only a sports bra and yoga pants in front of anyone before. Even during sex, I prefer to wear a shirt, keep my back snug to the sheets, and hide the rest of me beneath the covers. Plus, it was a tight squeeze to get into this bra, and I didn't have time to see how I fully looked before I left, but I'm probably spilling out of it. I already know I can't act the part of an experienced gym-goer, but I hate not even looking the part.

Stepping off the bus has my nervous system on high alert. Maybe I should just go home. But as I reorient my windblown bangs in the gym doorway, someone calls my name.

Standing in the cement-walled Dynamo Fitness Center lobby, Remington waves with his hefty gym bag wobbling over his broad shoulders. He's in thin black shorts and a taut black T-shirt with lightly rolled sleeves, giving me his same casual, half-up smile. "Hey, Lilibeth."

My name on his full lips stirs my belly into overwhelm. I grip my tote bag straps, but I'm smiling. "Hey, Remington. Sorry, I'm late."

"I'm just early. I haven't had a gym buddy in a while, so I've been looking forward to it."

My heart flips hard enough to lift my gaze. He was looking forward to this too?

Remington meets my elated eyes with an even softer smile. "Let's head in and claim a spot to warm up."

I nod, following after Remington as he hoists his heavy gym

bag over his back with one rippling arm. It stirs excitement in my belly that feels far too inappropriate for the first few seconds we've met today. I need to behave myself, so I stare at his heels as we walk.

This gym is busier than the one Gabby sent me to, and Remington was right; it seems far less hardcore. Women laugh together on the treadmills, speed walking at a breezy, reachable pace. A few men cheer another on at the bench press, a welcome change that surprises me enough to widen my eyes.

Remington veers off, but I only know so by his voice shifting to my left. "Lilibeth–"

He gasps, but I stop just before I crash into a column three times wider than me. Thankfully, it's padded, but Remington still races to a stop by my side with wide eyes.

I flush hot, no longer smiling. "O-oh, sorry, I– Sorry. I wasn't looking ahead of myself."

Hustling to the spot Remington picked out, I plop my tote beside his gym bag without lifting my head.

But Remington lets out a soft exhale. "I'm just glad you're okay. Are you nervous?"

"Yes." I dig through my bag for my refillable steel water bottle.

But when I peek at the bulky form blocking out the gym lights in front of me, Remington is still staring. "Am I making you nervous?"

I shake my head, standing next to him to face our reflection in the mirror. "I-I've been looking forward to this too. A lot."

I said it quietly, but Remington's eyebrows loosen in the mirror. Gripping my left foot by the toes, I stretch my quads, doing my best to fake calm despite Remington's sweet, gentle smile stirring powerful nerves in my belly. At least these nerves feel good: exhilarating, hyper, and anticipatory.

Remington copies me, bending his knee to grab his left foot. I wobble from watching his perfect form, and he holds an arm out for me. I grab it on instinct. Remington meets my eyes. His playful, sharp stare spikes my stomach to my knees. I burst into shy giggles, and Remington softly chuckles.

"I've been thinking we should establish some gym rules since that trainer fucked it all up for you," Remington says.

"Oh. Okay. Like what?" I wobble again. We finally switch legs.

"Like once you hit pain past a good burn, it's time to switch to the next exercise. Don't push yourself past it. That's how injuries happen."

I nod, copying Remington as he stretches his arms, pulling his elbow over his head. "Okay. What else?"

"I'll show you the ropes in terms of equipment safety, but I'm not going to be another mansplaining dick."

I laugh. "What if I need more explanation, though?"

"You can ask me anything, of course. But I think you've got this. From what I saw of you exercising, it seemed like you were underestimating your strength."

I drop my arm, ducking my head with it. Remington keeps his eyes trained on himself in my peripherals, but I still feel self-conscious. What if I disappoint him? With how much crap I get at work for how weak I am, I think *he's* overestimating *me.*

With my jaw clenched, I speak up with a racing heart. "I don't know. I still sucked at carrying the soup yesterday, and it was just as humiliating."

Remington drops everything to turn to me. "Oh, man, I'm sorry. Are you lifting with your legs instead of your back?"

I frown. "Yes. Everyone always tells me that, but that's what I don't understand – of course I'm using my legs. I'm standing when I pick it up, and putting weight on my legs. But when things get heavy enough, my back gets involved too, and my whole body strains."

Remington hums. "I think I might have an idea what's going on."

Within a minute, Remington and I have gathered dumbbells in various weights, some type of back brace from Remington's bag, and smaller wrist straps - all piled together on a workout bench. He stacks the smallest dumbbells before pushing the heaviest closer to me. "Do you think the soup's heavier than 25 pounds?"

Hoisting the dumbbell with one large end in either palm, I droop it between my knees, just like I would with the soup. "I don't know, actually. It might be similar to this weight, but the soup's just so big and awkward, and it's sloshing around and still boiling, so it's hard to carry without spilling or burning my legs on the sides of the pot."

"Alright, then, let's make it more awkward."

I laugh. "Oh. How?"

"We can try to lower your center of gravity with a different type of weight." Remington strides over to another weight rack, sliding off a 25-pound, donut-shaped metal weight with one arm. He drops it onto the bench, and it slips a little from its rounded edges.

"I see. Awkward," I mutter.

Remington whips his head around to me, letting out a sharp, quick laugh. "You're funny."

I can't stop myself from smiling. "I'm not."

"No, you are funny. And not in an I'm-making-fun-of-you way. In an I-didn't-expect-Lilibeth-to-be-so-witty type of way."

I bite back my smile, but my lip escapes my teeth's grasp anyway. "Do I seem too shy to be funny?"

Remington chuckles again, grabbing his back brace. "Oh, no. I know too many people to think it makes sense to judge at first glance. Especially with the shy ones - you all are secret tigers. Or maybe you're a panther with your black hair and those big, hazel eyes. Or are they green?" I bite my lip as he leans even closer - until he stops himself, zipping his focus away. "But anyway, I don't know, something about how you say your jokes hits just right. It's always unexpected in the best way. If I wasn't so pissed at that trainer, I would've busted out laughing with you and your dark sense of humor about that gift card."

Ducking my head, I laugh. If Remington keeps looking at me

with so much warmth in his dark eyes, I don't think my buzzing knees will last through our workout.

But his voice appears inches from my side, lighting my spine on fire. "Do you know how to put this back brace on?"

"N-no." I meet his eyes, and my heart flips.

I haven't been this close to him before, but now I can see a transparent silicone placeholder for an eyebrow piercing through his angular left brow. A swirly tattoo peeks from his hairline, covered by his choppy, short black hair over his forehead. Soft hints of his scent waft over me - a gentle mint from his toothpaste.

Taking the belted brace from him with shaking fingers, I loop it around myself, adjusting it on my waist to match where Remington strapped his on. "I-is that right?"

"It looks like it. Is it tight enough?"

I bite my lip. "I think? Can you— Can you check?" My heart spikes into my throat. This belt sits right over my mark, and I haven't let anyone touch my lower back since I was a kid. Why do I want Remington to? Should I take it back?

But Remington says, "Sure."

Stifling my anticipation, I hold as still as I can. Remington slips two fingers into the belt around my back, probably thinking it's the least offensive place to touch me. Really, it's the most sensitive place on me. The introduction of his thick fingers zaps my spine with a hot flash of nerves, expanding my ribs as I stretch myself taller.

Remington pulls away quickly, but I'm too flustered to check his expression. Why did that feel so nice? I'm left with a ghost of his touch tingling my back. Is it because I haven't been touched there in so long, or because it's Remington who touched me?

"Tighten it just a bit more, and you're all set." He circles back in front of me, nodding as I tighten my belt's velcro latch. "That'll help brace your back and hopefully take some pressure off."

My back does feel straighter. But I hum. "Normally, the

handles reach my shoulders, so getting it off the stove is even more awkward."

"Okay, then let's try something–" Remington hoists the weight higher, facing me like he's holding a metal platter at my shoulder height. "How about this?"

I'm nervous I'll embarrass myself by doing something terribly wrong. Remington's encouraging, firm nod convinces me to try anyway. Placing my feet at my shoulder width, I reach for the weight as if I'm grabbing the handles.

Remington smiles. "Okay, good news! I can definitely give you some ideas on how to lift easier when something is above your waist."

My heart soars. Remington demonstrates a way to place one foot in front of the other, rocking my weight from the front foot to the back to lift the heavy pot off the stove. The second I try it out with his advice, I hoist the weight from his arms with far greater ease.

"Holy shit, you've got powerful legs!" Remington announces to the gym. I peek behind us, and Remington covers his mouth. "Sorry. I got excited for you. But I don't think you're weak at all, Lily. You've got that in the fucking bag. Keep going - let's see how you carry it after."

His words boost my muscles, giving me the strength to carry the weight to the workout bench.

But Remington's expression shifts into stark seriousness. "Oh, Lilibeth— That's not painful for you?"

I drop the weight with an echoing *thud* through the gym. "I'm used to it."

His eyebrows furrow. "You must have a powerhouse back if you don't have regular injuries and can carry things like that all week."

I duck my head. "N-no. I feel really weak."

"You might feel that way, but listen— I swear it's not you, okay? Actually, have you even looked at the muscles that must be forming on your back from this? Look in the mirror." The second

Remington sees me tense from his suggestion, he waves off my worries with his hand. "You don't need to take your jacket off; just bunch it up in the front so the fabric is tight against your back."

Gathering my jacket in my fists, I look behind myself at Remington. Thank God my ass looks good in these yoga pants. If Remington checked me out, I didn't catch it in time: he's too busy gaping at my back.

I check a third time, making sure the mark on my back is covered. "W-what? Is it weird?"

"Dude," Remington rasps. "You're fucking *ripped*."

I sputter out a laugh. "I-I'm not!"

He gives me one quick, sharp laugh again. "Yes, you are! Look at you! Shit, what did I say, you're a badass. You carried so much soup that your back is stronger than mine."

My laughter bubbles out of me without warning, louder and higher-pitched than I'd normally allow in public. Remington laughs with me, and my heart soars. We attract a few stares, but it feels fitting; every second with Remington feels special. I meet his eyes, and more butterflies fill my chest than I've experienced with anyone else.

He pulls his eyes off me, hoisting the weight between his legs. Mimicking my awkward soup-carrying stance, he widens his knees and arches his back to hobble across the gym with the weight swinging wildly between his legs. "I better train up to match you."

"Don't!" I chase after him to grip his arm, stopping him as laughter steals the rest of my breath.

Remington takes one look at my hot red cheeks and rumbles out heavy, sharp laughter in quicker succession. It's such a sweet, goofy sound that my cheeks kill from how hard I'm smiling.

Refocusing ourselves, Remington gives me a sly grin.

"Just so you think I'm not saying anything creepy, I'll show you how to carry heavy things down low just by shoving your ass out behind you."

I burst into heavy laughter as Remington over-exaggerates the arching and flattening of his back, activating his legs just as he explained - by thrusting his ass out behind him. When I try it myself, I'm amazed.

And disappointed. "It was that simple? That's embarrassing."

But Remington crosses his arms. "What's embarrassing is that whoever trained you at work decided to give you shit instead of teach you. How are you supposed to know something you've never been taught?"

As I stand there, gaping at Remington's powerful form defending both my heart and body, I've never felt more loved.

We speed through the rest of our workout with an added perkiness to our movements. After the workout rushes by, I hate having to say goodbye, but Remington pulls out his phone in the gym lobby. After typing something into his phone, he shows me his screen.

Remington's phone number stares back. "Here. You don't have to text me, but feel free to take a picture of my screen in case you'd like to reach out sometime. I had fun with you today."

My heart flutters. I can't help but smile, even though my shoulders are rising. I feel like a dorky middle school girl again, unable to remember how to speak to reply to him.

"T-thanks," I mutter, opting to open a blank text message instead.

He opens his mouth to speak, but as I step closer to his side to copy his number, he stifles his breath. I hadn't realized how close I got to him until he froze, but now I can't move away without making it extra weird. Not that I want to. I don't know what this says about me, but even his light sweat smells alluring. I draw in one last inhale of him, my shoulder erupting into goosebumps beneath my jacket as his breath whispers down my side.

Sending him a quick text, I tuck my phone into my pocket. "I'll see you next week?"

Remington doesn't say anything. When I look up at him, he breaks into a sly smile. Except the gaze I just caught on him spoke of something else. A deep, desperate longing rumbles in my lower belly, heating my cheeks.

"Ready for another disgusting goodbye hug?" He opens his arms, and I laugh.

Tucking my cheek against his damp chest, I hug him a little tighter this time. "Yes."

Remington's heart gallops faster beneath my ear than I expected it to. Like last time, he gives me a lingering, tight squeeze, bringing a brighter grin to my smile-sore cheeks. "See you next week, Lilibeth."

He pulls away with a wave, spinning just before he bumps into a bike rack. We meet eyes and laugh, and that's the last I see of him this weekend.

CHAPTER THREE

Remington and I have a gym buddy system down: I complete the basic level of each exercise, and he adds weights or extra challenges to his, but we trade off performing each task together as a team before moving to another machine or floor exercise. The more I've settled into our groove, the more open I've felt around Remington.

Especially when he's so encouraging.

He nods to my lunges, even as he gulps massive mouthfuls of water. He breaks away from the bottle with a gasp, his wet lips creating an odd fuzziness in my stomach. "Hell yes! Look at yourself in the mirror, Lilibeth. Your movements have become so fluid lately that you look like a goddamn pro."

Catching my reflection, I boost through my next few reps with newfound pride; he's right. I look like a natural.

And I love pleasing Remington. I lunge a little deeper, aching to do a good job for him.

Except with my extra pushing, an acidic burn rages throughout my thighs, almost too heavy to withstand.

Remington's dark brows furrow. "You okay? You're doing more than usual."

"I'm fine," I huff, struggling to steady my heart rate.

But the second I bite my lip, pushing through the burn in my legs, Remington waves his hand.

"Okay, okay. Take it easy. You've done plenty."

I flush, dragging each heavy foot as I fetch my metal water bottle. When Remington breaks into his first lunge, my stomach plunges further; he's not smiling anymore.

"S-sorry," I mutter.

His eyebrows scrunch. "How come?"

"I made you upset."

He breathes evenly through each lunge, keeping his elbows slightly bent as he holds the dumbbells at his sides. "It's not about me. I'm just a little concerned, is all. I hope it doesn't feel like I'm pressuring you to push past your boundaries."

My heart flips. "O-oh, no, I–" Crossing one arm over my chest, I grip my opposite shoulder. "It's all me. It sounds silly, but I wanted to do a good job in front of you because I–"

I swallow hard. How do I explain that I not only want to please him, but also that I enjoy his praise? And "enjoying" doesn't fully cover it since I really like him too. Romantically.

But Remington's expression softens. My heart jolts at his serious, aching stare. "I'm sorry, Lilibeth. I don't think I made something clear: I'd rather you be safe because I'm *already* proud of you. You don't have to do anything except show up, and you should feel proud of yourself for it. If you need to stop early, that's honestly impressive too. It takes a lot of courage to know your limits."

My heart hammers harder than when I was exercising. As Remington stops lunging, we face each other directly. I can't bear to return to the mat's center for my turn, a magnetic pull tying me close to Remington's heaving chest instead. The longer my eyes zip over him, the deeper my longing is to belong in Remington's world.

I don't want to only be his gym buddy. I want to know what he likes, what he hates, and what he does when he's bored. And I've never felt like this with anyone else before, but I might even want to go to Club X with him to experiment my deepest fantasies.

But we're nowhere near that. With how awkward I am, I don't know how to bring us closer.

But I want to try. I swallow hard, landing on a terrifying question: even if Remington isn't on the same page, does he even like me back romantically? I don't know if I should voice it, but I don't think I can hold in my feelings for him any longer. It hurts.

If only I had an ounce of the cool, sly courage he carries in those broad shoulders. Rather than seeing myself as a badass wild cat, Remington is more of a panther than anyone I've met.

"Can you show me how to have more courage, in general?" My voice comes out soft and shaky.

Remington tilts his head, taking a step closer to soften his voice too. "What do you mean? Like, in all of life?"

But seeing him this close, my tiny shred of courage melts beneath his stare. I fidget with my waistband. "I-I don't know. Never mind."

Remington doesn't say anything for at least ten seconds, thrusting my heart into another gear. But then he places his overheated hand on my shoulder, passing behind me.

"Okay. No worries."

I can hardly breathe. Remington dropped the heavy subject for my comfort, but now that he's been extra sweet about my awkwardness, guilt stings my core for accidentally holding in other secrets: Remington still has no idea that I know he works at Club X, and I haven't known how to bring it up. What if he's angry when I tell him I talked about him with someone else? Or thinks I'm clinging to him just to fuck him?

He seems to trust me. The longer I wait to admit what I know about him, the higher the chance my accidental secret will expand into offensive territory. And I want to grow closer to him, not hurt him.

Remington has already moved to the pulldown machine to set up my weights. I fetch my tote, chasing after him.

Before I can overthink it, I sputter my first thoughts as I halt at his side. "I told my friend Gabby I met a nice Remington, and she said she knows you."

Remington freezes. When he looks at me, genuine shock freezes over his usual, neutral coolness. "Gabby, who?"

I swallow hard. "Gabby Ricchetti. We cook together at Salucci's downtown. She–" An unspoken knowing crosses Remington's dark eyes, and I'm terrified. But I have to keep going. "She said she knows you from Club X."

He still hasn't moved. Taming his expression, Remington's eyes drift over my parted lips, shifting eyes, and fidgeting hands. "What do you think about that?"

"Well, I'm–" I huff through light, fuzzy breaths. I'm not sure what his eyes are saying to me, but the way they're lingering makes me dizzy. "I'm curious."

Remington turns back to the weights with a hum. He slaps the barbell collar on one-handed like it's nothing when it's a struggle between the two of mine, then stands to face me. With less than a foot between us, I have to crane my neck to keep looking at him. His extra seven inches of height have never been so clear.

"If that's what you meant about finding more courage and figuring out your limits, I can tell you more about it sometime. Feel free to ask, okay?"

I open my mouth to speak, but I'm crushed by a never-ending bout of burning shyness. All I can mutter is, "Thanks."

We resume our workout as if nothing has changed.

Except it has. Remington didn't seem opposed to discussing Club X, which feels enormous. But he didn't invite me to play with him in the dungeon either. Although, that's ridiculous of me to hope for; from what I've researched, it could take months or years to build enough trust to play together, so our measly two months of knowing each other is nothing. Of course he wouldn't invite me to play.

But imagining Remington at the club - trusting me to hear more details about what he does there - stirs hope in me. I feel so safe around him that I don't want to stop opening up. I want to reach a place of security where I can confidently fling open that solid door in my heart, exposing my honest self to him.

And he just left one of his private doors open, just for me.

But I can't solve this now; I need to focus on my pulldowns.

Plopping onto the machine for my second set, I sigh. "It's still really difficult for me to keep my posture straight on these. I feel like I can't focus on everything at once."

"I hear you. It is pretty involved." Remington pauses as I reach for the bar. But when he steps forward, I freeze. "Hey, I have an idea. Maybe I can create a barrier with my hands around your lower torso to help you remember to activate your core?"

My heart flips. I want him closer to me, so I nod. "Okay, if you're okay with that, then thank you."

Remington kneels beside me, his head at my shoulder level. I keep my eyes trained straight ahead, hardly able to contain the rising excitement in my chest to have him so close. As he hovers one hand over my abdomen and the other behind my lower back, the mere suggestion of his touch flusters my breath from me. My heart refuses to settle in front of Remington, especially when I know he's watching me.

"Are you okay with me touching your stomach or lower back?" He asks.

Keeping my voice as even as I can, I force myself to sound confident despite my stumbling heartbeat. "Yes, I'm okay with it."

"Alright. Start your pulldown for me, and I'll check your posture closer." Remington's eyes track my core as I lower the bar. The body heat from his palms tingles my spine. As I finish the rep, Remington says, "Okay, freeze."

With my arms stretched above my head, I hold myself in place.

That's when Remington finally settles his palm over my stomach.

I suck in my belly, startled by the tingling rush his touch

bursts in my gut. But Remington's deep, satisfied purr redirects that excitement straight between my legs.

"There you go, now you're activating your core. Right away, I could see you've been arching your back too much. How about this: imagine your spine lengthening like I'm pulling a string from the top of your head, straightening you toward the ceiling."

Oh, God. The second I straighten my spine, my lower back bumps Remington's palm - right where I'm most sensitive. I catch a gasp just before it leaves my lips, distracting myself by adjusting my sweaty grip on the bar. I test out another pulldown, but in this position, the tugging pressure in my core amplifies from the bar pulling me upright. Dare I say this pulldown feels *good?*

Oh, no, it feels *really* good. As a cozy pleasure settles between my legs, Remington's warmth vibrates through my back, climbing to my reddening face. My rocky breath moves Remington's hands, shifting their pressure gently over my torso.

"You're doing so great. You're almost done, okay? You've got this," he says.

Oh, *no.* The bar's tugging sensation morphs into a deeper, tempting ache in my pussy. I chew on my lip, refocusing myself. What the hell is my problem? Poor Remington has no idea what's happening, and I absolutely wasn't planning on feeling aroused around him today - especially not in a public gym.

But my arms are pulled over my head, and Remington's mention of a string paints vivid images of being tied up with my arms trapped above my head. The longer I picture a rope pulling my torso straight, the more stuck I feel between Remington's palms. And that's not a bad thing. My lungs pick up the pace.

"Are you still doing okay?"

I clear my throat, steadying my voice. "Yes."

Get a grip, Lilibeth. I'm not going to let myself be aroused any further. I only have five more reps, anyway.

Okay, no. With the fifth-to-last pulldown, it's absolutely this exercise heightening this pressure in my groin, spurring my pussy into flexing in delight. Am I a total weirdo for feeling like this?

But I can't stifle it. My legs weaken, lifting my ass off the bench, but not for the reasons Remington might think.

His soft voice carries an extra allure to it from beside me. "There you go. You're doing so well activating your core. Can you try to keep your hips on the bench, or would you like some help holding down your body for the last few reps?"

Oh, maybe that would actually take pressure off my aching core.

"Sure, thanks," I say.

Remington's hand lifts off my belly, but his right hand on my back slides to my hip. The left settles on my other hip to match, and he applies firm pressure with it - pressing my ass tight to the bench. I breathe through my nose, doing my best to hide the luminous, raging fire in my belly.

"Ready," he says.

Okay, Lilibeth. You can do this. This is just an innocent physical exercise. Just a pulldown. It'll be over in less than a minute.

But with the slow, rooted stretch of my core, Remington's added pressure on my hips blooms a bubbling, expanding pleasure in my lower belly. I gasp for air, but with the rep's full stretch touching my most sensitive nerves, the extra effort this rep requires pushes a high-pitched, airy moan from my lips.

Shock erases all pleasure I'm feeling. My arms zip back up in fear. Remington looks me straight in the eyes in the mirror in front of the machine. I pant, unable to stop my entire body from flushing bright red.

"S-sorry," I breathe.

Remington hums. "It's all good, as long as you're okay. You've only got one more."

He knows that moan wasn't my regular workout exhale. He has to. Embarrassment stings my eyes.

Ignoring the heavy, pointed weight of his hands pressing my

thighs tight to the bench, I struggle through my last pulldown with a deep quiver down my spine. I've never let someone touch my back in that spot before, and his hands are so warm and big, and he's complimenting me, and it's all stacking onto the low, building ache in my groin.

What if it isn't the pulldowns after all, and it's mainly *Remington* making me feel this way - just with his eyes and words? Is this okay to feel? The pleasure in my pelvis expands to an almost unreachable level. What if I really am about to come? Panic strikes my heart again, and I know it's seeping through to my face.

"Pause. Don't finish that one."

Remington's sudden request zaps my nerves. I release the bar, allowing it to clatter to the top with a resounding *clang*.

Neither of us speak at first. I stare at Remington, wide-eyed and mortified as I anticipate his response to my inappropriate feelings, but his expression remains cool. He removes his pressure on my hips, but he doesn't step away, keeping one hand softly settled against my lower back. We're still gazing at each other in the mirror, even as I suck in an extended inhale at his buzzing touch on me.

"Are you sure you're okay with me having my hands here?" There's a silent, sultry question in Remington's eyes that throws my heart overboard. I don't want to lie to him. I can't.

"Yes. But I'm– I'm just a little flustered, since it feels nice to have your hands there," I whisper.

My body buzzes like I've been sprinting, clinging to the bench with clammy hands. I can't believe I just voiced that. Have I lost all blood to my brain?

But Remington hums quietly, his tone lower than ever. "It does seem sensitive."

He's speaking so softly that my pussy clenches. Thank God I can't get a boner. I open my lips, breaking into a pant. I can't stop my whisper from spilling out. "I have an embarrassing mark on my skin on my lower back, so I haven't let anyone else touch my back or hips on purpose before."

Remington freezes with a smoldering, pointed stare, effectively taken aback by my confession.

But he runs his thumb over my back, blasting pleasure up my heaving chest. "That's a real gift you've given me. Thank you. And I—" He lets out a quiet, slow exhale at my side before softening his voice even further. "I do like having my hands there too."

Remington's words ripple through me, stirring desire deep in my belly. I pause, giving myself a second to breathe. I feel so inexperienced and ridiculous for getting close from just words, simple touches, and exercise, especially beside who I'm fairly certain is a sex king. I hope he doesn't notice the depth of what he's doing to me - or if he notices, that he isn't grossed out.

But I don't want to stop staring at him in the mirror. Our eyes linger for far longer than usual.

He studies me for a while before muttering, "Do you want to keep going?"

I swallow hard, glancing at the bar over my head for mercy. "Yes."

He's not talking this time. Maybe I can handle my feelings without his praise amplifying them.

But a few reps in, Remington's hot breath on my back and the intensity of this workout creates a powerful, flourishing warmth in my groin - even more potent than the first time. Panic flips my heart. What's going on today? The next rep feels way too good, enough to replace the burn in my arms.

Am I really getting off on this exercise? Is that even possible? Glancing at the mirror, my anxiety amplifies from how close Remington is sitting to me. I've never let a man watch me come before.

My voice quivers. "I-I need a break."

"Okay." Remington immediately steps back, allowing me to stand and stop straddling the bench. My knees wobble as I pull back from it, and Remington grabs my searching hand before I tilt too far.

"Hey," he says softly.

I peek at him, still flustered from the radiating warmth in my groin.

But Remington smiles. "Thanks for being so honest with me about where you're at."

My gaze drops to the floor, but Remington says nothing else. He plops beside me on the ground as we rehydrate. I drop my head back and close my eyes, hoping the sensual ache dissipates. Nothing about Remington is helping, but I'm mortified that I feel this way without him knowing. I feel like a creep.

After a full minute, the feeling thankfully disappears. But when I open my eyes, I laugh at our reflection in the mirror; I'm a haggard, raccoon-eyed mess, and Remington looks like a tattooed, emo edition of Michelangelo's David. Remington looks at me with one eyebrow raised, then follows my gaze to meet our reflection. His half-up smile greets me.

He chuckles. "What's up, L.L.B.? You see something funny?"

I laugh. "L.L.B.?"

"Yeah - your new nickname. Unless you want me to keep turning you bright red every time I say Lilibeth."

I slap my hands over my face before erupting into giggles. "Remington…"

He rumbles through a quiet, deep laugh. When he speaks, I can hardly hear him. "I didn't say it didn't work on me when you say my full name either."

Tingles fizzle in my belly. I peek from my hands, unsure if I heard Remington correctly, but he's standing with his hand outstretched.

"Alright, I think we should switch to another exercise. You ready for more?"

I'm ready for more than he might realize. I've never been this attracted to someone before.

Taking his hand, I hop to my feet with a smile. "Ready!"

Remington pauses. As his gaze lingers on me, he gives me a smile I've never seen on him before: rather than lifting one cheek, he keeps his mouth shut as it curves on both sides. Except this smile reaches all the way to his eyes. Then he laughs. A gentle, brisk laugh that speeds my heart into a sprint.

"You're adorable. Let's go."

I bite my lip, strapping weights onto my wrists. Usually, people use words like "adorable" or "cute" to infantilize me, but the gentle, earnest way Remington speaks makes me feel like he saw all the way through me to the excitement in my heart and decided to meet it there.

"You're adorable too," I mutter.

Remington has his back to me, but the huff of air from his nose tells me he's genuinely smiling again. And the tremendous, building desire in my gut tells me it's too late to stop my heart from chasing after him.

CHAPTER FOUR

The next three weeks fly by, but I'm in agony. I can't stop thinking about the next time I'll see Remington, wishing away the days. So the next time I see him, I'm determined to make it count.

I want to challenge myself. Showing up at the gym with my jacket unzipped, I don't cover my form-fitting sports bra, and I switch to high-waisted exercise shorts I bought earlier this week that dip in a V-shape at the end of my spine to accentuate my butt.

Remington never comments on my physical appearance, and he doesn't comment on it today. If anything, I catch him staring just a bit longer when he thinks I'm not looking. I want more of it. On top of enjoying his attention, I've performed better without fears about my appearance, trusting him not to judge me.

But my physical strength has increased as much as mental, allowing me to steadily increase my workout regimen. Our agreement has stirred something deeper in me: a confidence I've never felt safe enough to express.

We took a break from pulldowns, so my *problem* hasn't repeated itself.

Until I lay back on the leg press machine, pushing the heavy slab of metal away from me with only my legs. Tingling sensations whisper between my legs on the third rep. By the fifth, it melts into a widespread ache in my pelvis. I gasp through my deep breathing, half from confusion and half from how quickly this pleasure builds.

Remington is still at my side. "Are you okay?"

Viewing him towering over me, a heavier jolt pierces my core. I retrain my eyes ahead. Opting to imagine boring, non-sexual things like cookies or flowers, I mutter a shaky "Yes."

"Are you in pain?"

I huff through another rep, and the pleasure blooms even wider now. "No."

Remington doesn't reply. When I dare to look at him again, he looks gravely concerned. "Let's stop and give you a breather for a second."

Oh, God, is it that obvious that I'm feeling different? I flush, hurriedly locking the machine to step off of it. But my core is still pulsing so rapidly that I stumble off the machine, my knees weak and panties soaked like I was just having penetrative sex. Remington has to catch me when I stumble, and I right myself quickly, speeding for my water bottle.

"You good?" He asks after me, setting up the machine for himself.

"Yes," I lie.

The orgasm that was building wasn't like those puny little ones I've had from rubbing myself on my pillow when I'm too tired at night after work. This one was deep - like the ones from my G-spot rabbit. After stopping and leaving myself intensely frustrated, I almost wish I had let myself secretly finish.

When Remington finishes his set, he suggests switching to upper body. We head straight for the pulldown machines. My feet slow.

Remington pauses. "Do you want to skip this one?"

I open my mouth to speak, but close it again. I don't want to skip it, but my reasoning isn't for the innocent workout we planned.

He frowns, stepping closer. "Are you sure you're okay?"

I drop my head, wrapping my arms over the small amount of bare skin on my lower ribs. "Y-yes. I just– I'm worried how it'll feel."

"Ah," Remington says.

My heart hammers into my throat. That "ah" was loaded far beyond what I was prepared for. How much does he really know?

But he lowers his voice. "We can skip this, seriously. Or we can keep going, even if it's– Even if you feel sensitive again."

I bite my lip. "You don't– You don't mind?"

The Remington I know would playfully shrug this off or make a sly joke. But the dark, longing eyes I find staring back flip my heart into my throat.

"I definitely don't mind."

Oh, my God. Does that mean what I think it does? If he likes witnessing me become aroused, my boosted hormones beg me to let him watch me exercise even more.

And I decide to listen, taking the initiative to finish leading us to the machines.

I've never done anything like this. Even when I've had actual sex, I've always made sure my partner felt pleasure first, or at the very least, at the same time. It's what I was taught men needed. But one quick glance at Remington's workout shorts leaves no bulge for me to see.

He's not aroused. Maybe he's not understanding that it's not simply a "good burn" and that I've actually been *sexually* aroused? Or maybe he's just plain not attracted to me.

My heart hurts. But this workout isn't supposed to be for sex. Shame compresses my sternum. I need to control my urges like an actual adult.

Diving into the workout, my melancholy thoughts erase all arousal in my body. It's not until my heart is racing on the last set that Remington spots my form wavering.

"Would you like me to help you correct it again?" He asks.

I'm still too bummed and anxious to feel aroused, so I nod. "Sure, thank you."

But with my heart rate elevated and Remington helping me to activate my core, it doesn't matter how disappointed I am: the introduction of his warm hands on my stomach plants a desirous seed in my core. Huffing through the workout, I part my lips as that same creeping pressure builds in my lower abdomen - each pulldown mimicking the sensation of my muscles stretched by a long, stiff object entering me.

"Good job," Remington says.

My pussy flutters.

"But don't forget to breathe."

Shit, I'm holding my breath to stave off the sensation. My nipples harden enough to poke through the thick fabric in my sports bra, and I have no idea if Remington has noticed yet. I have to breathe through my mouth, unable to suck in enough oxygen through my nose with my body's rising temperature.

"I-I'm sorry," I choke out.

Remington straightens to meet my eyes in the mirror. "What do you mean? Is it feeling sensitive again?"

I tremble through the tail end of the next rep. "Yes, I don't understand why. Is it weird for you? I'm so sorry."

"There's no need to be sorry. Do you want me to step away?"

I bite my lip, my eyelids fluttering as I let myself hang on the bar. I thought it'd relieve me, but the deeper stretch only makes my voice come out even breathier. "N-not unless you want to."

Silence hangs between us.

But Remington lowers his voice. "There's nothing wrong with it feeling good. It happens to more people while exercising than you think."

"R-really?" I whisper.

"Really. So please, don't push yourself. Either let yourself stop if you feel too uncomfortable or just roll with the feeling and enjoy it."

"O-okay," I whisper.

I've always kept sexual pleasure to myself, but the way he phrased that carried such ease that he erased all shame from my predicament. I settle into his touch, sinking into the pleasure swirling through my lower abdomen. This is human nature, isn't it? Maybe it's not as embarrassing as I thought to feel a little good, unexpectedly.

And maybe I can make it to the end without orgasming, anyway. I rarely ever orgasm in general, especially not without direct stimulation. But with just a single extra rep - now containing the knowledge that Remington is willingly watching me feel good - it feels like I'm having deep, delicious sex. I sputter out a heaving exhale, accidentally meeting Remington's eyes. It's almost enough to take me over the edge, so I quickly raise my eyes to the ceiling.

What the hell has happened to me? This is so unlike the old Lilibeth, but I feel so good that my judgment evaporates. I just have one more rep, then I'll be done. If I happen to come, so be it.

But just as I draw the bar to my collarbone, Remington lightly adjusts his hand on my lower back, sparkling fizzy sensations over my tender mark. It's just enough movement in just the right direction to nurture my tingling core. Pleasure blasts to my face, and before I know it, I'm having a deep, full-body orgasm. I'm so shocked by its force that I can't stop my weakened muscles from allowing the pulldown machine to hoist me into the air. I'm left hanging as I come, squeezing my knees together with a whimper and rock of my hips – all for Remington to watch.

Remington grabs me by the waist, holding me steady. "Shit, are you okay?!"

The second lust clears from my head, I crash to reality. Every shadowed possibility of what Remington might think of me tears through my mind at full speed - how slutty, repulsive, or classless I must appear. Mortification throws me from the machine. I crumple onto the bench with a thud, bursting into instant tears. I know it'll make Remington even more concerned, but I can't stop myself from sobbing. I can't bear to face him anymore, curling over myself.

Remington hovers over me, stroking the back of my head. "Oh, sweet girl, are you hurt?"

I shake my head no, too mortified to explain what just happened. Mainly because I really don't understand how it was possible. I haven't come in front of a man like that - not even when they've been inside me. Remington probably realizes what my body just experienced, and he seems okay with witnessing, if not enjoying it.

But I feel like something is wrong with me. I've never heard of this happening to someone else, and even though Remington acted like it happens to some people, I didn't tell Remington directly that I was about to orgasm. I should've been more explicit in case he didn't actually understand and didn't want to see it, but once again, I'm too weak to function the same as everyone else.

"What's making you so upset?" Remington's sweet, cooing voice over me pulls soft cries from my lips. He cups my cheeks, catching my tears. "Oh, Lilibeth."

"I'm sorry, I—" I shake my head. He's a friend. Just a friend. It hurts. How do you tell your gym buddy something like this?

Remington rubs my back softly. "Did I do anything to make you feel bad?"

I hitch through sobs, unable to meet his worried eyes. "No, I'm just embarrassed. Because I— It felt too nice."

Remington is silent at first. It terrifies me so much that I hold my stare on him, no matter how many nerves punch my gut when we meet eyes.

But I find a smoldering desire behind his black irises. It pulses my heartbeat into my groin in lusty aftershocks.

"So you *did*—" Remington halts his breath when I wince. "Sorry. It felt *really* good, I take it?"

Whimpering through another bout of tears, I drop my head. I can't bear to admit the truth.

Remington draws closer until his nose hovers beside my red cheeks. He softens his voice just above a whisper. "There's really no need to be embarrassed. It happens to some people from core exercises since it pulls on your pelvic floor. It's literally called a 'coregasm.'"

I choke out a sob. So he does know what happened. "B-but you didn't consent to seeing that. I'm so sorry."

"Well, you did warn me - multiple times. I'm no stranger to what was probably going on, and I kept checking in to make sure you wanted to let me watch. Did I misunderstand and make you feel violated?"

My lip wobbles. "N-no, not at all. I– You got everything right. I just still feel bad. Even if you don't feel violated, I could've hurt you if I was wrong and you didn't want to see." I groan, gripping my stomach harder. "I so wish I was better at expressing myself, Rem. I want to be, but I still suck at it. I don't want to be so incapable that I hurt your feelings."

With a sympathetic, sad sigh, he brushes tears from my soaked cheeks. "Oh, you're breaking my heart. I did want to see, just like I said, and I've been thinking you're better at expressing yourself more than ever lately. Are you sure nothing else is wrong? You're crying so much, L.L.B., and it's gutting me."

I've already fucked this up, so I might as well tell him the rest. My heart lurches, sending me into deeper, hitching tears. When I speak, it comes out weak and sad. "I *really* like you."

Remington melts into the sweetest smile. "I really like you too."

I hold my breath, halting my tears. Huffing out a laugh, I wipe my cheeks. "Oh."

He chuckles, dissolving into his sly, half-up grin. "Which means you actually gave me a fun surprise just now."

I bury my head into his shoulder with a gasp. "*Remington!*"

His chuckle rises, but he hurriedly rubs my back. "Sorry, sorry, I won't tease you. But I don't want you to feel bad about it, okay? This might be a lot to say, but I feel really strongly about you. And as long as you're not hurt, I'm all good. Or, actually, I'm really happy. I'm so excited we feel the same."

My heart throbs into my throat. Is this really happening?

Yes, it is. My core is still aching, I'm encompassed by Remington's embrace, and my heart floats in bliss. With fresh tears, my voice comes out wobbly. "I'm really happy we feel the same too. B-but I'm still a little sad now."

"How come?"

"I wanted to at least go out to dinner with you before either of us came."

Remington lets out a sharp, loud laugh, hugging me closer. "Holy shit. You're so fucking funny and adorable." The harder he laughs, the more I burst into tiny giggles. Remington sighs, stroking my back. "That was great. But there's really no problem here, Lilibeth; I'd *love* to go out to dinner with you - make up for lost time."

I gasp, sitting back to face him with a rising smile. "Really?"

He laughs, wiping the mascara from beneath my eyes. "Yes, really. You didn't think I would? I just told you I liked you – a lot, a *lot*. Even your little snot nose."

Before I can realize what he's doing, he swipes mucus from my upper lip. I yelp, smashing my face back into his chest to hide again, and he laughs even louder. His laugh is so boisterous and goofy that I have to belly laugh with him, uncovering my messy face from the safety of his chest. We clean the last of my tears with my temple against his shoulder, and I feel calmer by the second.

"Thank you," I whisper. "I'm sorry for crying."

"You're okay. Let me ground you a little, sweetheart," he purrs. Remington pulses firm, loving squeezes down my arms and back. A soothing buzz in my chest covers more and more of me until I slump into him. He hums through a soft smile. "Good job."

I hum back, softly rubbing his chest in gratitude. But with the sudden lack of space between us, the massive shift in our relationship finally sinks in.

My eyebrows arch through my smile. I'm simultaneously

elated and aching. "So I don't have to wait a full week to see you anymore?"

Remington's eyes soften. "Oh, poor L.L.B. You were feeling bummed about that? Fuck, I should've asked you out sooner. I was just afraid of losing you if I moved too fast."

I shake my head. "I-I wanted to move faster with you too, even if it's scary for me."

His genuine, soft tone warms my heart. "Then I'm right there with you, and we're right where we're supposed to be."

I love the sound of that, beaming with my fullest smile. "Then how's the Ruby Bistro, Thursday night at 6?"

Remington's deep chuckle gives me goosebumps. "You're trouble. Thursday it is."

CHAPTER FIVE

I can finally lift the soup. Rocking between my feet, I call out, "Order out!" Gabby whistles as I widen my stance, keeping my chin lifted to carry the massive pot to the pass for plating. Giuliano pauses a whole two seconds to watch me cross before returning to his lasagna with a disparaging head shake. I stifle the pride in my chest, allowing myself my moment; the fact he didn't say anything at all is just as good as the praise he'll never give me. I'm really doing it.

Maybe I can lift Mom.

"Thanks, thunder thighs." Ben laughs as I drop the pot on the pass.

My heart stings, but I don't allow him to see it, lifting my chest higher. Ben does a double-take at my glare. He gapes like he doesn't know what to say, so I channel a little Remington through me, darkening my stare and lifting one eyebrow. He breaks into laughter, latching onto Paolo as he dashes by.

"Dude, look at Lily. She actually looks pissed."

"Leave her alone," Paolo snaps. Ripping his arm from Ben's grasp, Paolo leaves Ben gaping.

He turns to me with wide eyes, and it's my turn to huff out a small laugh. Hurt crosses his features just before I turn my back to him, returning to the stove.

"Behind." I dash to Gabby's side. She stops stirring three soups, allowing me to share the load.

Gabby leans in. "I was hoping you'd let that tough girl side out a little someday. Told you you're a bombshell all around."

I can't stop smiling. Maybe I do have more courage in me than I thought.

I wish Remington was here to see it. My heart flips. I'm not sure if he's technically my boyfriend now or what mutually liking each other "a lot, a lot" means for our weekly workouts, but I want to know more about him too. Does he also have sides of himself that he's too afraid to show anyone? Does it have anything to do with why he almost never smiles with both cheeks?

But before I can see him again on Thursday, I need to visit Mom to make sure she's okay. Last month's visit was annoying but not terrible. Maybe it'll go smoother this time too, now that I've learned how to respect my limits even more.

From the second I shift the car into reverse in my apartment complex's parking garage to two hours later, when I'm hobbling on shaky legs in front of my childhood home, my stomach burns like hot acid, steeping in my anxiety. The choppy sidewalk to the front door seems to stretch into the distance, so I turn back to my car. I lean against it to reground myself, pretending I'm fetching my keys in my tote bag in case anyone is watching from the window.

No one comes outside to greet me. Dad must be napping. I know not to knock and wake him once he's finally getting a chance to rest, so I slip my key in as quietly as possible.

But when I open the front door, Dad shuffles down the hall towards me. I stiffen from head to toe, gaping up at him.

He quirks one eyebrow with his smile, opening his arms. "Good morning to you too."

I huff out a relieved laugh. "S-sorry. Hi, Dad."

He pulls me in for a glomping hug, but I keep my side to him, busying my focus on removing my shoes and dropping my tote.

"How have you been, Lily? Mom's been hoping to see you."

My heart stings so sharply that I have to swallow it. Is Dad saying that to guilt me, or was Mom genuinely upset that I missed our usual time for a monthly visit last week?

My voice shrinks even quieter than usual. "Sorry, Dad. I've been really stressed with work."

"Come in, come in. Go grab yourself a drink and settle down on the couch."

He guides me down the hall with an arm over my shoulders, and I'm tempted to step back. I give him a soft laugh, lifting my refillable metal water bottle. "Thanks, Dad. I'm okay; I have water already. Where's Mom?"

Releasing me, Dad points down the hall. "Resting in her room."

I rush down the hall before he can catch up to me - even though I expect his footsteps clodding after me from behind.

Approaching my old bedroom still feels weird. I'm just grateful Mom and I were able to convince Dad that Mom needed her own room to sleep in for her sleep apnea machine - since it's hard enough for Dad to stay asleep between caregiving. They've seemed to settle into this new setup, Mom happily watching sitcom reruns on my old, rattly TV from the late 90s. Her bed tray stands on the mattress over her blanketed legs, holding her phone and an old plate over her lap.

"Lilibeth!" Mom beams when she sees me. It's not until I see her bulging eyes in hollow sockets that I can tell she's thinner than last month. She opens her arms. "Hello, baby!"

I smile, fighting against my desperate need to cry. Side-stepping Mom's wheelchair, I lean over the bed for a hug. Wrapping my arms beneath her back, I'm relieved by how toasty her pillow feels. At least she's staying warm.

"Hi, Mom," I mutter.

She hugs me as tight as she can. I don't know if it's my fears kicking in, but her grip feels looser than usual. What if tomorrow, the muscles in her esophagus prevent her from swallowing correctly, and she chokes and dies? What if this is our final hug?

Squeezing my eyes shut hard, I take a deep breath. I can't think about that now.

Dad plops into the armchair beside Mom's bed, and the leather groans in complaint. "Lily says the restaurant has been stressing her out."

Mom gasps, releasing me. "What? What's been going on?"

Shaking my head, I give them a light laugh. "It's nothing new. Just regular work stress."

"Is it just as busy as always? Even with how expensive those meals are?" Mom asks.

"Busi*er*. Sorry I couldn't come last week."

"Oh, no, it's fine, sweetheart! Come, sit. Tell us what else is new." Mom turns to Dad. "Honey, can you lower the volume so I can hear Lily better?"

Dad lays his head back on the armchair's headrest. "You've got the remote right next to you, Lia."

My jaw clenches tight. Mom reaches for the remote with a shaky hand, but I lean over her to grab it first. The TV snaps off with my hard press on the red button.

"Thanks, Lily," Mom whispers.

I don't meet Dad's eyes, but I've memorized his body language enough to see his taut beer belly in my peripherals - a warning sign his patience is running out. I never know which minor insult will be the tipping point between his regular, stewing annoyance and a full-blown outburst, so the sight stiffens my shoulders.

Sitting on the bed's end with my back to him, I smile at Mom. "I haven't actually been up to much else. I made a new friend, but that's it."

Mom's eyes brighten. "That's *it?* That's so exciting! You were just telling me it'd be nice to find more friends. It's so hard to find more as a working adult, isn't it? What's her name?"

I giggle at Mom's long string of thoughts. "He's actually a guy. His name is Remington, and he's my workout buddy at the gym."

"Oh! How unexpected! That's so great you've been able to get to the gym! I know how long you've been wanting to do that."

But Dad straightens. "How are you affording it?"

My ribcage tenses. "My friend Gabby gave me a gift card—"

"Honey, she's in her thirties. She can use her own money to take herself to the gym." Mom snaps at Dad.

He clenches his jaw. "You think I like having to rely on our youngest daughter for rent?"

Mom gasps. "Joe!"

"What? It's no secret."

Mom scowls at Dad, ready to argue back, but I sit straighter. "And rent is almost due, I know, and I lost track of the days last week. I'm sorry to worry you. The envelope for this month is in my bag, by the door. I'll get it for you in a minute."

Dad stands. "I'll get it myself."

Rage simmers deep in my belly. My heart screams to chase after him, yell at him, rip my money from his hands - anything but continue to sit here like I have most of my life. But Mom's shaking hand lands on my arm, reminding me I can't. It's not safe.

Dad takes care of everything alone. He's generous and hardworking, but his patience will be tested beyond his limits if I don't help them with rent. I'm afraid his temper tantrums will leak from just targeting me to also including Mom. What if he hurts her worse than he means to, like he's done to me? Mom doesn't have the youth or body I do. She might survive her disease despite suffering through it for the rest of her life, but if she sees what Dad's really like when he gets angry, I'm afraid she could die from pure heartbreak.

"Ignore him. He's just hurt that I gave him a hard time this morning," Mom sighs. "Actually, Lilibeth, do you think you could help me to the bathroom? I think your dad accidentally forgot I asked thirty minutes ago."

I can hardly school my fiery breath. "Thirty whole minutes ago? And he's complaining about turning the TV off for you?"

She laughs. "Oh, Lily, it's fine. He's just an old, tired man."

"It's *not* fine," I whisper.

"Okay, well, either way, I need to pee," she laughs, and my shoulders soften. "And I rested a lot today. I might be able to stand just long enough to sit in the chair without him picking me up. I just need your help keeping steady."

My stomach tenses. I open my mouth to speak, close it, then open it again, but the words won't come out.

Mom's whisper comes out desperate. "Lily, seriously, I need to go. Let's try before he comes back. You know what they say - it's easier to ask for forgiveness than permission." She laughs again, but I can't even smile.

"Maybe I can give you and Dad a break soon. I've been working really hard at the gym. I think I can lift you now, Mom."

Mom freezes. Her placating smile is gone.

She glances at the open door over my shoulder. Her whisper softens even lower. "You really think you can?"

"Yes. Can I try?"

She waves me on. "Hurry, hurry."

Scooping my arms beneath her emaciated torso and thighs, I breathe through my pounding, frantic heartbeat. I have to do this. Please, let me be able to finally do this.

But the second I have a good hold on her, we hear footsteps parading back down the hall.

Mom gasps. "Stop, stop, Lilibeth. He'll be even more hurt–"

I pull my arms from her as fast as I can, but that's easier said than done with how weak her core muscles have grown, unable to keep herself in place. I have to be careful not to carelessly roll her over, no matter if her bulging eyes zip from me, to the door, and back to me in pure panic.

But just as my hands slip out from under Mom, a voice appears behind me.

"What are you doing?"

I scour my mind for an acceptable answer, but Dad steps in front of me. I instinctively take hurried steps back, bumping into my old dresser and knocking over two of my collectible cat figurines.

Mom laughs. "No worries, honey. I just really need to pee and asked Lily to help."

My heart feels like it's been dropped in battery acid. Mom covered for me again.

"You should've just asked me to take you. I said I'd be right back." Dad's brisk tone remains sharp despite our efforts to pacify him. "Am I not doing something right, again?"

Mom gasps. "Joe, honey, stop. You're doing wonderfully. Thank you for your help."

Dad ditches Mom's wheelchair, heading to the bathroom without it. There's no reason to leave it behind, especially since it means Dad will have to lift Mom not only off the toilet, but also back to her bed, all while not allowing her muscles a chance to retain their strength.

But that's exactly why he did it.

My internal switch shifts from fear to teeth-clenching anger. Without her chair, Mom can't move around the house without Dad's help. It took me a whole year to save for the chair - the only assistance I could afford for her, since I can't afford a repeating payment for a caregiver after paying part of Mom and Dad's rent. I'll never forget how relieved Mom looked to roll herself forward a few feet. And how stern Dad looked, blaming it on the football game that day not going his way.

Dad never expected his life to go like this. To become Mom's caregiver.

He hides his resentment from Mom, excusing his moods as fatigue or annoyance over minor problems they bicker through, but I know better: Dad expected to become more of Mom's third child to clean up after, so no matter what we do to placate him, he feels like he's been stolen from. For this destruction of their life plans to feel worth bearing, Dad needs to feel important - singularly vital to Mom's survival. Whether it's a wheelchair, extended relatives, or his daughters, Dad can't handle our help.

But this wheelchair is Mom's autonomy. If she has autonomy, Dad sees his efforts as wasted. Yes, he helps her night and day, expending every ounce of his focus and efforts to support her, but beneath the surface, I can't help but feel it's vile; he'd rather Mom have nothing if she doesn't have him.

I'm not okay with that.

Lifting Mom's wheelchair, I storm down the hall after Dad.

Mom laughs in the distance. "Besides, there's so much to remember when it comes to me. You just forgot, so I reminded Lily, is all."

Dad doesn't respond.

He hears me coming behind him - I know it. But he won't turn around, so the second he settles Mom on the toilet, I block the doorway with her wheelchair. "You forgot Mom's chair."

Dad's neck tenses. "She doesn't need it. I can carry her."

"I bought it so you wouldn't have to as often, and she could take herself around."

Dad and I stare each other down. This is my cue to back down, but I refuse. The raging fire in my heart has grown too large to bear, and this has gone on for far too long. Not even Annabella, my estranged older sister, wants to talk to me anymore, thinking I side with Dad's abusive outbursts by paying his rent. She always believed cutting Dad off was the only way to rescue herself, and therefore, anyone who associates with him has to go - no matter if I was the one person who truly understood what she went through.

But what the fuck else can I do? How else can I help Mom out of this imprisoning cycle, other than picking her up and running out the door?

Not even that will stop Dad from getting her back — he's the only one who knows her caretaking routine, inside and out, and the only one of us who can lift her dozens of times per day. Mom is trapped here. Just like I was.

After looking back and forth between us from the toilet, Mom laughs, waving her hand at Dad to shut the door. "Oh, stop, you two. Let a poor old woman pee, won't you?"

"You're not old," I mutter.

But Dad closes the door, bumping the wheelchair against my shins.

Without the bathroom light, the hallway dims. I can't track Dad's eyes.

But he simply points down the hall.

My heart beats so quickly that each pulse physically hurts. He's about to snap.

But I won't move. If I move away from this door, out of Mom's earshot, he'll be able to do much worse.

Clenching my fists, I lower to a whisper. "I just want to help Mom."

"And not me, huh? We all know what you're really saying. Even after raising you, your ungrateful sister, *and* my wife, I'm never doing anything well enough for your liking."

Guilt creases my confidence, but I can't show it. I won't.

He puffs his chest. "I have this handled. You've done plenty, paying part of the rent for your feeble, old parents. You don't need to keep playing the hero."

Venomous words attempt to belittle me. It's working. It always works. It never stops hurting, no matter how silent or loud or strong or weak or obedient or rebellious I've made myself appear, just like Annabella. She attempted to overpower him with even bigger fits, but Mom only saw her teenage rage, and Dad knew how to avoid Mom's gaze or guilt us into keeping quiet - until Annabella allowed herself to be the villain and "abandon" us early. I know she still hurts, even though she left. She was the abandoned one.

And secretly, I feel abandoned too. It never stops hurting because *Dad* never stops. He never will, not until the day he dies.

"I just want to help Mom," I repeat myself calmly, like I'm talking to a three-year-old throwing a tantrum.

Dad steps closer, shooting my frantic heartbeat through the roof.

But Mom shouts from behind the door. "I'm done!"

I reach for the handle, but Dad sucks in a tight breath. I

flinch away. Dad turns the doorknob to help Mom wipe, flush, and wash her hands.

Biting my lip, I force down hot tears. I can't let Mom see me upset and make her feel even worse. Stepping into the shadows behind Dad's back, I duck my head, using my bangs to keep my eyes out of sight. As my parents exit the bathroom, Dad's tall shoulders hide me from Mom's view. He strides down the hall back into my old bedroom.

Snapping out of my daze, I grip Mom's chair, dashing down the hall with it. Even if I can't lift her, I need this chair by her side. I need her to live - at least long enough for me to finally become strong enough to take her home with me.

But as I breach my doorway, Dad steps out first.

He closes Mom's door.

"Is everything okay?" She calls through it.

"One second," Dad calls back.

There's an edge to his voice. Before he even acts, I know what's about to happen: after bottling every minor insult or inconvenience in his life for months, his resentment has compiled high enough for everything to spill over in a seething rage.

Destruction clouds his eyes. He's staring at the wheelchair, reaching for it. I gasp, shooting my hand in front of the chair.

"Don't!" I cry.

He grips my hand instead. I freeze, zipping my focus to him to read every one of his minuscule facial shifts to know how to protect myself. But he hasn't stopped scowling.

And he hasn't let go.

Dad hasn't physically hurt me in almost fifteen years, but the veins bulging on his forehead tell me I won't escape today without it. Panic floods my throbbing veins. What's he going to do next? Now that I've pushed him far enough to snap, I don't know. I never know.

"You really think you can do this better than me? That I haven't sacrificed my life enough for her? You know better - you're not strong enough to carry her. Leave it to me."

He grips even harder. I gasp, tempted to scream, but I don't want to upset Mom. She worsens from stress. I pull at his fingers instead - struggling to tear them off me and prevent him from crushing my wrist and half of my palm with his wide grasp.

But I can't stop him now either. I feel young. So feeble.

"Are you listening to me, Lilibeth? This is your final warning. Stop meddling," he hisses.

Before I can stop myself, my face contorts into ugly, frantic tears. I'm breathing harder by the second, hardly able to choke out my words. "T-that h-*hurts*."

Dad blinks, gaping as if he just realized his hand was wrapped tight around me.

Snapping his hand back, Dad's eyebrows contort. "Shit, sorry, I— I didn't mean to–"

When he meets my wide, panicked eyes, Dad can't bear to witness how small he's made me feel for more than a millisecond. Darting away, he leaves me to stoop over my hand, babying it to my chest. Dad dashes to the kitchen for wine, followed by the rattle of keys and a resounding thud of the front door slamming.

I release a slow, heaving exhale. Every heartbeat rips through my aching wrist and hand, but at least I'm okay. I'm alive.

"Lily, are you out there?" Mom's fear squeaks from her voice, even from behind the door.

"Coming." I use my jacket sleeve to hurriedly dry my tears and wipe my nose before pulling my other sleeve over my shaking hand. It hurts so badly that I'm too afraid to move it yet and discover how badly he damaged me.

Crossing my unharmed arm over me to awkwardly open the door, I shuffle in with a weak smile.

"Lilibeth, did you two have another disagreement?"

Dropping myself into the armchair beside her, I feel too heavy to move. Too weak to carry Mom. If I didn't know Dad was drinking away his guilt on the porch, I'd force myself to jump back up and kidnap Mom to safety.

But either way, Dad sucked out every last flicker of energy in my cells.

"Sweetheart, don't mind him. You know how he is, and it's best to just not even start." She sighs. "You know his dad treated him so badly, and it really changed your father. Thankfully, your dad's nothing like his dad with those tremendous, alcoholic rages, forcing poor Elizabeth to replace every window in the house. At least your dad's not abusive."

"He is," I whisper.

Silence hangs between us.

Fuck, I shouldn't have said that.

As expected, Mom sniffles through tears. I rush to her side, but she's still smiling. "I'm so sorry, Lily. I know he says hurtful things when he gets mad. I swear he doesn't mean it."

My lip wobbles. She still has no idea the extent to which Dad has hurt me, but even this breaks her heart. What if I don't know how badly he hurts her either?

Either way, she hasn't stepped back far enough to realize what I have; no matter Dad's reasoning, there's no reason big enough to lay a hand on us.

All I can do is hug Mom. Hold her while I can. "I almost have enough saved to take you home to stay with me and take the stress off you both. I'm sorry it's taking so long."

"Oh, sweetheart, stop being so hard on yourself. Look at me."

I can't. Keeping my head bowed and my throbbing hand limp in my lap, I pull back from our hug. Mom tucks my hair behind my ear.

"Lilibeth, I want you to live for yourself, not for me. Keep working your way up at that restaurant like you're so good at, and forget about the rest. I'm happy for you that you've made a new friend. Can you tell me about him?"

I swallow hard, still reeling from my dad. My relationship with Remington feels like an entirely separate world, and I'm struggling to reorient myself in all of space and time. "He's really sweet. Sweeter than anyone I know - other than you."

Mom laughs. "Are you pregnant?"

Nothing reorients me faster than that question. I sputter out a laugh. "Mom, no! I still have an IUD, anyway."

She laughs. "You just have this glow about you, but maybe it's because you're in love."

Biting my lip, I giggle. "I– um– Well, we just officially scheduled a real date, but I haven't felt like this before."

Mom's genuine smile ages her backward. I'm so relieved to see it that I settle into our conversation with loosened shoulders - and Mom has plenty of questions about Remington.

By the time I'm heading out the door, I regain a bit of the confidence Dad stripped from me. He tracks me as I pass by on the porch.

"Bye, Lily," he mutters.

"Bye," I grumble.

"Wait."

I freeze on instinct, but I immediately regret it. Dad stands from his porch chair, and I allow myself to peek back despite rushing faster to my car.

"I said, wait, jeez." Dad quietly chuckles, as if it could soften the blistering tension between us. He's leaning over the porch railing, holding out an ice pack.

Staring into his worried eyes, I'm tempted to remind him why I need one at all. But I know what he'll say: he snapped because *I* meddled, pushing him past his limits.

To spare myself further hell, I take the ice pack.

"Love you." He gives me puppy-dog eyes.

Gritting my teeth, I open my car door and chuck the ice pack into the passenger's seat. "You too."

I zig-zag a few blocks until I find a random enough street to stop where Dad wouldn't expect to find me. It's awkward to drive with one hand, especially making so many turns, but I'd rather be safe than see him pull up behind me ever again in my lifetime.

I wanted to drive home before the sun fully set, but I still feel like hell - a hangover-like exhaustion weighing down my chest, enough to prevent me from sitting straight. Plus, I need to assess the damage on my hand: whether I need to call in sick this weekend.

But as soon as I shakily spread my fingers, I heave a sigh of relief. I'll definitely have bruises by tonight, but nothing is broken.

Tears spill. Not in sadness, but in an immense, building rage. It shreds through my panting breath, begging me to act.

I don't know what to do when I get like this. How to let it out. I want to go back in time and smack Dad's hands off me. Better yet, I want to punch him in his bitter fucking face.

I smack my steering wheel with my good hand instead, letting out a sharp scream.

Shock freezes me in place. I never hit things.

I'm not becoming like Dad, am I?

No, things have just changed. I'm not 18, I have my own place, away from Dad, and I've finally been working out.

And now I have Remington.

I'm not used to being treated like shit anymore.

My hands shake as I open our texts, tapping Remington's number. It rings a few times as I struggle to breathe through leftover rage, and my stomach wavers. It's past seven, so he's probably at Club X. Maybe I should just let him work.

But just as I drop my phone from my ear, his low voice rumbles through the speakers.

"Hello?"

My whole body slackens. I drop my forehead onto the top of my steering wheel, raising my phone back onto my ear. "Hey, Rem. Sorry to bother you, I just– I just wanted to say 'hi.'"

Distant shouts echo in the background of our call until it's suddenly silent. With the rush of wind into the receiver, Remington softens his voice. "Sorry, I was still on my way outside. Are you okay? I'm really worried."

My heart flips. "O-oh. How come?"

"Your nose sounds stuffy like it does when you've been crying. Did something bad happen?"

I exhale hard, closing my eyes. "I really don't know how to explain."

Remington hums. "That's okay, sweet girl. I'm here for you, okay? Want to meet after my shift for a hug?"

Warmth floods my chest. It's such a startling difference from the dark, hollow ache there that I need a second to breathe through it. When I can finally speak, my voice wobbles through soft, weeping tears. "I'm out of town, and I just needed to talk to someone I feel good around."

Remington huffs through a soft laugh. "That's too damn sweet. Now I'm dying to hug you even more. Are you sure you'll be okay?"

"Yes," I whisper. "I'm excited to see you tomorrow."

"I'm excited to see you too."

I hang up with my smile restored despite my sore heart.

CHAPTER SIX

It's the first time I've seen Remington's eyebrow piercing in, now that we're not meeting just to work out. The hardware adds a striking intensity to his dark eyes, stirring longing low in my belly.

Remington is decked in black: sleek pants belted with black, jingling chains and a silky button-up with the first two buttons open, baring more of his gorgeous, branching chest and neck tattoo than I've ever seen. But best of all, Remington's grin feels ten times warmer now that I know it's for me - for our first official date, in particular. With our tight, excited hug, I'm smiling wider than ever too.

"Would you like to hold hands?" Remington extends his palm for me.

My heart flips in giddy delight. I hold out my right hand, living purely in the moment. But I freeze; I almost gave Remington my injured hand.

I try to laugh off my awkward pause. "I'd love to, but can we switch sides?"

Remington smiles, raising the opposite eyebrow to his one lifted cheek. "Sure. Is your left hand better for some particular reason?"

I laugh. "Oh, no. I just got an injury on my other hand."

Remington stops walking. "Oh, no, can I see? Was it from work?"

I hesitate; it's absolutely not from work, and the visible finger marks on my hand and wrist prove it.

But I don't want to hide the truth from sweet Rem. I cautiously raise my hand, allowing him to see. "Um, there's not much showing since I put makeup on it."

At least, I thought there wasn't. But even under the hazy streetlamp, the bruises still show a sickly teal beneath three layers of foundation.

Remington's eyes sharpen darker than when he chased Josh out of his own gym.

After a painfully silent second, Remington's heated breath lowers his voice. "Who grabbed you hard enough to bruise?"

My shoulders raise. "I wanted to visit my mom since she's not well, but my dad and I don't agree on how to take care of her."

Remington stares at my hand, unblinking for what feels like ages. Then he grabs his hair, letting out a helpless sound. "No, Lilibeth, really?"

I hate seeing him so sad, and it's all my fault.

I shrink, but Remington turns back to me with contorted eyebrows and a panicked stare. His voice comes out strained and quiet. "Oh, this is *so* awful. How often does he do this?"

"Not often - at least, not physically. It's been many, many years, actually, but I think it changed because I– I was feeling braver lately, thanks to you– O-or, us. If there's an us?"

His eyes soften. "I'd love there to be."

I beam. "Me too."

"But what does that have to do with being brave?"

"I set him off by standing up to him for once. I'm sorry," I rasp.

Remington stoops as if I've physically crushed him. He delicately grabs my cheeks. "Sweet, sweet girl, never apologize for this. I can't imagine why anyone would feel the need to do this to you, let alone a dad to his own daughter. He's supposed to protect you, not bruise you."

Oh, my heart felt those words - a gnawing ache appears,

rooted deep in my soul. I look down, unable to withstand the sorrow in Remington's stare. Seeing it from a distance, I know what he's saying is correct, but after visiting my parents, I fell right back into the panicked, fragile state my dad put me in when I left home at 18, especially since he did feel guilty, and he did try to repair it in his own way. It's so confusing - receiving care from someone who turns violent in a flash. That's why Remington's touch, his words, and his gentle voice feel so new, no matter how many times he washes affection over me. His affection doesn't rely on a threat.

Remington's soft sigh carries an ache that stings my heart. "Can I rub out the bruise for you throughout the night?"

I bite my lip, tears pricking my eyes. I've never had anyone else help me do that before, but that's exactly what I planned on doing before bed so I didn't have to keep wasting makeup.

But I nod. "T-thank you. That would be nice."

His shoulders soften. "Okay."

Gingerly placing my hand into his palm, he lays my fingers flat before applying gentle, circling pressure along the bruise.

"Is this too painful?" He whispers.

I shake my head, struggling even more to keep myself from crying. My heart feels so protected by him.

Remington's breath shakes. "Oh, God. Do you need a hug or some space? Are you still okay to eat dinner?"

I softly laugh, blinking away my threatened tears. Stroking Remington's cheek, I give him the best reassuring smile I can manage. "Really, Rem, I'm okay. You sound more upset than I've been over it. Let's just go eat dinner."

He grows exceptionally quiet, straightening. But as we grasp hands, resuming our short walk to the restaurant, he mutters, "I wondered why you didn't seem to stay traumatized for more than a day after what that trainer did. But of course that asshole trainer's abuse didn't feel any different to you. You're swimming in it already, probably your whole life, so it was just another day."

I don't know what to say. He nailed down an aspect of myself that I've struggled to put together for a long time. Why I'm so quiet, so guarded, and so unable to do the things I want.

And I'm still at a loss on what to do about it. How to fix me.

All I can do is huddle my whole side against Remington's tattooed arm, keeping my head lowered as we walk. Just before we enter the restaurant doors, Remington slows to a stop.

"Hey, can you look at me for a second?"

My heart flips, but I want to. Especially now that I know there's an "us."

When I peek up at him, he softens into a gentle smile. "There you go. I'm sorry we started off the night so heavily, but it's not your fault, okay? You don't have to believe it yet, but please at least listen to me; you deserve better than this."

I huff out a smile, hurriedly blinking away my watery eyes. "Thank you. You're the actual sweet one."

"Oh, *I'm* the sweet one? Are you sure about that?" He hums, turning to wrap his arms around me. I'm so relieved to see his half-up smile that I giggle, softening into his embrace.

"Yes, I'm sure," I whisper.

We hold each other outside the restaurant, beaming. At one point, Remington sidesteps to allow another couple into the doorway, swooping me out of the way. "Sorry, folks. I got a little distracted by this rockstar here. Seriously, where did you get this sick studded jacket? I want one."

My bright giggle warms his smile into a three-quarter grin, this time with teeth. I've never seen it on him before, so I can't stop my eyes from widening.

Remington blinks fast when he looks back at me. "You look like you're up to something."

I laugh. "I just have a cute– A cute gym buddy, um, boyfriend?"

His sharp, startling laugh swirls through my heart. "I cannot *believe* someone this cute exists. You really want to be my girlfriend?"

I give him an extra squeeze. "Of course. Are you teasing me?"

He chuckles, bending just enough to kiss my forehead

through my bangs. My heart genuinely stops for a split second, restarting with a leaping sprint. Remington pulls back to find me breathless and stunned silent. He sputters into laughter. "Alright, in this case, I'm taking my girlfriend inside before she starves to death."

Remington loves to knit. I never thought to imagine those powerful, inked arms weaving yarn into delicate, beautiful patterns, but the second he's honest with me about his hobby, I can see it perfectly; his hands on me range from whisper-gentle to deliciously firm, speaking of his sensitivity to the material or person he's touching.

But he's right. If this is what real love feels like, I don't feel hurt by Remington. Love shouldn't hurt.

Maybe it's too soon to call it love, but the more questions we ask each other about our hobbies, favorite shows, and random stories from our childhood, the more I ache to watch candlelight glimmering in his black eyes for years to come.

Remington catches me staring, shifting into a gentle smile. "You look beautiful in the candlelight."

I bite back my smile. "You stole my thoughts. I was just thinking you look beautiful too."

Remington's eyebrows soften into startled seriousness, and a jolt snaps through my chest. If I called my high school ex beautiful, he'd hate me for feminizing him.

"U-um, sorry–" I sputter.

But Remington's seriousness shatters into a tense concern, his eyebrows arching. "Oh, no, sweet girl. I thought it was sweet. Just surprising to hear someone say that about me. But not– Not bad."

"Oh," I whisper.

As my shoulders soften, the more vulnerable Remington

looks: less of a panther and more of a sad kitten. I want to hold him.

But Remington drops my stare, looking at my arm. "Can I hold your hand again?"

I break into a smile. "Please."

Lifting my bruise-less hand, I reach for Remington. But then I remember he wanted to rub out my bruises tonight. Flushing deep, I switch hands, passing over my injured one.

Remington doesn't move at first. When I glance at him, the surprise on his lifted eyebrows quickly snuffs out - like he didn't want me to see. Shit, maybe I understood incorrectly. What if my bruise is triggering or disturbing for Remington to see too?

But his soft, sweeping touch scoops up my hand, settling our palms together. He's so careful with my hand that a fuzzy warmth seeps up my arm, settling my tense shoulders.

Remington softly skates his thumb over my bruises. "Does it hurt to hold hands?"

"No," I whisper.

Within seconds, Remington has me laughing again, chatting about nothing and everything. But all my focus is on our hands; it's never felt so powerful and warm to hold someone's hand. I run my thumb over him in return, hoping he feels just as good.

"I want to take care of you too," I blurt out.

He chuckles, rubbing my thumb back. "That's sweet, but what exactly do you mean by taking care of me?"

"You've helped me feel more secure, and I'd love to help you feel the same, somehow. E-even though I'm not sure how, or if I can."

He looked touched until the last part, a crease forming between his brows. "What do you mean, you don't think you can?"

"I don't know how to say nice things to make you feel good, like you do. Or how to ask hard questions, even if I care about the answer - or care about the people I'm asking about, with my whole heart."

Remington breaks into a sly grin. "Is that a deeper confession than the one we already had at the gym?"

I flush, ducking my head. What do I even say to that? The answer in my heart screams "yes," but that feels too massive to share this early.

Remington chuckles. "Sorry, I had to tease you back a little. You have no idea what you're doing to me."

I peek at him. "I want to know."

"Oh?" Remington leans back in his chair.

He looks so cool and casual, relaxing back so fluidly that his long arms seem to stretch on forever - still able to softly hold my hand. The butterflies in my belly flutter even lower. I have to cross my legs to relieve the aching desire between them.

But Remington happily sighs. "Listen, I find you so endearing, sexy, and sweet. You might not think you're capable of being supportive verbally, but you do a lot for me without needing words. You help me feel safe just by being yourself."

I lean in until I'm pressed against the table. "So do you, truly. That's why I'm so curious about you. Like about what you want in life or don't, and what you enjoy, a-and also about—" I check over both shoulders before softening my voice. "About how you feel about where you work and— And what your interests arc there."

He studies me for a while, leaving me to fidget in silence. "Am I hearing right that you'd like to go to the club with me?"

I shrink. "I don't know. I think so, but it's new for me, so I don't know what I'll actually feel. But I've also been curious for a long time. Like, since Gabby and I started talking about it - and that was a few years ago."

Remington's half-up grin appears. "Have you been talking to Gabby more about the club then?"

My heart flips. "Yes, but— But my worries are the same as always, and they're not about you. I don't know if I'd like being around a lot of people for these types of things, but- um— privately might be okay, maybe–"

Leaning forward, Remington stops me before my rising shoulders hit my ears, his gentle touch brushing my arm. "Hey, hey, it's okay. There's no rush to share anything intimate right away. You don't have to tell me anything unless you want to — and also feel ready."

His words should relieve me, but I drop my focus to our empty plates, a sense of defeat dropping like a bowling ball in my gut.

But Remington's voice deepens. "Although, if you were already interested in what Gabby and I are into and feel ready to just take a peek, maybe I can show you around soon."

I gasp, jolting upright. His gaze flickers over me, so I grip my napkin for support.

He dropped his offer as if it were a casual invitation, but I know it's not. If Remington trusts me to visit Club X with him, that's opening yet another heavy door between us that I've been craving to look behind.

"Y-yes, I– I'd like– I'd *love* to."

Remington settles back into his chair with a bright laugh. "You really are so sweet. How about next Tuesday night, when there's not as much of a crowd?"

I smile. "Oh. Thank you. Yes."

"Of course. But just to be perfectly open with you, it's a personal rule of mine to keep things vanilla until we've discussed formal consent in detail."

My chest loosens. "Okay, yes, I like that. And I expected it. I've researched this a lot."

Remington's eyebrows raise. "Oh, yeah?"

"Yeah. Before we met, but also lately. Just in case we– um– dated, and you wanted to do anything like this with me and were okay with me wanting to keep it private."

He grins wider with my every word. "Now I *really* can't wait to talk about this more with you on Tuesday."

"Can we have a discussion about formal consent there?" I blurt out.

Remington looks just as surprised as I am for asking such a tremendous question to rocket our path forward.

But Remington melts into a heavy-lidded smile, drawing warmth into my lower belly. "You're that interested in playing with me?"

I nod. "B-but if you're not, or it's too early, I understand."

He shuts his eyes before leaning forward with a groan. "Oh, no, sweet girl. I can just feel that pull between us, and I'm still worried I'll want to go too quickly for you. If you hadn't suggested it first, I'd keep questioning myself if you wanted to go this far, maybe ever."

"I do," I whisper. "Is this not normal?"

He brings my hand to his lips. The soft kiss he plants on my bruised wrist steals my breath. "No, not for me. I almost never play with anyone. Only two people in my adult life."

I suck in a tight breath. My racing heartbeat throbs in my groin. "T-thank you."

"Thank *you*, Lilibeth. This is kind of a big deal for me."

"For *you?*"

He laughs, sitting back. "My job title might make that confusing, but I mean it. I'm—" He hums, twisting his lips. "It takes a lot for me to want to open up."

As his dark stare dissolves into pure vulnerability, my heart tears at the seams. He's trusting me, even though it's scary. Just like I'm trusting him.

I break into a smile. "T-that makes me feel special."

"Good," he rumbles. "Because you are."

Huddling together, our chat extends beyond just some extra sexy fun; I feel like we've shifted our friendship into the most romantic friendship I've ever experienced.

We're growing into each other's presence by the minute, laughing just as much as we settle in to whisper secrets. I wish tomorrow was Tuesday.

CHAPTER SEVEN

Gripping my black bomber jacket with clammy palms, I hunch over myself on the bus, trying to will away my nausea. I can't back down now: I know I don't want to. I already texted Remington photos of my latest STI test results, just like he did. We flirted heavily afterward, leading me to have to hide from Celeste, hopping into the shower to properly fantasize and quell my arousal. I want this, and I want Remington; I'm attracted to him enough to erase the sexual anxiety that usually prevents me from climaxing. All I have to do is think about his hands applying firm pressure to my hips again, and my toys hoist me over the edge with squirming legs.

But now that Tuesday is here, I'm gut-wrenchingly anxious.

I probably care too much about what Remington thinks, but I can't help it. No matter how hard I try - wearing my faux-leather platform boots, a ruched black top that flaunts my cleavage, and the coolest jacket I own with patches, chains, and even more studs than my last one - I'm still about to look like an awkward, lost doe at Club X.

Who am I kidding that I could actually be entertaining enough to play with someone as experienced as Remington? He'll probably think it's a nuisance to have to teach me every little nuance he's known for years.

But the second I step off the bus, Remington's brightening stare erases my thoughts. Chains grace his hips, a collarless and ripped black T-shirt hangs low on his chest, and a string is the only thing tying together the front of his tight pants. He looks like a lead singer, but he's gaping at me as if I'm glorious.

I laugh, dropping my head, but Remington steps closer. Hugging me tight, his deep, welcoming hum sends a happy shiver down my back.

"You look *gorgeous*, L.L.B." He pulls back to look me up and down again in his arms, and I smile wider.

"You look amazing too, Rem."

But Remington pauses, biting his lip.

My heart drops. "What's wrong?"

"You've looked incredibly cute every time I've seen you, no matter what you wear. I just hope you aren't trying to change your style for my sake."

"Oh," I mutter. Glancing at my boots, my heart hurts.

"Fuck. Sorry. I hurt your feelings." Remington rubs my shoulders, but I shrug.

"No, I– I knew I tried too hard to fit in. I haven't had a chance to wear this in a while–"

"Fuck, yep, you owned this outfit already. I shouldn't have assumed you weren't walking around like a badass every day. Way to be big-headed and make it all about yourself, Remington." With every passing word, Remington's sentences race faster. "Actually, I should've known you'd look like this. You look sicker than me, and you aren't even inked. God, I sounded like such a dope. You think you don't fit in here? No, you could own the goddamn club–"

Sputtering out a laugh, I give his arm a squeeze. "Remington, it's okay!"

He groans, playfully rocking me back and forth by the shoulders. "No, no, it's not. I just– I brought my own baggage to that comment and fucked up our greeting. Let's try again. Stay right here."

Before I can speak, Remington flips away from me and speedwalks down the sidewalk. My feet beg me to chase after him, but I remember he told me to stay put just in time, halting myself in place. I laugh when he glances over his shoulder, pretending to catch sight of me with an over-exaggerated, gaping jaw.

"Lilibeth Norris?! Is that you?"

A genuine laugh rises from me as multiple strangers turn to watch us reunite on the sidewalk. Opening my arms, I allow Remington to crash against my chest. Except he comes barreling faster than I expect, glomping onto me heavily enough to nearly take me out. I shriek through laughter, clinging to his back as he steadies me on my feet.

When he pulls back with his sly half-grin, I beam at him. Our noses are just an inch from brushing each other. I hadn't realized we lingered this closely until his quick, huffing laugh tickles my lips, flipping my stomach upside down.

"You're cute," he whispers.

"You're goofy," I mutter. "In a cute way."

Remington stares for a second too long. Except that second extends into another. And another. I'm still in his arms, but neither of us moves to let go. A tremendous pressure in my chest begs me to lean in and kiss him for the first time. But I've never done something so daring. Or been the first one to kiss a man. Would he be okay with it?

But as excitement ignites behind Remington's soulful, jet-black eyes, I suddenly feel like I'm about to be attacked by a golden retriever. My mouth pulls into an even wider smile.

Then I'm forced to blink.

"*Boop.*" Remington pokes the tip of my nose. Then he whips away from me. "Alright, now that you've been booped, you've been granted official entry into Club X. You're welcome here, you belong here, and no one can argue with it."

He puts his arm around me, guiding us straight for Club X, and my heart flips. I thought I'd be terrified entering these doors, but instead, I'm laughing.

Club X sucks us into a moody, electric dimension, hot pink

LEDs lining the ceilings with not much else to light our way. Faces form as blurry shadows while my eyes adjust to the darkness, but Remington nods at everyone we pass, chatting up a few of them. They're eyeing me; I'm tucked against the Dungeon Monitor's side. But I'd rather stick close to Remington. There are far more people here than I anticipated for a slow Tuesday.

A sweaty man in only leather short-shorts and boots passes close by us. His back has been patched with gauze, but blood still seeps through. My stomach plunges. I'm not sure I'd be into anything like that.

Music drowns out the party that appears to be raging at the hallway's end: the dungeon. Even after all my mental preparation, I'm not sure I'm ready to see what's behind those steel, crackle-painted black doors. I grip Remington tighter.

But he veers us to a short hall on our left. At the end of the hall, a few people chat on a tufted couch. They're in each other's laps, cuddling in a playful chat. One woman, clad in leather, catches sight of us. The second I see her commanding, sharp stare through her mask, I know she's a dominatrix.

But before I can worry that I'm disturbing her happy place, she cheerily waves to us, giving me a sweet smile. My shoulders settle, and I brightly wave back.

As Remington opens the door to a private room, he leans in to whisper in my ear. "Holy shit, you got a smile out of Miss X."

"Oh. No wonder I feel like I've been blessed," I mumble.

Remington's sharp, abrupt laugh echoes into the private room, hardly muffled by the emerald green tufted couch or cushy bed in the corner. I bite back my smile, unable to fully relax as the door shuts behind us; that "cushy" bed also has icy metal cuffs hanging from all four corners. The dresser beside it must be full of flogging toys.

The sudden silence brings my pounding heartbeat into focus. I track Remington as he fluffs pillows, plopping himself on one end of the couch. Trailing after him, I drop my purse on the matching emerald ottoman, sitting as close to Remington as my heart can manage. We're just sitting side by side, but now that I have him all to myself, even leaving 6 inches between us feels startlingly intimate.

I know it's obvious I'm nervous. Remington chatters away with me, shaking off the nerves as we discuss his job at Club X and how my shifts at Salucci's were this week.

Once we're settled in, Remington's lowering voice rumbles across the walls. "Before we jump into our formal talk, I have a bit of a difficult question for you."

My heart flips. Is this when Remington admits he's not sure I can handle this?

Remington glances at me, clasping his hands in different directions in a nervous fidget. "What makes you interested in doing this with me?" Anxiety spirals throughout my body, but Remington rubs his thumb joint. "Sorry, I– I know it's a big question. And I know we like each other. That's no secret. But I guess I'm trying to ask, why me? Like is the end goal in this mainly sex, or…?"

Silence hangs over me - a million times heavier than ten soup pots. I curl into myself, unable to translate my thoughts into words.

It took far more than sexual desire to get me here. I've been terrified of expressing myself sexually for so long that I never even considered visiting Club X, even with Gabby's peer pressure. But the second I saw Remington, a deeper part of me opened up, wanting to be seen by him.

No, not just be seen by him - to see him too.

But how do I explain that in Club X terms?

"I want to please you," I blurt out. Remington's body language from the corner of my eye gives no hints as to what he's thinking, but I know he must see my shoulders curling into themselves.

"Sexually?" He asks.

I don't want to lie. "Yes, that's one part of it."

Remington doesn't say anything. I peek at him to find him staring. He's so serious but so neutral that I can't read him.

So, I continue. "B-but not *just* sexually. Like, I like how it feels when you say good things about me, and I want you to be able to feel how nice it is too."

Oh, he's too stunning - an extra sharpness to his black hair today with that piercing and decked-out skin, crowning him a badass king on this emerald throne of a couch. I can't bear looking anywhere near him, so I duck my chin.

"I-I guess what I meant to say is, I want you to feel nice, happy, and fulfilled. And I want to be the one you feel that way around since I– I feel that way around you. And I'd be really happy if that included sex someday too, but even without it, it's been amazing just getting closer to you. I guess what I really mean is, I like seeing you pleased."

Remington's shoulders soften. After a long pause, he turns to me. "Sorry, I'm just gathering my thoughts since I'm feeling oddly shy, myself. Can I play with your hair?"

Loosening my wound shoulders, I break into a smile. "Yes."

With a delicate trace over my cheek, he tucks my hair behind my ear. His fingers follow a straight line to the back of my head, softly stroking my hair at its roots. My eyelashes flutter, and Remington hums. By the time he reaches the back of my neck to give it a gentle massage, I'm burning inside - enough to flush to my chest.

Remington's voice is low and soft. "You're achieving that right now, Lilibeth - treating me back with a warm and fuzzy feeling. I'm *so* pleased by you. Thank you for sharing your thoughts with me."

I duck my head.

"Are you uncomfortable with eye contact?"

Remington's abrupt question sends a jolt through my chest.

"No," I say. "But also yes."

"Hmm. Can you tell me more?"

"S-sure. No, I'm not uncomfortable since I like it. But yes, I'm uncomfortable, and that's also because I like it. I like it a lot."

"So you feel big feelings when we look at each other?" He asks.

"Yes," I whisper.

"I feel them too. That's why I felt shy."

My heart throbs so hard that my stomach won't stop somersaulting.

But I choose to look at Remington anyway. It feels ten times more intense knowing that he could feel even a fraction of the excitement, anxiety, and delight I'm experiencing.

He tilts his head. "So, just to clarify, when you said you'd like to please me, you meant in other ways than sexually?"

"Yes, in as many as you'd like. S-so I wanted to ask during our formal consent discussion about what types of affection you like. And about anything else that makes you happy. Like why you enjoy working out."

He hums, fiddling with the edge of his jacket. "Why I like working out is complicated. I want to feel physically powerful enough to protect people I care about."

I hum, just like Remington. "That sounds like you. B-but what about the affection part?"

He laughs. "I love how tenacious you are. You're not letting me get away with sharing unequally, huh?"

I bite my lip, but this time, I don't look away.

Remington holds my gaze. He doesn't smile. Instead, he softly touches the bottom of my chin. "Look at you. You're doing so well in such a short time, and I'm so goddamn impressed." His voice drops as he leans in. "I'll tell you a secret: this is the type of affection I like most. Watching you slowly unravel beside me. Trusting me enough to witness it."

I feel like my insides have been lit on fire. I don't know how to speak or breathe. I just know I want to be close to Remington. Touch him.

"C-can I hold your hand?" I ask.

Remington's eyes sharpen. "Yes."

He opens his palm for me. Even though I hesitate, I drag my

fingers up it. He's so warm. Calluses line the top of his palm, but the rest of his hand feels ridiculously soft. Remington adjusts to meet my touch until our fingers slip together. Giving me a slight squeeze, Remington stokes the fire in my belly.

"Big feelings" doesn't cover this. My heart screams that I'm holding a hand I want to hold for ages. Even if it's not forever, a tugging, guiding pull in my chest overpowers everything except now. Without the future in the way, all I want is to be beside Remington in the present.

Rubbing the back of his hand with my thumb, I sputter out air, unable to put words together to describe the sensations in my chest.

Remington brushes my cheek again, sending tingles down my neck. "Talk to me. Even if it comes out wrong."

"I want to touch you more," I blurt out.

His eyebrows raise. I blink a few times, struggling to catch up with reality. Why did I say it like that? That sounded much more sexual than I meant for it to - and right after Remington sounded concerned about me only wanting him for sex.

But Remington uncrosses his foot over his knee, placing both soles on the ground to scoot closer to me. There's no gap between our thighs now.

Running his free hand down my arm, Remington softens his voice just above a whisper. "There you go. You've got yourself all wrong, Lilibeth. I see you working so hard to achieve more and more of what you want, but you're actually taking the hardest steps that most people wouldn't dare. Ever since we've met, you've been a little powerhouse."

"Still little, though."

He laughs. "I'll give you that."

His hand slides to my lower back, drawing a line of pleasure down my core. I suck in a tight breath.

Remington freezes. "Should I stop?"

I don't know what to say. I like it, and I like that he remembers how sensitive it feels for me, but his touch on such a vulnerable area feels overwhelming today - while we're at Club X, in particular.

But I've already let Remington touch my lower back before. And what if this is a test? What if he's a dom, like I'm suspecting? Does he want me to say "yes?"

Either way, I've taken too long to reply. Remington removes his hand, and I deflate. "Sorry."

"There's nothing to be sorry about. You're allowed to say 'no.'"

I loosen in relief without meaning to.

But Remington becomes startlingly serious. He turns to face me directly.

"I want to be clear about something. You have full autonomy, and you always will."

My heart hammers into my throat. "And you too, right?"

Remington swallows hard. The intensity behind his stare dims, and I fidget a little, unsure if I should be feeling such a deep need in my lower belly during this serious discussion.

But Remington speaks even softer. "Yes, if we're good partners toward each other, we'd both have full autonomy, even during any extreme type of play. And let's say you're interested in pursuing some type of kink or BDSM together. Everything we'd do would be discussed and agreed upon, and forever changing. Even if we end up doing something for years, you could still change your mind one day, and I wouldn't do it again unless you asked."

I tighten my belly to stifle my excitement. "Y-years?"

He chuckles, copying my eager lean with a slow, drooping weight into his arm over the couch's back behind my shoulders. "That's another big secret I'm afraid to share with you. Because I don't do these things with just anyone. I wouldn't have even brought you here if I didn't feel strongly about you. I'm just shy as fuck about how hard I'm crushing on you, L.L.B."

Biting my lip doesn't stop my elated giggle. "Just a crush?"

"Okay, yeah, 'crushing' is really underselling it. I really, *really* like you."

I can't stop smiling. "I really like you too, Rem. A lot, a lot, like you said."

He groans. "You're so cute. It's totally derailing my focus from our formal discussion. But did you hear me about agreeing on everything beforehand and still being able to change your mind?"

"Yes. And I'd do the same for you."

He strokes my arm. "Good. I'll remind you while you're still new to the process, but I want to make sure you're comfortable and understand as we go."

Heat rises between us as we remain closer than ever. Remington's gaze wanders over me, leaving tingles in its wake with just his eyes.

But then he hums. "I'd also like you to be able to say 'no' to me before we try anything kinky. Do you think you can?"

I hesitate. Where I grew up, that wasn't an option. With how heavily my heart wavers in defeat, I'm terrified my fears are coming true; I'm nowhere near Remington's level of communication.

But Remington places his hand over my knee, sparking warmth up my thigh. "Hey, it's okay. If that's too scary for you, this all can wait."

My heart sears in my chest. "O-oh. You don't want to do this anymore?"

"Breathe. I'm still right here." Remington cuddles closer, softening his voice. "I do, but kink and BDSM can be hardcore, and your heart is precious. I can't do anything with you unless I know what you do or don't want. If I went ahead anyway, I wouldn't deserve your trust."

My whole body softens into him. "You're sweet, Remington."

Remington shakes his head. "This is the bare minimum, so if you've never had it like this, you deserved better before. I had to learn that too."

I don't like how he phrased that. If he meant he struggled to learn consent like other men who were taught they're owed everything, I feel like he would've called himself out, as usual.

Someone must've betrayed his consent. But the tense way he's avoiding my eyes tells me he's not ready to open up about that just yet.

"C-can I hold your hand again?" I whisper.

A soft smile pulls at his lips. "Yes. You don't have to keep asking me about that one, if you'd like to establish that now."

I perk up, and Remington laughs. I laugh with him, unable to stifle my excitement. "Yes. You can hold my hand anytime too."

He grins. "Okay. Sounds nice."

As our hands reattach, my heart soars. Remington beams at my widening smile, the light glittering in his observant eyes. But having him so close has me feeling extra brave.

"Can we try again to discuss this? I– I just need some help learning it's safe to say 'no.'"

Remington's entire posture loosens, drawing close enough to waft his scent over me. "Fuck. You're teaching me things too. I didn't catch that, so thanks for telling me so clearly. You're doing so, *so* well. God, I just—" He bites his lips. Releasing them with a groan, he cups my cheeks. "You're just so wonderful. Be honest with me— Are you okay with me calling you pet names?"

My breath heightens, heating the gap between us. I feel terribly shy still gazing at him, but I don't want to stop. His gaze flickers across me, taking in my reddening chest. But I allow him to look.

"Yes," I breathe. "P-please."

He shuts his eyes with a hard exhale. "So. Fucking. Brave. Seriously, I don't know how to contain my excitement around you, baby girl."

His words hit my soul, shocking my nervous system with such tender affection that I gasp.

Remington's stare darkens. "Oh, you liked that. It's written all over you. I'm going to have too much fun, so we better get you saying 'no' to me."

Still struggling to catch my breath, I swallow hard. "I-I'm afraid of being hurt from saying 'no.'"

Remington winces. But he shakes his head. "Not here. It's just you and me, baby - none of those old shadows who taught you that."

My heart twinges just as hard, but this time, it stings my eyes with raw emotions. I so badly want to believe Remington. That it's safe to say "no" to him, and that he actually *wants* me to.

"Go all in, Lilibeth. You can do it." Remington whispers. "Do you know what soft and hard limits are?"

"I-I think so. Like the soft limits are things I'd be unsure about trying, but would be up for discussion, and hard limits are no-go-zones?"

Remington smooths my hair off my cheek. "*Exactly*, baby."

It's the third time he's called me "baby," but the word sinks its teeth into me; he means every letter, heaping affection laced into such a small word. I have to blink a few times to refocus.

His fingers sweep down my neck. "I'm going to ask you a few basics to gauge what you're interested in, and I want you to tell me what you're curious to try, as well as your soft limits. Except when we get to the hard limits, give me a direct 'no.' I'm going to throw some wild ones in there as a challenge, and I want you to be honest, even if you think it'll offend me, disappoint me, or hurt my feelings. The more you say 'no,' the easier it'll get. You've got this."

My heart flips. We're already practicing?

But I nod. "Okay."

"Okay. Are you interested in flogging?"

My chest tightens. Remington breaks into a sly grin, and I wince. "N-no... Why the first one, Rem?"

His sharp, loud laugh dissolves me into giggles. "Sorry. I'm not really into it either, but I'd be fine with doing it if you were. How about CBT?"

"W-what?"

His grin grows even more mischievous. "Cock and Ball Torture."

As my eyes widen, Remington laughs even louder.

But he's also waiting for me to answer seriously.

"N-no," I whisper.

His sharp, huffing laughter comes out in bursts. "I'm so sorry, gorgeous. You're doing such a good job for me that I'll give you a break. What about role-playing fantasy scenarios?"

I open my mouth, then shut it again.

I didn't think it would be even harder to say "yes."

But Remington freezes. "Not necessarily dom and sub scenarios, by the way. Just like, anything. Like the wild stuff you imagine alone in bed at night, except we'd reenact them in character."

I bite my lip. "Yes."

Excitement races past his eyes. My heart hammers faster, but I can't stop my curiosity.

"What about you?" I mutter.

"That's my favorite," he says. "But not many people have matched my tastes. I like the passionate, saviorism ones the most."

He analyzes the whirring emotions on my face. I have no idea what I look like, especially when I'm feeling a mix of everything. I've never had someone to share these vulnerable thoughts with, so it feels like I've already leaped a mile, and we haven't even moved beyond simply speaking about it.

But I want to.

I sound choppy and awkward, but I share all I can. "I have a certain type of fantasy just like that. Like, I'll rewrite old fairy tales in my head where someone comes to rescue me away from a dungeon or danger, but I'll make it– um– *very* sexy."

Remington grins. "Care to share how?"

"L-like–" I bury my face in my hands, but I can't help but grin with him. "Like, usually fairytales surround virgin princesses locked away to keep them pure, so the only way to rescue me is to have sex and ruin my worth."

Remington's hum hits differently this time - trailing between my thighs. "I see. That is quite the sexy fairytale, baby girl. I love it."

I'm surprised by how tenderly my heart just ached at Remington calling my silly fantasy "sexy" - as if he held me at my core. As warmth fills the silence between us, I understand why; I've never had anyone affirm my innermost thoughts like this before.

"God, I love how much you're trusting me to open up. You're doing such a beautiful job." Remington's purring words pulse heat to my groin. He traces my rising chest with his eyes before lifting his focus back to my face. "What about praise?"

The sultry tone to his words tells me he's seen right through me - probably for *months*. I nibble on my bottom lip. "Y-yes."

Remington breaks into a broader smile.

But I'm not done. "B-but a big, *big* yes."

His breathing pauses. Then he sucks in a deep, shuddering inhale. "Fuck. I had no idea how this would go today, but so far, we have a lot of shared interests. We could have a lot of fun, if you feel up to it."

My heart flips. "I do. I– I really want to try, even though it's a little scary."

Remington shakes his head in disbelief, but he's not smiling anymore. "I'm so proud of you, baby girl. So, so proud of you."

He flusters me speechless. Remington laughs, rubbing my arms until I can giggle with him again. Once I regain my bearings, we get to work narrowing down our common interests and throwing out our hard limits. So far, it sounds like he's not as interested in some of the hardcore kinks that I expected he might be as a Dungeon Monitor. I'm relieved I won't make him miss out on too much.

A world opens up to me that I've never imagined possible - one where Remington might be willing to accept me at my most vulnerable. And as he leans in closer, whispering his own secrets, I'm dying to be the one to accept him too.

CHAPTER EIGHT

As we fizzle out of ideas, Remington looks me in the eyes, gathering my focus.

"Hey, before we go any further, I want you to know something important: these things can trigger a lot of emotions, so even though you're showing me how good you're getting at saying 'no,' it's okay if you have trouble with it again when you're feeling a lot. If you reach a point where you feel like you can't say 'no' out loud, do you think you'd feel comfortable enough either giving my hand a tight squeeze–" Remington demonstrates with a hard, fast squeeze of my hand. "Or by using a red light, yellow light, green light system?"

My shoulders soften. "Yes, I think so."

"Okay, then we're golden for today. We'll come up with a safeword together too."

With my hopes restored, I smile. "O-okay. I'd like that. For you too. I want you to feel safe."

My words seem to catch Remington off guard. But it's not a bad thing: a giddy lightness traces his eyes, loosening his laughter and widening his smiles.

We adjust to face each other as we continue to chat casually, tracing each other's hands. But Remington's tan skin looks so beautiful against my light olive skin that I place his forearm in my lap, tempted to give him closer attention. My fingers shake, but I trace the wispy ink at his wrist, following it down the back of his hand. Remington droops into the couch with a hum. I peek up at him in concern, but he gives me an encouraging smile.

"That's nice," he whispers.

I nod, dropping my palm to trace wider, tickling circles over his whole hand. He shivers, and I giggle beneath my breath, trading my tickling sweeps for a gentle massage.

"I forgot to say I want to try Shibari," I mutter.

Remington's eyes flutter open, only to find me wide-eyed and petrified.

He laughs. "Did you surprise yourself?"

I drop my forehead to his hand with a groan. "Y-yes."

That sharp, bright laugh morphs into something warm and intimate, pulling me back in. My shoulders soften as I meet Remington's gentle smile, deciding to lean against the couch with him until our heads are tilted just the same.

Remington slips his hand from mine to steal my palm, opting to massage it for me instead. "What about Shibari makes you curious?"

He gives me a long pause to answer. My breath speeds, but Remington is still waiting. Listening.

I grow even quieter. "You said we'd have to also talk about traumas, right?"

Remington's sharp stare grows serious. But he's soft with me, reaching across the small gap between us to stroke down my arm. "Yes, when you're comfortable. And I'd be there to hear about what you've experienced, even if we don't move forward with this."

"I really want to listen about what you've experienced too."

Remington stares at our hands for a long time, smoothing his body heat over the back of my hand with tender strokes of his fingers.

I'm recognizing his pattern; every time I acknowledge keeping him safe in return, he grows far too quiet for his playful self.

When we finally meet gazes again, his irises peer back with a powerlessness I haven't seen in him yet.

"My sweet, sweet girl," he purrs.

My heart rate leaps out of control. I think I just made Remington feel safe despite whatever is whirring around in his head - and he called me *his* girl. When my lips part in desire, Remington's eyes zip right to my mouth.

His stare morphs into a sultry warmth, just like his voice. "Come here."

Nerves tingle down my limbs, but I scoot closer. "Where?"

Remington opens his arms, and I clamber into his lap. He doesn't seem to mind my awkwardness; he releases a delighted sigh, swirling excitement through my ribcage. As his arms wrap around me, I buzz all over, unable to fathom how close I feel to him already. It's not just everything we've experienced together in this short time - it's how his low voice grows so delicate when I'm beside him. It's his doting gaze, swelling my heart with affection. I already feel close to him, and the feeling expands into deeper intimacy by the second.

With his arms wrapped around me, Remington nuzzles into my hair. "I'll tell you more about my past experiences too, but I want to make sure you have your chance to finish. Do you feel comfortable sharing more about what you were saying first?"

I swallow hard. "W-well, I- I know a lot of people get claustrophobic in small spaces, and it feels natural for them to hate it, but I've wanted to try Shibari for a while because I— I like feeling trapped in small, hidden spaces. A-and there's a reason, um—"

My voice shrinks until I cut myself off. But Remington hums, rubbing my arms.

"Good job, baby. I'm right here," he whispers.

Relishing in his tender patience, I huddle in closer. Remington alters our snuggle pile until I'm curled in his lap with my knees to my chest. It feels so reassuring that my secret spills out.

"If I'm squished into a small space, it feels like a big, safe hug, but a deeper one. Like a hug for my heart," I whisper. "I like it because it feels like no one can reach me to hurt me."

Remington huffs out a pained breath before squeezing me in the most tender, tightest hug. As his compression grows strong enough to make my lungs fight to flex, I sigh in delight.

"*Good,*" Remington breathes. "You're so brave for sharing this with me. Thank you so much."

Hot tears prick my eyes, but I'm smiling.

My eyelids flutter shut. "It feels so nice. You're giving my heart a big hug right now too."

"Good. I was trying to. I've got you." Remington strokes my side, softening into a whisper. "Can I ask you something difficult about this, baby girl?"

"Okay," I whisper.

"Do you feel like your dad could come find and hurt you now?"

Biting my lip, I hide my eyes against Remington's neck. "No. It's only when he loses his patience after bottling things up for a while."

Remington hums. "Then what about your mom? I know you've mentioned she's sick, but is she safe with him?"

My fists tighten. If I tell Remington about Mom, I'm not sure what he'll think of me or my situation. What if he thinks I'm right to feel guilty, and that I should've done more to protect Mom? Or that I'm being too lenient and should cut myself off entirely from Dad?

But as my shoulders rise, Remington adjusts his cuddle on me, enveloping me just as warmly. "Baby girl, if you're not comfortable talking about it, you're more than welcome to say 'no,' remember?"

Every inch of me loosens. Closing my eyes, I mutter the shaky truth. "O-okay, thank you. I'd rather not talk about it yet."

"Thank you for telling me, gorgeous."

I smile, stroking the smoky tattoos up his collarbone and neck. We cuddle in silence for a while. With my ear against his chest, each airy pull of his lungs reminds me that this is real, and he's this special to me already. How could he be single?

"Rem?"

"Yes, L.L.B.?"

My heart flips. "You don't have to answer, but why aren't you dating or playing with anyone else?" I gasp. "W-wait, no– That came out badly. I just mean– I don't understand who wouldn't want to be with you."

Remington's breath heightens against my cheek. I don't know what he's thinking, but I can hear the nerves in each tender inhale. He strokes my hair, and I nuzzle my head into the nook between his chin and collarbone.

"I don't want to spend too much time talking about it today, but my last partner was into non-consent play, and as you now know, that's a hard, *hard* limit for me."

I've never heard Remington's voice sound so small. "O-oh. And you broke up because of it?"

He sighs, loosening his grip on me. I straighten in concern, but he doesn't look at me, his chin tipped to the ceiling like he's laid back and relaxed. The taut muscles of his neck tell me it's the opposite. "Only after she tried to force it on me over time. It slowly broke my fucking heart."

Acid burns my chest. I instinctively place my hand over Remington's heart, only to find it racing.

But Remington keeps talking. "I really do like role-playing, but I felt like she was sexually harassing me to be sexually harassed, and how do I even explain that to anyone? I lost so much enjoyment in playing that I gave up on participating, moved, and just became a bouncer to protect others from feeling that way. I didn't expect to meet you and feel this way again, so— So it's kind of new to me to trust again too."

I feel so deeply for him. This must be why he never fully smiles.

But I'm missing a big piece in this equation. "What is it that you'd prefer the most instead for role-play?"

His head pops up. He shakes his short, dark hair, still not meeting my eyes. "I really like feeling needed, so role-playing rescue scenarios as the hero is my favorite. But it kind of scares me - allowing myself to have that selfish title of a hero. So it's a little thrilling, but also holds a lot of shame for me. Which, of course, that asshole trainer made fun of me for wanting to play the hero with you on that first day we met without knowing how deep it cut." Remington laughs, but I rub his chest.

"You *were* my hero. And it wasn't roleplay. It was real. You saved part of me that day I didn't know needed saving."

He finally looks at me. My lungs swell, filled with courage from the deep trust in his stare.

My voice quivers. "I feel like you're saving my heart now too. It's been so scary to challenge my fears about how I look and sound, but the more time we spend together, the freer I feel to exist."

Shutting his eyes with a heavy exhale, Remington breathes, "*Lilibeth*. God, you're such a sweetheart."

His hand on my shoulder urges me back for another cuddling hug, and I happily return my cheek to his chest. But this time, I tilt my head enough to keep staring him in the eyes. He gazes down at me with a soft chuckle, nestling me closer before tucking a strand of hair behind my ear. The longer we stare, the deeper the need I have to kiss him.

But Remington breaks into a devilish grin. "As your next challenge, you can be the one to kiss me first."

I groan. He's right; I'm absolutely terrified to kiss him myself. "I really want to, right now, but..." I sigh.

He giggles, stroking my cheek. "That's fine. We've got time."

We whisper about the rest of our plans for the week for a while, mere inches from each other's lips.

But before we leave, panic strikes my heart.

Remington freezes. "What's wrong?"

My heart aches. "I'm so sorry, I– I didn't get to ask if you also had another reason for wanting to feel like a rescuer before you broke up or if it started with your ex. I– I know that's a lot, but–

But I wanted you to feel heard too. I'm so, so sorry I missed that at first."

Remington stays perfectly still, allowing the silence to stretch between us. The longer I sit facing his shocked, gaping stare, the deeper my heart aches.

Did he really not expect me to care about him back? Have I touched on something too deep?

But when Remington speaks, his tone remains even. "Sorry, I still have a really bad habit of deflecting all focus off me after all that happened with my ex. My therapist thought I was trying to protect myself by being funny or distracting or something, but all I know is that I just cause more problems that way in the long run when someone actually cares. Except I— I still feel like it's rare to find someone who genuinely does, like you do, so I almost don't know what else to do."

He still doesn't move, so I remain motionless with him, keeping him held close. I don't know what else to do either.

"But yeah, there's something even deeper that started my interest in all this too. I'll tell you about it sometime soon," Remington mutters.

The sorrow laced into his voice guts me.

All I can do is stroke his back. "Okay. Thank you."

CHAPTER NINE

Remington hesitates outside my apartment complex. We couldn't bear to part after our heavy discussion, so Remington took the bus with me to walk me home. We're still gripping each other's hands tight, neither of us making any moves to let go on the rusty red brick porch.

"Are you okay?" I ask.

Remington's Adam's Apple bobs with his swallow. When he speaks, his low voice rumbles even deeper than usual. "No."

I tense, ready to burst into panic. Is he having second thoughts? Remington meets my petrified eyes.

He sucks in a sharp breath. "Sorry, not in a bad way. I mean—"

Remington shakes his head, but I step closer. I'm so concerned for him that my heart thumps into my ears.

But he lifts his worried eyes. "I just mean I don't want to have to say goodbye yet. I really like spending time with you."

I'm surprised even *Remington* seems shy about asking to spend more time with me. Maybe coming home with a date isn't normal for him after what happened with his ex.

And I've helped Remington feel safe enough to change that for him. My elation spills over so fast that before I can stop myself, I dash into his chest for a hug. A puff of air escapes his nose with my impact, but it's followed by a deep chuckle.

Remington's warm hand settles behind my head as he wraps my upper torso in a satiating embrace. I snuggle in, taking a step closer. Remington does the same, settling me softly against the brick wall behind me.

But the longer we cuddle against the wall with our thighs snug, what I find bumping my belly startles my breath out of me. Remington freezes. But when I don't move away, instead leaning in a little closer to tease his forming erection, Remington's fingers on my head slowly weave into my hair. My eyes flutter shut as he gives my scalp a soothing rub. I hum, and his shaft flexes against me in response.

My heartbeat rages faster. I'm not sure how long Remington has been staving off arousal, but just the feeling of his warm, firm shaft through our clothes ignites a fire between my legs.

I pull back, desperate to stare into his brooding, black eyes beneath my apartment porch's crappy lighting. His tattoos sneak through the shadows, sprawling over his neck to guide me to those plump, parted lips. I can't stare at them for too long, my feet shuffling in a yearning to press my hips a little deeper into Remington. But I'm afraid if I give in, we won't be able to contain ourselves, and someone in my building will walk up and catch us.

But I've stared at Remington's lips for far too long. His fingertips drag over my pulsing jugular before settling against my cheek. My eyes zip to his, and I realize he's been beaming down at me this whole time. He's not smiling with his lips, but his eyes - slanting like they're toying with me. There's a sultry, crouching fire behind his irises - a black panther ready to pounce.

I part my lips to match his. But I've never been this nervous to kiss anyone in my life. It might be just a kiss, but with the reality-shattering emotions I feel around him, I know it's more. An anchor hooks my heart, dragging me closer to binding myself to Remington. And I know it's already too late; I dove so deep that a part of me will feel deeply for him for life.

A sour, realistic voice inside me warns this could be another one of those moments: a man taking me inside, having a little fun, getting bored of me, and leaving me alone in the morning.

But with how cherished I feel in Remington's arms, I want to feel every second of this moment with him. Even if it's just for tonight.

The tips of our noses make the lightest contact, brushing over each other in a gentle, tickling dance. Remington's eyes lose their tension, and my belly somersaults.

He's waiting for me to kiss him first.

I grip fistfuls of his leather jacket, but he still doesn't move. My thighs rub together, teasing Remington in the process, and Remington releases a low, humming exhale.

"Lilibeth, if you're too uncomfortable—"

"C-can I—" I suck in a breath as his shaft prods me again. "Can I kiss you?"

"Yes," he purrs.

Wobbling on my toes, I take Remington's cheeks in my palms. He holds me steady, hugging my waist flush to his by my sides - still avoiding my lower back. But he doesn't make the first move, allowing me to take my time. Which is nice, since I'm still too terrified to kiss him. My breath pulses over his lips, and my anxiety skyrockets past the top floor of my apartment building.

But as my eyes flit between his, the affection I find staring back spurs me into action. I ease one of his hands behind me, allowing his hot palm to caress my sensitive mark.

"I-I changed my mind. I like it, when I'm not overwhelmed," I whisper.

Fire burns behind his eyes. Remington swallows hard before rumbling, "Thank you for telling me, baby girl."

I can hardly resist indulging in the soothing buzzing his voice creates in my lower belly, but when he sends a flurry of tingles through me with his soft, sweeping touch on my lower back, my forced calm snaps. Gasping against his lips, I arch my back into his hand. I want him to keep touching my mark. He's the only one I've felt safe enough with to allow it, but he's also the only one to be so lovingly gentle with my body to help me feel safe enough in the first place. It makes even the slightest brush of his fingertips feel like he's pleasuring my deepest nerves.

And tonight, every corner of my body and mind begs me to kiss him. With a galloping heart, I press my lips into his - just a light peck at first. But Remington hooks one arm tighter around my back, pulling me in. I suck in a hitching, frenzied breath as the full weight of those lips settles over mine, shooting fireworks of buzzing, tingling bliss down my spine. I grip his cheeks tighter, pulling him closer. I want more.

And Remington certainly gives me more. He releases my cheek to cup the back of my head, just in time to protect it as he smushes me against the brick wall. My eager hips buck on instinct, and it's only with his rumbling, pleased groan that I realize that he's bending his knees to stoop low enough for me - placing his hot shaft in the perfect position to nudge my clit.

Running out of air, I break our kiss with a sharp inhale. But I don't budge an inch. Remington's breath beats against my lips as he stares into my eyes, our foreheads pressed together.

"You're so brave," he whispers.

Hot, whirling tingles shred through me, flexing my core. Oh, my God. His praise really does something to me.

I grip Remington's jacket collar, the studs icing my hot fingers. I struggle to speak between flustered breaths. "Rem, I— We're outside, but— But I like this too much to want to stop."

He nudges my nose with his, pressing his chest against my breasts until my shoulder blades meet the wall. Wait, is he squishing me because he remembers I like compression? That thought is so sweet that I can't help myself, smashing my lips against his. This time, our searing breaths meet as we open our lips. We kiss heavier and heavier until our tongues touch, flickering further over each other with each successive, deep kiss. His shaft nudges me again, and I inhale hard through my nose; I'm so damn sensitive to this man that my core can't stop flexing in response to him - especially as he draws gentle circles over my lower back, tantalizing my nerves from every angle.

Remington breaks our kiss with a heavy exhale. "You still okay, Lilibeth?"

I nod furiously, still catching my breath.

He softens his voice, but it rumbles through my chest, vibrating to my lower belly. "Do you feel good?"

Slipping my hands into his open jacket, I grip the back of his soft T-shirt. "Y-yes."

"Good. You look and sound like you feel good, but I want to make sure. Do you want more? Even though we're outside?"

My heartbeat pounds into my ears. I check over Remington's shoulder, but the late-night streets are just as empty.

"Y-yes," I whisper.

"Do you like the thought that we might get caught?"

I clench the back of his shirt in my fists so tightly that my nails press into my palms. "F-for some reason, yes."

Our eyes meet just as Remington's curious stare hardens into a sharp, desirous focus. Tilting his head, Remington covers every inch of my lips in such a delicious massage that my heart squeezes tight. Gripping his shirt harder, I hug him closer. We mush together in a hot, full-body kiss.

Remington hums through his exhale. When he speaks, his voice sounds just as airy as mine. "Good girl."

He covers my lips just in time to stun me silent. Bending his knees and arching my back, Remington grinds his shaft over my clit. My lungs restart at how warm he feels. But as he gives me another soft, slow hump, my thighs jolt with pleasure. My breath hitches again, but this time, it's accompanied by a tiny, exhaled moan. As my knees widen, my grip releases Remington's shirt, leaving it crumpled. I cling to his taut back muscles just as hard, urging his waist closer.

"You feel really good, don't you?" Remington whispers, and I whimper against his lips. He kisses me, giving me a heavier rub between my legs. I shudder a heaving breath into his mouth, lifting my hips to meet him. I can't believe how close he's made me, but heat floods my chest, heightening the expanding pleasure in my core. As he settles his palm over my sensitive mark with deeper pressure, I'm seconds away from coming.

But Remington stops. "I don't know what your noises mean yet, sweet girl. I'm not moving until you're clear with your words about what you want."

I grip his hips, struggling not to slink down the wall from how good it feels to press against his body. "Y-you have a big, *big* green light."

Remington's chuckle against my lips sends sparks down my chest. "Fuck, what a good girl. Thank you."

I whimper into his mouth as we crash into another heavy kiss. As my thighs pulse open, Remington's hands slide lower, spreading warmth down my back until his palms cup my ass. He squeezes me tight, rubbing against me slower and deeper but keeping his pace consistent. I gasp, diving for his chest in a tight hug.

"Remington–" I huff into his sternum. If he keeps going, I'm going to come in his arms, right outside my apartment complex door.

Tucking his chin, Remington presses a kiss against my temple. "I've got you."

My breath turns choppy, each sharp, vacuuming inhale punctuated by a tight hold of my diaphragm as warmth balloons between my legs. Remington hums against my cheek, his deep voice buzzing through my chest, and I let out a soft, genuine moan.

He sucks in a surprised breath, but he rocks a little faster. "You good, sweet girl?"

"Rem–" I gasp, dragging my forehead over his collarbone. "You're–"

Massaging my lower back, Remington teases tingling pleasure into my core from every angle. When I let out another pleading moan, he hastens his slow rocking until my legs quiver at his sides. "I'm, what?"

I drop my head back until we're nose to nose, my chin tipped to gaze straight into his eyes. "You're about to make me– Even though we're outside– I'm–"

"Fuck, you're so brave. This is hotter than anything I imagined with you, and we're just–"

Remington's sharp breath cuts him off as I gasp, open-mouthed against his lips. Each breath is followed by a moan as pleasure rises in my belly, expanding beyond my control. Gripping the back of my thigh with one wide palm, Remington lifts my leg just enough to rub his shaft directly against my clothed labia. I'm so wet that the heat of his shaft spreads through my soaked jeans, sending me over the edge. I let out a soft cry against his lips, my knee slamming shut against his hip as I squirm through an eye-fluttering orgasm. Remington's grip keeps me smushed against him and on my feet as he rubs every last drop of pleasure from me.

I'm left shaking from excitement and nerves, letting out soft whimpers as I slump against Remington's chest. Stroking my bangs off my forehead, Remington kisses my clammy skin over and over.

"*Good*," he breathes. "You did so well, baby. God, I'm so amazed by you."

His words raise my shoulders through the giddy, fluttering aches he creates in my chest. I'm so delighted that I'm weak, hardly helping Remington to keep me upright. But he keeps my back safely pressed against the wall, humming soft, reassuring noises over me between gentle kisses on my cheek. He's harder than ever, still prodding between my legs. I jerk with leftover pleasure each time his shaft taps me, too breathless to know what to do about it yet.

But the thud of nearby sneakers on the sidewalk sends me flying from Remington's arms. I sloppily jerk my wallet against the complex's lock system. The half-second it takes to open seems to take forever. Snatching Remington's hand, I thrust the door open the instant a whirring, metal buzz and a sharp beep tell me the door has successfully unlocked.

Remington's boots clod after my sloppy footsteps, bolting

up one flight of stairs to my apartment door. I crash against it, hardly able to breathe.

But as Remington comes to a chuckling stop behind me, I turn to him with a gasp.

"S-sorry! I– I kidnapped you. Do you actually want to come in?"

His grin softens into that genuine smile of his - the one that crinkles the corner of his eyes. "I was hoping I'd get to be extra cozy with you tonight. But especially now, after…"

He zips those black irises over my overheated body. I bite my lip through the powerful, residual ache his playful eyes spark in my groin.

I'm also buzzing with nerves. Is Remington talking about letting me experience proper aftercare for the first time?

Wait, no, that's ridiculous. A quick dry hump must seem like child's play to Remington - not worthy of full aftercare. Especially because I've left him unsatisfied. My eyebrows draw together, and Remington's smile fades.

It hurts my heart. "S-sorry, I'm a little worried I didn't do the right thing."

He frowns. "What do you mean?"

"I'll let you in first, sorry."

He rubs my back, tickling my cheek with his breath as I sloppily push my keys into the door. "You don't have to keep apologizing to me, baby girl. I'm right here with you."

My belly flutters. But when I open the front door, we're greeted by a little *mew*.

Flipping on the light, I giggle at Celeste's swanky walk to greet us. "Hello, baby."

I get to work dropping my bag and unzipping my boots, but Remington gasps behind me.

"Baby girl number two!?" He whispers.

I turn around to find him crouched as low as he can, his fingers outstretched for Celeste to sniff. To my surprise, she has no fears about rubbing her cheek over his knuckles, allowing those gentle, inked hands to stroke her black fur.

He hums. "Hi, pretty girl. You look just like your mommy."

My heart nearly explodes. I watch them from a distance, my sweet cat nuzzling my favorite person, and I'm startled by how well Remington fits into my life. My messy apartment with black, purple, and red decor envelops him like he's the one who lives here. It's not until he glances at me with a gentle smile that I realize how beautiful this moment feels for me: loving who I've brought home.

Oh, God. I love him.

"That's Celeste," I whisper.

"How cute. Almost as cute as you." He carefully slips off his boots, giving Celeste another reassuring stroke. She toddles after him as he rises to meet me. "Celeste - like *Celeste?* A little heaven-sent, celestial beauty?" He pronounces her name how I would in Italian, widening my eyes.

"Yes. Do you speak Italian?"

He huffs out a laugh. "Not with anyone but my unhinged family, so mainly only a few vulgar words that stuck in my head."

I laugh. "Same here. Just from my mom's side - and angry co-workers."

"So baby girl number two *is* heavenly, like you." Remington grins.

I laugh. Grabbing his outstretched hand, I don't know what else to say; I can't grasp my bearings. I've never been so nervous and excited yet deeply soothed to have a man over.

I guide him to my dark room, flicking on only my pink salt lamp to give the room a radiating, moody glow. But, of course, this reveals the giant mess of clothes I forgot I left on my bed.

Remington chuckles through a groan. "Oh, what a sweetheart. You worked so hard to look nice, only for me to be a dick about it."

Before I can brush off his concerns, he bends to collect my shirts, skirts, and pants.

"Ah, it's okay! I-I've got it." I rush to his side, placing my hands over the pile in his arms.

But Remington's beaming smile stops me. "I really meant it; I want to take care of you after you worked so hard to please me. Relax on the bed for me, okay, baby?"

God, I think he *is* considering what we did downstairs as enough to constitute aftercare. I want to experience it with him, but I hesitate at my bedside, my fingers fidgeting with my jacket zipper. Is it okay to continue to let him neatly gather my clothes? To let him do a favor for me after I was the only one who climaxed? He places a stack of clothes on my empty chair in the corner, unaware of my racing heart until he turns to find me still standing.

Remington freezes. "Oh, baby. What's wrong?"

"I didn't please you… fully."

He catches me eyeing his remaining erection and grins. "Ah. You don't have to get me off to please me. Honestly, I forgot to tell you I have a kink about forcing myself to wait to get off until I can't stand it, for one. And, second, I would take care of that myself, not make you do it - unless we happened to be in the mood together. But, third, I really did get spoiled. I told you the affection I like most is watching you unravel."

Shuffling in place, I burn hot. Truthfully, I want to unravel more. Especially if it means I get to watch Remington unravel on top of me too.

But his eyes widen. "That's right– What did you mean outside your door? You were worried you didn't do the right thing, as in when we were making out downstairs, or something else?"

"Y-yes, I– It was that, and leaving you frustrated. I haven't seen men have a lot of patience before. I normally just lay down for them, and they come in me and leave. I don't know if I'm good at this stuff compared to you."

Rapid emotions flicker across Remington's face. But when he settles on an intense frown, my chest burns with anxiety. "Are you telling me a guy's never made you orgasm before?"

I bite my lip, dropping my head. Fidgeting with the skin on the back of my knuckles, I lower my voice. "I-I don't know, not on purpose, I don't think. I get so nervous that it feels impossible. One time, a guy got me close, but it was taking a while, so I just pretended it happened so we could stop because he looked really bored and frustrated with me."

Remington's jaw tightens. "So, do you get nervous, or is it actually that no one took the time for you to feel safe enough with them?"

My heart flips. I never thought of it that way.

He sighs, gripping his forehead. "God, that hurt my heart. Before we get to anything too intense, I think you need some good vanilla sex, L.L.B. You're capable of feeling pleasure, and you deserve it."

I drop my head, willing away fresh tears. But Remington strides around the bed, hurriedly enveloping me in his embrace. I nuzzle into his chest, hiding my face.

Remington kisses the top of my head. "Come here, baby. Let's lay down and cuddle for a while."

That sounds amazing, so I hurriedly pull away, crawling onto my bed. Remington chuckles behind me. His weight pressing into the mattress beside me for the first time flips my heart. He helps me remove my stifling jacket, stripping his right after. My heartbeat pulses into my throat, unsure how much more we'll see of each other.

But Remington lays down in his T-shirt and pants, opening his arms wide. The second I return to his embrace, every ounce of anxiety melts away, aided by his gentle touch sweeping my bare upper back.

"Does that feel good?" He whispers.

I nod, my eyelids drooping.

"Close your eyes. I'll give you a little massage."

The second he runs gentle pressure between my shoulder blades, I can't keep my eyes open. Giving Remington a soft hum,

I'm delighted by the sound of his warm breath; I can hear the breezy smile in it.

But after Remington melts me into my mattress, I open my eyes with a gasp. "Can I trace your tattoos again?"

"You look so sleepy, baby girl. It's okay for you to enjoy yourself."

"I am, with you. But do you not want me to take care of you ever too? It matters to me that you also feel good and safe."

He grows quiet. "Sorry. I might just want to cuddle together for a while then."

Settling into him, I bite my lip. "Sorry if I said that meanly."

"No, you were sweet. I just need to absorb what you said. It's been a long time since I've heard something like that from anyone other than my best friends."

The thought of Remington not receiving enough love kills me. I gaze at him, breathing through the raw ache in my heart. "I want you to hear it."

He's silent for a while again. When he speaks, his whisper is quieter than ever. "Thank you."

I decide to trace his smoky, spiraling neck tattoos on my own. As my fingertips roam over each flickering stripe of ink, Remington's blinks deepen.

But our eyes remain on each other. Our rhythmic breaths link in perfect time, creating a quiet, peaceful softness between each inhale and exhale. A coziness unlike anything I've ever experienced settles in my heart; it might be the first time I've truly felt everything is okay in my world.

Soon enough, Remington copies me by tracing my features. He skates around my eyebrows, down my nose, and over my sensitive lips, leaving behind tingles that make me shudder. Breaking into a smile, Remington hums.

"I don't want to sleep," he whispers.

I smile, huddling in closer. "Me neither. I just want to lay here all night, living in the moment with you."

Remington traces a soft line down my cheek, following my

jaw. His fingertips land on my pulse, and he silences his breath. I let him feel my fluctuating heartbeat, jumping whenever we meet eyes. After a comfortable silence, he scoots closer to plant a relaxed, plush kiss on my lips. I breathe in his body heat, holding his torso flush against mine as I kiss him back, but nothing about this moment feels overtly sexual. We settle in, nose-to-nose, and I couldn't be happier.

"What's happening right now?" Remington whispers. "Is it just me?"

"No, it's something, for sure, but I don't know what."

He huffs out a soft laugh. "Me neither. But I love it."

"I'm so glad," I whisper.

Brushing light touches down his face, I smile as Remington closes his eyes. I decide to whisper something new. Something I'd never say, but Remington always does.

"D-do you… feel good?"

His dark eyes flicker back open. Whatever he sees on my nervous face melts him into a sedated grin. "*Very* good. I'm loving this moment with you."

"Me too. I'm here too, Rem. Let yourself sleep."

His hum comes out as a drowsy purr, stirring every nurturing nerve in my heart. As Remington's eyes droop shut beneath my gentle brushing down his arms, my heart aches. I don't want this to be another short fling. I don't want him to disappear, ever, even if he doesn't feel the same about me. I thought I knew what love was in high school with my first boyfriend, but I never had someone listen to me like Remington. Witness me like him. Understand me like him. Or misunderstand and try his hardest to better understand me like him. And I've never felt such a deep longing to do the same.

I might actually be in love with him.

No, I'm sure of it. The longer I hold Remington's limp body, the more I cherish his innocent, sleeping breath. I want to hear it as long as he'll let me.

I want to be his rescuer too.

CHAPTER TEN

My sleep is muddied with nightmares that I've just been sleeping all alone in my parents' house, waking up to find Remington just a figment of my desperate, trapped imagination.

But every time I stir in reality with a racing heart, Remington's sweet, sleeping face is still mushed into my pillow.

I love it, but it's also killing me. What if this relationship won't last?

I guess I better enjoy it while it does. Snuggling up to him, my heart flutters as he wraps me in his arms in his sleep, mumbling nonsensical words and forcing me to hold in a laugh.

But when I open my eyes to see the light from the window and no Remington, I shoot upright with a pained gasp.

"Hey, hey," a voice rumbles beside me.

I flip around to find Celeste leaping off Remington's chest, bolting from the room. Remington gazes up at me, his eyes still bleary with sleep.

He lets out a low chuckle before tackling me back to the mattress. I yelp in surprise, but as he glomps onto me like a huge bear, rolling me over in a tight cuddle, I break into uncontrollable giggles. Remington lets out a low, growling hum, pulling me even closer until my entire backside - from shoulders to feet - is pressed against his front. "Did you forget I was here?"

"Oh, God, no," I gasp through a laugh. "I was terrified all night you wouldn't be here when I woke up."

He hums, scooting higher to press hard kisses into my cheek. Almost all of me is coated in his hot skin, but he rolls up and over me with his leg thrown over my hip, enveloping me until just my head is barely poking out for air. I burst into heavier laughter, making Remington chuckle through his kisses. "And why would you think something like that, baby girl? Did I not love on you enough last night?"

My heart flips. Love? He didn't mean he already loves me, did he?

But I might.

I swallow hard. "No, I– I think I need to tell you something."

Shit, that sounded bad. Remington releases me, turning to look at me directly. He looks so worried that I stroke his tense forehead and cheeks.

Thankfully, he softens a little. "What's wrong, L.L.B.? Are you having second thoughts about us?"

I gasp. "No!"

Remington blinks rapidly before erupting into giggles. "Looks like you learned how to say 'no' really well."

Letting out a surprised laugh, I softly squish his cheeks. "Remington! I'm trying to be serious."

He laughs. "I know, but you look so petrified that I'm trying to lighten the mood. Are you sure nothing is seriously wrong?"

The second fear crosses his eyes, my heart hurts for him. I can't make him wait any longer.

"It's just– I have *really* deep feelings for you, Rem. 'Liking' you isn't big enough."

My heart throbs at my confession, especially as Remington's chest freezes with his sharp inhale. We stare at each other for a long time. Anticipation crawls up my arms, tempting me to believe in my worst fears. Is this when he'll leave?

"Say something, please," I whisper.

Remington lets out a frantic breath, sorting out my bangs. "Fuck, I'm so sorry, I didn't mean to freak you out. I'm just– I'm panicking a little, because I have *really* deep feelings for you too,

Lilibeth. So big, it's scaring me also. I was already thinking hard last night about how right you were - that I wasn't as open as you've been with me - and I felt really bad for you. I'm terrified of somehow breaking your heart - of someday losing this bliss between us and becoming like my angry, arguing family."

I face him. He looks even more gorgeous in the daylight with his rumpled T-shirt and messy hair, churning my stomach. Is there a rift between us? I don't want there to be.

But as Remington's shoulders rise, I realize there's no rift at all; we're on the precipice of deciding whether to fully meld together, and if we both feel this strongly, that's *huge*. Remington really meant it when he explained he's petrified to take the leap, so maybe he's telling the truth: that he doesn't want to lose me either, and that's exactly why it's scary.

"What do you mean, you haven't been as open with me? You told me so many secrets lately, especially at Club X," I say.

He huffs, stroking my arm. "Fuck, I'm scaring you. I'm so sorry. I'm dying to stay close to you, Lilibeth. Please, before we continue talking, just know that."

My shoulders soften. "I'm dying to be close to you too. Can we sit closer?"

He rushes for me, pulling me into his lap. Wrapping my legs around his waist, I hug him tight, holding the back of his head to me as he tucks his chin over my shoulder. My heart shatters; I hadn't realized he was shaking until I had him in my arms.

I rub his back. "You're so scared, Rem."

"I know, I'm sorry. I guess after my ex, I'm also just afraid to allow you to be affectionate back to me too much. And I didn't do it intentionally, but I realized last night how much I've been deflecting your care out of fear instead of just enjoying this with you. But part of me is still afraid that the next time I deflect, you'll realize my feelings aren't what's actually important to you, and you'll leave me really hurt too."

I gasp through his words, holding him even tighter. "I couldn't imagine that. That's not me."

"No, I know. Sweet isn't a strong enough word for how empathetic you are towards me. You're such a sweetheart to keep bringing up my needs, so I'm sorry I've been so difficult. I— I *really* want to be close to you."

I lean back, and Remington clings tight to my waist. Squished in his lap, I raise his chin toward me until I can finally see his sad black eyes. They're rimmed in red, shattering my heart further.

Running my fingernails through his hair, I soften my voice. "You haven't been difficult. You've been so kind to me. I just worry you aren't getting enough love from me in return, when I want you to have it all."

The second those words leave my mouth, I'm breathless. Fuck, why did I say it like that? Telling Remington I had deep feelings for him was enough to freak him out, and now I just implied I love him.

He's still staring back, but he hasn't said anything. My heart races into my throat.

But as his eyebrows arch, his sudden tears spill over.

"Oh, *Rem?*" I cup his cheeks, my heart galloping. "Did I upset you more–?"

Remington's lips crash against mine. I gasp through my nose, pulling him closer. His hungry hands on my back squeeze me tight, sending a flood of fuzzy, elated warmth to my heart.

When he pulls back to breathe, he can hardly scrape his words out. "I'm only scared because I love you, L.L.B. I love you, way too much already."

I choke on my breath, gaping at him. The sunlight clings to his hair, revealing traces of crystalline brown in his black eyes. If he's this terrified, I want him to remember how I truly feel - to soothe his heart with my words, like he always does for me.

Combing his hair back, I lean into Remington's desperate embrace until we're nose-to-nose. "I'm here. You're safe. I want to be here for you because I love you too. I really do."

A fire flashes behind Remington's stare. We rush into a heavy kiss, our hands gripping each other's heads and backs. I gasp against his lips, unable to contain the rising emotions in my chest. When he leans in to kiss me even deeper, I let out a soft, needy moan. Remington purrs, adjusting me in his lap, and I moan again; I'm not sure if it was on purpose, but his hard shaft just rubbed against my aching pussy. I kiss him twice as heavily, and his breath hitches.

He's not crying anymore, but he's certainly feeling something; his shaking, powerful grip roams over me, massaging pleasure into my sensitive lower back. I squirm in his lap, leaning even further into our makeout. His hum comes out as more of a growl as his hips lift into my shifting pelvis, pressing pleasure straight into my core. The second I widen my knees for more, Remington's hands adjust to protect my head and waist - just before he tackles me onto my back.

I squeak as I hit the mattress, but I'm smiling. There's a breezy playfulness to Remington's eyes above me, flooding me with relief.

And his soft smile reaches his eyes. "I want to feel even closer. Can I help you feel good, baby?"

I run my fingertips down his chest. "I want to help you too."

He swallows hard. "Okay, that would be nice."

The strained quietness of his voice tells me that was vulnerable for him to say out loud. But as it lifts my heart into giving me a big smile, Remington melts above me.

"But this time, it wasn't a deflection. I meant what I said last night: I want you to be able to experience how good it feels to come with someone you love," he says.

Nerves flash through my core. "Thank you."

Remington adjusts me beneath him, sliding his hand down my side. As his hot palm skates up my shirt, tracing my bare skin, I rush into another kiss, unable to stop feeling shy. There's no escaping the sunlight illuminating our bodies, so if we remove our clothes, Remington will be able to see all of me — including my mark.

But I want to see all of him too. And a deeper, braver part of me is dying to be seen by him.

As he trails his fingers down my stomach, my breath settles into a heavy, shaking rhythm, forcing my lips to part.

"You okay?" He whispers.

"Better: I'm really good," I whisper.

He smiles, dragging gentle fingers over my bare belly and leaving a tingling buzz in their wake. "You okay with me touching you even lower, then?"

I flush down to my chest; just his question flexed my pussy. I nod, rubbing Remington's shoulder. He drops onto his elbow, pressing a smooth kiss into my lips. I chase after his warm pressure, opening my mouth until our tongues press heat down my spine.

But as Remington's adept fingers pop open my pants and slip inside over my underwear, I gasp through open lips. My breath shakes from how good just his light touch feels outside my panties. My hips are tempted to lift, so I dare to let them. It deepens Remington's kisses.

When my chest heaves faster, Remington's fingers stop on my clit. He gives it a quick circle, and I jolt from how strong it feels, breaking our kiss.

Remington softens his voice against my lips. "You're so sensitive, baby. Do you touch yourself much?"

I gasp, my hips bucking as he spreads another tingly circle over my clit. "N-not much usually, but more the past few months."

A mischievous grin spreads over his cheeks - both of them, yet again. "Because you're imagining us together now?"

I nod, my cheeks flaming hot.

But Remington grows serious, just before tackling me into another fiery kiss. The pressure of his lips doubles the pleasure he whispers between my legs, curling my toes. As his fingers slip lower to circle my labia, I can't help but push my hips into him for deeper contact.

He hums, breaking our kiss. "You're so wet, baby. I can feel it through your underwear."

My breath shakes. "I want to go further."

"Oh, what a good girl. Thank you for telling me. How about I play with you directly? Would you like my fingers inside you?"

I nod furiously, even though I feel super embarrassed to have all the focus on me. But I want him so badly that I grip his shoulders, clinging on as he gently pulls my pants and underwear off.

With nothing to cover my bottom half, my breath triples in speed. What if he thinks I look or feel gross?

Leaning closer to drag his nose over my ear, he softens into a gentle whisper. "Shh, I'm right here too. Just like you are for me. Thank you for reminding me."

"Thank you too. And I— Are you okay if I touch you too?"

With a soft kiss on my cheek, I can hear his smile in his whisper. "Yes, baby. Thank you for asking."

The second my breathing slows, he slides his bare hand down my naked thigh to find my soaked core. Remington hums at my shuddering response. He toys with me, jerking my hips with swirling sweeps until he lightens his touch. But even his gentlest circles create slick sounds I've never heard from my body before; I've never been comfortable enough with someone to get this wet around them.

But as he slips the tip of his finger into me, all I can think about is how nice it feels. I open my knees with a hard breath, searching out his hard cock with shaking fingers. When I find him just as wet as I am through his clothes, my gasp escapes as more of a breathy moan.

"Yes, fuck, you're doing such a good job. I love seeing you express yourself, so don't hold back your breaths or moans, okay? They're beautiful." Remington's low voice flexes me over his finger.

I smooth gentle pressure over his shaft, breathing even harder as he slips deeper inside me. Sedating, pulsing warmth expands in my pelvis. His gentle entry feels so good that I might come in less than a minute, just from his finger penetrating me.

Remington swallows my needy breaths, his lips brushing mine as he whispers into my mouth. "Have you figured out where your G-spot is on your body so I can give you an extra massage?"

I gasp as he pulls softly out of me, stroking my soaked labia before entering me again and leaving me breathless. "I-I don't know, isn't it always on the rough part? But that spot usually hurts when I rub it too much."

He carefully brushes the textured inner wall of my pussy, only an inch or so inside me. As usual, I wince.

Remington freezes. "I'm sorry, baby. I don't think that's the right spot, then. It's different for everyone."

My heart flips as he slips even further. I stroke his erection through his tented pants, aching to make him feel just as good. I think it's working; he shudders just before he speaks.

"Do you like any toys?"

"I do like my G-spot rabbit. But I have to shove it all the way in for it to feel nice."

Remington's sly, sultry smile clenches my core. "So, it's deeper. That's normal too, baby."

I can't respond; he slips deeper, but now he's prodding me, curling his fingertip toward my belly. It feels better and better the deeper he pulses, until he reaches an even deeper spot that drops my jaw. I grip his working forearm to beg for more, breathing harder than I would for my G-spot toys.

Remington's voice is rough with pleasure, and I'm not even touching him anymore. "There you go, baby girl. Is it too strong?"

I can't speak; he's genuinely giving me an internal massage, pulsing the most thorough, blooming pleasure I've ever felt through my body until it reaches my face. I moan, arching my back, and he pauses.

"Can you answer me, gorgeous? Is this okay?"

I grip his shoulders, desperately tugging him closer. "Green—"

He pulses inside me again, and I gasp out. "Green, *green*—" Moans replace my words as my hips buck in desperation.

Holy shit, I really am about to come. But Remington doesn't even have his pants off.

I gasp hard and fast, my eyes wide. "Red," I choke out.

Remington freezes, removing his hand with wide eyes. "Shit, are you okay?"

I'm struggling to catch my breath. "I don't want to enjoy myself without you— unless— unless you don't want to either, but—"

His tip has leaked so much precum that I can see the pool of it spreading through his black pants.

"Do you mean you'd like to use your hands on me?" Remington asks.

"No, I really want you inside me, i-if you'd like to be."

He stares at me for a moment before letting out a hard breath. "Oh, I'd love to be. Do you have a condom in your drawer I can grab? Otherwise, I'd have to escape your clutches to get mine in my jacket."

I laugh, realizing I'm gripping Remington's shoulders so hard that my fingertips are white. Releasing him, I collapse back into the comforter with a shaky laugh. "S-sorry. And I do have condoms if you want, but I—"

I swallow hard. Remington's eyebrows raise, awaiting my next words.

"I know you like sentimental things, and maybe this won't seem like a big deal to you, but it is for me. When I said I only use condoms during sex, I meant with everyone else. I don't usually tell guys I have an IUD because I know they'll try to convince me to be bare inside me when I don't want them to be, b-but with you, I— I'd like it. Love it."

He's motionless for a full ten seconds, leaving my heart to pound wildly. When he speaks again, his voice is raspy. "L.L.B., that's a big, *big* gift you're offering me. Are you sure?"

"Yes, very. I really do love you, and I want you to feel it."

Emotions crease his eyebrows. "You really touch my heart. I'm sorry, I-" He swipes over his eyes.

I cup his cheeks, so worried about him that my heart aches with his shaking breath.

But Remington gives a soft, wet laugh. "I'm okay. I just really love you too. I love you so much."

Remington dissolves back into tears, pulling a pained whimper from my chest. I place my hand over his heart, dying to protect it.

"Breathe with me," I whisper.

We stare at each other, the only sound our anxious breaths. But the more we relax our bodies into each other, the slower our breaths melt. Tilting my head, I leave my open lips gaping over his, intentionally inhaling his air. Remington's shoulders rise as he draws me in, softly placing his lips against mine until we exchange breaths almost solely from each other's lungs.

I don't know what compelled me to start this, or why, but the desperation in his hands tells me Remington must feel the same; there's a tender intimacy in sharing our life force that I've never experienced.

A tremendous ache grows in my chest, yearning to feel Remington all over - until I can't take it. My lips collapse into his, and Remington softly moans, flipping my heart. He cuddles me so tightly that when he kisses me twice as hard, wetness gushes between my legs. I spread my knees for him, bucking to rub up on him.

Remington breaks our kiss with a sharp breath. "Can I take the rest of your clothes off for you, baby? If it's too scary, I understand."

Cupping his cheeks, I huff through my speeding heartbeat. "It's scary, but I want to feel you against me. I've- I've never shown anyone my back, either. I always keep it hidden against the mattress."

"Fuck," Remington breathes as he sits back. "How did I get so lucky then?"

I pull my arms and knees in, feeling shy without anything covering my bottom half. "Because I– I love you."

He smiles. "I love you too, baby girl. Are you shy about anything other than your back?"

I bite my lip. "I think my boobs look too heavy. I feel like guys haven't expected them to hang so much."

"Then, do you trust me not to judge you if you sit up for me while I lift your shirt over your head?"

I can hardly breathe. But I sit up. "Yes."

After flipping his shirt over his head, Remington scoots closer on his knees. I gape; his neck tattoo doesn't start at his chest. It starts below his waistband, drawing a thick line up his stomach and sternum until it explodes in beautiful, fiery geometry over his chest and throat, a collection of different patterns I'm dying to memorize. I run my shaking fingers down that center line, leaning into his touch as his palms caress my sides, rolling the base of my shirt. I shiver, meeting his eyes - just before I have to lift my arms.

I tense with nerves. I trust him not to judge my breasts, but I still judge them.

Remington makes quick work of stripping my top, flipping it over my head like ripping off a band-aid. As my breasts droop from their support, I hold my breath. I'm kneeling on the mattress in front of him, fully naked.

But Remington's shaft visibly twitches in his pants. I loosen my shoulders, struggling to process it. Is he really that turned on by my bare body?

As he scoops one hand behind my head, drawing me in for a sultry kiss, I assume the answer is yes. I grip his forearms hard. They ripple beneath my palms, lifting his hands to softly stroke the heavy underside of my breasts.

I shudder hard enough to break our kiss, open-mouthed as he shifts to stroking over my nipples.

"You didn't think you were absolutely stunning, baby girl?"

An avalanche of heat crashes through my core, flexing

my pussy as Remington resorts to tender, all-encompassing massages over my breasts and nipples. All I can do is moan, my hips shifting on the bed. I didn't know I could get this turned on by someone playing with my breasts, but I'm absolutely weak from it, my back arching and thighs quivering.

"Can I see your back?" He asks. "Not if you're not ready. But so that you know from now on, I won't judge it."

My heart flips, but I grip his palm flat against my chest, craving a deeper squeeze. He gives it to me, and my eyelids flutter. "Y-yes, but– But it's definitely not cute. Please, just don't say anything."

"Okay. But I'm confused what you mean by a mark. Is it a birthmark, or–?"

Remington pauses when he peeks over my shoulder, witnessing my bare back in the morning sun. He says nothing more. My heart drops through the mattress. This silence is worse than I imagined, and not what I had in mind when I told him not to say anything.

CHAPTER ELEVEN

When I feel a delicate tickle over my mark, I jump at how sharp and intense it feels.

"Oh, I'm so sorry, gorgeous. I was about to pet your back to reassure you, but I didn't want to hurt you, in case–" Remington swallows hard.

In case it still hurts, he must be thinking. I shut my eyes, gripping his hand on my chest tighter. He realizes why I'm so vague about my mark, doesn't he?

"Y-you're probably wondering what happened." My whisper shakes.

Remington sits back on his knees in front of me, cupping my cheek. "You don't have to tell me anything. Just let me know if it's sensitive in a bad way, especially without clothes on."

I drop my head, clinging to his arms. "It doesn't hurt anymore. It's just– I don't want to lie to you like I do with everyone else. It's not a birthmark like people assume when I say it's a mark."

Remington is silent for a good ten seconds. "I know, baby. It's a scar, yeah?"

"My dad threw boiling water on me." My whisper comes out hot, scraping my chest on its way up. Remington holds perfectly still, unspeaking. I'm too afraid to check his expression.

"How old were you?" He mutters.

"Eleven. He didn't like that I told him he was making spaghetti wrong since they don't snap noodles in half in Italy,"

I huff out a shaky laugh. "He made me promise to convince my mom it was an accident. The hospital too. I was in the burn unit for a while."

My nervous system buzzes so fast that I feel like I'm floating. This truth has never left my mouth before. Not since it happened.

I drop my head into Remington's chest, breathing a loud sigh.

Remington springs into action. Scooping me up, he brushes my hair out of my face. "Oh, baby... Are you okay?"

I bite my lip, staving back the confusing mix of shame, elation, and love in my chest. "I feel really, really exposed. But that's what I wanted. I wanted you to see all of me."

As I sit fully naked in Remington's arms, my heart raw, I allow him to drag his stare down me. To my surprise, my body relaxes into it. I loosen my limbs, laying back to give him a clearer view, and Remington's stare darkens. He drinks in my image with a heavy swallow, running a hot palm down my chest until I shiver.

Remington's jaw clenches. "Fuck. You're too good to me. Lay back on the pillows for me, baby girl. I want to spoil you."

My heart flips. I crawl to my spot on the bed, my groin aching at the thought of what we'll do next.

"Are you hitting your limit?" I blurt out.

Remington glances over his shoulder as he struggles with the knot tying his pants. "God, you *are* a little panther. If I say yes, I don't want you to think it's yours to solve."

"Okay. But I want to this time. I exposed myself to you for me, but also for you. Since you– You like to watch me... un—"

I can't say it.

But Remington freezes. The second I lay back, Remington crawls over me until his hands beside my shoulders sink me deeper into the mattress.

His sly smile appears. "Are you telling me you're torturing me on purpose, baby girl?"

A smile plays on my lips. I bite it back, giving him an innocent shrug. "What? Is it a kink of yours, or something?"

Remington grins wider - just before he tugs me lower by the

hips. It inspires such a sharp thrill through me that I let out a loud giggle, spreading my thighs for him. But Remington doesn't lay himself over me yet; grabbing one of my pillows, he lifts my back, propping up my hips.

It's the perfect position to drop my knees open for him, no matter how terrifying the idea sounds. I can hardly breathe as my thighs wobble, tempted to part. But with how tightly Remington's jaw clenches with desire, my heart tumbles over itself, dying to unravel even more of myself to him.

When I drop my knees wide open, Remington's focus zips to my exposed pussy. I'm tempted to shut my legs, afraid of what he'll think, but a rising fire builds behind his eyes. They skate back up to meet me, dark, brooding irises glittering fireworks in my chest - just before he swoops in to kiss me.

Our lips crash over each other, ten times fiercer than they have all day. I pant through our open-mouthed makeout, my hips squirming as we build heavier and heavier pressure in my teased core. When Remington skates his fingers down my belly, swooping past my clit to rub my labia, my back arches high off the bed, tingles blasting to my nipples.

I whimper through our kiss, especially as Remington's low voice hums through his gasping breath. He feels good too. Unable to bear the thought of stopping our delicious makeout, I run my hands down his chest, seeking his waistband. He must've been far more flustered than I thought; he still hasn't managed to untie his pants.

To his credit, they're knotted tight - especially with his flexing cock swallowing all remaining wiggle room. Before I can fumble with it for too long, Remington yanks his waistband past his ass in a frenzy, his cock springing free with a gentle tap on my belly.

I gasp through my nose, kissing him faster. I wrap my fingers around his warm shaft, delighted by how soft he feels. My spine alights as Remington shudders from my gentle stroking, but it's not only my spine that feels it. A potent, spreading ache swirls through my groin, deepening my kiss. The more I stroke him, the more I crave his reaction, massaging in longer, steadier strokes, making sure to rub extra attention over his leaking tip.

But as Remington suddenly settles himself over me for a heavy hug, I relish his weight over my chest.

We're both out of breath.

"I adore you," Remington whispers.

I hum in delight - until our bare hips brush. I flinch at the burst of sensations in my pussy. His tip has nothing to cover it - already the first to touch me there, bare. That thought is enough to send me clenching uncontrollably. I'm unable to imagine how stunning it'll be to feel him directly inside me, reverting to heaving breaths.

Remington pauses. "You still okay? You won't hurt my feelings by saying no to anything during sex, okay?"

"Same for you, Rem. I want this, but please let yourself say 'no' too."

"You're such a sweetheart, baby girl. I don't know what to do with myself."

Remington spreads deep, flat-palmed rubs between my wriggling legs until my fluids coat his palm. My pussy blooms wide, begging him to enter me. But instead of stopping and trading his hand's attention for his cock, he glides two fingers in, pushing deep.

I choke out a gasp.

"Sorry, baby. Was that too much? That's why I wanted to do this first."

I shudder, widening my thighs. Remington pulls out, but then he pushes even deeper in one swift movement. This time, he presses deep enough to push heavy, orgasm-inducing massages against my G-spot. Jerking in his arms, I lift my hips high.

I sputter out a gasp. "Rem, *Rem*– You'll make me come if you don't stop."

He pauses. "Fuck, sorry. I'm just getting you ready so it feels really good from the start when I enter you."

I huff out a soft laugh. "Oh, I'm ready."

"You are, baby. You got so wet and opened up so deep for me. It's so gorgeous."

Anticipation ripples through me as he covers his shaft with my fluids - right in front of me. When he lines himself between my legs, we grow quiet.

"Are you okay? Give me a light too," I say.

"Green," he whispers.

I gasp through hard, anxious breaths; I'm preparing for it to take work for him to enter me - maybe even hurt a little. But as he pushes in, I'm already so worked up that he glides far past my pelvic opening. I let out an uncontainable cry, accidentally digging my nails into Remington's shoulders at the rush of pleasure he thrusts up my whole being.

Remington's eyelids flutter shut. "Fuck, are you okay?"

Gasping faster, I grip a handful of his ass. With my desperate tug on his hips, he pushes even deeper. His bare skin drags unbelievably plushy pressure deep inside me - enough to burst all the way up my chest, giving my heart a tight squeeze.

I breathe hard and fast. "Rem, it's– I-it's so nice that I– I feel it in my heart muscles."

"Fuck, good. You're doing so well." But Remington groans, flexing inside me. "It's going to be really hard to last longer than a couple minutes. You're so soft and reactive that it feels stupidly good."

"You're soft too. So warm."

I shudder out a wispy breath as he slips halfway out again, just to plunge back in to introduce a deeper, more delicious flood of pleasure.

"Remington–" I cradle his head, my voice shaking.

"I've got you, baby girl."

Remington kisses me between gentle thrusts, loosening my tense shoulders. But just as I lean deeper into our heavy makeout, he slips his hand under my sensitive back. I break our kiss with a breathy gasp, and he lifts my hips higher, adjusting the angle he's gliding into me until he slides the deepest he has yet, his hips meeting the base of my pelvis. Fluttering, expansive pleasure strikes my gut, dropping my jaw. A genuine, whiny moan escapes my lips.

Remington purrs. "There it is. What a good girl."

I gasp, unable to reply; he's slowly thrusting that delicious spot again and again. My knees raise to my shoulders on their own, but that only makes him hit deeper, pulsing rhythmic, intensifying pleasure up my abdomen. And his sly, heated stare tells me he knows exactly what he's doing to me.

"*Remington—*"

His jaw clenches. "Fuck, baby, it's the first time I'm trying so hard not to come in under a minute."

I let out another moan. "Please do, I'm about to—"

I choke out a gasp as Remington thrusts a little heavier, stirring an expansive warmth within my belly. He repeats the action until I moan with every breath, my voice rising - until the bubbling heat in me spills over in an uncontrollable wave. My pussy flutters over his shaft, doubling each stroke he drags in and out of me. As my legs squirm at Remington's sides, I come with heaving, breathy whines I've never heard from myself.

"Good job, good, *good* job, Lilibeth. Oh, my sweet girl—" Remington whispers, pumping every last moan from me until I stop clenching over him rapidly. My body reverts to meeting each continued thrust with one hard squeeze, perfectly in time with Remington's hips.

Remington's jaw hangs in delight, flip-flopping my heart. I want him to feel good. His shuddering reaction pushes another sated moan from me, adoring how blissful he looks. Remington's breath deepens into hard, heavy bursts as he slows to penetrate me deeply. It still feels so good that I smash my lips into his, unable to thank him with words.

His cheeks are clammy and his breath shaky, but his hardening, swollen shaft tells me he's about to let me feel what it's like to have him come inside me for the first time. That thought alone makes my pussy ache so badly for more that my muscles weaken, allowing his deep, tender thrusts to sink straight into my most pleasurable nerves.

But a sudden burst of liquid between my legs startles me silent. Did I just pee? I'm mortified, but Remington is still breathing hard on the edge and only starting to speed up. I don't want to ruin his fun if I ruined the bed.

It must show on my face; Remington slows, softening his voice. "You okay?"

"S-sorry," I mutter.

Remington stops moving. "Hey, what's wrong?"

My heart throbs into my throat. "Sorry, I did something embarrassing."

"When you came? It was gorgeous, baby."

I flush. "No, just now. It felt really good, and I got so relaxed, and—" Biting my lips, I shrink into my pillow. "I couldn't control it. I think I peed a little."

Remington softens into a sly smile, heavy-lidded eyes burning with intensity. "Ah. So I *am* hitting the right spot, huh? No, I think you squirted."

I realize with his next thrust that he's been aiming for my G-spot on purpose - and absolutely succeeding. Each pulse of his hips caresses that same tender nerve, and it hasn't stopped feeling good: each prod of his shaft only strengthens its pleasing effects on me.

"*Remington*," I breathe.

"I've got you, baby. Don't be embarrassed. I'm so proud of you for letting yourself feel good."

I gasp, widening my legs for him. "I'm proud of you too. I want you to be the first to come in me."

He sucks in a tight breath. "Fuck."

His hips restart with extra vigor to each thrust, flipping my heart until my inner walls swell tighter around him in delight. The faster Remington works me, the greater effort I make to squeeze his shaft. His heavy-lidded eyes and shaking breath paint a clear image of how good he must feel to slip in and out of me. I moan from the raw intensity of it, but Remington dashes in for a sloppy, frantic kiss.

"Fuck, thank you. Thank you—" He gasps.

I moan again, startled by how hard he suddenly feels. Remington grabs me with a sharper gasp, pumping faster by the second. I loosen my body for him, allowing my breasts to bounce and knees to spread wide, giving him room to pound into me. And it's more apparent than ever that he's barely hanging on, his elbows dipping as he huffs hot air over me. Imagining him bursting within me any second pushes a heavier wave of pleasure up my core, widening my legs for everything he can give me.

He shudders a gasp on my lips. Rising over me, Remington buries his shaft so deeply into me that his pelvis presses against my clit. He comes with a soft, gorgeous moan. I didn't expect to feel a deep warmth inside me so clearly, but as he shudders again, I realize he's coming a lot - another wave of warmth spilling inside me. Witnessing his pleasure is so hot that I flutter on the edge for him, my inner walls squeezing every drop of cum from his shaft as my legs squirm. I've never felt this close to someone before.

"Thank you. Thank you so much," I say, repeating Remington's words.

Remington shudders, brushing my hair off my clammy forehead with arched eyebrows. "Oh, my baby. Do you feel okay?"

I whine, writhing on the edge. "Sorry, I know you might feel sensitive after, but it was so nice that I'm close again."

"Okay, I've got you. After I breathe for a second, I'll be happy to keep going. It still feels good for me too." And I can feel it; he's softer than before he came but still firm enough to remain inside me, continuing to prod me with hard flexes.

Still, I expect him to pull out and touch me with his hands once he catches his breath. But Remington releases his grip on my back, pausing to skate his fingers down my breasts. I shiver as he flicks over my nipple, but instead of traveling to my clit, he sweeps his palm back up, massaging back and forth over both breasts. I huff from the startling intensity of it; my breasts feel even better now that I'm heavily aroused, his touch spreading a soothing warmth throughout my ribcage.

Remington places a soft kiss on the tip of my nose. "Can I squish you up into a little ball so you feel held?"

My heart aches at the tenderness in his words. He remembers how much that meant to me. I feel so seen that my eyebrows arch.

"O-oh. Y-yes, okay," I whisper.

Pulling one arm tight to my chest, he squishes my breast with it. Stretching his pinky, he fetches my other wrist while retaining his grip on the first, smushing them together as tight as he can against my sternum. Just this firm hold on me flutters my eyelids; I feel wrapped up beneath him in heavy bliss.

"Hold your hands there for me for a second, please," Remington whispers.

I do as he says, my heart racing. How will this feel? But when he gathers my knees to pull my legs in, he compresses my chest with his weight, carefully laying himself on me to pin me down. I struggle to breathe - not because he's crushing me, but because I've never felt such an intense, flourishing burst of oxytocin through my veins.

"How's this?" Remington whispers.

My eyelids droop in bliss. But when Remington tests out one thrust, I choke out a needy gasp; I feel so protected and covered, yet so deeply ravished, that all I can do is moan.

"Please?" I rasp.

He doesn't move. "Please, what?"

"More," I breathe.

He restarts his hips, but this time, he buries his shaft even deeper, digging his hand between my back and the mattress to elevate my hips with one arm. The more he thrusts, the more warmth builds from him intentionally hitting my G-spot. I realize it's his cum inside me that's making me extra wet, smoothing the movements between us. It builds such a speedy, delicious buzzing in my pelvis that I squirm beneath him.

But squirming isn't the right word; I'm pinned, unable to move beneath him beyond the weak jerking of my pleasure-limp limbs. I love it.

I whine through my hard breaths, sharpening Remington's stare.

He softens into slower, deeper pumps. "Are you—?"

"More, *please*," I breathe. "Please—"

He thrusts faster but keeps his hips sunken in close; rather than hammering in and out of me, he's kneading his soft tip against my inner walls. As a heavy orgasm builds, I squirm harder against his weight, but he presses firmer too, keeping me trapped in place.

He's not just hugging my heart now, but massaging me from the inside out, coating my body with a fuzzy warmth. I cry out from how delicious it feels.

"You still okay?" Remington asks.

But I can't answer; I'm panting through high-pitched moans.

"Give me a light, baby girl."

"Remington, it's green– It's so nice—"

"Fuck," Remington rasps.

As he stretches over my knees to kiss me, he plunges just hard enough to set off a shuddering, powerful orgasm through me. Removing all weight off his arms, Remington squishes me with his hug, speeding his hips until I'm mewling out my moans. My toes curl at how safe and secure I feel beneath him. His intense pressure on my chest pushes me to flex even harder over his shaft - except he's so engorged that I can hardly squeeze him, giving me a delightful, filling, internal hug too.

By the end of my orgasm, Remington suddenly grunts and pins himself deep into me, releasing another wave of soothing heat in my belly. My eyelids flutter; he just came in me again.

This is better than anything I've fantasized about, especially because it's Remington. My heart swells so wide that I can't stop myself from whining through fresh tears.

Remington releases me with hot, heaving breaths. "Oh, my God, sorry– I got a little rough at the end."

"No, I'm just so happy. I wasn't scared or nervous at all, Rem. I felt so good with you."

"Oh, my poor, sweet baby," Remington chuckles. "Cry it out for me."

Finally releasing my knees from my chest, Remington drapes his loose body over me, cuddling me into a deep, sedating kiss. I hiccup through happy tears, letting myself cry, and he doesn't attempt to stop me. Instead, he strokes my hair with purring, acknowledging hums to reply to my whimpers. Crying has never felt so comforting. Within a minute, I settle into a sleepy bliss.

Loosening into the silence, we lay with our ribcages nudging one another in a rhythmic dance. We smooth slow, grateful palms over our bare skin, indulging in our collective warmth for minutes on end.

When Remington eventually props himself over me to softly brush my bangs back into place, I smile.

"I've never felt this close to someone," I whisper.

"I know, same here. That's why I got scared earlier, but not in a bad way. I'm not used to feeling vulnerable like this."

"I want to be here to support you through it. So whenever you feel scared about anything at all, please tell me, okay? It won't change how much I love you."

A touched flicker of emotion creases his forehead, but Remington reverts back to his quiet side. Collapsing back into me for a heavy hug, Remington kisses my neck. "Sweet girl."

All I want to do the rest of the day is snuggle into Remington. Thankfully, he's feeling just as clingy, unable to keep his hands off me even as he carries me to the bathroom, ensuring I don't get a UTI.

After a morning of cuddling and kissing, I hobble to work on sore legs.

The second Gabby sees me, she laughs. "You've got a sex glow."

I can't deny it, so I bury my chin into my chest, smiling for the rest of my shift. It's far, far more than a sex glow. Remington unraveled a piece of my heart I didn't know I had, unlocking pure pleasure - and it was all born from me daring to finally show myself to him.

He didn't judge me; he loved me back.

CHAPTER TWELVE

For my birthday, Remington gifted me a gym membership. I wouldn't let him pay for more than a year, but he insisted on at least one, especially so we can keep spending time together at least once per week.

But that hasn't been difficult for us. It's been over six months since we met, our initial, new relationship energy settling into a fuzzy sense of peace and security that I can't get enough of. Whenever I'm in Remington's arms after a long day, I wake up refreshed and ready to take on the world. Even Celeste meows a little brighter, adoring our combined attention.

Today, I'm leaving Celeste at home with plenty of food and fresh litter. Remington keeps his big hands pressed over the cheap Halloween costume he picked, hiding the design from me, but I have to turn my back to hide mine.

"Stop looking already," I laugh.

He groans, throwing his head back. "I can't. I'm dying to picture you in it."

Thankfully, I don't have to continue to dissuade him; it's his turn to check out.

Except he swipes my costume from my hands to pay for it, keeping his eyes off the design as he tucks it beneath his costume.

I gasp. "Rem!"

He chuckles, greeting the cashier. They quickly ring up the

costumes, and I accidentally peek at Remington's costume choice.

We agreed on equally "cheap, slutty Halloween costumes," but I didn't expect Remington to be able to find an outfit for himself that's this revealing: his knightly "armor" only covers the tops of his shoulders and chest, leaving his abdomen exposed. Rather than pants, there's just a floppy little skirt to fit around his hips, padded with fake armor over a rich, red loincloth.

Remington hums. "Lilibeth Norris."

I bite my lips, quickly averting my eyes. "I– I saw nothing."

His sharp, huffing laugh makes the cashier blink a few times, spurring Remington into even more laughter as we exit the store.

"Answer me honestly: did you see it?"

I shake my head. "Not on you, so it didn't count."

He laughs, pulling me to his side with a big hand on top of my head. Leaning down to mutter into my ear, Remington deepens his low voice. "Naughty girl."

My stomach flip-flops. I really do feel naughty, considering what we're about to use these costumes for.

By the time we've settled back into Remington's apartment, my gut rumbles with anticipatory nerves. Remington's moody, vampire-chic bedroom suits our medieval costumes perfectly; his pillows are bloody shades of wine red, fluffy black blankets drape over his black bed frame like pelted coats, and a collection of various leather harnesses hung on the walls add an extra believability to the "dungeon" atmosphere. With candles lit, Remington and I separate to put on our outfits.

The second I see him in his skimpy knight costume, my heart flips. His tattoos are on full display, as well as his athletic thighs and cold, perky nipples, leaving my imagination to run wild.

But Remington's eyes dart away from me. "Fuck, L.L.B.–"

I squirm against my tiny costume, struggling to choose between keeping it pulled up over my nipples or down over my ass. "S-sorry, I– I think it's a little small."

The second we meet eyes, we erupt into giggles.

"Yeah, I–" Remington clears his throat, his hands zipping between his legs. "I'm getting a little too eager just looking at you, clearly. If I'm not careful, something's going to pop out of my clothes too."

I sputter out a laugh. Dashing to meet him, I huddle against his bare chest.

Remington isn't only proficient in knitting yarn; as we run through our scene, he knots a gorgeous flower pattern over my chest, cupping my breasts and crossing over both shoulders in a satiating, squeezing knot behind my back. I feel so held, my body buzzing with blissful warmth.

My eyes droop shut as Remington circles me to assess his work. "Thank you."

"You're doing so well, baby girl. I'm trying not to look too closely so I can have the effect of rushing up to find you in our scene, but just your softened lips are doing wild, dangerous things to my poor heart."

Biting back a smile, I open my eyes to find Remington's tender stare. Stooping to plant a leisurely, cushy kiss on my mouth, he flips my heart three times over.

"I feel spoiled already," I whisper.

Remington hums through a smile. "Good. What's the safeword, baby?"

"Alligator."

"Good girl." Fetching three more ropes for simple ties around my thighs, ankles, and wrists, Remington completes our preparations. "I've got you the whole way through. We can stop anytime - and I want you to use that word. Don't hold back for me, even if I'm about to come."

"Okay. I'd be happy to stop whenever you need to too, even if I seem like I'm having the time of my life."

Remington chuckles. "Thank you, sweet girl. Are you feeling nervous at all?"

With my thighs squished together tight, I take a deep breath, allowing Remington to pull and prod my loose muscles as he gathers my wrists together, completing my final bindings. "I was, but now that I have you here against me, I feel really good."

Dark, curious eyes zip to mine as Remington hugs my bound wrists to his chest, dropping his chin to kiss my knuckles. "That makes me feel even better too. I love you."

"I love you too."

"I'm going to lift you, baby. Okay?"

I smile. "Okay."

Easing me into his arms, Remington carries my bound body from his bathroom, settling me softly on my feet at his open bedroom doorway. Candlelight from his dresser flickers off his tattoos, creating an animated illusion with the sharp, black illustrations.

Hopping one step forward, I line myself beneath the pull-up bar secured over Remington's doorway, ready to secure my wrists over it.

Remington's hand trails over my lower back as he side-steps past me, sending a shiver up my spine. He keeps mere inches between us, his even, warm breath sweeping over my bare skin as he tests and re-tests the pull-up bar for stability.

But he looks startlingly serious.

"Are you okay, Rem?" I whisper. "Do you feel ready?"

He hums. "Very. But I feel like I need to reiterate something."

"Okay, absolutely."

Slowly extending my wrists over my head, Remington gazes deep into my eyes. "It might seem like on the outside that I'm holding all the power and control over you right now, but I want to be clear about why." Hooking my wrists to the bar above us, Remington tugs my arms into a deep, tingling stretch. "You've gifted that control to me for the night. Any power I hold over you now is still yours. It will always be yours. And it's hard to explain just how beautiful it is that you've trusted me to hold it for tonight."

My heartbeat pulses wildly enough to thump into my ears. "Remington, I didn't think I could ever play this out in real life.

Thank you for being so patient in practicing to get me here, and accepting my secret fantasies in the first place. I'm so, so grateful to have a chance to do the same for you."

Remington groans, giving me a hurried peck. "Good thing I get to come back to you in a second to ravish you. I better hurry and run away before either I kiss you dizzy or your arms get too tired."

I laugh. "Should we start?"

"Yes. See you soon, baby girl."

"See you, gorgeous knight."

Remington's footsteps fade down the hall behind me. I lower my weight until I hang by my wrists, closing my eyes to set myself in the mood.

This is a big scene we've worked on for a long time now. At first, we giggled while planning it together, but we grew far more serious as we developed a deeper, darker message beneath the scene to heal our hearts. In order for this scene to work, I have to begin by remembering the "evil dragon" who tortured me for 18 years, binding not only my body, but my soul.

A deep melancholy fills me, producing a spark of genuine anxiety in my chest at the thought of Dad grabbing my wrist again. I squirm a little against the rope around my wrists, pushing myself to feel even more of this fear - challenging my limits. Last month, I cried when Remington tied my wrists gently, but we gradually worked up until I could finally handle this scene.

I need to get this out. I'm ready.

A knight races down the hall right on cue, rushing toward me in the dungeon. I gasp, imagining the fear I feel every time I don't know who is approaching my back.

"Who's there?" I ask.

"Oh, Princess," Remington breathes.

My heart lifts; I'd recognize the voice of my long-lost lover anywhere. "Sir Remington, is that you?!"

"Yes, I've come to save you." My knight in shining armor circles me, his hand on the small of my back. I squirm faster, desperate to reach him. He steps into my view with burning eyes, taking in my restrained form. Wild runes scour his body, far more than I remember him having in our youth: a sign he's overcome numerous curses placed upon him on his journey to find me.

Sir Remington tugs on the ropes at my chest, jostling me with a single hand, but the ropes won't budge. "My poor princess. What did that demonic dragon do to you?"

"He—" To my surprise, tears prick my eyes, stealing my breath.

Remington pauses, studying my face.

But I choke out my line.

"He hurt me," I whisper. Remington's forehead warps at my shaky words. "He burnt my skin, leaving a permanent mark on my back. Then he bound me. But that's not the worst part: I'm stuck feeling his pain."

He cups my cheeks, softening his voice. "I'm so sorry he did this to you, Princess. Thank you so much for telling me the truth." My lip wobbles, and Remington catches my tears. "Tell me, what color is the candlelight beside us?"

He's checking if I'm okay with continuing. I take a deep breath.

"It's a beautiful green," I whisper.

"Good - that's what I see too. And that green is a good omen that I can rescue you even sooner. Just breathe through it for me, okay, Princess?"

I slowly exhale. "Okay, Sir."

"You're doing so well, sweet princess. Allow me to try to cut your restraints with my most blessed knife."

Fuck, I finally did it; I made it past the worst part for me. Smiling in relief, I allow the leftover shakiness in my voice to give Remington an extra boost in his favorite kink. "Please save me, Sir Remington— Only my true love can. I've longed for you desperately."

"Your true love is here. Keep breathing for me, Princess Lilibeth."

He drops to one knee, skating his hand down my bare thighs, the fluid movement interrupted by the ropes squeezing my legs into bulging around them. His fingertips halt on the rope binding my ankles, pulling at it to test its strength. Whipping a knife from a holster strapped over his thigh, Remington slips its chilly blade between my ankles. I breathe faster through its suggested danger, but Remington's hands smooth down the back of my thigh, pressing my skin to his mouth. His gentle lips shoot pleasure up my legs, swirling between them.

Remington stands, lowering his voice. "My sweet Princess, I'm afraid there's dark magic sealing these ropes, and I don't know the spell to release you."

"I do, Sir," I breathe.

Glancing up at my red hands, Remington slips both arms beneath my ass, lifting me to give my taut arms a break. Blood rushes back into my hands, pushing heavy, relieved gasps from my lips.

Holding me against his chest, Remington softens his voice. "You do? Then please, Princess, tell me how I can save you. I'll do anything."

Our noses brush over each other, fluttering my heart. I stray from our scene to press a long, sultry kiss into Remington's lips. He purrs, adjusting his arms beneath me to allow one hand a massaging squeeze of my ass.

Once the heat of our lips trickles to my groin, I break our kiss. "Sir Remington, I've saved myself for you, and the dragon desires a virgin's blood. Defile me. Make me worth nothing."

That line strikes my heart harder than I expected it would, carrying shame I've had placed on me my whole life; the longer I've dated Remington, the more I've realized I viewed my main purpose as a girlfriend was to supply sexual pleasure. But this pleasure also carries taboo, warping me into an unholy, wicked creature no matter how "pure" or "impure" I make myself.

But if I'm an inherently vile creature, Remington stands at the gates of hell with me, ready to face all wrath. That line also means what I want it to for our relationship: I chose Remington to take more firsts from me, including enacting this private fantasy. And he has welcomed all of my flaws and secrets with open arms.

Both of us breathe hard and fast, our air mixing between our gaping lips. Remington kisses me again, but this time, it's because he's nervous to say his line.

Beyond the main storyline we're sticking to, we improvise our role plays to keep them fresh. But there are a few lines in particular we're sure to mention: for Act One, there's "I've come to save you," "He hurt me," "Save me," "Defile me," and Remington's final line in this act. The one he's holding me higher for, knowing my arms can't take it if he waits too long.

But as he settles my toes back on the ground, he looks me in the eyes. "If these are his wicked tricks, then perhaps I understand this spell better than I believed. After all, I've fought my own dragons to meet you here."

My heart shreds at the quiet, strained tone of his voice. I still don't know who his other dragon was - other than his last ex - but I don't need to know. I'm happy to help him through this in any way I can.

I breathe out the pain in my heart. "Sir Remington, I'd never wish this on you."

He bites his lips. After a hard swallow, he kisses me softly. "It's alright now; I've made it through. And now I can use everything I've learned to rescue you in whichever way it takes."

We did it. We made it to Act Two.

"But I dare not defile you, Princess. I'll love you with my seed, so the only thing I'll defile is your dragon's fun. You'll be worth nothing to him, but everything to me."

I bite back a smile. That wasn't planned, but I love it. Maybe I can get creative too. "Then, Please, Sir. These ropes are bound over my heart. I only wish for them to be released by you, my true love."

A smoldering flicker in Remington's eyes sets my nerves ablaze. "They *are* bound over your heart, aren't they? That simply won't do. I've made a silent vow to take care of that heart of yours."

Remington stoops before me, sweeping his hands down my restrained form. The cool, cheap fabric of my tiny dress chills my burning abdomen, but the heat of Remington's palms sears me once he reaches my compressed thighs, giving them rough squeezes. I squirm beyond my control as tingles race up my body.

The pressure of my arms being pulled taut is working its magic on my core again. I droop my weight a little deeper, squeezing my knees together to rub my clit.

Just watching me squirm, Remington purrs like he swallowed a mouthful of something delicious. His hands skate back up, flicking the flimsy skirt that barely covers my pussy. As he meets my eyes again, his fingers trace the ropes tied beneath my breasts. "Are you sure you wish to give yourself to me?"

"Yes, Sir Remington. You're my hero."

His dark eyes flicker from my words. I planned that myself, hoping it'd break his cool.

With a shaky breath through his nose, Remington steps closer. I hang frozen, awaiting whatever he decides next; Act Two only ends once I tell Remington I can't bear hanging here any longer, requiring me to utilize our safeword. I'll be gathering the courage to use it without overthinking - the most extreme "no" I could give him during our scene - and in the meantime, I've given Remington full permission to tease, kiss, or penetrate me at any angle he'd like.

One second, he's still. The next, he yanks the front of my dress, exposing both breasts. I yelp in surprise, followed by heavy, pleased breaths as Remington massages his thumbs over my bare, hardening nipples. Just his caressing touch on my breasts ripples buzzing pleasure down my abdomen, restarting my heartbeat; I've never been genuinely restrained to this level, adding a tremendous excitement to Remington's every shift in touch. Especially as I stare into his fierce eyes.

Remington hums at my gaping lips. "Gorgeous, naughty girl. That feels good, doesn't it?"

Leaning forward, I rub my breasts against his hands. "Y-yes, Sir Remington. Please, I want more of your hands on me."

"Perhaps you're not as pure as your dragon wishes. Have you ever touched yourself, Princess?"

I huff out sharp, panting breaths as his palms sweep faster, switching from dragging down my hips to brushing just above my pubic bone to heavier, pulsing massages over my bare breasts.

My voice comes out airy and weak as my core clenches. "Secretly. In my bedchambers."

Remington purrs. Dragging his fingertips down the center of my torso, I flinch in delight when he lightly sweeps over my clit. Circling my body, he keeps his warm hands on me at all times - letting me feel how close he remains against me since I can't turn my head to watch him. Each sweeping touch over my thighs, up my back, and down the curve of my ass heightens the goosebumps on my limbs. Wet heat pools between my legs.

When he grips my hip bones from behind, pulling my ass out behind me, my heart hammers faster. I know my skirt does nothing to cover me, rolling higher by the second. Whipping my panties down, Remington has to pause to peel their center off my soaked core. As my breath speeds, Remington's low growl amplifies the tremendous tingles buzzing through my rapidly numbing arms. He drags his fingers down my exposed labia, rubbing a delighted jerk out of my hips.

"Naughty Princess. You're absolutely soaked." He clicks his tongue. "And here I planned to tease you over the edge first."

Two of his fingers press into my pussy from behind. Sputtering out a gasp at how heavy the pleasure roots into my gut, I jerk on my restraints. The doorframe creaks in complaint, and we both look up.

I choke out an accidental giggle. "I-is it okay?"

Remington's deep chuckle tickles my spine just before he kisses the back of my neck. "Yes. You're safe. Even if it fell, I'd catch you."

Plunging his fingers deeper, Remington spreads warmth over my bare upper back with his heavy breath. As he curls delicious pressure into my G-spot with thick fingers, I part my lips, forcing Remington to hold me steady as I thrust back into his touch. His erection bumps my squirming ass, hitching my breath; he's wet too.

Shoving my skirt all the way up to my mid back, Remington exposes my full mark. "Does that feel good, Princess?"

As I lean into the stretch, fucking myself over his fingers while the rope pulls at my core, I release a soft moan through my exhale, closing my eyes. "So good, my knight."

He hums, kissing just below my neck to send a thrill down my spine. "I thought so. You feel ready for me– Look how deep I can stretch you."

Adding a third finger, Remington glides deeper, dragging right over my G-spot until his knuckles squish into my ass. I choke out a moaning breath, my legs shaking from how desperately my body wants to spread my tied legs for him.

But as he curls his fingers a few more times, spurring heartier moans from me, I'm surprised by how eagerly I thrust my hips back for more. Remington breathes hard behind me. Soft, slick sounds separate from the ones he's creating inside me tell me he's stroking himself in preparation for me.

I twist through the burn in my arms, my pussy gripping his fingers beyond my control. "Sir, you're– You're about to make me come too soon–"

Hooking his hand around my hips, Remington pulses one set of fingers inside me, and the other set stroking in every direction over my clit. Pleasure strikes me so deep that I hop, my lungs heaving in time with each penetrative curl of his fingers. My moan escapes as more of a small yell, shocking even me.

"Fuck, yes, Princess. That was hot as hell. Keep going."

As Remington pulses faster, I hang lower, bucking my hips back over him. The raging fire in my arms makes me lightheaded enough to quiver on the edge, presenting my ass higher for deeper attention.

Just before I come, Remington's fingers slip from me, replaced by his hot, stiff shaft. He plunges deep in one thrust, pushing a harsh gasp from me.

Remington groans. "Fuck, you're squeezing me so hard–"

With one wet hand smashing my ass into him and the other hooking around my hips to swirl around my clit, Remington spurs me into frantic, gasping moans. The pull-up bar groans in complaint as I wriggle over Remington's shaft, but neither of us cares about it this time, pleasure crawling up my belly until my climax spills over. I melt into his thrusts, all my weight carried by my wrists. I'm whining through every breath, but I cry out in delight as Remington softly pats my clit in time with his rapid thrusts, extending my orgasm.

"Good girl, Princess, keep–" He moans alongside me. "Keep going."

I've never been this loud, but the sound of my own voice echoing off Remington's walls doubles the thrill of how I imagine I must look - wrapped up just for him. His delicious, heavy strokes inside me slow with my shaking, exhausted breaths.

Remington drags his hands over my lower belly, stepping closer with a low purr. "God, you did so fucking well, Princess."

His words inspire a hard squeeze over his cock, forcing him to grunt. But now that he made me come as hard as I could, pain bursts through my arms, no longer numb from pleasure.

For a second, I hesitate. Is this pain bad enough to use our safeword for? Is it really okay to stop him? Maybe I can bear it.

But as Remington hugs me closer, slowing his hips into tender nudges, another blast of pleasure between my legs conflicts with my worries. I want to enjoy this with him, but I can't.

Wait, of course my pain is enough reason to stop. That's the whole reason why we planned the scene like this.

Even after validating myself, my heart screams through anxiety; I'm still hardwired to fear a no's wrath.

I'm hardly able to speak up, my voice quivering. "Sir Remington, I-I see an alligator outside."

Remington freezes. "*Good girl.* What a good, good job." His hands zip to my wrists, pulling them a bit higher to unhook them. I whimper at the deeper stretch, but Remington coos behind my head. "Keep breathing, baby girl. Bear with it for me for one more second– You've got this–"

I wince, stretching as high as I can with my limp, blood-drained arms. It's just enough for Remington to be able to shove the rope off the hook, gasping with me as my arms drop against my thighs with a thud.

"You did it," Remington rasps, frantically squeezing life back into my arms. I drop back against him, heaving my breaths to the ceiling as I shudder through the buzzing pain of my blood returning to my limbs. As he steps even closer, bending to hug his hips tight against my pelvis, his deep flex inside my core shocks my breath out of me.

Now that I said "no," having him inside me feels ten times as delicious.

"Oh, Rem– I-I want more."

"Yeah? You feel okay for Act Three?"

"Yes," I breathe. "I feel so close to you."

Turning over my shoulder, I meet Remington's wild, dark eyes. He sweeps his palms down my breasts and belly as he presses a deep kiss into my lips, fluttering my pussy over him. His delighted purr flips my heart.

Breaking our kiss, Remington stares me down with a sultry grin. "You broke the spell on one of your bindings, Princess, but now it's my turn. Bend over."

Squeezing my wrists to my chest hardly stifles the thrill Remington just shot through me. But as I bend at the waist, his hand settles around the knot behind my upper back, gripping utter control over my torso with a single palm.

My jaw drops; he lifts me just enough to pull my ass flush against him, burying himself deeper than he has yet. Except with such a tight knot around the front of my chest and a tender, slow press directly into my G-spot, he's giving my heart the deepest hug I've ever felt. I roll through the pleasure flaming low in my belly, allowing it to spill from my open lips.

After reflecting on the fear within my back and wrist injuries, the pure bliss Remington kneads into my core from tying me up startles rapid gasps from me.

"Oh, Princess," Remington breathes. "Are you okay? I've never heard you like this."

"I— love you," I gasp, unable to speak another word as my eyes flutter shut.

Remington hums, pulling me closer with a sharper tug. My body is so loose for him that I roll into him, my ass mushing against his hips. He sweeps gentle pressure over the sensitive scar tissue on my lower back, introducing a cascade of shivers through my chest. I shudder through them aloud, peeking at Remington over my shoulder.

His dark irises stare back between deep, pleased blinks. The sight of Remington indulging in himself over me, his hands squishing firmer into my skin as his chest heaves in bliss, flexes me over him tighter.

But as he applies harder pressure to my chest, yanking me tight against his rocking hips, he moans in time with me, opening his eyes to meet mine. "I love you so much."

An intensifying buzz sweeps my body - just in time for Remington to bend over with me, hugging me around the hips. He smushes heavy palms over my sides and breasts, fluttering my eyes shut with how cuddled I feel. Keeping our hips bound, Remington pulses deep pressure into my lower belly rather than slipping in and out of me. Each little nudge of his shaft massages every inch of my pussy, spilling such heavy tingles over my whole body that my nipples harden.

Remington is close, and I'll never get over the sweet, giddy rush I get from his tell; he always huddles into me as close as he can just before he comes, desperate to kiss me. With his chin tucking against my shoulder, I lift my bound wrists just enough to touch the edge of his jaw. Through our colliding lips, we moan in time to Remington's slowing, deepening thrusts, his hard breath shaking through his nose.

He breaks our kiss to wrap one arm around my hips and the other around my chest, gripping the knot over my sternum as hard as he can before curling me tight into his chest. Cuddled from all angles, I cry out in bliss. With my pussy flexing rapidly over him, Remington's grip grows tighter. His lips open against mine, and he shudders through a heavy orgasm, nearly toppling us over as his cum floods the space between my thighs. Righting us with a quick tug on the ropes on my back, Remington delivers such delicious friction that I wriggle beneath him.

"Remington—"

"Oh, you were such a good girl for me. Lean into it, baby." He heaves through heavy breaths, shocking my nervous system with a tender rub over my mark. As he grabs my hips in both hands, Remington tilts my core to reach as deep as he can, each speeding stroke rubbing fuzzy pressure over my G-spot. Fluid gushes down my legs at the extra massage.

"Yes, there you go. Picture it for me, baby girl. Picture us loosening these ropes around your heart, freeing you to express every side of you these dragons say is shameful."

My heart pounds wildly as I do as I'm told, imagining my heart opening with each crash of our hips. I moan from my gaping jaw as Remington smooths his thrusts, meeting my shaking thighs with rolling tenderness. As I quiver on the edge, my knees threatening to buckle beneath intense pleasure, Remington rushes to keep me upright, hugging me as hard as he can. With his arms locked around me in a tight embrace, each rub over my G-spot spills over in a sugary, blossoming warmth, my fluid splashing between my thighs as I come. Remington's soft kisses against my cheek throb loving pulses through my heart, carrying me through my orgasm in an overwhelming mix of emotions.

By the time Remington has massaged me into a breathless, mushy ball, he can't speak either. Shaky hands rush to untie my legs, leaving me desperate to turn around and see his sweet face.

"I've got you–" Remington rasps, hastily yanking the knot loose around my wrists.

As I groan through the sudden freedom, Remington grips my hips, slipping himself out of me. We both gasp as a combination of our fluids spill from me, but Remington swoops in to lift me.

"Oh, sweet baby girl–"

Settling me on the bed, Remington swipes a towel over my soaked thighs with frantic, rough precision. But the second I see his eyes rimmed in red, I throw my arms around his neck, kissing him hard.

Remington clings to my back, sucking in sharp, shaky breaths through the start of fresh tears. I stroke his head, unable to grip enough of him. I'm still bound over my chest, but I don't realize it until he grabs a fistful of the knot on my back, squeezing my ribcage to push a flood of loving, cuddly pleasure through my chest. My muscles soften, drooping me against him, and Remington hums.

"I'm so fucking proud of you."

I whimper at how raw his voice sounds. "I'm so proud of *you*, Rem. I feel so soft with you."

Remington gasps over me, cupping my cheeks. We stroke each other's heads and cheeks, staring into each other's eyes. I didn't expect to feel this emotional with him after this scene, but I can't get over how deeply trusting he was of me - and how safe he helped me feel in one of my most vulnerable moments.

As we clean and massage each other, Remington and I take a long time to slow our breaths. We peel our sweaty costumes from each other, interlocking sweaty, naked limbs on top of Remington's bed.

Remington's considerate fingers smooth delicate pressure down my sore wrists and thighs. "How are you feeling now?"

"Good," I whisper. "A bit more grounded. What about you?"

"I'm still floating a little. I probably will be forever."

I laugh, pressing a lazy kiss into his mouth. Our lips remain locked for a few breaths, inhaling each other's air before pulling away to resume looking into each other's eyes.

"You're not going to want to release me so I can ice you, huh?" Remington grins. I giggle, shaking my head, and he chuckles. "Then let's go over what we liked, and what we'd like to do differently next time."

I bite my lip, unable to contain a smile at the thought of there being a next time. That we could continue to play and heal like this as long as we wish. But as I skate my fingertips through Remington's sweaty hair, I know exactly what I'd like better.

"I'd like to see your eyes more next time," I whisper. "I felt like my heart was in it even more whenever our eyes met behind my shoulder - when you bent over to kiss me to tell me without words that you were enjoying yourself. It made me feel extra connected to you."

Remington freezes. It's only after I give him a few quick squeezes down his arms that he resumes his gentle touches over my back. "I didn't know you understood that so clearly, but I– I feel really seen. So taken care of."

My heart lifts above the bed, holding him there with me. "I'm so happy to hear that."

He blinks through a giddy, touched smile, snuggling in even closer. "And, L.L.B., I have to say– I really loved that you could say 'no' to me. I know you might still see it as an inconvenience for me to have to stop, but to be honest, you saying 'no' actually makes me feel way more relaxed that I really do have your consent."

I'm stunned silent. My heart restarts as I blink, piecing together everything he just told me. I knew saying "no" was necessary for my own safety, but I never thought so clearly about how it grants Remington his. What I perceived as rejecting him was actually protecting his sense of security. My "no" doesn't hinder him; it rescues him.

My heart tumbles over itself as Remington massages my sore wrists, quieting his breath as he gives me room to process. But the more he applies gentle, loving pressure there to replace the hurt my dad caused me, the more I crave feeling Remington all over me.

"I miss the feeling of being held up by you. It was so nice," I whisper.

Remington breaks into a massive grin. "God, I'm so fucking happy to hear you telling me what you like so openly these days. Come here, baby."

Balling me up on the bed against his chest, Remington snuggles me into his bare skin before draping his fluffy blankets over our cooled, damp bodies. As he nestles me into the deepest sleep I've ever experienced, it's with the knowledge that someone in this life has seen more of me than I knew I had within me, unraveling it for both of us to see. I hope he feels just as safe.

CHAPTER THIRTEEN

I've graduated to pull-ups.

Remington's bright stare meets me in the mirror. "You've got it, you've got it! Just one more!"

I huff through my nod, my muscles boosted by his encouragement. As I hoist myself higher, Remington's phone rings for the third time in the past three minutes. I've rarely heard it ring once in the eight months we've known each other, so I peek at Remington.

"Are you sure it's okay?" I grunt through my fifth rep.

"I'll check it after. You've totally got this. I'll just give you a tiny boost for the last one."

With his hands on my waist, Remington boosts me just enough to be able to do a sixth pull-up. I hop from the bar with a bright smile, excited for Remington's glomping, celebratory hugs.

He laughs, giving me an extra squeeze. "I'm so fucking proud of you!"

"Thank you," I huff. "I couldn't do this without you. Like so many things."

His wide grin lifts my heart. "Same for me, baby girl. Same for me."

While I guzzle down water, Remington digs his phone out of his gym bag. But when he grips the back of his neck, I freeze. His back tenses beneath his soaked gray T-shirt, kickstarting my heart.

"Rem? What's wrong?"

Before I can rush to his side, Remington buries his eyes into his forearm, hitching out a sob. My heart drops. I've never seen him so upset. I rub his back, but he walks in a circle, glancing around us like someone might be watching.

"Come here," I whisper, guiding him to a more private corner where the mirror ends.

Squatting behind a weight rack, Remington lifts his shirt collar over his nose, rubbing his eyes with the fabric. "Sorry, I haven't cried over this in a long time."

"You're okay - just keep breathing, okay? Can I see the text?"

Keeping his eyes hidden in his shirt, Remington passes me his phone.

Natalia: I tried to call but I don't want you to have to pick up the phone to hear it from anyone else. Uncle Ernesto died.

My stomach drops. "Oh, God, Rem, I'm so sorry… Were you close to him?"

He flinches. Sitting unmoving for a whole minute, Remington stares into the distance - even as I vigorously rub his back and arms, whispering his name and reassurances.

Until Remington stands, striding to his gym bag. "I need to go home."

I chase after him, close behind. "Did I say something wrong?"

"No, I need to be with you, alone. I'm panicking, hardcore."

I knew he was gravely upset, but he's right; I've never seen every muscle in his body so taut and his forehead so strained. And after knowing him intimately, I've also had many chances to recognize that his anxiety shows up as silence.

Rushing to the parking lot, I keep my arm around his waist. "We're almost to the car."

He nods.

What do I even do? Am I making this worse for him? Missing something that could be helping him?

Focus, Lilibeth. This isn't about me; it's about Remington. I open the passenger door of Remington's car, and he glances at me as he steps in. "Sorry."

I lean in after him as he puts his seatbelt on, sorting his sweaty hair over his forehead. "Please, don't be sorry. I'm here for you too, baby. Okay?"

He warps back into tears, shredding my heart.

I give him as big of a hug as I can. "Rem, I'm so sorry you're hurting. I wish I could take it away, but I know I can't."

"Thank you," he whispers.

He doesn't say anything else the whole drive home. I cling tighter to the steering wheel, unable to stop checking on Remington in my peripherals. But by the time we're a block from his apartment, Remington closes his eyes, slackening into his seat.

"Are you okay?" I whisper.

He gives a low hum. "Tired."

After parking, I rush to help Remington from the car. But he's already out, heading for the parking lot elevators. Dashing after him, my stomach drops. I knew his heart was heavy, but his dragging, clodding footsteps tell me his body carries an equally unbearable burden. I've never seen anything hit Remington so hard.

We lay together in the pitch-black darkness. I snuggle up to Remington in his bed, doing my best to be a grounding force, but he's far from relaxed. His heart races beneath my palm, just as stressed as his heavy breath. His eyes are closed, and he hasn't said a word since we got home. He said what he needed was to be alone with me, but I still feel helpless; all I can do is lay here with him as he rides out his anxiety.

It takes an hour for him to speak again. His voice is rough with exhaustion. "L.L.B.?"

"Yes?"

"I didn't ever explain to you why I got into kink and BDSM, and I'm sorry about that. It's just not something I like going over."

"Okay. Do you feel like you want to share it? I don't want you to feel like you have to."

He hums. "Baby girl, you're too good to me."

I prop myself on my elbow to face him in the total darkness, running my hand down the thickness of his torso that I can only feel rising beside me, not see. "You've done the exact same. I really want to be there for you, so I'm sorry I'm not too good at it."

"You are," he whispers. Remington's swallow is followed by a deep hum, but it's not as soothing as usual; there's a dash of stress in his strained voice. "I wouldn't have done any of this with you if I didn't feel safe around you."

I smile, even though my heart still aches for him. Leaning over his chest, I dip to plant a soft, smooth kiss over Remington's lips. He breathes into me, dragging a heavy hand across my back in slow sweeps. Goosebumps trickle down my spine, easing my body against him. Remington adjusts himself to face me, and I adjust with him until we lay nose-to-nose in the pure darkness.

"I don't know how to say this to anyone. It's weird to just say on a whim," Remington whispers.

I smooth my hand down his neck before planting a small kiss on his jaw. "Maybe you might need to just say it, even if it comes out wrong - like you have to say to me."

He chuckles. "Maybe. Then, first off, I have diagnosed PTSD from this, and my ex made it worse."

My heart flips. Of course I know what PTSD is, but I don't know-know its symptoms. I'll have to research it later.

Remington sucks in a sharp breath, then holds it.

I rub his chest. "K-keep breathing."

His exhale shatters as it exits, tearing at my heart. Flipping onto his back again, he grips my hand to his chest. "We used to have the whole family stay over on Christmas Eve, especially with my cousins. Almost everyone would get wasted after the kids went to bed - or before, to be honest. But either way, there's one time–" He huffs. "One time in particular was extra bad."

I cling to Remington tighter. I'd be afraid of where this was going even if I didn't know him, but since I do, the pieces are falling into place in the worst way.

"Y-you're doing so well," I whisper.

He blows out a long breath. "Sweet girl. I don't want to make you listen to this."

"What if I want to?"

My heart pounds almost as hard as Remington's beneath our clasped palms. He shuffles beside me as if he's itching in his own skin.

Until finally, he whispers, "My uncle got blackout drunk every year. And there wasn't enough room for all of us, so my sister and I slept in the same bed, which was fine since I was eight and she was only ten. But my uncle came in to–" I wince, and Remington clears his throat. When he speaks again, his voice is unusually flat. "He came in to touch Natalia, or who knows what else. Anyway, I stopped him, and he didn't like that, so I offered to take her place, which– Which was not something I wanted, but all that I knew to do to keep her safe. I played the fucking hero and fucked myself up for life. But I don't know if it was even worth it. I can't decide if Natalia would've felt worse having it done to her or if she feels worse now from the guilt of trading places with her baby brother and having to hide in the corner to watch us."

I can hardly breathe. I'm so horrified for Remington that I don't know what to say. He hums again, rubbing my back.

"You okay, baby girl? I know you have your own dragons–"

I choke out a heavy breath. "Remington, no– I'm so sorry you were subjected to this. I just hate that he did that to you so much that I don't know how to put it into words, I just–"

Remington hums, pulling me into a hug. "It's okay."

But I straighten in his arms, cupping his cheek. "No, Rem. It's not. It never was, and it's not your fault, even if your sister has trauma now too. It's all his fault– And I wish I could help you."

My voice waters beyond my control. I don't want to take away from him, but Remington's sweet brushing over my head holds so much more meaning now. He's not playing the hero because he was unsuccessful at rescuing someone; he's playing the hero because that little eight-year-old hero needed rescuing too, but no one came to save him.

"You do help me," he whispers. "You're grounding me more than you know. I can't believe I'm relatively okay right now."

"Even if you're not, it's okay. Thank you so much for telling me this, but–" I breathe hard, terrified I'm about to say something insensitive. But I have to try. "I don't want you to be strong for me. You can be my rescuer while we play, but what if, at least once, we try a scene where I can be your rescuer too?"

Remington lets out a soft, smiling chuckle. It's not until I hear the nasally sound of his laugh that I realize he's been silently crying. "Lilibeth, I'm literally telling you you're rescuing me right now. You're not seeing how sweet you're being towards me."

"It's not enough. I wish I could rush into your room and protect that little Rem. Go back in time to save you. I so, so wish I could - to at least be there to hold you and heal you after. To be the one who actually showed him love."

Remington falls quiet. I cup his cheeks, worried I've triggered him worse.

His body shakes beside mine, and my soul plummets. I sit up taller, ready to spring into action to help him, but Remington thrusts himself across the bed, tackling me into a hard hug. His breath shudders as he settles into deeper, heart-wrenching tears, but at least I can hold him. I hug his head to my chest with one hand, squeezing his back as hard as I can with the other.

"Thank you." His voice quivers. "Thank you for always remembering me too."

"We don't have to do this," I say.

Remington hardly dressed up for his uncle's funeral. He's been alternating between moody, weepy, and numb all weekend, but now he looks plain ill.

"I have to. I know I sound like a monster, Lilibeth, but I have to see him dead to feel safe in this world."

My heart flips, but I understand. I'm just shocked that someone else voiced the secret thoughts I've had about my father for decades.

Gripping Remington's hand, I nod. "You're not a monster. You've been running from a dragon since you were eight, and everyone knows you have to make sure you see how the villains die to make sure they're truly gone forever."

He shuts his eyes, but a slow, weary half-smile appears. "You're right, baby. You get me." Opening his eyes again, Remington tracks his family members as they pass by our car. He ducks his head out of view, kissing my knuckles behind the steering wheel's cover. "Let's just get this over with."

We stand in the very back of the small ceremony. As Remington's family sniffles and shares various memories about Ernesto, Remington stares at his uncle's coffin, his expression perfectly flat.

But I can feel the rage brewing beneath his hot skin. It's a rage I know well.

As they lower the coffin into the ground, everyone moves to say their final goodbyes.

Except for us.

I stand in silence beside Remington, staring at everyone's agonized backs.

"Do you feel okay sharing what you're thinking with me?" I whisper.

He clenches his jaw. "I feel like a shit person, but I hate seeing everyone so sad over him. So, basically, I'm standing here, wondering what's wrong with me."

"I think hating this makes perfect sense. It's insulting to see your loved ones support someone who hurt you."

Remington's eyebrows flinch, but he turns to me. "You understand, don't you. *Really* understand."

I swallow hard. "I do. I love my mom, but I've felt tremendously abandoned by her for a long time for not rescuing me from my dad."

Remington scoots a little closer, and my heart flips. Just that little step was enough of a shift to feel like we're standing here as a unit, creating our own loving, protective barrier over our hearts.

It's only once the dirt piles over the coffin that Remington's shoulders finally settle. I can tell by the way he's fidgeting that he's sick of being here.

The second it ends, we don't stay to stick around and chat with family, even turning away from Remington's grieving parents.

But his sister, Natalia, approaches us. She didn't cry the whole funeral, but with one look at Remington's blank expression, she bursts into tears.

Remington finally softens. He dashes to his older sister, pulling her into his arms.

"I'm so sorry, Remi."

I bite back my own tears at Natalia's breaking voice. I wish I could hug Annabella like this too. To tell her I'm sorry I made her feel just as abandoned, and that I believe her with my whole heart.

"No, don't blame yourself ever again," Remington mutters. "I mean it. I'm okay. He's finally gone."

She nods, pulling back. "Can I go back to Mom and Dad's with you?"

He gives her a half-up smile. "Hell yeah. Now I get to ride with my two favorite women in the world."

Natalia breaks into a smile, extending her arm for me. The

three of us walk to Remington's car with our arms around each other, smiling despite heavy hearts.

Thankfully, Remington's sister is a safe face amongst the chaos of their parents' house. But chaos might be underestimating this. Remington has hardly moved: a silent column in a room of shouting, criticizing, and mocking laughter.

Outside of his playful aspects, I consider Remington a soothing person. But his silence today is far from calm. He almost looks unfamiliar, devoid of emotion and unwilling to participate in conversations beyond a few simple words.

At first, I felt horribly sad for him. But the more his family harasses him for not speaking, his cousin even pushing him back into his seat to keep him from leaving, the faster my simmering anger bubbles.

Is this what I looked like all those years, amongst Dad's chaos? Snuffing the life out of myself until I fell utterly silent, unable to even say "no?"

I grip Remington's hand, squeezing a few times - our silent safeword. He doesn't squeeze back, so I lean in as close as possible to whisper, "Can you tell me what color the stoplight was while we were driving, earlier?"

He blinks a few times, as if I'm snapping him out of a haze. "I think… yellow."

So he's okay, but on the brink of "red."

"Let's just leave," I whisper.

But his cousin spots us whispering, shouting across the dinner table. "Ahó, cugino! You still into that fucked-up sex shit?"

My heart flips. I can't believe he said that in front of the whole table. Remington ducks his head, and my gut churns - shame radiates off his tense shoulders, which is the last thing I'd want him to feel about what we do together in private. But with how tightly Remington clenches his jaw, I'm afraid of how this will play out.

Natalia rubs his arm, muttering what Mom used to say to me when I'd get myself too worked up. "Scialla, scialla–"

"She your new toy?" His cousin laughs, lifting one finger from his crossed arm to loosely point at me.

The whole table falls silent. I don't know what to do or say, my shoulders rising to my ears as everyone turns their eyes on me - and not in a good way.

But Remington lifts dark, piercing irises to his cousin, sending a chill down my spine. His voice shifts from a low growl to a yell. "*Vaffanculo!*"

My jaw drops. I certainly remember that Italian word, but I've never heard it spoken so wholeheartedly - to the point where I'm not looking forward to how Remington's cousin responds.

Thankfully, multiple men hold his cousin back as the whole family erupts into a shouting match. The volume rises loud enough to crackle my eardrums. I flinch into Remington, and he does a double-take.

"Fuck, my poor girl," he says, tucking me close. "That's not how I think of you, okay? Please, don't listen to them. I'm sorry for yelling."

Staring Remington's raw fear in the face, I clutch him harder. He's not okay. Squeezing pressure down his arms as fast as I can, I quiver through my words. "I know, Rem, I know. I'm taking you out of this place, okay?"

When I stand, Remington sucks in a tight breath.

And I raise my voice louder than I have in years. "Hey!"

Everyone freezes, turning to me. Maybe I really have gained some real confidence.

I clear my throat, softening my voice. "I've had enough of this conversation now. We're going home. Thank you for dinner."

A gasp resounds from the table's opposite end.

A sea of eyes zips their focus to Remington's mother. She's beet red. "You can't go! Ignore these idiot men – we haven't finished eating!"

I remain standing. "And I've had enough of this conversation now. We're going home. I hope you have a nice rest of your night."

I've kept my back straight and chin high, but when I peek at Remington still sitting beside me, his eyes are wide.

But they're filled with hope. That eight-year-old boy sits beside me through his adult body, begging someone to come rescue him.

I steel my jaw, puffing my chest. Truthfully, I'm terrified, but I want to be strong for him. I will. I am.

A sudden calm washes over Remington's eyes.

His mother leaps from her seat. "Remi, please! Don't do this to your mother."

Remington doesn't spare her a glance. He stands, facing me, and softly smiles. Not his half-up smile, but the gentle one that reaches his eyes. "Sorry, Ma. You heard my girl; we're leaving."

Wrapping his arm over my shoulder, Remington chuckles as we stride for the door. His family calls after us, but we keep our eyes locked, smiling wider the further we step away.

"God, you're such a badass. I'm so proud of you for speaking up so strongly, baby." Remington kisses my cheek. "Thank you so much for being there for me."

I smile, ducking my head. It's been a long time since I stood up to someone I initially wanted to impress like that. I'm a little shy to admit I feel proud of myself too, but I'm especially proud of Remington; as we speed walk down the sidewalk to the car, he lifts his head to the night sky, closing his eyes with a tremendous sigh - as if we just set him free.

But once we settle into our drive home, Remington remains quieter than usual. We're holding hands over the center console, and I drive as smoothly as possible, hoping he can relax.

About thirty minutes in, he mutters, "Thank you. I'm okay, just tired."

I bite my lip. I don't know exactly how to say what I want to say, but I want to try.

"Rem, I'm here for you, always. But it's okay to still be upset. I know leaving early or me having your back doesn't take away all the awful things they said to you."

He sighs, kissing my knuckles. "Sweet girl, it's really okay. I was in a bad place, so I lost my cool, but I have a high tolerance. They've said and done far worse. That was nothing."

Stopping at a red light, I hunch into the steering wheel, breathing through the tremendous ache his words created in my heart. Remington strokes my hair, ready to soothe me, but I grab his hand, holding it to my chest.

My voice comes out fragile. "They've done worse to you, baby? I'm so, *so* sorry. You didn't deserve that. Any of it."

Remington bites his lip, dropping his head. The light turns green, so I grab his hand, refocusing on the road. But he pulls our hands into his lap.

"You're a sweetheart," he breathes. I can tell he's trying to hide it, but the wetness in his voice is apparent.

I pull my hand from his, focusing on the road as I stroke his head beside me. He settles into my touch, breathing through soft sniffles as we drive in silence. I continue to rub him the best I can: down his back, across his shoulders, and soft scratches over his scalp.

After watching him be hurt by his family, it kills me to hear him hurting without being able to hold him. I want to be there for him. I want to be his hero too.

But I can also see why it might feel too vulnerable for him to be the one being saved. Showing weakness felt deadly under that roof.

Just like it feels around Dad.

"Can I give you a bath when we get home?" I mutter.

I can't help it. Maybe it's selfish, but I want to be the one who's there for Remington, anyway.

He blows out a whistling breath. "Sure. Thank you."

With Remington in the bath, my heart softens a little; at last, he's safe. Dragging a washcloth down his beautiful arms, I smile as Remington closes his eyes, allowing his limbs to nestle limp in my hands. I give every inch of his shoulder, bicep, forearm, palm, and fingertips a rolling massage, loving the way it parts his lips in pleasure. My heart feels nurtured just watching him enjoy himself, allowing himself to be gently jiggled back and forth - his muscles loose as I rub soap over his broad chest.

"I think you've fought more than two dragons," I blurt out.

Remington's eyebrows crease as if my words were both shocking and confusing.

"It's not your fault what they've done and are continuing to do," I say.

He's silent for a while as I trickle warm water over his chest, massaging him between delicately tracing the dark black line down his sternum.

But he scoops up my cheeks to give me a small kiss. "I'm worrying you."

"No, I just don't know if I'm making it worse or not when I really, *really* wish I could help you feel better."

He swallows. "It's not you. I got silent because I'm afraid to ask you a favor."

I sit on my heels, leaning against the tub's edge. "Then all the more reason to ask."

He gives me a soft chuckle, his focus flickering between my eyes. "Can we–? Um–" He takes a deep breath. "Can we try the scene?"

I'm taken aback. He's never seemed hesitant for any of our established scenes before. "Which scene?"

Fiddling with my fingers, Remington's voice remains soft. "The one you came up with when I told you what he did."

My breath shakes as I stare at his rising shoulders. Remington is referring to the scene where I come in to rescue him instead.

"Absolutely. But when? It's still so raw, Rem."

His hard breath sounds startlingly close to a cry. Pulling my hand to his chest, Remington's tension shoots my heart into overdrive. "I feel physically sick from carrying this, L.L.B. I can't bear it any longer."

I choke out a sharp breath as tears prick my eyes.

But Remington continues. "I feel like I have to try. I want to get this out of me, especially now that he's gone. I don't want to rot with him."

As he lifts his chin to find my warped, sobbing expression, his eyebrows arch.

"Oh, baby, please, don't worry. I'm ready to start trying to let this go, finally. I'm tired of holding it alone. And I trust you. I trust you with my whole heart."

My heart swells until I can't stand it anymore. The bath sloshes as I push a wet kiss into his mouth, hiccupping through tears. His hot hands soaking my upper arms remind me that he's okay. He's here, and he's giving me the power to support him in a tremendous, raw way.

Hurriedly swiping the tears from my cheeks, I smile. "Sorry. I just feel for you so deeply. But I trust you too, and I want to be there for you so badly."

He softly smiles. "I know. I can feel it. It helps more than I think you realize."

I fetch the giant, fluffy, white towel Remington usually saves for me. "T-then, do you mean you want to work on this now?"

"Please." He eyes me up and down. "If you feel like your heart can handle it tonight too."

As I gently rub him dry, I steel my heart. "Okay, my sweet Rem, I'd love to try. Lay down and get cozy in your bed, and I'll turn off the lights when you tell me you're ready. Is that okay?"

"Yes. Let's do a quick run-through first, please."

Setting the towel aside, I hand Remington clean boxers. "Okay, here's what we'll do: after I turn off the lights, you'll be alone in bed. I'll leave the kitchen light on, so you'll see my shadow in the doorway. You won't know who it is looking into your room yet, and it might feel very scary. But when I step in, you'll see it's just me. I'll be there, by your side, to keep you safe in the dark."

Remington nods, seeming to want to cry again.

"It's okay to cry, okay? You're just feeling a lot, which is so good."

"Thank you. I'm getting in bed."

He suddenly seems so young that I feel nauseated with him. But I know how much my fairytale role play genuinely did break the ropes binding my heart. I'm dying to help him untie himself.

Once I've given him a minute to get in bed, I step into the hallway with a racing heart.

"Remington?" I whisper.

"I'm ready," he calls out.

"Okay. I love you."

"I love you too."

We fall silent - my cue to flick off his bedroom light. I don't look at him lying there, popping my head in just enough to spot the light switch, but his silence is heavy. As I disappear back down the hall, my eyes squeeze shut. How did Remington tolerate binding my wrists again and again, even when it triggered me into heavy tears? All I want is to bring his smile back.

But he's giving me a chance to rescue him tonight.

With a slow, shaky exhale, I turn around, striding down the hall with louder footsteps. Stopping in Remington's doorway, I can see him, but he can't see me. I didn't think of it so clearly - that this is what his uncle must've seen. Rage thrusts my heartbeat throughout my body. I breathe through it, hating how Remington is laid out on his back, trusting his bed to keep him safe enough to sleep.

I can't believe Remington braved these feelings for me too.

But as he tugs his blankets higher, my heart shatters.

"Hello?" He whispers. His voice comes out so small.

Everything in me begs to protect him. I grip the doorway for stability, dying to be his hero. "Remington? Are you okay, sweet boy?"

He's silent for a long moment. "No. I'm scared someone will come in."

My heart flips. "Can I come in to hold you?"

There's another silence. This time, it's broken by choppy, laborious breaths. "Yes."

I'm tempted to run. But I know that might startle Remington, so I open my arms, softening my footsteps. To my surprise, he opens the blankets. But he doesn't just allow me into his safe space: Remington scoots over for me, giving me the spot he warmed.

I huff out the loving ache in my chest, climbing into bed beside him. "Oh, sweet boy."

Remington huddles into me quickly, pressing his forehead against my collarbone. The second I stop moving, I'm hit with a wave of his anxiety - physically experiencing his trauma shakes with him. I wrap my arms around his back to protect more of him, squeezing my watery eyes shut.

"I've got you. You're safe."

Remington finally allows himself to let out a soft, vocal cry against my chest. "Sorry."

"Breathe, baby. I've got you now."

Nodding, Remington breathes deeper, his frantic grip softening into a firm squeeze. Every muscle I rub on his back is rock-hard, and I know it's not from our workouts. He's uncomfortable, but he's allowing me to see it. I love how vulnerable he is with me: this big, athletic, tattooed man, trusting in me to witness him reliving his darkest moments. It makes me feel so special to him.

"Sweet boy," I whisper. "You're so precious. You deserve to feel safe."

He shudders through a tearful breath, wrecking my heart.

I cuddle him closer, kissing his forehead. "I'm here to protect and save you now, the best I can. No one can come in to hurt you without anyone to stop them anymore. You're not alone."

After a few hard, tense swallows, his voice comes out fragile. "Thank you."

My heart pounds wildly. All I know to do in traumatic moments is burrow up and hide, just like I would when I was a kid. Normally, that would seem immature to suggest in our thirties, but as Remington quivers beside me, maybe he really is leaning into that younger side of himself, and little Lilibeth has the best idea of all.

"C-can I hide with you under the blankets?" I whisper.

He lets out a soft, smiling huff. "Okay."

Lifting the blankets for us, Remington waits until I sink deeper into the covers with him before tucking them over our heads.

I feel for his hand in the muffled darkness, squeezing it tight. He lets out a slow, steady breath.

"Good job," I whisper. "We're safe in here together. It's okay to cry or feel scared."

The whimper that erupts from him bristles my nerves. He rushes for me, frantic hands scooping around my waist to press me hard against his chest.

With our torsos compressed, every desperate heave of his lungs rattles against my ribcage. I stroke his head, struggling to quiet my fear.

"Rem? I'm checking in, baby."

He chokes out a hard sob. "I— I don't know, I'm freaking out. I'm—" He groans in vivid frustration. "Alligator."

Throwing off the blankets, I sit up with wide eyes. Clicking on Remington's bedside table lamp as fast as I can, I whip my focus back to Remington. His hand is placed on his heaving chest, but he's clinging to my shirt like he's desperate to keep me close.

"Look at me, Rem." I pulse loving, quick squeezes down not only his arms, but also his whole chest. When he meets my eyes with a frantic stare, I do my best to smile. "I'm sitting beside you on your super cool bed, with all sorts of harnesses and toys on the walls - definitely your adult bedroom." He gives me a soft, weary chuckle, and I smile even wider. "There you go, sweet boy. It's done. You're okay. You made it."

He nods, loosening his grip on me as his forehead relaxes. But it warps just as quickly as his shaking hand stretches to brush my cheek. "Fuck, thank you, L.L.B."

I bite back fresh tears as Remington shifts into softer, aching ones. "Thank you for letting me try to rescue you back."

As he huffs, Remington attempts to give me a sweet smile. "Come here, baby girl."

Diving into his open arms, I cuddle Remington as closely as possible. He shifts to meet me, melding our bodies as our legs wrap as tightly as our arms.

Placing a wet, shaky kiss on my lips, Remington smooths his hand down the back of my hair, deepening our kiss. My lungs swell in adoration, cherishing this moment; he made it here to be with me. He survived, just like I did.

We hold each other for minutes upon minutes, staring into each other's eyes. We've stopped crying, but the bewildered look in Remington's eyes tells me we share a similar sense of awe.

Remington breaks the silence with his fingers brushing down my cheek. "I feel so close to you. I've never let anyone else rescue me. I trust you so much."

I breathe out the heavy, grateful ache in my chest. "God, I feel so safe with you too. And I never used to let anyone else rescue me, either. I'd usually pacify things to smooth everything over, but being around you helped me realize I'm tired of that. I want to say 'no.' I want to let you say 'no' too. I want to be loved by you just as much as I want you to feel loved by me."

A sense of peace washes over Remington like I've never seen before, erasing every minor evidence of stress from his features. Closing his swollen eyes, he breaks into a genuine, sweet smile - his body drooping into mine like I eased him back into a warm, safe bath. As he allows me to witness his pure comfort, I feel like his hero.

CHAPTER FOURTEEN

The more we repeat the scene, the more Remington smiles with both cheeks. I'm so relieved that I laugh lighter alongside him, celebrating as his joyous, playful spirit shines.

But one morning, Remington stops in my entryway with a contemplative hum - just as I'm strapping on my boots to head out the door for work.

"Maybe you also have more dragons than you thought," Remington mutters.

I peek at him with one foot still in the air, my eyes wide.

He chuckles, looping my scarf around my head. "Sorry, I just can't stop thinking about how badass you looked cooking breakfast. I know it's a rough industry, and I don't know jack shit about cooking compared to you, but I don't know - it's in the way you hold yourself in front of that stove and have no second guesses about which spices you're throwing in, or how much of each ingredient to add no matter what we're cooking. Or when you knew the legitimate chemistry behind why I burned my fucking eggs again, and then just casually dropped the bomb that you learned all this *yourself*. It's just— I want you to feel acknowledged for how hard you've worked. You've worked beyond hard, baby girl. Harder than you should've as a sous chef. Maybe it's not you, and they're just dragons."

My heart hammers wildly as I stare at my bleary-eyed

boyfriend in only his T-shirt and boxers, spouting what would've been life-saving words for a younger Lilibeth.

What if he's right? I've already climbed the industry years longer than Gabby, Paolo, and Ben, which is why I'm the sous chef beneath Giuliano.

Yet he treats me like I'm incapable.

But is that really on him, or is it still my own doing? Maybe I'm doing something wrong?

"Hey." Remington lifts my chin. "No matter what, I see it: you're a fucking rockstar at what you do. Take care of your heart for me while you're at work, okay?"

Biting my lip, I nod. "Thank you, love. T-that means a lot."

Standing on my toes to meet his lips, I cup his cheeks to sink into a lingering kiss. His warm hand swoops behind my back, tucking me closer with a quick, soothing squeeze. When he releases me, I see it: the warm, tender confidence in Remington's eyes when he looks at me.

I'm capable to him.

Why am I not capable in my own eyes?

Is it Dad's abuse clinging to me, or is it my own, based on how he taught me to see myself? Do I also believe I'm everyone's punching bag?

It terrifies me. I grasp Remington's hand. "Rem, I don't want to just be head chef. I've always wanted to open my own restaurant. I want to nourish people with my own food."

Blinking rapidly, Remington gapes. Then he bursts into the most vibrant, wholehearted grin.

With just that one look, I feel like my dreams have already come true - that someone else can see it, so it's already in the works. It's possible. I beam from ear to ear, letting out a joyous giggle.

Remington softens into a touched, gentle smile. "You've never shared that with me before. It makes me so fucking excited for you, L.L.B., you have no idea. I can't wait to see you achieve it."

His words boost my soul so electrically that I feel like running a mile. Except I can't; I have to hurry before I miss the bus to work.

I've never felt so earnestly seen by anyone except Remington. After 15 brutal years of grinding my way up the restaurant industry from fast food to luxury, he's one of the few people who have acknowledged my efforts. But he meant every word. His bright, beaming black eyes stick in my mind the whole bus ride to work, forcing me to hide my smile in my scarf.

So the second I see Ben muttering snickering insults into Paolo's ear when I clock into work, it's a stark, horrifying difference from how Remington and I treat each other. Fresh alarm bells ring in my head that stopped sounding three years ago - when Giuliano convinced me this was "just how it was" in professional kitchens.

My jaw tenses with Paolo's shoulders. He's not defending himself, either.

And I've had enough.

Marching up to Ben, I harden my resolve. "Ben, what are you doing?"

Ben whips around, searching for the voice questioning him. When he realizes that voice belongs to me, his wide eyes soften into laughter.

"Dude, Lily, chill out. You have no sense of humor—"

"*Enough,*" I say.

Gabby stops chopping celery to look at me with wide eyes, sending a jolt through my chest. Am I doing the wrong thing? Should I not have spoken up for once?

But as Ben chuckles, opening his mouth to say something else, Remington's words click into place; Ben isn't the only one treating me poorly. Paolo stands up for me occasionally, but only when someone drags him into it. Gabby pretends nothing bad happens at all, just like Mom. Servers and bussers follow Giuliano's lead, using sharp, angry words the entire shift, making it ten times more exhausting to hand orders to them and have to listen to them fight while I'm hoping to cook customers warm, loving meals.

And of course they all act like this. Our head chef treats me the same way in front of everyone, and I'm supposed to be his right hand.

Gripping my fresh apron, my voice shakes as I interrupt Ben. "I said, enough. What do you think you're accomplishing right now?"

Ben's jaw hardens. "What the hell is your problem today?"

Giuliano clocks in, still tying his apron as he stomps through the doorway. "Why the fuck is no one cooking?"

The dragon horde has gathered in one place. Sucking in a fiery breath, I picture banishing them from my inner kingdom, loosening my shoulders.

That doesn't mean this isn't terrifying.

I quiver as I turn to Guiliano. "Why? I'll tell you why."

His eyes widen. No one dares to move. Even a few servers freeze in the doorway, awaiting my next words. My eyes bulge just as much as theirs, but a protective rage settles into my chest. If it were little Remington who I was protecting, I'd have no qualms. But Remington helped me realize that whenever someone crushes the cook in me, they're sinking their claws straight into little Lilibeth - the one who dared to save her own life by joining this industry, even if she'd be a laughingstock. I don't want her to suffer anymore.

Tears prick my eyes. "I'm sick of how you treat me. Treat each other. I know I don't say much, and I can be awkward, but do you have to treat me like absolute shit for this kitchen to function? I just want to fucking *cook!*"

Gabby's shoulders droop. "Lily..."

Giuliano continues to gape, but when he opens his mouth, I stand taller.

"This is not how things should be run. When I cook for our community, it's because I want to nourish their bodies, and hopefully help them experience one moment of delight in this cruel world. And what are your bitter comments accomplishing? You really don't think it makes our muscles weaker, distracts our minds, and tears at our hearts? And maybe you don't feel the same, but I see my job as to nurture through food. How can I do my job properly in a hateful environment when all I want to do is share love?" I huff through hot, aching breaths. "Just let me cook in peace. Let me live."

No one has moved. Not even Gabby seems to know what to say, her arms limp at her sides. Do they all think I'm crazy now?

Snatching a cleaning cloth, I wipe one of the steel tables.

"G-get back to work," I mutter.

Everyone bursts into action, hustling to their next task without a single word of complaint. I freeze, gazing at the determined focus around me.

They listened.

I want to feel proud for finally speaking up. But as tears cloud my eyes, my forehead warps from the pain in my chest.

Why can't I convince Dad not to hurt me? What am I doing wrong?

I haven't visited Mom and Dad since I showed Remington what Dad did to me. Witnessing someone else's shock over my injuries hit a deep nerve, reminding me that no, this isn't normal, and I can't afford Dad seeing his physical force as a reopened door. Remington assured he'd be at my side as a buffer the next time I visit, but I still hate that Mom has no choice. She's trapped in a prison she didn't mean to enter, maybe for the rest of her life.

Turning away from the table, I swipe at my gushing eyes with my apron, hating that I'm crying in front of everyone here. But I crash straight into Guiliano's chest. I gasp, taking a few steps back. "S-sorry."

I try to circle around him, but Giuliano blocks my way with a hand open in front of me. "Come into the back with me for a moment, please."

My heart flips. What's he going to say? I undermined his

authority in front of our whole staff. He can't fire me over this, can he?

Ducking my head, I follow Giuliano's swift steps to the back room. At least the speed we're walking prevents me from having to be witnessed for too long.

But when the door shuts behind us, Giuliano snatches a tissue and whips around. "Lift your chin."

Defensive fear tightens my muscles. But as I take the tissue from Giuliano, I find his face startlingly neutral. Turning my side to him, I do my best to quickly clean myself up and stop crying.

But I can't help it. A well has overflowed in my heart, aching at all the time and joy Mom and I lost to Dad's will.

Giuliano crosses his arms. "I want to retire."

I gasp, meeting his eyes. "What?"

"I've been waiting for you to speak up so you could take my place. They'll trample you if you don't keep that chin up, and I don't want to see a good cook lose their passion. Not many in the industry have the heart behind their work to back up their skill."

Is he finally acknowledging me? Telling me I'm still his one and only choice for head chef?

I always thought I'd feel a sense of validation if this ever came true, but as I face Giuliano, I grit my jaw. "So you decided to harass me into shape? How well do you think that worked?"

He tenses. To my surprise, he drops his head. "So, what? Are you quitting?"

I sigh. "No. I need this job to keep my family alive. I'm going to keep cooking."

"Good."

Silence stretches between us. But my tears resurface, refusing to be shoved down anymore. I fetch another tissue, struggling to tame my breath.

"Are you sure you're okay, Lily? Is something else going on?"

"Maybe," I mutter.

"How about you go home, and I'll cover for you. Do you need a few extra days off this week?"

My stomach flips. "Oh. That would be nice."

"Go home, then. Take care of yourself."

Giuliano rushes back to the kitchen to take my place, leaving me in a daze. I slowly fetch my things, returning my apron to my locker. Is he really taking in my words?

Or is he getting rid of me for the week to force everyone to forget about what I said? My hopes plummet. Dashing back into the kitchen, I hold my breath, expecting to see utter chaos.

But it's silent. Calm.

Giuliano speaks low at the cutting board as everyone works. "You heard our sous chef. Things need to change around here."

My heart is just as sore, but my shoulders loosen just enough to propel me out the doors.

All I can think about is Annabella. She went through the process of cutting ties with Mom and Dad, all alone as a teenager. Dad always faced me alone, but I similarly have no idea what he did to her. I only know she survived him long enough to leave him behind on her own, and that her rage was only evidence of how badly her heart hurt through every waking moment.

Pacing across the sidewalk in front of work, I open my phone's contact list. I stop at the nearest bench when I zip up to her name. It's been two years since I've dared to contact her, especially after she made it clear she was furious with me for paying Dad's rent. She didn't let me explain the full situation - that I was still on her side, not Dad's.

But explaining myself isn't what's most important anymore. Even if she hates me for calling, I want to try to apologize for hurting her from the bottom of my heart. To tell her I love her, at least one last time.

Trembling on the bench, I'm wide-eyed as the dial tone rings. I cling to my scarf, shivering in the icy January wind. The longer it rings, the more I feel like a horrible person. I'm breaking her consent, aren't I? Should I have asked Remington what he thought about this first?

But the second I hear Annabella's frantic breath on the

phone, I clutch my scarf tighter, missing her enough to warp my eyebrows.

"What's wrong? What did he do?" She snaps, her fear prickling my skin.

"N-nothing, well–"

I swallow hard. If I tell her he bruised me recently for the first time in 15 years, she'll lose it.

Closing my eyes, I open my heart. "That's not why I'm calling. Annabella, I love you. I'm so sorry I hurt your feelings so drastically. No matter what everyone else says, I'll always believe you in what they put you through, and I hate that you might think otherwise. I'd never, ever want to hurt you more after all you went through, but I did, and I'm so sorry. I'm still on your side."

Pure silence stretches on the line, long enough for me to remove the phone from my ear to make sure we didn't disconnect. I'm dying to jump from the bench, to run from the stinging fear in my heart that I might've hurt Annabella even more, but I'm frozen in terror. I don't want to lose her forever.

Finally, Annabella sighs. "Lilibeth, I love you with my whole fucking heart, but I'm still furious with you. How could you be on my side when you're paying for his alcohol?"

I gasp. "What?! No, Annabella, you never let me finish explaining what I meant when I said I was paying for their livelihood. I'm not cutting them a small check to just do whatever with; Dad can't work because Mom can't do anything herself, so I'm paying their rent - to the penny. He has to use every last bit of it to keep a roof over their heads."

Annabeth groans. "You seriously think he's not still using it to buy booze and going into debt? That he's not the one making her constantly on the edge of homelessness in the first place?"

My teeth clench. "I don't know, but what am I supposed to do, let Mom die?"

She scoffs. "I don't know. She'd still choose him over both of us either way, so that's her problem."

My stomach drops to the bench beneath me, leaving me reeling. The hurt in her words wasn't just directed at our parents this time, but me. "Do you seriously think I actually, intentionally abandoned you too? After all we both went through together?"

"No– Well, I don't know." Her breath hitches. "It felt like it that day. I guess I didn't know all the details. Maybe I was a little harsh to cut you off without letting you explain, but–" She tightens her tone back into anger. "It's more than that too. I just can't stand to watch you hurting yourself more by going back to him. I just don't understand it."

I can hardly process the thoughts flooding my mind before my sister seethes through her teeth.

"It makes me sick to my stomach that you know what he does to you, yet you're continually putting yourself in harm's way in front of him for Mom - when she doesn't even want you to."

My heart flinches like she left a searing scratch over it. "W-what? How could you say that? She's trapped, she can't walk–"

"Lily, for God's sake, you're not okay. It's like those plane safety rules - put on your own damn oxygen mask first. How can you save Mom when you need saving, yourself?" She raises her voice, but her quivering tells me she's crying alongside me. "You didn't abandon me; you abandoned yourself."

Annabella single-handedly strips the air from my lungs. I gape on the bench, my heartbeat hammering. This is just like what I discovered about little Remington - why his adult self loves playing the hero. And why I love taking my power back by letting him borrow all of it.

But I can't give up on Mom.

Annabella's anger fades by the second, her voice wavering through gut-wrenching pain. "I couldn't save you either, Lils. I tried so hard, but here I am, having to hear that man probably hurt my baby sister again? How do you think I feel?"

Tears spill before I can register them. I swipe them away, only for three more to gush out. I laugh through my stuffy nose. "A lot like I do, I guess. So pretty shitty."

She huffs in annoyance. Then she laughs. I break into weepy giggles with her until we're both laughing, only separated by Annabella's groans.

"You drive me crazy. But not like Dad. I love you, baby Beth. Thanks for apologizing, but don't worry so much about me, okay? I just want you to be happy. To feel safe."

She sounds just like Mom.

"But I miss you." My lip wobbles as horrendous, longing tears wrack my gut.

Annabella sniffles through the silence with me. I can hear the pain in her shuddering breath, forcing me to shut my eyes hard to swallow it down.

"Fuck, I'm so sorry. I really hurt you too," she whispers.

I don't know what to say. She did, and I didn't realize how badly it stung until now.

Her clothes shuffle against the microphone, painting a clear picture of her squaring her shoulders, as always. She hardens her voice to feign confidence, no matter how deeply she's hurting. "Okay, Lilibeth, here's what we're going to do. I'm going to keep talking this through with you, okay? We'll figure this out together once we're in a better headspace. In the meantime, just get out of his immediate reach. Please."

I huff, swiping thick tears from my eyes. "I will. I decided it was finally time, and I have a really sweet boyfriend who will protect me, but still– I'm scared."

"I know. I still am too."

My heart drops as her true feelings click into place; Annabella wasn't pulling away from me. If she breaks her vow to cut contact with Mom and Dad, it will break the power behind her "no."

Yet she still picked up the phone for me. I'm not her dragon.

After I annoy her with three more I love yous, I promise to tell her what happened between Dad and me to make me call -

since I can't get away with hiding anything from my older sister - and I hang up with a tumultuous heart.

My head spins. I know what I have to do, but can I? I might have slain multiple dragons today, but I've left the biggest one for last, and I'm terrified that I'm not strong enough to face him alone.

I need to see my knight.

By the time the next bus can take me close to home, Remington will be twenty minutes into his shift at Club X. I switch bus lines, opting to find him there instead. Maybe I'll be interrupting and distracting him from his job, but this feels like an "alligator" moment, and I don't want to trudge through it with anyone except Remington.

But just like Remington waited until he felt safe enough to share details about his uncle, I haven't shared all the details about Mom's health with Remington. He knows she placates Dad and that I want to pay their rent to keep Mom alive while she's trapped, but he doesn't realize the additional gravity of it. I've been so afraid that if I tell him she can't even walk, he'll reiterate the fears I've had to face my whole life: as long as Dad is alive to reign over Mom's life, she's trapped forever.

But I can't agree with Annabella that Mom doesn't want my help. I saw how quiet Mom became the last time I was there - when I said I might be able to lift her now. Maybe she's ready to leave. If I ask her directly for the first time, telling her the truth about what Dad does to me and that I'm scared he's hurting her too, maybe we can be done with *him* forever, instead. Annabella doesn't know I've worked hard with Remington to craft my own oxygen mask.

Adjusting to the club's darkness, my chest clenches tighter by the second; I can't find Remington in the halls. He's in the dungeon.

Without thinking, I make a beeline for it. But I stop at the door. I've never entered those doors without Remington allowing me to watch. Is this a private party today, or have they not started yet? Just as my hand lands on the door to take a peek, a gloved hand appears above mine.

I snap my hand back with a gasp, smashing my back into the hallway wall.

Miss X's eyebrows raise beneath her mask. "Oh, sweetheart, are you okay?"

With her soft touch on my shoulder, my last semblance of composure snaps. I erupt into tears, grasping her hand. "Where's Remi?"

"Take a deep breath for me, okay? I'd say I'd fetch him for you, but Remi's a good boy - he's already spotted you through the doors, and he's rushing over like his life depends on it." Miss X smiles, staring through the window. "Maybe it does. Clearly, you're his heart."

Her words lift my soul. Can she tell? How powerful it feels just to look into Remington's eyes, finding him staring back with just as much pure love?

Miss X slips from my grasp with a wink, opening the door for Remington.

Rushing to my side with wide, panicked eyes, Remington cups my wet cheeks in his big palms. "What is it? Something happened."

"I need to carry my mom," I whimper.

Remington's brows furrow. "You've said that before, haven't you? When we first met."

I let out a panicked, despairing cry. "It's been too long. I don't know what to do. I never have."

Remington's expression hardens into determined neutrality. Slipping his hand into mine, he guides me from the dungeon, unlocking the first private room he can find. Closing the door behind us with his back, Remington pulls me into his arms for a tight, reassuring squeeze.

"Breathe, baby. Tell me from the beginning."

I tell him everything: how it wasn't as severe at first, but Mom deteriorated over the years, how she was eventually diagnosed with MS, but they said it was showing up worse for her than most, how I pretended Dad didn't hit me so Mom couldn't stress more, but Mom deteriorated more anyway until she couldn't walk, how Dad decided he was worth nothing unless he was Mom's one and only source of life, and how when I had to leave home because I wanted to either leave or kill myself from feeling like a burden, Mom told me she would be fine without me, so I took the chance to restart my life - saving myself.

"I thought I needed to become strong enough to carry her *home*. But I finally called Annabella."

Remington blinks a few times. "No way."

"I know. We made up, I think. But Annabella thinks our mom genuinely doesn't want my help, and I'm so scared she's right. But I can't accept that yet, Rem. I think I need to say goodbye to my dad one last time, tell my mom the truth, and hope she actually wants to come home with me. To leave him with me." I grip my head, steadying myself in Remington's solid focus. "But fuck, even if she does, nothing has really changed. I can't afford a specialist for her. She can't care for herself, and I can't afford a caregiver, so all she has is my dad. He does everything for her, but that scares me. I don't know if he hurts her when he's frustrated too."

"*Fuck*, your dad is just—" Remington grips his forehead almost as hard as he clenches his teeth. "Okay, so if this were the best case scenario, what would you want to do instead?"

I let out an exasperated sigh. "I-I don't know. I can't offer her to live with me if I can't afford to care for her. How could I have time to work and be her constant caretaker at the same time?"

"Then do you want to take her home to live with you alone, or what if she comes home to live with *both* of us? We could share the load together. Split one rent payment, care for her, and probably even afford a caregiver."

I gape at Remington, unmoving. When I realize he's serious - that this moment is real, and I didn't die and go to heaven - tears slip from my eyes. "Oh, my God, you're a sweetheart."

Remington pulls me closer, cupping my cheeks to wipe tears from my eyes. "No, I just love you. And I'm really serious about this offer. I–" He softens his voice. "I want to spend my life with you."

Elation strikes my whole being, weakening my knees. I lean into Remington, scooping up his sweet face in my hands. "Oh, God, yes, Rem. So do I."

This time, the tears escaping my eyes are filled with pure joy. I hop on my toes in excitement, arching Remington's eyebrows as he gives me the sweetest, most emotional smile. Crashing into a fierce kiss, we cling to each other with our full hands, squeezing like we can't get close enough without melting into one.

Remington breaks our kiss with an elated, breathy laugh. "God, you're so sweet. Are you as happy as I am, baby? Because I feel like my life was just made."

I sigh through a watery smile. Stroking my thumb beneath Remington's eye to catch a joyous tear, I float in the clouds. Is this really the same man who was afraid to let me love him, terrified we'd warp into the same monstrous familial relationship he grew up under?

"Rem, I'm so many things. My heart is so happy, my soul feels safe, and I feel so, so proud of you for allowing yourself to be here with me."

Melting into a soft smile, he draws me into a gentler kiss. We linger, holding one another in a blissful silence.

Remington seals our kiss with an even deeper press, easing his lips off mine. "You rescued me last, so now it's my turn to rescue you from the dragon, L.L.B. If we visit your parents, and you decide you feel ready to take your mom home, I've got your back."

As he settles me onto the couch to ground me with loving, sweeping touches, I know he has far more than my back; he's holding my whole heart, and I'm holding his.

CHAPTER FIFTEEN

"Are you okay?" I unbuckle my seatbelt, tearing my eyes off Mom and Dad's empty porch out the car window to look at Remington.

"I should be asking you that, not the other way around." He sighs. "I'm okay. But I don't know if I can pretend to like him, L.L.B."

"Just be yourself. We don't have to talk to him much, and I'll mainly just want to say hi to my mom before I–" I swallow hard. "Before I propose our offer to her in private."

Leaning over the center console, Remington eases a soft kiss onto my temple. "I'll be right here by your side. If she says yes, we'll come up with a safety plan to get her out first. No one's laying a hand on either of you today."

Chewing on my lip, I nod. "I-I do feel safer this time. Thank you."

He gives me a soft smile, but nothing can settle my nerves as we step out of the car. Glancing back at Remington one last time, I hesitate as his jaw sets.

I stop beside the rusting mailbox. "Are you sure you're okay?"

"No, L.L.B., I'm not. I don't want to say anything to him if it makes you uncomfortable, but…" He sighs, softening his voice as his eyebrows arch in sorrow. "I don't think he should be allowed to think he can continue to do this to you. It's long overdue for someone to stand by your side, and I'd feel like a shit person if I kept this secret for his comfort - and therefore sacrificing yours."

I swallow hard. I've never had anyone visit Dad who knows what he does to me, so I almost don't know what to say. But I trust Remington. "Okay, thank you. I don't mind if you say something to him; just don't say anything around my mom. I need to tell her when I'm ready."

Remington strokes my shoulders. "Okay. I've got your back."

He does. I can feel it in his steady gaze. My torso unwinds - just in time to hear the click of a lock unlatching.

Dad opens the front door, greeting us with a bright wave.

My heart stings. I didn't expect to feel as guilty as I do from Dad's unsuspecting smile. I know my offer for Mom will hurt him. But he made the choice to hurt me, over and over again. That truth guts me, just like it has my whole life. Why wasn't I good enough for him to keep safe?

But what if I'm over-exaggerating how bad he is? When he's smiling and waving so sweetly, he doesn't look like a dragon.

As we approach, I force myself to smile, opening my arm for a side hug. "Hi, Dad."

Dad hugs me with both arms. "Hi, Lily. And Remington - it's so nice to meet you, finally!"

Remington's deep hum buzzes behind my head as he places both hands on my shoulders, keeping close. "Hi, Mr. Norris. Thanks for having me."

"Oh, no need to be so polite. Call me Joe." Dad chuckles, extending his hand. But I know Remington far better than to think he's being pleasant; if he's not at an excitable puppy-level of a greeting, he's unhappy.

Remington stares at Dad's hand for a lingering second, shooting my heartbeat into my throat. I can only imagine what he's thinking; he's the only one who knows what Dad's hands have done.

As Remington takes Dad's hand, Dad chuckles again. "Wow, you've got a strong grip."

Remington's jaw tenses, and Dad's smile fades.

"*I* have a strong grip?" Remington's voice is quiet but sharp, piercing the space between us.

My heart beats wildly. I don't know what to think or feel. I knew Remington wouldn't be able to hold back - he has that venomous "vaffanculo" look in his eyes again - but no one has stood up for me to Dad before. No one has even *noticed*.

Dad's eyes have never been wider. But he furrows his brow with a light chuckle, his forearm tense in Remington's grasp. "What's going on here?"

Remington hums, but it's not a kind hum. My teeth clench as he steps closer, lowering his voice. "I had the unfortunate experience of discovering just how strong your grip is, *Joe*."

Dad blinks a few times, and I shuffle in place. I don't know how to exist in a world where he's facing the consequences of what he does to me, and it terrifies me. A frantic urge tells me I should run and hide, petrified he'll turn to take his frustrations out on me again - blame this all on me, somehow, but even worse. Deep down, keeping Dad's secrets has always been more than not wanting to hurt Mom; I've been afraid to discover what happens when I find out I'm not worth protecting to Mom cither.

Just like poor Remington experienced when his family kept Ernesto around.

But Dad sputters, fear blanching his cheeks. "I-I don't– I don't know what you–"

"You don't remember the clear finger silhouettes you left me to find on my girlfriend's arm?"

Dad pales. Then his eyebrows warp in sorrow. He turns to me, opening his mouth with a sharp inhale, but Remington hums.

"No, don't look at her to bail you out of this. There's no fucking reason in the world to lay a finger on this literal angel on your doorstep. You're lucky she stuck around at all, especially after that scar you left on her back."

Dad winces, and my heart beats wildly into my throat. I've never seen him look so guilty.

But Remington's jaw only clenches harder. "I'm only going to make this clear once: you're never laying another fucking hand on your daughter again, you hear me?"

My head spins, terrified of what Dad might say. But most shocking of all, I'm the most afraid of how awful Dad must feel. Even though he hurt me, I don't want to hurt him.

But Dad shuts his mouth with a meek, "I'm so sorry."

My squeeze on Remington's hand softens his set jaw. The second he lets Dad go, Dad races back into the house, dashing past Mom as she slowly wheels herself down the hall.

I'm numb with fear. Did she hear any of that?

She blinks a few times, turning her head the best she can to call after him. "Honey, where are you going? Is everything okay?"

Dad doesn't answer, slamming his bedroom door with a *bang*.

Mom furrows her brows, looking between Remington and me as I remain dazed in her doorway. "Lilibeth, are you alright?"

Remington tenses. "Sorry, I–"

I release a slow, shaky exhale. "No, I– Yes. I'm–" The more I breathe, the lighter I feel. I'm not alone. I let out a soft, disbelieving laugh. "I-I'm good. Really good."

"Thank goodness." Mom beams, clasping her hands together at her chest. "Oh, it's so good to meet you, Remington! Lilibeth hasn't brought a boy home since high school."

I peek at Remington with a giggle, but as we meet eyes, I find a hint of agonized sadness behind his dark irises.

He gives Mom his half-up smile. "That's quite the compliment. Your daughter is the sweetest woman on the planet."

Having Remington here makes it real for me - how fake these pleasantries feel, leaving me to wait for the inevitable storm. And now that I'm not left to face it alone, it's sinking in how disastrous this has all been. I have to live my whole life with Dad's scar on my back, yet I'm *still* keeping it hidden for him; even though Dad knows his secret has been exposed to Remington, it's kept safe from his wife.

We shuffle inside, and I wheel Mom down the hall. As Mom chats with us, Remington releases a slow exhale beside me. We meet eyes. The pain behind his harrowed stare shocks my heart into restarting. I lean into his touch as he smooths his hand over my back, but as the ache in my heart only grows, Remington's eyebrows arch to match my expression.

Heat stings my eyes. This has nothing to do with him, but he's visibly aching like his heart was the one my dad hurt. He understands.

"My hero," I breathe out an almost inaudible whisper.

He softly smiles, mouthing, "I love you."

But as we settle onto the living room couch, facing Mom's smile, dark thoughts consume my focus. Can I really do this? Ruin Mom's sense of peace with what I've been through? I swallow hard through the sudden onslaught of emotions crushing my chest. Remington stiffens beside me, his eyebrows knitted, but Mom speaks up first.

"Lilibeth, something is wrong today." She's speaking low enough to capture my focus; her tone is specifically low enough to keep our conversation from Dad behind his closed door.

She's right. Something is wrong. The dam I've built around my secret has broken, spilling out like hot oil scalding my heart.

Or, rather, boiling water. Vivid images of the deep, horrifying pain of Dad burning me enter my mind. It killed so drastically that my brain protected me from remembering the physical pain, but I can't forget the mental torment he caused when I looked up at him, realizing he hurt me drastically, on purpose. I thought I might die, and all I could see was a repeating image of his determined, disgusted glare as he tipped the pot.

But my back was turned; I had already learned I needed to run from him.

My body shakes, even as Remington grasps my arms to ground me. Mom rolls closer, her eyes wider than ever.

And my worst fears tumble from my mouth.

"Mom, does Dad hurt you?" I rasp. Shock ripples over her forehead, but as she sucks in a breath to speak, my chest tightens. "Physically. Does he hurt you, physically?"

Remington freezes beside me. I quiver in his arms, the acidic, burning sensation spewing deeper into my heart as I await Mom's response.

But she continues to gape. As she takes my hand, she shakes her head. "What are you saying, Lilibeth? No, he doesn't. No, how could he?"

I sputter out a sharp gasp like I'm drowning. Remington jolts into action, resuming his grounding squeezes, but I didn't expect this to hurt this badly. If Mom isn't lying, that means his daughters are the exception. That this really is personal. To Dad, I'm not worthy enough to protect.

Tears spill with my rasping hiccups. This isn't how I wanted to ask Mom to live with me. I wanted to look strong enough to carry her.

But as Remington shakes his head beside me, Mom turns her focus to him. "Remington, what's going on?"

Remington only shakes his head faster. It sobers me; no matter how angry Remington is with Dad, he's not giving away Dad's secret, just because I asked. It's not fair - to me, either.

Or to Mom.

Straightening, I steady my weepy voice. "Sorry, I just need to talk to you about something. This isn't how I wanted to ask you, but before Dad comes back, I have a question."

"Okay, please, what is it, Lilibeth? You're scaring me."

I swallow hard. "Remington and I talked a few things over. We're already spending so much time with each other that moving in together and splitting the rent would save us money. But that also means we could support you however you need to, and even afford a caregiver together. We wanted to offer for you to live with us, if you'd like."

Mom blinks a few times, her focus racing between

Remington's somber expression and my reddened eyes. "Wait, what about your father?"

My shoulders raise. I lean in, softening my voice. "Mom, you and I both know he's abusive."

"What? Lilibeth, it's not like that."

My blood burns. "We agreed on it last time, and there's a reason why I didn't visit for months after that day."

Jutting back by the chin, Mom only widens her eyes further. "Well, I don't understand. We don't argue like the two of you do. He's not all that bad to me, and he doesn't mean the hurtful things he says. I still love him."

As I gape at my mother, I can't believe what I'm seeing; she's choosing him, just like I was afraid of. Does she really think all Dad does is get into petty disagreements with me? She's so set in her mindset that I almost fall back in with her: what if I'm the one giving too much attention and weight to what Dad treats me like? Maybe I should just be quiet and get over it.

But the second that thought crosses my mind, I stiffen.

No, I've had enough of sitting back and taking it. Remington's sturdy grip on me proves it further; if Remington's praise has taught me anything, Dad's verbal abuse damages my soul, just like his physical abuse. Dad didn't hurt me physically for years, yet my self-esteem around Dad is the polar opposite of the Lilibeth I can be with Remington. With Rem, I can exist without overanalyzing every blink, breath, or word. Even if I had never met him, the blissful, utter relief I felt holding my apartment keys for the first time at eighteen speaks volumes.

And my knight taught me that my safeword isn't reserved for when my pain "matters enough." My pain is worth acknowledging, even if it's hard for Mom to hear.

Whether Mom believes me or not, I believe me now. My father is abusive.

And Mom hasn't stopped staring, wondering why *I'm* acting like this.

As reality sets in, I'm just as nauseatingly horrified as I am furious. I clench my jaw. "Wait, so you want to stay with him, forever? This isn't just the only option you have?"

Mom's shoulders droop. She leans in, placing her cool palm over my knee. "Yes, honey. I'm okay. I'm happy here."

This can't be happening. My eyes flood, but as Remington huffs out fury with me, Mom only gives me a sympathetic, sad smile, stroking my knee.

"Lilibeth, I've told you time and time again that I don't need you to worry so much about me. I want you to live your life for you now, not for me. I really mean it."

She doesn't get it. I didn't even have a chance to tell her everything Dad did to me. How can I, when she doesn't even believe me now?

All I can do is shake my head in disbelief. "So, that's a no?"

Mom rubs my knee. "Yes, honey. That's a no."

Another voice appears behind us. "What's a no?"

Every muscle in my body tightens in defense. Remington holds me tighter, and I follow his gaze over my shoulder.

Dad stands in the doorway. His belly is taut, brows furrowed, and mouth pressed in a tight line. Just catching a millisecond glimpse of him on the edge sets my nerves on fire, my body begging me to bolt from the room.

But the image of Dad upset over my justified heartbreak is the final drop in 33 years of pent-up rage.

I don't bolt from the room. I stand.

"Do you hurt her too, Dad?" I hiss.

The words rip from my lips before I can stop them. Every shuffle of clothes in the room, tick of Dad's jaw, and shudder from Mom threatens to tear my pounding heart from my chest, but I only grit my teeth harder as Dad tightens into a scowl.

"What are you even saying, Lilibeth?" He snaps.

I freeze.

Disappointment crashes over my heart; the sight of his rage still poisons my resolve, no matter how strong I can build myself up. Will I ever be free from him?

But Remington lets out a low hum, breaking me from my trace. The visceral disgust I hear in his tone validates me to my core.

Except Mom hasn't moved. She's gaping at Dad, hardly seeming to function from shock.

Oh, God, it's finally hitting her. Anxiety sears my veins. What will she think when she processes the truth?

When Dad tightens his fists, my body hardens.

"You heard me." I grit my teeth, unable to keep my voice from raising to a yell. "Do you hurt your wife too?"

Dad's eyes bulge like I've thrown a bucket of ice water over his head. He sputters out nonsense syllables before his stare finally lands on Mom.

She's still frozen, but tears gush down her cheeks. She knows.

Guilt creases every inch of Dad's face, withering away his age by the second. He hesitates, glancing at my seething boyfriend. But as he returns his gaze to my shaking, furious form, his eyebrows arch in sorrow.

"No," he rasps, shaking his head. "No, I… No."

My jaw quivers. I don't know what to think. I'm afraid if I breathe, this will feel too real, but my lungs force me to release cutting, rapid exhales.

But as Mom breaks into a sob, my focus zips to her.

She can hardly croak out her words. "Oh, my God, does he hit you, Lilibeth? That's what this is about?"

Mom's eyes are fractured - unfocused and scattering over me. It terrifies me so much that I can only see Remington's grounding squeezes of my limp hand, not feel it.

But as Mom looks to Dad for the truth, my heart drops.

My dad is a frail shell of himself, fear stripping him to bones before my eyes.

It's infuriating.

Hot gasps sputter from my lips as I burst into violent tears. "Why do you always get to be the one who gets to feel bad?"

My shrill tone echoes throughout the living room, but no one can answer my question.

I shake as I choke out harder tears. "If you realized you shouldn't hurt her, where was my mercy? Why was I different?"

Dad just stands there. I can't bear to look at him another second, repulsed by his empty guilt. It didn't stop him from bruising my wrist mere months ago.

Mom's voice comes out creaky. "Lilibeth, has he hit you? Answer your mother."

Dad still hasn't moved. I'm afraid if he does, he'll keel over. Mom's answer is right there, in his shame. She just has to finally notice what's in front of her.

I turn to Mom, afraid to face the growing ache in my chest as I look into her eyes. But as she genuinely searches me for the truth, my heart breaks.

"Would it even change your answer?" I whisper.

Mom's gaping jaw wavers as she stares me in the eyes. I know the truth is written on my face now, and it's not that Dad was the only one who hurt me.

"Sorry," Dad rasps.

My focus zips to his hanging head. Did I imagine he said something?

No, I didn't. Dad chokes out a soft sob. "I'm so sorry, Lily."

Remington's breath has been steadily heightening, but with Dad's apology, he grips my hand hard, forcing me to blink. I realize it's because I've been clinging to him for life until my hand was nearly numb.

But now I know exactly what to do. Even in this terrifying, gut-wrenching confrontation, I'm safe. I'm not alone anymore.

I give Remington's hand a soft squeeze, releasing him to stand stronger.

"I don't believe your apology. I can't," I say. "Maybe ever."

After a scathing silence, Dad just nods. Mom dissolves into true weeping, clinging to her chest as she stoops over.

I close my eyes. "I need to go home."

The second I say the word, Remington's arm swoops around my side, bolstering my strength. His deep, shaking voice soothes my nerves as he turns to my mother. "Lia, if you change your mind, or he ever comes close to laying a hand on you, we'll be here to care for you in a heartbeat, no questions asked."

Mom doesn't answer. She can't; all she can do is shake her head in disbelief, her quivering fist clamped over her lips.

Remington gently rubs my side, softening his voice. "Let's go home, baby girl."

As I meet his dark, nurturing eyes, his pet name hits harder than it ever has. My chest collapses from the pain. Sobs erupt from my lips as Remington guides me down the hall, keeping me standing - giving me the strength to finally walk down this hallway for the last time. He's supporting me to set myself free.

Footsteps chase us. But they come to an abrupt stop as Remington whips his head around, his rib cage expanding against my side. A flash of fear tenses his muscles, and I suddenly remember Josh's final outburst on the first day we met - the way it stiffened Remington into fear along with me. Now I know it's from Ernesto.

I have to hold my heart to not feel like it's dissolving in my chest. Before Remington has to speak, I harden my tone. "Stay back, Dad."

Dad's eyes are wide, as if I'm about to tear out his lungs. "Lilibeth, you have no idea how sorry I am. It's not you, I just have anger issues, and things just pile up. This isn't how I expected my life to go."

I have to cling to Remington's arm, but with his firm grasp on my side, I find the strength to look Dad straight in the eyes. "This isn't how I expected a father to treat me either."

A pained exhale escapes Remington's lips. The sound shatters me, allowing me to voice the heart of my pain as my forehead contorts.

"When Rem saw my wrist, he described it perfectly for that little girl in my heart. She just wanted—" My voice shatters.

I hiccup through tears as I continue. "I just wanted— to be protected, not bruised."

Dad's sunken expression dissolved into nightmarish guilt and horror.

It's maddening. Even now, he gets to be the one who feels bad. The one who gets to feel hurt, forcing me to carry his pain for him.

As I stare at his worn frame, I realize nothing he can say to amend this will ever feel satisfying enough. He still hurt me, and I can't change that.

I allow my face to contort into my ugliest cry. The only sound echoing throughout my childhood home is my sharp, angry tears, but I don't feel shame in them anymore; I feel the power in them. Instead of pretending to be invincible, I'm finally showing how deeply Dad scarred me for life, not just physically, but throughout every form of my essence. I can hear my heart's pain, releasing from tears of pent-up grief over little Lilibeth's sense of safety.

I can do this. I can finally leave.

But my heart wavers as Mom panickily wheels herself down the hall, crying with me. She raises her quivering voice. "I'm so sorry I didn't notice."

Closing my eyes, I lean into Remington, tempted to collapse as my heart snaps.

But Mom grasps my hands, holding me upright with Remington's warm hands on my waist. "I need to talk this out with your father, and hold him accountable for it all. I need to take time to understand this, for all of us. But please, listen to me: I understand if you never come back here, Lilibeth. I won't hold it against you. The least I can do is allow you to live for yourself now, just like I've been hoping for you. Please, whatever you decide, just be free, my love. Be free."

She props herself up just enough to swipe a tear off my cheek. I grasp her hand tight, hugging it to my chest.

"I love you," I rasp. "Both of you."

It's confusing, but I mean every word. Mom gives me a soft smile despite her longing eyes, knowing this is goodbye for quite some time. She allows me to leave with Remington, pinning Dad in place with a tense shake of her head.

Remington closes the door behind us.

I can't believe this just happened. I'm so shell-shocked that I can't remember the walk to the car, snapping back into my awareness in the passenger's seat.

Remington's thumb sweeps over the back of my palm as he shares the silence with me. As I peek into his eyes, he gives me a somber smile.

"There you go, baby girl. I'm right here. You did it. You really did it."

He's been softly crying this whole time. As my tears return, Remington strokes my head with an even wider smile to mirror me - I'm grinning from ear to ear despite my lips quivering.

"Thank you, from the bottom of my heart. I couldn't have done this without you," I say.

He shakes his head, and I only smile wider; I've memorized this conversation already after training my heart alongside him for nearly a year. He doesn't need to reiterate that we're happy to be there for each other, no matter how painful life's worst moments may feel.

Which means it's time for aftercare. "Can you drive two blocks over, please? There's a really pretty park I want to show you."

Remington laughs through his stuffy nose, kissing my hand before slipping from my grasp. "Sure thing, my gorgeous little panther."

The further we drive, the freer my heart feels - just like Mom hoped. Except it's still so heavy with pain and disappointment that I can hardly bear to suck in each weighty inhale.

Bitter nostalgia seeps through my core as we pull up to the park, childhood memories flooding my mind. The good ones hurt just as much as the sad, frantic anxiety I'd feel for making

Dad take me to the park while Mom didn't feel well. I've avoided this place because of it.

Except this time, I made the right choice in returning anyway; Remington's presence refreshes my soul to create a new, healing conclusion to those confusing, lonely days.

Remington leads me to a cool patch of grass. We settle in side by side, watching the sunset lower the clouds into ice cream pastels across the sky.

"I'm so proud of you. So amazed by you." Remington takes my hand. "I've never met anyone so brave, and I'm so honored you let me be by your side to witness you owning your power."

My eyes flood with tears. We snuggle closer, Remington's cheek pressing against the top of my head as I nuzzle into his chest. Even though my heart hurts, I'm smiling.

"Thank you. I feel so seen by you," I whisper.

But when Remington sniffles above me, my heart flips. Lifting my head to check Remington's expression, I'm surprised he doesn't attempt to hide his tears from me. I let out a soft whimper as a droplet rolls down his cheek, but Remington dives for my lips. Our kisses are rushed and sloppy, startling us into laughter as we have to gasp for air from our stuffy noses. Swiping each other's faces with our sleeves, I cherish every second of the earnest giggling he inspires in my sore chest.

I sigh. "I'm so disappointed. I really thought Mom felt trapped too, but she chose my dad even before I was born, and she kept choosing him. I only believed she was trapped because I felt like I was, all my life. But it really was just me. I really was as alone as he made me feel."

Remington hums, tucking my hair behind my ear. I scoot closer, glancing back to the sunset as it deepens into blood orange.

My voice shakes. "Rem, I never realized it as deeply until today, but she broke my heart along with him too."

Drawing me to him gently, Remington kisses my forehead.

"I know, I watched it hit you, and it broke my heart too. I'm so sorry."

Burying my head against his chest, I warp into heartier, yearning tears. Remington holds me tighter, securing me in place. We breathe through the heartache together, but after a silent minute, I laugh.

"After all that effort to get stronger, I didn't even have a chance to carry her once."

Remington doesn't laugh. He straightens, turning to face me in the grass. "Was that all it was for, though?"

I furrow my brows, plucking a piece of grass. When I first joked to Remington about my failure to carry Mom, I thought that was why I worked so hard to get here, besides carrying the soup. But he's right: now I'm not so sure it was the soup, either.

Sweeping his fingertips down my back, Remington hums. "Maybe one of your goals was to get stronger for your mom, but I saw it as more than that the more I got to know you. Having a reason to work out opened up a door for you to be able to step into yourself at your core - and shed so much shame. Except you took it a step further, Lilibeth. That little panther I saw hiding beneath those bangs came out in full force against her life's worst hunter tonight, baring her teeth even though it made her whole body shake. Fierce isn't enough to describe you. Especially as you let yourself cry raw, real tears, in front of all of us."

My heart gallops along with Remington's wild words. As I stare into his eyes, his faith in me has only strengthened after today. I'm not only capable to him, I'm his hero too.

And I know the reason I saw myself as worth the tears, pain, and trauma shakes tonight was because of the freedom Remington and I created together - just like Mom hoped for me. I'm already living freedom, staring into these eyes.

But my heart flips into my throat. We're not taking Mom home anymore. What does this mean for our plans?

I'm terrified to ask.

That's exactly why I will.

I grip Remington's hand, swallowing hard. "Rem, I know we talked about living together to support my mom, and I know that might change without the same urgency, but I– I'd still really like to…"

Trailing off, I gape at the grinning, tattooed man before me. He's smiling wide, both cheeks extending joy to his crinkling eyes.

"Lilibeth, that offer still stands for me too. There's nothing I'd love more than to wake up beside you, cry beside you, chase boredom away beside you, laugh beside you, and struggle beside you for as long as you'll have me there. As long as I get to love you, I'm happy."

The sunlight casts a deep pink glow through his black eyes, reflecting the blissful, soothing warmth his words wash over my soul. I drop my nose against his, gazing into his eyes as I ease our lips together. We hold each other for ages, softly kissing as the sunset fades to a dim purple. Not even the fresh night breeze can cool my elated blood pounding through my veins.

Drawing Remington close, I soften my voice. "Being with you feels so big, but so calm at the same time. We're building something together that feels so healing for our hearts, including our younger selves, and I almost can't believe what we can accomplish because of it. We have the power to heal both the past and present for each other, just by existing. I've never seen anything more beautiful."

The sigh Remington releases from his nose heals my heart just the same; I can hear him setting himself free alongside me.

Splitting rent is one thing, but having the opportunity to build our own home with Celeste, creating a healing environment in which we can all thrive, is beyond my previous imagination of what I'd want in life. As we lean into each other for another soft, lingering kiss, I trust the life we'll create alongside each other will be even greater than I can imagine now too.

I know I will heal there with him, but my heart flutters as I realize what it means for Remington too: I can hold space for him, showing him over time that I'm not going to dissolve into someone who hurts him the way he was hurt. And I know he'll teach me the same. He already is.

Remington's sharp, huffing laughter spills from him, breaking our kiss. He's still tearing up, but I understand exactly what he means; the joy emanates from the glowing purple sky in his black eyes, promising another day to come. And it's one where we'll be here to face it all - together.

ACKNOWLEDGMENTS

If it weren't for Kayla Vokolek's willingness to jump in and devote her time and energy to edit this story, it might not have even existed. Thank you, Kayla, for providing crucial, foundational support for this project from the moment it was a creative whim to the eleventh hour when I was overthinking everything (and overthinking it again).

My family and friends have held such a wonderful space of excitement for me throughout this story's creation that touched my heart.

Thank you, Mom, Dad, and Blake, for rooting me on through this process - including 24/7 care when I became suddenly and horrendously sick in the middle of writing this story. The selfless kindness you share with me and everyone you know amazes me and inspires me to share even more sweetness with my readers.

Thank you, Julia, for your encouragement, for joining me in sharing secret, honest thoughts about life that help me feel human just as much as my characters, and for taking the time to always support my creations.

Thank you, Hannah, for giving me the gift of continually seeing through to the heart of my stories and, in turn, helping me feel seen too.

Thank you, Layla, for cherishing our friendship as much as I do, making literally any moment hilarious (including falling obscenely ill), and always making those around you feel welcome and valued.

Thank you, Ren, Jamee, Helen, Roman, and Lukas, for checking in about my writing progress and cheering me through it. Your excitement boosted my spirits through every single word.

A huge thank you to my incredible Patrons on Patreon who have helped my stories come to life by providing direct, immensely generous support: Lukas, Katy, Anonymous, E the Cat Caterer, Mitchie, Phoebe, Courtney, Drask, Jennifer, Kim Warren, Stacie, GenderBender LLC, Cass, Leyth, and Sarah.

Throughout my life, LGBTQ+ groups and fellow queer community members have consistently advanced my education about bodily autonomy. Thank you, chosen family members, for helping me retrain my brain until I realized that all versions of my "no" matters too.

Thank you, Reader, for granting Lilibeth and Remington's story a moment from your precious life. I wish you all the best in stepping into yourself more and more throughout the years. I'm so proud of you, just as you are.

RESOURCES

You deserve support and free access to knowledge. Please utilize the resources below whenever you need them. The world needs you here.

International Society for the Study of Trauma and Dissociation
https://isst-d.org

RAINN (Anti-Sexual Violence Nonprofit)
https://www.rainn.org

International OCD Foundation
https://iocdf.org

Psychology Today - Find a Therapist (International)
https://psychologytoday.com/intl/counsellors

Trans Lifeline
https://translifeline.org

The Trevor Project
https://thetrevorproject.org

International Association for Suicide Prevention
https://www.iasp.info

MORE BY RIVER KAI

BOOKS

My Shy Alpha: Book 1 of the Steamy Shifter Romance Series

Freeing My Alpha: Book 2 of My Shy Alpha, the Steamy Shifter Romance Series (June 2024)

Book 3 of My Shy Alpha (Winter 2025)

GRAPHIC NOVELS

Resonance: Space Gays Vol.1

What-Sexual?? Vol.1

What-Sexual?? Vol.2 (2024)

For current updates, follow River Kai on social media

@riv_kaii

@riv_kai

River Kai

River Kai Art

or sign up for the River Kai Art newsletter at
riverkaiart.com

ABOUT THE AUTHOR

As a bisexual and transgender creator, River Kai specializes in LGBTQ+ Romance, Sci-Fi, and Fantasy with mental health and disability representation, creating stories for readers like him to see they're not alone. While he writes in multiple Romance sub-genres, his stories share three recurring themes: empowering character arcs about healing from trauma, authentic representation of transgender or bisexual main characters with depression, anxiety, PTSD, and OCD, and a sweet-but-spicy emphasis on consent.